Riding Shotgun

Riding Shotgun

Racquel Williams

URBAN
BOOKS

www.urbanbooks.net

Urban Books, LLC
300 Farmingdale Road, N.Y.-Route 109
Farmingdale, NY 11735

ISBN 13: 978-1-64556-361-7
ISBN 10: 1-64556-361-8

First Trade Paperback Printing August 2022
Printed in the United States of America

10 9 8 7 6 5 4 3 2 1

Distributed by Kensington Publishing Corp.
Submit orders to:
Customer Service
400 Hahn Road
Westminster, MD 21157-4627
Phone: 1-800-733-3000
Fax: 1-800-659-2436

Riding Shotgun

by

Racquel Williams

Chapter One

Akila

"Damn, nigga, hurry up and come," I pleaded through tears to Mari while digging my fingers into his bare skin.

My legs were up on his shoulder, and, as usual, this nigga was digging deep into my guts. His big-ass dick was hurting my insides. This wasn't new. I knew his dick was too big for me from the day I met him. I had no idea why I kept fucking this nigga when, for days, I walked around with a sore pussy, scared to wash with soap. I would try using cold water, but that only made it worse, stinging the hell out of me.

"Open up, shawty. I'm about to bust. Oh shit . . . Open up," he said for the thousandth time, and I knew damn well it was a lie. He thinks he's slick. Each time he got close to busting, he would pull out his dick, slow fuck me, and then sink his dick deeper in.

I was near tears, so I closed my eyes, bit down on my bottom lip, and braced myself as this nigga ripped through my pussy wall. He didn't seem to care that I was in pain. Instead, he ignored my cries, lifted my legs higher in the air, and dug deeper into my guts. I backed all the way up until my head was against the headboard. I grabbed ahold of it for support and tried not to apply too much pressure. I was scared I would break the brand-new bed that I picked up from Ashley Furniture about a week ago. The pain was unbearable. It wasn't even fun anymore. I wanted to push him off me, but I tried my best not to act like a crybaby. To some, sex was pain, but this shit was downright torture.

"Aargh, I'm busting. Fuck, bitch, who pussy is this?" He rammed me harder.

"Yours, daddy. It's your pussy, daddy." I stroked his ego as I tightened my pussy muscles around his dick. I was hoping this would help him to bust faster.

His dick got bigger as he thrust harder inside of me. He put his hand under my ass and pulled me closer to him. "Damnnn, aarghhh . . ." He pulled out just in time to bust all over my stomach.

"Why the fuck you keep doing that nasty-ass shit, nigga? You know I hate when you come all over me," I shouted.

I jumped off the bed, slightly irritated. The truth was, I wasn't irritated because of him busting on me. I'd been trying for a year and a half to have this boy's baby, but he wasn't having it. I mean, come on. We'd been dating for two gotdamn years, and I had proved my loyalty to him, so why the fuck did he act like I wasn't good enough to have his seed? Shit, I was good enough to suck his dick at night. I was good enough to wash his dirty-ass clothes and cook him a hot meal every gotdamn night. Yeah, the nigga made sure I wore the latest designer clothes, he made sure he paid for my classes to become a massage therapist, and I always had money in my pocket, but I wanted more. I wanted a family, a little me running around, calling, "Mommy, Mommy." I shook my head. I had no idea how to get this nigga to bust inside of me.

I walked out of the room with an attitude. Then I closed the bathroom door, jumped into the shower, and washed off. As usual, I cringed as the Dove soap hit my sore pussy. I gently washed off, scared that my skin might peel off if I did it too hard. When I walked back into the room with the towel wrapped around me, he was sitting on the bed smoking a Black & Mild while counting the money he'd made the night before. He looked up when I walked into the room, put the Black & Mild in the ashtray, and looked at me with a grit on his face.

"Yo, B, what's wrong witcha?" he asked.

"Why? Ain't nothin' wrong wit' me," I replied nonchalantly while I walked away.

I went to my closet and pulled out a pair of Levi's and a white shirt. I had class at 1:00 p.m. and didn't want to be late because the instructor would go ham if we were. I was this close to graduation and couldn't risk fucking up. Shit, the way Mari been acting, I'm going to need my own money soon.

"Yo, B. You need to loosen up a little. We used to have so much fun together, but lately, all you want to do is argue. You make it hard for a nigga to be around you." He held his head down while he continued counting his money.

"*Really*, Mari? You got some fucking nerve coming at me like this. Don't play dumb, nigga. You know where this shit is coming from. You're right. We used to have fun when we were just fucking around. Then we decided to make it official and become a couple. It's been two damn years, and it seems like we're going backward. We are *not* getting any younger, and all you want to do is have fun," I lashed out at him.

He threw the bills on the bed and looked at me. "Yo, B, don't tell me you back on that baby shit again. I mean, come on, B. I done explained this shit to you over and over. I mean, look at us. Yeah, we got nice rides, nice clothes, and I got a few dollars stacked away, but not enough for no seed. Plus, I be in the streets too much. I want to be able to be around my seed all the time, not part-time like my daddy was. I never seen that busta except on weekends—if that. I don't want my seed to go through that. We're happy together, so why the fuck you trying to trap a nigga for?"

"Trap you? Nigga, *you* pursued *me,* even when I told your ass I wasn't ready for no relationship. You said you were ready to settle down. All of a sudden, you got amnesia." I looked at him and shook my head in disgust.

"Come on, B. You know I ain't mean it like that. It just came out. I love you and want a future with you, but right now, you're just being selfish 'cause we ain't ready for no baby."

I heard his gums yapping, but I wasn't listening to any of that bullshit that he was preaching. We had more than enough money because I watched him count stacks upon stacks every night. Shit, the nigga just blew twenty grand at the MGM Casino a few weeks ago. If you ask me, he was full of shit. This conversation wasn't getting anywhere, so I walked away to finish dressing. I brushed my weave into a ponytail, put on a little makeup, then walked back into the room. He was still sitting there, smoking and acting so nonchalantly.

"Listen, either we make a life together, or you get the fuck on, for real. I'm not going to be no damn fool sitting around and just waiting on you. You better act fast before I get the fuck o—"

Bap! Bap! Before I could finish my sentence, he flew off the bed, slapped my face, grabbed my neck, and threw me up against the wall. He then took out his 9 mm Glock and pointed it at my head. "Bitch, who the fuck you think you talking to like that? Bitch, *I* took you out of the motherfucking slums. *I* fucking gave you every-mother-fucking-thing, and *this* how you talk to me?" He squeezed my neck so damn hard my vision got blurry.

"Get off me." I tried to bring my hand up to hit him, but I couldn't reach him.

"You better quit playing, Akila. I fuckin' love you, B, but you stay bitchin' in my fuckin' ears. Keep it up, and you gon' push me into the arms of another bitch." He started kissing my lips, but it was more like he was biting them.

I pushed him, and he finally let go of me. "Get the fuck off me. What the *fuck* is wrong with you, dude?"

"Sorry, baby, but you know how crazy you make me when you talk like that." He tried touching my face.

I looked at him and dashed into the bathroom. I checked my lips and noticed a little blood, so I grabbed a piece of tissue and dabbed it. My anger rose as I saw what that nigga did. Tears rolled down my face. Then I dashed into the room. He was back sitting down, acting as if nothing happened. I grabbed my stuff and ran out of the house. I trembled as I sat in my car for a few minutes, trying to get myself together. This nigga had gone too far this time. I felt anger and disappointment. This was the nigga that I was loving. How could he treat me like this? After a few minutes of sitting in the driveway, I wiped the tears away, got my emotions under control a little, and then pulled off.

As I drove to school, I couldn't help but reflect on my life. I was born and raised in Jackson Ward Housing Project in Richmond, Virginia, to be exact. I didn't know my parents because I heard they had been cracked out for years. I also heard that the minute I was born, my mother gave me to my maternal grandma, and no one had heard from her since. I grew up feeling alone because I didn't really have anyone but my grandma, and she was old and sick. I gave her props, though. She did the little that she could do for me. Her only form of income was the SSI check that she got once a month, and after the bills were paid, nothing was really left. My clothes mainly came from the thrift store or when I borrowed my homegirls' clothes. My grandma ended up passing when I was 17, and I was left to fend for myself.

With no family or anyone to turn to, I quickly turned to the streets. First, I started boosting designer clothing and selling it to the dope boys in my hood. Shit was sweet until I caught my first case. I was walking out of Macy's, padded with a lot of shit. I was almost out the door when the robocop at the door approached me.

"Miss, can I check your bag?" He stepped in front of me.

"Nah, why? Is there a problem?" I stepped away from him, thinking about an escape plan.

"Ma'am, please, come with me."

"Hell no, I'm not."

He said something on his radio, and a few seconds later, I saw two uniformed police approaching me. I knew then shit was about to get real. I shook my head and stood there as they questioned me about what was in the bag. When I couldn't present receipts to them, they escorted me to the office, a female cop searched me, and they discovered everything. I was hauled off to Richmond City Jail. My bond was $2,500.

I called my homegirl, Ariana. It took about four days before she hustled up the money. I was later given probation and a strong warning from the judge. Those four days were hell for me, and I vowed I wouldn't never go back to boosting. So, with boosting out the window, I started struggling. Got me a job at Hardy's, but that didn't work out. Life was rough for me. I started fucking different niggas to get some money to buy the things I needed.

I was at the Canal Club celebrating my eighteenth birthday when I met Mari, and we started chopping it up. I already knew who he was because his name rang bells in the streets of Richmond. He was one of the hottest dope boys. He was from Virginia Beach and fresh in the city. It was rumored that he was the go-to man for some of the rawest dope in the city, and he also had the weed game on lock. We met by accident. I was coming out of the ladies' room, and we accidentally bumped into each other. I excused myself and walked back to where my homegirl was standing. A few minutes later, one of the bartenders brought me a drink, letting me know that the gentleman at the bar had sent it. I looked over at the bar, and there he was, standing, smiling at me. A little later, I decided to walk over to him and thank him for the drink. We sparked up a conversation, and before you knew it, we were exchanging numbers. I knew he was out of my league, but shit, I still decided to try.

I told my homegirl to go home without me, and I stayed back with Mari. He took me to a hotel on Broad Street. With the help of the alcohol and his fine ass, I fucked him on that first night. The next morning, he dropped me home. Once I sobered up, I figured I had made a mistake. I mean, this nigga was a high roller, so what did he want from little old me? I know I got some good pussy and sucked his dick good, but there are plenty of bitches out here that do the same shit.

I was shocked when he called me the next day, telling me how much he enjoyed the previous night. He invited me out to dinner later in the evening. At first, I pretended like I would be busy, but with a little convincing from him, I gladly accepted the invitation. I played it cool, though, like I wasn't pressed. I knew that nigga was my ticket to get out of the hood and to a better life.

It was easy for me to pop this pussy on him and suck his dick like I was famished and needed his cum to nurse me back to health. Before long, we became inseparable, and my life instantly changed for the better. About three months into our relationship, I told him that I needed to move. He agreed and decided to move me out of the projects. He told me to start looking for a house. After weeks of searching, I found a nice three-bedroom, ranch-style home over on Patterson Avenue by the city's West End. About two weeks later, with the help of the real estate lady, we moved in.

The honeymoon didn't last long. Soon after moving in, I started to see another side of him. He started staying out all night, and when he did make it home, all he wanted to do was fuck and go to sleep. He barely took me out with him anymore. When I would question him about it, he would make up all sorts of excuses. Mainly, we lived together, but we didn't have to hang out in the streets. I started feeling lonely at home all the time by myself until it finally became the norm. I was shocked at his sudden change of behavior, but I learned to shut my mouth and focus on bettering myself as time went by. I knew he had lots of money, so I went to him and told him I was trying to go back to school. Surprisingly, he agreed that was a good idea and gave me the money. After that, I turned my focus to school and tried my best to live with the situation.

I dried my tears as I pulled into the school's parking lot. This was my ticket to a better life. I planned to finish up soon, get a job, get some experience, and then open my own business.

I glanced in the mirror and made sure my makeup was not smeared. My hair was straight, and the lip gloss was popping. Not bad for a chick that just got beaten up.

Mari

Damn, why the fuck did my ass move in with this bitch? I love her, but her fucking mouth was in the motherfucking way. See, I wasn't your regular-ass nigga. I was fine as fuck, my dick game was on point, and I'm heavy in these streets. Born and raised in Virginia Beach, I was exposed to street life early. Money was running at the Beach, but shit was getting hot. Plus, I heard money was in Richmond. I would get the work from New York and bring it to Richmond. I had niggas out in Virginia Beach and Newport News, so we were moving the work with ease. With all this money I was making, bitches came around like roaches. I ain't bragging, but shit, I could fuck a different bitch every night of the week, and most times, I did just that. I didn't think it would be affected when I moved in with her until she started bitching at a nigga.

I met Akila at the club one night. She was cute, and I felt like I could fuck her. Getting the pussy was easier than I thought; we fucked the first night. I should've let her go after that, but truthfully, I was feeling her. Pussy was tight, and she sucked my dick good. She wasn't like the other bad bitches that I was used to, but me and her hit it off, and I started feeling comfortable around her. Akila should've considered it a privilege when I called myself fucking with her little hood ass. I wasn't going to lie. It was supposed to be just a fuck, but when shawty latched on to my dick like a young pit bull, I had to hurry up and cuff that ass. I loved fucking pussy, but getting my dick sucked was my specialty thanks to that crackhead bitch Brenda, who sucked my dick at 10 years old for that five-dollar bill that I promised her ass. She was geeking for that piece of crack. That bitch sucked on my little-ass dick with those bare gums and had me experiencing some out-of-body shit. When she finished, I threw that bitch the ten-dollar allowance mom dukes threw me earlier. That was the first time, and I hadn't stopped tricking yet.

Everything was cool at first 'cause Akila was quiet and seemed humble. She never questioned me or blew up my phone, which was a plus. I've fucked with bitches that never understood a nigga in the streets all hours of the day and night. Shit seemed good, so when she came to me and suggested we live together, I quickly obliged. Big fucking mistake. About a week later, the complaining and whining started. I tried to explain to her that I got to be out in the streets. She didn't seem to get it, so I stopped explaining myself. Shit, either she was going to live with it or get the fuck on. Even though we lived together, I kept several bitches on the side. Shit, I was a young nigga, and I was going to fuck until the day my dick couldn't stand up. And then I would continue getting my dick sucked.

I pulled up at the shop to get my car detailed. My brother owned the shop, and the business also helped us clean up our drug money. I parked my 2017 Range Rover and hopped out. My brother spotted me and made his way toward me. "Whaddup, my nigga?"

"Can't call it, playa." We exchanged daps as we walked back into the building.

Rio was my older brother and the one responsible for getting me started in the dope business. He was my nigga and my heart, the only nigga I could count on in these streets and vice versa. So when I told him about the move to Richmond, he jumped on it, and here we are together.

"Yo, who working? I need my bitch cleaned out."

"Which one of yo' bitches, nigga?" he joked.

"Old Becky need a good detailing."

"Yo, Rahu, get this," he hollered at a Middle Eastern cat. "Yo, let's go to the office."

We walked into the back, where we handled most of our business. "So, how that run looking? Are we still on?"

"Hell yeah, nigga. Got to re-up. Ain't got shit but a key left. The first coming up, so you know it's gonna be jumping."

"Hell yeah, 'cause I'm almost out of the shit that I took yesterday. Man, when I tell you my phone was jumping last night, you would've thought it was the first or something. I ain't go in the crib 'til six."

"Oh yeah? I know old girl snapped on that ass." He busted out laughing. I swear, he got a kick out of that shit.

"Man, fuck her . . . You know I went in and dicked her down as usual. Then the bitch went off this morning talking about she gon' leave and shit if I don't tighten up. Shit, bro, I choked that ho out. I was about to shoot that bitch, ungrateful old ass."

"Yo, yo, I told you about putting your hands on that bitch. You done fucked up and moved in with the bitch, and her ass know too fucking much now."

"Man, fuck that bitch. Her ass ain't goin' nowhere, and she know I will beat that ass if she ever run her mother-fucking mouth."

"A'ight, li'l bro, but a scorned bitch is a dangerous one. All she needs is another nigga to be all up in her ear. Trust me, these bitches ain't loyal these days."

"Damn, nigga, you blowin' me wit' all this preaching, bro. I got these hoes. You just focus on running the business." I chuckled, but I was serious as fuck.

I loved my brother, but he was always soft for those bitches. That was why his ass was married with three fucking kids. That nigga swore to God he was happy, but I knew different.

"Nigga, hit this loud and shut the fuck up. Mama used to say a hard head makes a soft ass," he said and handed me the blunt.

The mention of Mama made me smile. I swear I miss that woman. I know she was up there smiling down at us. Fuck cancer. I would do anything to get her back here with us.

I took a long pull off the fat-ass blunt he'd rolled. That nigga missed his true calling—counseling. We smoked two more blunts and then got down to serious matters. Business was definitely booming. We just had to be careful in these streets. A few Richmond niggas try to bring some heat our way, but we sent a strong message by shooting up one of the nigga's baby mama's house. Since then, shit died down, but we were not letting our guards down. War could start any day, and we need to be ready to square up with these bitch-ass niggas.

Chapter Two

Akila

I didn't want to be in class after what had happened earlier. I couldn't believe that nigga put a fucking gun to my head and bit my lip like he was a fucking animal. I wasn't going to front; he'd put his hands on me before. I really thought we were way past that after he cried to me and begged me to give him another chance once I packed my bags and was almost out the door. But that nigga shocked the shit out of me when he jumped off the bed like that earlier. Tears welled up in my eyes as I remembered how that shit played out.

"Yo, you good?" Tyrone, one of my classmates, asked as he walked up to me.

"Yes, I'm good," I smiled at him. Tyrone had been crushing on me since the first day of school. I wished I could just lie on his shoulder and cry it out. My heart was broken, and I needed a listening ear.

"Well, you know if you need to talk, I'm here, right?" he said before walking off.

"Thank you, hon." I tried to use my hand to hide my busted lip.

He looked back at me, smiled, and continued to walk away with that turned-up ass swag. He was a cutie-pie and had that country accent. He told me he was born and raised in Georgia. He sent chills through my veins whenever he spoke. I wasn't going to lie. I'd entertained the idea of going on a date with him. But Richmond was so small, and Mari had connections and ears out in the streets. I knew I couldn't make a move without him finding out about it. I quickly dismissed that idea because it was not worth me or that boy losing our lives behind that nigga and his jealous ways.

After class was over, I thought about going straight home, but I felt down and didn't want to go into the boring-ass house. So I got into my car and dialed my bitch Ariana's number. I hadn't seen her ass in a few days and could really use some girl time.

"Hello," her loudmouthed ass hollered into the phone.

"Damn, bitch, must you be so fucking loud and unlady-like all the time?"

"Listen, you little heffa, you called *my* motherfucking phone, so state yo' business or get the fuck on." She busted out laughing.

"Bitch, you is stupid." I couldn't help but also start laughing.

"Where the hell you been, nigga? Oh, I know. Laid up with that boy and forgot all about your bitch."

"Where you at? I'm leaving school right now."

"I'm over here at the Marriott by the airport."

"What the fuck you doing over there? Selling pussy, bitch?"

"Shit, a bitch got to get it how she live. You comin' through or nah?"

I hesitated. I had no idea what the fuck she was doing over there, but what the hell? I needed to see my bitch.

"Text me the address. I'm on the way."

Before I could pull off, someone knocked on my window, which startled me. I looked up and realized it was Tyrone. I let the window down to see what this sexy-ass nigga wanted.

"I noticed you were still sitting here, so I wanted to check on you to see if you're good."

"Yes, I was on the phone, but thank you, though." I shot him a smile.

"Oh, a'ight. Cool. Aye, take my number and hit me up sometime."

"Why would I do that? I got a man." As soon as it left my mouth, I regretted it.

"I ain't tryin'a date your nigga. My only interest is you. And from the looks of things, I don't think you're too happy wit' that nigga."

His boldness turned me on instantly. "What's the number?" I looked at him, surprised at his statement. I thought I did a good job hiding my pain, but I guess I didn't.

"You gon' call, right?"

"I'll think about it." I shot him a half smile.

"I hope you do. You deserve so much more."

I didn't say anything. I just started the car. He looked at me, and without saying another word, he walked off. I kept my eyes on him until he got on his motorcycle. That boy was very persistent. *I kind of like that. It's cute,* I thought as I pulled off.

I looked at my phone to get the address of where Ariana said she was. Then I turned the music up to help ease my mind. Part of me was fed up with Mari and his bullshit, but I loved that nigga's dirty drawers. I loved the way he spoke to my soul. I just wished he would get some help for his anger. If he did, we would be so happy together. That was one of the reasons why I thought if we had a baby, it would make him calm down some. Now, I was second-guessing. I no longer knew if I wanted to be with him, not after what he did to me today.

I noticed that I was approaching my exit. I turned off to where the GPS took me, then pulled into the parking lot and dialed Ariana's number.

"Hey, boo."

"I'm here. What room you in?"

"Room 204. Come in and turn to the left. The elevator is on the corner."

"All right." I grabbed my purse, got out of the car, and walked into the hotel.

On the way up to her room, I kept wondering what the hell her ass was doing in a hotel. It wasn't like she didn't have her own place. Her ass was probably up to no good. The elevator stopped. I stepped out, walked to room 204, and knocked on the door.

"Hey, bitch." She opened the door dressed in a sexy bodycon dress.

"Hey, boo," I said as we embraced.

"Come on in."

I walked in and looked around, curious about what was going on. I noticed that no one else was present, which was good but suspicious.

"Bitch, sit your ass down. Why you look like you been through hell?"

"Girl, you have no idea. Mari is back on his shit again." I broke down crying.

"Bitch, I done told yo' ass to leave that nigga the fuck alone. He ain't gon' never change. How long you been dealing with that shit? I know the nigga got money, but that shit ain't worth the way he treats you. You can make money without him."

"I know, but I thought it would be different now that we've been together for years. But to be honest, shit only got worse. It's like he doesn't respect me no more."

"I told your ass I heard rumors that nigga was fucking with a couple of other bitches. But yo' ass decided to stay with him. I love you, boo, but you deserve so much more than what that nigga be dishing out. Shit, there are lots of other niggas out there with good dick and money.

You're a queen, and you deserve to be treated way better than that."

Her words were stinging hard like alcohol in an open wound. Everything she was saying was all things that I knew, but it was so hard to leave him. No one really understood that I was deeply in love with him. He was the nigga to show me a better life. Living in the projects, not knowing where my next meal was coming from, was hard as hell. Now, I wear nice clothes, eat good, and I don't worry about money.

"Well, those are all rumors. You know how bitches are always claiming they fuckin' with a trap nigga, but in reality, they be lying. Unless a bitch got proof that he fuckin' them, I ain't trying to hear that shit for real."

"Bitch, please stop making excuses for this nigga. I have a feeling the proof could be hitting you dead in the face, and you still ain't gon' leave that nigga. Bitch, I hope that nigga don't lose it and kill you."

"I know . . . I just be hoping and praying that nigga will see that I love him, and he'll change his ways toward me." My face saddened as those words left my mouth.

"Well, you know you my bitch, so if that nigga is who you want, then I ain't got no choice but to support you. I don't fuckin' like it, but I love you. You feel me?"

That was one of the qualities that I love about Ariana. We'd been rocking with each other since middle school and always had each other's back. I loved that bitch for real because I could always count on her to keep it one hundred with me. She's the kind of bitch that will tell me what things are even if my feelings are hurt.

"Well, bitch, enough about me. What the hell's going on? Why you up in here dressed up like this?" I shot her a dirty look while I smiled.

"Hmmm. How you think I make my money to buy a brand-new car and keep up my lifestyle?" She looked at me.

"Bitch, I don't know. You said you were making good money being a waitress at the bar up in Richmond, right?" I looked back at her for confirmation.

"Well, you know you my bitch, my sissy, and my rider. But there's something that I've been hiding from you. . . ."

"What, bitch? Spit it out."

She took a seat beside me and started talking. "Well, I haven't been working at the bar like I told you before. I've been escorting."

I shot her a surprised look. "You mean you been selling pussy, bitch?"

"Damn, you ain't got to say it like that. I go out with rich men, and in exchange, they give me money and buy me expensive things."

"Bitch, we from the hood. I *know* what the fuck an escort does, so you can pretty that shit up all you want, but it has the same meaning. You sell pussy to niggas."

"All right, whatever you say. You asked me a question, and I told you. Now what?"

"You my bitch. I don't give a fuck what you do. Shit, it's your pus—"

Before I could finish my sentence, someone banged on the door. "Who's that? You expectin' someone?"

She didn't respond. Instead, she walked over to the door and looked through the peephole. "Dang, that's one of my clients, Ramon. He early as fuck." She looked at the time on her phone.

"I can leave now so you can handle your business." I stood up, about to grab my things.

"Nah, you good. I'm just gonna let him in, so we can talk for a few minutes."

Without waiting for a response, she opened the door. A tall Puerto Rican dude entered the hotel room. I felt very uneasy being in here with this stranger, but I trusted my girl's judgment. I hope she knows what she was getting herself into. Escorting was a dangerous business. Often, girls end up hurt or dead.

"*Hola, mi amor,*" he said in a thick Spanish accent.

"Hey, babe." She hugged him. I watched as he cuffed both of her butt cheeks. "Papi, have some respect. We have company," she said while she wiggled out of his grip.

They walked toward where I was sitting, and Ariana took a seat beside me.

"Oh, excuse my manners. Who is this pretty lady?"

"This is my best friend, Akila," Ariana said.

"*Bonita,*" he said as he smiled at me.

I smiled back at him while thinking he seemed like a weirdo. For some reason, I felt like his accent didn't sound authentic. I blew it off because Ariana was talking and laughing with him. I guess I watched too many ID channel shows.

I felt my phone vibrating, so I took it out of my purse and checked the message. It was from Mari.

Babe, I just want to apologize about earlier. I love you with everything in me, and I don't know why I act like that. Please forgive me.

Why did that nigga have to text me right at this moment? I was doing good not thinking about him for a minute, and now he was all back up in my head, messing with my mental. I didn't believe shit he was saying. He's done this too much and thinking if he says he's sorry, it's supposed to be all good. I'm not going to lie. I've forgiven him in the past, but this time, he really fucked up.

"So, pretty lady, you want to join me for some fun?" Ramon walked up to me, grinning.

"No, I'm good. Matter of fact, I was just leaving."

"Leave her alone, Ramon. Mommy got all the sugar you need, daddy," she teased.

This felt awkward and somewhat creepy. I stood up and grabbed my purse. I was going to tell Ariana that I was about to bounce. I didn't knock what she was doing, but I wasn't into being in hotel rooms with strange niggas.

"I want some of her too," this fool said and grabbed my arm.

"Let go of my arm." I yanked it away from him and started to walk off.

"Stop it, Ramon. What are you doing?" Ariana yelled out at him.

"Bitch, shut up." This nigga turned around and smacked the fuck out of her face. She fell backward on the dresser, hitting her head.

My heart started racing. I needed to get out of here, but this bastard was a step ahead of me. I tried to run, but he placed his foot in my way, tripping me. I fell to the floor and looked up. Before I could get up, I noticed he had a gun pointed at my face.

"Bitch, get up. I said I wanted some of this pussy. Now, take off your fucking clothes." He dragged his words out in slow motion. The fake accent was gone. Now he spoke perfect English.

He grabbed me by my hair and yanked me up toward him. He had a cold look in his eyes. I could tell the nigga meant business, and only God knew what the fuck was about to take place in this room. I started praying to God to help me get out of the situation alive. I started crying, hoping he would change his mind.

"Bitch, take off your clothes and open your fucking legs," he demanded loudly as he shoved me down on the bed.

"No, please, don't do this. Do you want money? I can get you plenty of money," I pleaded, even though I was sure he wasn't after money. I was saying that, hoping he would fall for it.

I trembled as I unbuttoned my pants. I've never been raped before, and the thought of this nigga raping me had me wishing I was dead.

"Hurry the fuck up, bitch." He pressed the gun to my forehead.

I quickly realized that there was no way out. I reluctantly unzipped my pants. The entire time, I kept my eyes closed. I didn't want to see what this nigga was doing to me. I was hoping someone would come knocking at the door. I waited in vain 'cause nothing happened. No one was coming to save little old me.

"Open your motherfucking legs before I blow your fucking brains out on this bed." He pressed the gun against my forehead again.

I began crying louder and started to pray in my heart to God. This savage-ass nigga ripped my shirt open and started roughly fondling my breast with his hand. I squirmed as he placed his mouth on my breast. My body tensed up as I began to feel nauseated. My stomach turned, and vomit blew out of my mouth.

"Get off her!" Ariana finally came to and jumped on his back.

He got up off me and used the butt of the gun to hit her in the head. She tried to run, but he grabbed her and started choking her. He then used the butt of the weapon to beat her in the head again. Blood started splattering on the wall. I wanted to run, but it would be impossible to go by him without him grabbing me.

"Noooo, noooo," I started screaming out loud. Maybe the people next door would hear me and notify the police.

"Bitch, shut up, or I'll kill this bitch."

He continued beating Ariana in the head until there was complete silence. I feared the worst. She was no longer screaming or fighting. I only hoped my bitch wasn't dead. After he was satisfied that she was no longer a threat, he turned his attention back to me.

"God, please, just take me now. Please, God," I pleaded through busted lips.

This nigga grabbed my legs and yanked them far apart. "Please, don't do this. Pleeeease," I pleaded with everything in me while I tried scratching his face.

"You gon' love this dick, baby. You'll see." He grinned as he rammed his dry-ass dick inside of me. "Damn, this some tight pussy you got here," he whispered in my ear as he thrust in and out of me.

I wasn't wet, so I could feel my shit being ripped apart. The more I fought, the harder he pushed inside of me. I finally decided to stop fighting and screaming. I wanted to die at that moment and had no idea why God wasn't listening to my cries.

"Aargh, aaargh," this nigga grunted as if he were having the time of his life.

I had to endure what felt like a lifetime of hell on earth. Finally, he pulled out and came all over his hand.

"You liked it, didn't you?" He smiled at me with a devious grin plastered on his face.

I wanted to respond, but my mind wasn't willing, and my soul was hurting too bad. I just lay there helplessly. I was feeling numb, wondering what he was going to do next.

He pulled up his pants, then stared at me. "Listen, little bitch, don't you think about running your mouth to no police. I'll be watching you, and if I find out you talked to anyone, I will come back and kill you. Trust me; you don't want to play with me," he said in a cold, serious tone.

I didn't say a word, scared that he might kill me. I watched as he opened the door and walked out of the room. I waited a few seconds, praying that that monster was gone.

What seemed like forever was actually only a few minutes. I could barely move, so I struggled to pull myself farther up on the bed. Finally, I picked up the phone, dialed 0, and waited for the operator.

"Front desk, how may I help you?"

"Please send the police to room 204. We need help," I said as I dropped the phone.

Mari

After kicking it with the niggas all day, trying to secure the bag, I was ready to roll up in the crib. I was tight as fuck because I'd been calling and texting Akila's phone all gotdamn day, and that bitch didn't answer. I even stopped by the crib earlier, but her ass was nowhere to be found. Now, that bitch knew I would put my motherfucking foot up her ass, so I had no idea why she kept playing with me. I knew she was mad at me earlier, but that didn't give her ass a right to be playing those childish-ass games. It was damn near 2:00 a.m., and that bitch still wasn't picking up the phone. I tried to think where she might be, but I was coming up short.

I sped down the highway as my anger level elevated. I hated the fact that I let this bitch have me feeling like this. Where the fuck could she be? I lit a blunt that I was smoking earlier. I took a few pulls and turned up Kevin Gates's music. I was trying to calm my nerves and not snap on that bitch when I see her. Now, I noticed her car was not in the driveway. She probably was parked in the garage or, worst-case scenario, the bitch still had not come home. I parked my ride, jumped out, eagerly opened the door, and ran upstairs.

"Akila, Akila, where the fuck you been?" I yelled out as I rushed into the bedroom. The room was empty, so I ran into the bathroom. There was no sign of her. I hit the bathroom door, trying to release some of my built-up frustration.

Finally, I walked back into the room and sat on the edge of the bed. Where the fuck could that bitch be this early in the morning? She had never pulled this fucking stunt before, and I had no idea what the fuck she was doing. Trust me; if a bitch was out that time of night, she was out selling pussy or laid up with another nigga, plain and simple. I dialed her number again, and instead of it ringing, it went straight to voicemail this time.

"Aye, yo, I know you see me calling you. Where the fuck you at? Yo, get at me." I left her ass a voicemail message.

My nerves were torn the fuck up over not knowing where that bitch was. I decided to grab some liquor and roll another blunt.

Chapter Three

Akila

The physical pain I was feeling was nothing compared to the mental anguish I was dealing with. I still couldn't believe that I got raped by that nigga. This nigga took my pussy and then threatened me. I'd been careful my whole life, but the one day I let my guard down because of my bitch, look where the fuck it got me. Oh my God, what happened to Ariana? I started to cry. The last time I saw her was when the paramedics were wheeling her out of the hotel room. I hope she's all right because I couldn't take it if anything happened to my bitch.

"Hey there, how you feeling?" the Asian doctor walked in and asked.

"I'm a little sore but much better than when I came in earlier."

"Good. You were beaten pretty badly, but your X-rays look good. You have no broken bones, just lacerations on your face and buttocks. Also, you have a rip in your vagina. While you were still sedated, we went ahead and put some stitches in—"

We hadn't finished talking when I heard a knock at the door. I panicked. What if Mari found out where I was? Before I could get my thoughts under control, a police officer in uniform and a woman in plainclothes walked in.

"Doctor, are you finished here? We need a few minutes with the patient."

"Yes, sure . . . Miss Jones, I will be writing you prescriptions for the pain and some antibiotics. I'll be back to talk with you after the officers finish."

"Miss Jones, I'm Officer Simmons, and this is Detective McKinney. We understand from the doctor that you were assaulted earlier. Can you tell us what happened and who assaulted you?"

I looked at them with confusion on my face. "Uh, who?" I asked out loud while trying to remember what the fuck the nigga said his name was. I felt so embarrassed that I'd got myself into a fucked-up situation like this. I searched my mind, and after a few seconds, I remembered the name Ariana called him.

"His name is Ramon. . . ."

"Does Ramon have a last name, and how do you know him?"

I went on to tell them what had happened. I tried to leave out the part about my girl being an escort. There was no way I would throw her under the bus like that.

"So, let me get this right. This gentleman was a friend of your friend, Ariana Gayle?"

"Yes, it was my first time seeing him."

"And did your friend tell you what she was doing in the hotel?"

"No, not really. I just stopped by to say hi because I've been busy with school, and we haven't been able to really kick it like that lately."

"Well, Miss Jones, we know that Miss Gayle was exchanging sex for money with different men. She's been under our radar for a minute after one of the johns complained she stole money from his wallet. What we're trying to understand is why a college girl like yourself would be in the same hotel room as a working girl and a john? Are you in the prostitution business as well?"

"I told you I went to see my girl. Why don't you ask her why I was there? Shit, she'll tell y'all. I ain't never sell pussy a day in my life. I go to school," I lashed out. I was offended that they would think I was a prostitute.

"Wait . . . You don't know?" The female officer looked at me strangely.

"Know what?" I looked at both their faces for some sort of explanation.

"The young lady that was in the hotel room with you didn't make it. Ariana Gayle passed away on the way to the hospital. The perp beat her severely in her head."

I felt a lump form in my throat. I tried to swallow, but I couldn't. My body quivered uncontrollably. Tears welled up in my eyes as I tried to grip what they'd just told me. This is my bitch . . . my sister and rider they're talking about. This has to be some kind of mistake.

"Y'all trippin', man. Go check on her. Y'all see that she's good. She good, I promise y'all. We leaving up outta here together. . . ." My voice trailed off, and tears rushed down my face.

"I'm sorry, but Miss Gayle didn't make it."

I looked at them. I could tell by their expression that they were as serious as a heart attack.

"Oh God, no. This can't be. Noooo, y'all lying," I screamed out. I grabbed my pillow and buried my face into it as I bit down on my lip, forgetting it hurts.

"I'm so sorry about your loss. If you can remember anything more about this individual, it can help us to arrest him and get him off the streets."

I wasn't trying to hear anything else that they had to say. Instead, I pulled the blanket over my head and let the tears flow freely.

"She introduced him as Ramon when he first walked in. At first, he had a Spanish accent, but when he attacked me, he spoke clear English. He looked Puerto Rican, but he was definitely born here." I racked my brain to think of anything that I was leaving out. I needed this murderer and rapist off the streets.

"The hospital was able to get DNA from you, so that will be tested. You think you can help our sketch artist? I'm pretty sure this isn't the first time he did something like this. It's imperative that we get him off the streets. Your life could still be in danger."

"Yeah, sure." To be honest, I could still see that nigga's face in my head. I could smell his stank-ass breath as he breathed down my neck while he raped me.

"Miss Jones, again, I'm sorry about your loss. I'm putting my card on this table. Give us a call if you remember anything about this individual, and you can come down by the station as soon as you're discharged. I want to get his picture out there immediately." Officer Simmons placed his card on the table, and they walked out.

I didn't even bother to respond. I threw my head back down on the pillow. This shit can't be true. I grabbed my phone off the table and dialed her number. The phone rang out and then went to voicemail. I tried it two or three more times before I threw it on the bed. That was the worst fucking news ever. She was so fucking young and full of life. That bastard killed my fucking ace. He could've just raped her like he did me. Instead, he had to kill her. His face flashed across my mind. While he was raping me, I made a permanent note of his face in my memory. It was a face that I'd never forget.

"No, God. Please, help meeee," I cried out loud while I held my head.

"Are you okay, Miss Jones?" the nurse asked when she ran into the room.

I couldn't respond. Instead, I cried and cried. I trembled as I tried calming myself. The nurse was worried about me, so she went for the doctor.

"Miss Jones, the police told me what happened. I'm sorry for your loss. I'm going to give you something for the pain, and it will help calm you," the doctor said.

I still didn't respond to him. I really didn't want to be bothered. They both walked out of the room, and I slid all the way under the cover. A few minutes later, the nurse walked into the room. She gave me a shot of morphine that helped calm me. Within minutes, I started feeling dozy. This was the first time that I welcomed sleep so quickly. My bitch's face flashed across my mind. I closed my eyes, trying to get rid of the image.

When I woke up, I was hoping this was some sort of nightmare . . . that someone would tell me this was a mistake. I waited, but no one came bearing good news. I grabbed my phone to log on to Facebook. It took me a few moments to scroll to her page. Then there it was. Reality hit me. Ariana's page was full of RIP posts. I lay there staring at her profile pic. Tears started flowing as I read her last status, made yesterday. She was so happy, and baby girl had no idea this would be her final status. I couldn't take seeing this, so I quickly logged off because it was too much to deal with right now.

After logging out of FB, I realized that I had over twenty missed calls and a bunch of texts from Mari. My heart sank as I prepared myself to listen to his voicemail and read his texts. Just as I'd imagined, he was going off about where the hell I was. I swear, that dude had no idea what I'd been through today, and I was pretty sure he wouldn't even try. I wish our relationship were different 'cause I so needed him right now. But I know him. He would try to switch this up. I threw the phone down and slid back under the covers. *Fuck my life,* I thought. I cried so much that my chest started hurting.

***

The following day, I was discharged from the hospital. The doctor wrote me a prescription for hydrocodone for pain and gave me some numbers for doctors that could counsel me. That was cool, but physical pain was the least of my problems. I felt dirty and disgusting from that nigga raping me. I had so much rage. I swear, if I knew where that nigga be at, I would kill him for what he did to me and for taking my girl's life.

I got dressed and was ready to leave when it hit me that I didn't have my car. The ambulance had brought me here, and my car was parked at the hotel. Damn, what the fuck was I going to do? The last thing I wanted to do was call Mari, but I had no choice. It wasn't like I had any family out here. Before I could dial his number . . . Wait, hold up. Tyrone always said if I needed him, I should reach out. I searched for his number on my phone. His phone started to ring, and I began to panic. Before I could end the call, he answered.

"Yo."

"Hello . . ." I gasped for air.

"Hey, babe. Damn, it's about time you hit a nigga up," he said, laughing.

"I need a favor from you, please."

"Sure. What's good, ma?"

"I'm at the hospital and don't have my car. I need a ride someplace."

"Hospital? You a'ight?"

"Nah, I'm not all right, but I need you to come pick me up and take me to my car."

"OK, text me the hospital and the address."

"Thank you, boo."

"A'ight. I'll be there shortly."

I can't believe I asked him to pick me up, but I was desperate, and calling Mari was not an option. I gathered my things and walked out to the front to wait on him. I was nervous seeing him because I knew I looked a hot mess. I ran my hand through my tangled weave, trying to straighten it out a bit.

About fifteen minutes later, his car pulled in with the music blasting. I stood up and waved so that he could see me. He pulled up, and I got into his ride. I couldn't help but notice how clean his ride was. It smelled like new leather, and his music was thumping hard.

"Yo, you a'ight? How long you been in here?"

"Since yesterday. I had a bad headache, so I came up here," I lied.

"Damn, ma, you need to take care of yourself."

"I am." I managed to squeeze out a smile.

"Where you going?"

"My car is parked at the Marriott by the airport."

"Okay, bet."

The entire ride was quiet. I had a lot on my mind, especially the death of my bitch. I tried my best not to break down in front of him. Then I heard my phone ringing. I grabbed it out of my purse. It was my other homegirl, Tesha. I already knew what she was calling about.

"Hey, Tesha, I'm busy right now. Let me call you back in a few."

"A'ight, babes." I could tell by the tone in her voice she was crying.

I let out a long sigh, disconnected the phone, and placed it back into my purse.

He pulled up at the hotel. I got out and walked to the front, where I had parked. I noticed that my car was gone. I looked around at the other parking spots, but it was nowhere to be found.

"Hold on. I'll be right back," I leaned into the car and said to Tyrone. Then I walked into the hotel.

"Hello, may I help you?" the clerk asked.

"I parked my car here yesterday, and now it's gone. Do you have an idea who moved it?"

"Are you a guest here?" She shot me a suspicious look.

"No, an incident happened here yesterday, and I was one of the victims. The ambulance carried me away, and my car was left in the parking lot," I said with an attitude.

"Oh, okay. Wait one minute. Let me get my manager." She walked off toward the back of the office.

I waited patiently as an older man walked to the front.

"Hello, ma'am. My clerk told me that you were inquiring about a car left in the parking lot. Well, it's the policy of the hotel to have all vehicles towed if the owner is not a guest at the hotel."

"What the fuck you mean? I was assaulted in *your* hotel, my best friend got murdered, and the *best* you can do is tow my shit? Where the fuck is my car at?" I yelled at the top of my voice.

"Ma'am, it's an unfortunate situation, and we're deeply sorry that happened to you and that other young lady. We are working very closely with the Richmond Police Department to help bring this criminal to justice."

"Man, whatever. Y'all so fucking sorry, y'all couldn't wait to tow my damn car. Just give me the information so I can get my shit out," I yelled and shook my head. I was freaking disgusted. *This* is how they treat me after *they* let a fucking rapist walk through their door?

"Yes, ma'am, sure." He walked off.

Minutes later, he returned and handed me the info with the towing information. I snatched it out of his hand and walked out, cussing under my breath.

"What they say, shawty? Where's your ride at?" Tyrone asked when I walked up to his car. He was standing outside texting on his phone.

"At the fucking tow yard. My head is killing me, and I'm fucking tired. Please drop me at the pharmacy and then at my house."

"If you want, we can go grab your whip real quick. I'm off work today."

"Thanks, but I'm tired, and I don't feel too good. I'll get it tomorrow."

After getting my medicine from Walgreens, I ran off the address to him. I knew I was making a fucked-up decision because Mari's ass might happen to be there, but I was tired and didn't give a fuck right about now. I just needed to crawl into my bed. After all, Tyrone and I were only friends. But in Mari's deranged mind, he will swear to God I was out fucking around.

"Yo, shawty, you sure you a'ight?"

"Yes, I'm fine. Just a little irritated," I lied to him. I really wanted to let him know I wasn't okay. I could use a hug right now.

It felt so good to be around someone who gave a fuck about me. I just had to be careful not to get caught up in his kindness. You know how niggas are when they're trying to get with you. Shit, look at how sweet Mari was when we first started out.

"I don't know what's really going on, but I can tell you're going through some shit. I want you to know you can talk to me about anything. I won't judge you, and if you need a nigga to be there, I'm the one. Shawty, every nigga ain't the same. . . ." He reached over and touched my hand.

I tried to remain still in the seat, but his touch sent chills through my body. I finally managed to move my hand away from his.

"Thank you, but I'm good." I smiled at him, trying to assure him I was straight.

He entered my neighborhood, and my anxiety shot up. I hope that Mari wouldn't be around. As soon as Tyrone pulled up, I wasted no time. I jumped out of the ride.

"Thank you so much," I said before closing the car door.
"No worries. Hit me up if you need me."

I looked at him, smiled, and dashed off. I prayed he
hurried up and drove off. I watched as he pulled off down
the street, then let out a long sigh.

I was at ease when I noticed that Mari wasn't home.
I rushed up the driveway, scared to look back. It was a
relief to be at home alone, even though I knew it might
be short-lived. I rushed up the stairs and turned on the
shower. I needed to scrub my skin the proper way. I even
thought about using bleach to cleanse it.

The water felt great on my body, and the Dove body
wash helped me wash that nigga's smell off my body.
That's when everything hit me. My bitch was lying on ice,
and I would not be able to see her anymore. I was crying
for her and also for myself. How was I supposed to live
with the fact that I was raped? The worst part about it
was that nigga didn't use a condom. I bawled harder as I
thought about how nasty that shit was.

I must've stayed in the shower for almost an hour,
scrubbing and washing between my legs. It got to the
point where it started to burn when I touched it. I finally cut off the water and got out of the shower. After I
got dressed, I made myself a cup of hot chocolate. Then
I took two of the hydrocodone that the doctor had pre-
scribed for me. My body was still sore from that beating I
took from that bastard. Finally, I climbed into bed, hoping to fall asleep right away.

I didn't know how long I'd been asleep, but I knew I
was awakened by Mari poking me.

"Yo, shawty, where the fuck you been?" he yelled.

"Boy, come on. What time is it? You waking me up out
of my sleep," I said in an annoyed tone.

I knew shit was about to get real, so I sat up in bed and
braced myself for what was about to take place.

"Man, answer my fucking question. Where the fuck you been? I been calling yo' ass and texting you with no response for a whole fucking day," he yelled in my face while spit flew everywhere.

"I got raped, okay? I was at the hospital," I blurted out. Shit, that part was the truth.

"Bitch, you think I'm a fool. You go fuck a nigga, and now you screaming you got raped? What nigga was you laid up with?" he yelled louder.

I looked at him good. I just told the nigga that supposedly loved me that I was raped, and all he could do was accuse me of fucking around on him.

"What are you talking about? See, there you go being paranoid and shit. Just because *you* are a ho don't mean *I'm* a ho. Check the fucking news. I got raped, and Ariana got murdered. Now, cut off the light and let me go back to sleep. I'm tired." I tried to lie back down.

He grabbed my arm and pulled me closer to him while pointing his gun at my head.

"Ha-ha, you must think I'm a chump. See, bitch, I could just blow your fucking brain out, but what's the point? A ho gon' always be a ho. I've always known you was fucking around on a nigga. Yo, B, that nigga can have you, 'cause I'm done fucking that nigga's old lady."

"You're cold and sick. You think I would make up a story about being raped? But you're too selfish to see that I'm hurting. A nigga *violated* me and *killed* my bitch. You know what? I'm done with this old stupid-ass relationship."

"What the fuck you want me to say, B? I been telling you, your friend was selling pussy, but what you do? Accuse me of not liking her. What I want to know is, were *you* selling pussy too?"

"Fuck you, Mari. I can't believe I ever loved you. I fuckin' need you, and this how you act. I swear your ass better not ever need me in this life 'cause I ain't gon' be there. You hear me?" I yelled as the tears rolled down my face. It hurts like hell that he wouldn't take my hands and find out what happened to me.

He turned and walked out of the room and down the stairs. Everything in me was yelling for me to get up and run after him. I wanted to tell him about what I'd been through. How that nigga took my pussy without my consent. I needed him to hold me, to tell me it was going to be all right, and he was going to get the bastard that hurt me like that. My heart was willing, but I couldn't move. Then I heard the door slam, and a few minutes later, his car pulled off. I buried my head into my pillow and just cried. There was nothing else to do but pray and cry. I just needed God to ease some of the pain I was feeling.

After the fight with Mari, I drank some wine and when to sleep. Around 2:00 a.m., when I woke up out of a nightmare, I realized that Mari didn't come home. This wasn't really that bad at all because I was tired, and I didn't have the strength to keep fighting with him. I also didn't want to hear him accusing me of all sorts of shit that wasn't even true. I would've shown him my discharge papers, but fuck him. My word should've been good enough. I knew his ignorant ass would get on me about going to the hotel in the first place. He already insinuated that I might be selling pussy too. Since my bitch was dead, I was the only one that could say what happened, and I knew he wouldn't believe me.

I stayed in bed for days, crying about my pain and missing my best friend. We've been through everything in life together, from our first periods and our first boyfriends to our first heartbreaks. I wish I could've saved her, but I know in my heart there's nothing I could've done. I kept taking multiple showers, trying to scrub this nigga off me. Yesterday, I scrubbed so hard my skin started burning. I felt dirty, and each time I closed my eyes, I smelled that nigga. I felt like I was losing it and didn't have anyone to help me get through it.

It was Saturday and Ariana's funeral. I grabbed the phone a few times to call her mother to let her know I couldn't make it, but I hung up before she answered. I didn't go to the wake yesterday 'cause I couldn't drag myself out of bed after a night of drinking and popping pills. But I knew today I had to show up for my girl. The church was packed. Ariana was well known in Richmond, not because she was selling pussy but because she played basketball in high school and was also on the track team. Everyone thought she would go on to play in college, but her senior year, she got sick. We later found out she had sickle cell. From then on, she was always in pain or admitted to the hospital.

I walked in and took a seat. I really didn't want to deal with the crowd. I know people heard we were together and probably guessed that I was selling pussy too. The pastor started preaching like he knew her. That shit kills me. When she was alive, no one gave a fuck about her. Now that she's gone, everybody loves her. Shit was so fake that I couldn't take it anymore. I got up and dashed out the door. I was heading to the stairs when I heard someone yell my name.

"Akila."

I stopped and looked back. It was Miss Lela walking toward me. Shit, I thought I could just sneak up out of here without anyone noticing.

"Hey, Miss Lela." I quickly wiped the tears from my eyes.

"Hey, there, baby. We missed you yesterday at the wake." She reached over and hugged me.

"I'm sorry. I didn't feel too good."

"Baby, listen, you and Ariana were closer than most sisters. I know you're hurting as bad as we are. I love you like you're my own, and I don't want you to be no stranger. You're welcome to stop by anytime. We're family now." She hugged me again.

I hugged her back and let the tears flow. I could feel her warmness in her touch.

"I love you, baby. Stop beating yourself up. That animal did this to my baby, not you. My baby knows that you would've helped her if you could've."

Her words were soothing, but my tears wouldn't let up. I needed to get out of here and get to a place by myself.

"I got to get back in there, baby, but stop by soon. She has a lot of things that I'm going to need help packing up."

"Okay, I will," I squeezed out between sobs.

I watched as she walked off. Then I ran down the stairs and out of the building. I welcomed the fresh air that hit my face. A minute ago, I felt suffocated. I ran to my car and got in, then rested my head on the steering wheel and let it all out. I wished I could stay longer and celebrate my girl's life, but I wasn't strong enough to face her. I felt like I had let her down. I let our friendship down. I wiped my tears and pulled off.

Mari

I'd heard a lot of fucked-up stories that bitches be running on their niggas, but what's crazy is Akila would try to run some of those same lame-ass games on me. I could smell that bullshit a mile away. I knew that bitch couldn't be trusted but was just shocked that she would try me like that. I would've snatched that little bitch up any other time, but not this time. Matter of fact, I looked at that pitiful bitch and just walked away. It was time to run up in some different pussy.

My side bitch, Dreema, had been blowing up my phone all gotdamn evening, but I was in the streets. It was easy to get distracted by a bad bitch, but I knew the consequences. I'd seen a lot of niggas become casualties to the streets because pussy had them losing focus. I've been fucking shawty for a good year and a half now. She was the total opposite of Akila, who was book smart. Dreema was straight hood. Sometimes when I make my runs, shawty would be the one driving the whip. Anything pop off, I can call on her. And trust me, she coming through with the burner. She was as hood and thorough as they come, but I couldn't wife her 'cause she's the kind of bitch that ain't loyal to nobody but the money.

I dialed her number as soon as I pulled off from the crib. "Aye, yo, what's good witcha?"

"Nigga, fuck you. I've been calling you all motherfucking day, and you just now want to answer my call?" she said with an attitude.

"Baby girl, cut it. You know a nigga be in the streets handling business all day long. How the fuck you think I can afford all them Gucci purses or those MK shoes you be wantin'? Get the fuck out of yo' feelings, shawty," I demanded.

"You right, babe. I'm just in my feelings 'cause my pussy was throbbing, and I needed you to come over and fuck me real quick." She switched up real fast.

"Shit, what you got on now?"

"You know I'm always naked. Got to let the pussy breathe."

"Well, I'm on the way. Make sure that pussy stay wet 'til I get there."

I disconnected the phone without waiting for a response. My dick was already rock hard and poking through my sweatpants. Shawty was a certified freak, and I loved fucking her. I had never met another bitch that could take dick like she could. The way shawty fucked and sucked me, I had no problem dropping a couple of stacks on her at any given time. Shit, matter of fact, I thought about cuffing her ass a few times, but she'd been around, and I didn't want no nigga clowning on me like that.

I stopped at the Wawa and grabbed a few blunts on the way over. I was going to get fucked up and get fucked. The goal was to get that bitch Akila off my mind. I parked my car and tucked my nine in my waist. She lived by Southwood Apartments, which was a hot spot for crime right now. I jumped out of my ride and locked the doors.

"Yo, open the door. I'm on the way up." I hung up before she could respond.

She had the door opened by the time I got to it. I kissed her on the lips and squeezed her booty as I walked into the apartment

"You straight, boo?" she quizzed.

"Yeah, I'm good. Nothing that I can't control." I took out the blunt and started rolling.

"Well, while you do that, I'm about to jump in the shower and get this pussy right for you, daddy." She leaned over and grabbed my dick.

"Yeah, you do that." I shot her a dirty look while she massaged my dick through my pants.

I trailed behind Dreema, watching her ass clap while she led the way to her bedroom. *Damn, I can't wait to tear up that pussy,* I thought as my dick got hard thinking about how badly I wanted this pussy. After finishing showering, she walked out of the bathroom and stopped in front of me. I wrapped my arms around her body and started kissing the side and the back of her neck.

"Hmmmm, don't start nothing you can't finish," she said, placing her hands on top of mine, rubbing them. If she only knew. Whatever I started, I was capable of finishing. I continued kissing the back of her neck while grinding my hips on her soft, fluffy ass.

"Mari, you better stop it unless you—" she cut herself off.

"Unless what?" I ran my tongue around the inside of her ear. I felt her entire body shudder.

"Unless what?" I asked again.

"Unless you're gonna fuck the hell out of me."

Soon as I unwrapped her from my arms, she turned around, facing me. Her hazel-brown eyes spoke volumes. "And don't waste my time." She tugged at my pants, unbuckling my belt.

Waste her time? I thought to myself. As long as I wanted to hit the pussy, I surely wasn't going to waste any time. All I was going to do was put in overtime because the Lord is my shepherd, and he knows what I want. I pulled off my shirt and stepped out of my shoes. She stepped back, sizing up my dick.

I smiled. "You don't have to worry about me wasting your time." I chuckled because I was going to fuck the hell out of her.

"You better not," she stuttered, swallowing her spit. I stepped up in front of her, ripping the towel away. This time, I had to step back to get a better look at her bedroom body that God handcrafted himself. "What are you going to do? Look at me or fuck me?"

"Fuck." I stepped back up to her, scooped up her sexy, petite body, and laid her on the bed. Her neatly shaven pussy was purring, looking at me. I was so excited and anxious at the same time. I didn't waste any time easing my hard dick into her wet, warm pussy.

"Easy easy easy," she moaned out as I slowly inched my head into her tight pussy. She held on to my back, squeezing the fuck out of my shit. I could feel her nails digging deeper into my back with each thrust I took. "Ooooh, shit. Mari, it feels so good." Her claws dug deeper into my shit.

I wanted to stop, but the pussy was so good that I continued penetrating her. I swear, she was drawing blood from my back, but I endured the pain and grinded my hips until my nut sack slapped her pussy lips. Sweat dripped from my chin as I sped up my strokes, trying to rip out her insides. Her pussy was so wet, good, and tight as she squeezed her muscles around my dick.

"Sssss, shit, girl," I hissed.

I swear her pussy had me floating on cloud nine. The sweat on my back had my shit burning like it was on fire, but I didn't let that stop me from exploding inside Dreema's womb.

We were now ready for round two. I stood up and slid her over to the edge of the bed. Her legs were on my shoulders as my dick penetrated inside of her walls. Her titties bounced back and forth with each thrust. Her moans grew louder as she begged me to fuck her harder. I leaned over, dropping my weight on her, and then slid my arms under her back until they made their way to her shoulders. I locked my hands on her collarbone and penetrated harder into her pussy.

"Ayeeee," she grunted, taking as much dick as possible. Deema's head was motioning no, but that only made me fuck her harder.

"I'm about to bust, Mari."

As soon as I pulled out, clear liquid shot out of her body, hitting my midsection. She lay there trembling, mesmerized by what her body had just experienced.

I stood back on my feet, looking at the welts on my back in the mirror. *Fuck,* I thought.

Dreema

It's funny how pussy will have a nigga acting like a straight clown out here. Mari's name was ringing bells heavily in the streets of Richmond. But our paths didn't cross until one night at the Canal Club. Me and my bitches were out partying, and I was dancing and enjoying a vibe when my bitch, Yanique, grabbed my arm.

"Look, bitch."

I turned around, trying to see what the hell she was pointing at. This nigga smelled like straight money from a distance. He wore dark blue jeans with a nice buttoned-down shirt and a pair of Tims. To top it off, he had on a NY Yankee fitted cap. His swag was off the chain.

"OK, bitch, who is that?" I asked with an attitude, pretending like I was curious to know the answer.

"Bitch, that's the famous nigga Mari from Virginia Beach."

"You lying. You talking about the moneymaking, taking-over-these-streets Mari?" My face lit up as I stared him down.

Our eyes locked, and he nodded at me and smiled. I wasted no time. I sashayed my ass over to where he was standing.

"Hey, handsome."

"Whaddup, ma?" he grinned, showing his pearly white teeth with one gold cap.

"I'm Dreema. What's your name?" I said as I straightened his shirt.

"Are you always this friendly to every nigga you come across?" He stared me down.

"No, but I saw a nigga that caught my attention, so here I am. Are you gon' tell me your name or what?"

"Damn, ma, chill out. I'm Mari. Nice to meet you, Dreema."

"It's my pleasure, love."

After we got the introduction out of the way, he offered me and my bitch multiple drinks up in the VIP area. We partied together the entire night. We were definitely the envy of all other bitches that wished they were in our spots. When the club shut down at 4:00 a.m., we decided it was too early to call it a night. We got rooms at the Marriott on Broad Street. Mari and I in one room and Yanique and his boy, G, in another room. Not sure what my bitch was doing over there, but my ass was sucking, slurping, and fucking. It's not often that I get to meet a nigga with as much street cred as him. Rumor in the street was this nigga's money was long. Fuck the rumors. I was trying to find out for myself. So, I did what I had to do to make sure this wasn't just a one-time fuck.

The next morning, we woke up, took a shower, and fucked some more. I was surprised how the nigga sucked on my pussy before he fucked me. I hope he didn't have a bitch 'cause the way his beard was buried in my pussy, there's no way she's not going to smell pussy juice all over him.

We started fucking around on the regular, and the nigga started spending stacks on me, took me to the outlets a few times, and even took me to New York on a shopping spree. It didn't take me long to start catching feelings for him. Old people say that if it's too good to be true, it's not true. So one day after we finished fucking, I decided to talk to this nigga about taking our relationship to the next level.

"Hey, boo, I know we've been fucking around for a minute now, but you never said I was your girl. I was wondering if we could start claiming each other."

"Yo, B. I fucks with you heavy, but I got a girl."

"You got a what?" I jumped off the bed and got in his face.

"Yo, chill out. I got a girl, but that don't stop nothing."

"You fucking lied to me. Oh my God, I've been stupid as fuck."

"Chill out wit' all that. I never lied to you. You never asked me if I had a girl. I thought it didn't matter. Shit, why should it? I fuck you like you my bitch and spend money on you like you my bitch. That label shit don't mean nothing. As long as you keep that pussy tight and don't let no other nigga run up in you, you my bitch, and I'm your nigga."

I couldn't believe what I was hearing. This nigga sat there so nonchalantly, acting like he didn't notice the tears rolling down my face. See, I done fucked a bunch of niggas before, but I knew I was only after their money. No strings attached. With Mari, it was different. I let myself slip, and I fell hard for him. After all the time we spent together, where did he find time to have another bitch? Who the fuck was she, and why she ain't wondering where her nigga be at during the night?

"I can't do this. I'm too good of a bitch to be a nigga's side bitch. I fuckin' love you. I'm sure that bitch can't love you like I love you. You really don't need her, boo." I grabbed his hands and stared into his eyes.

"Chill out, ma. You ain't got nothing to worry about. I got you."

He stood up and started kissing me while fondling my breasts. Within seconds, I stepped out of my drawers. He threw me on the bed, parted my legs, and sucked on my clit until I had multiple orgasms. Then he slowed fucked me, reaching every single inch of my body. Soon after he left, I crawled into bed and started crying. I wondered if he left to go be with her. Why wasn't my fuck good enough to keep him around?

Later that night, I called Yanique. She was my best friend and the only one who would understand what I was going through.

"Hey, girl, I ain't heard from you at all. Mari must be keeping that ass on tight ropes."

"Yanique, you and G still talking?"

"On and off. G's ass in too much freaky shit. The other day, the nigga asked me to do a threesome. Don't get me wrong. I don't knock the shit, but it ain't for me. Ever since I told him no, he hardly hits me up, and when I call him, he always acts like he so busy. Girl, fuck him. Why you ask? He said something?"

"No, I ain't hear nothing. But, girl, I found out Mari got a bitch."

"Where you hear that from?"

"He told me with his own mouth."

"Bitch, you lying. So, this nigga just come out of the blue and tell you he got a bitch? That's some crazy shit. You my bitch and all, but did you expect that nigga *not* to have no other ho outside of you?"

"Bitch, yeah. I know what the fuck I bring to the table, so, yeah, I expect a nigga to only fuck with me. Why would I think he got another bitch when we're always together? Shit, we fuckin' without condoms, and he eating my pussy. Does that seem like a nigga that's in a relationship?"

"Well, you have some good points, but you know how dirty these niggas are. All that shit don't mean a damn thing. You better pray his bitch ain't got no STD or something worse."

"Bitch, I'm so mad at him, I don't know what the fuck to do with myself. That nigga could've told me he had a bitch," I vented.

"What would that change from the night you met him? You still would've fucked him. Look at it like this. The nigga been spendin' hella money on you. Shit, he even takes you on trips and shit. That's way more than I got. I only got a fucking meal at Outback Steakhouse. Bitch, you better quit complaining. Plenty bitches wish they were in your shoes right now. Him having a bitch don't mean a damn thing. Let that dumb bitch keep playing house while her nigga and you live life to the fullest. You need to boss up and play your position. Shit, he might even forget about that ho."

I sat there listening to Yanique spit some knowledge to me. One thing about her . . . She never let nothing get her down. I wish sometimes I was like her with that "I don't give a fuck" attitude.

"You know what? You're right, Yanique. I mean, I never seen the bitch, and he never answers his phone when he's around me. Well, fuck her."

"That's my bossy bitch. Listen, for years, these hoes been fucking our niggas behind our backs. Shit, it's our time to fuck the niggas and let them hoes worry about what their niggas doing."

"You're so right. I'm not going to worry about who he's fucking. Shit. Instead, I'ma play my position. My goal is to get a house out of this nigga and a phat-ass bank account."

"Now you talkin', bitch. And please don't forget about yo' best friend when you go on these shopping sprees."

"Bitch, you know I got you."

We talked for about twenty more minutes, then hung up. I'm happy that I called Yanique 'cause I feel so much better now. Mari was mine, and that's how I would carry it from now on. Fuck that bitch, whoever she is. Hopefully, she'll find out about us and decide to leave him. In the meantime, I will be fucking and sucking him whenever I want.

Chapter Four

Akila

It took me a few minutes before I could pull off from the church. I wasn't in the best frame of mind to be driving, but I had no choice. I thought about going to the burial ground, but I knew I wasn't strong enough to handle it. My girl has to know if I could, I would be there. About two blocks up the street, another car was in front of me, so I drove slowly. I spotted a car that looked like Mari's car parked by a detailing shop to the right of me. The closer I got, I knew for sure it was. I spotted him right away, dressed in black and white. He was standing beside his car with a light-skinned bitch hugged up on him. I pulled over to the side in a rush and jumped out of my car, leaving the engine running. They were so deep into each other that they didn't see me running up on them.

"Yo, who the fuck is this bitch?" I ran up to him, asking as I grabbed his shoulder.

"Yo, shawty, what the fuck you doing?" he asked with a shocked look.

"Mari, who is this bitch? Better yet, you need to get her before I drag her ass all over these streets."

I turned around, and without any words, I popped that bitch in her cute little mouth. "Bitch, I'm right here, so how about you try beating my ass." So I started pounding that bitch's face with my fists.

"Yo, chill the fuck out, yo. What the fuck you doin', yo?" That nigga grabbed me up and threw me up against his ride.

"Fuck you, bitch. If you were fucking him right, he wouldn't have to be over here sucking on this sweet pussy," his ho teased and smiled.

"Man, Dreema, chill out wit' all that," he yelled at that bitch.

"So, this is the tramp you were with for the last couple of nights?" I got back into his personal space.

"Yes, he sure was, bitch. Tell her how you was sucking on this pussy and licking my ass while I called you daddy, babe." She grinned. I could tell this ho was basking in my pain.

I lunged toward that ho again, but Mari jumped in the middle, grabbing me up again. He pinned me against his car. "Nigga, put me the fuck down." I tried clawing at his face.

He gripped my arm so tight it started hurting. "You better listen to me, shawty. Take yo' ass home. What the fuck you out here acting like one of these regular-ass bitches for? Man, get in your fucking car and go home." He yelled like I was nothing to him.

Tears flowed from my face because I felt betrayed and humiliated. I'd just caught that nigga with a bitch, and *that* was how he talked to me? I felt so fucking hurt and just wanted to get the fuck away from him.

"Man, put me the fuck down," I demanded.

"Not if you gon' be out here showing out. You need to get in yo' car and go home."

That nigga picked me up and carried me to my car. I tried my best to get out of his grip, but I was no match for his strength. He opened my car door, threw me inside, and closed the door. I thought about jumping out and running to the bitch again, but I knew it would be hard to get around Mari. So I stayed in the car and rested my head on my steering wheel. I was so upset that I was shaking. I watched as he walked back over to the bitch and started talking to her. I could tell she was cussing him out. It broke my heart to see my nigga standing in front of me with his side bitch instead of over here with me. Finally, I couldn't take it anymore, so I started my car and pulled the fuck off. That nigga had crossed the fucking line. I wondered how many other bitches he was fucking, or as that ho said, "sucking on pussies." The thought of that nigga out there slinging dick everywhere, and he had me sucking his dick made me sick. My stomach was so upset that I pulled over and threw up. Then I sat there for a few minutes before closing the door and pulling off.

K. Michelle's song blasted through the speakers as I drove through Richmond's streets heading home. That was where I really didn't want to be, but I had nowhere else to stay. *God, I need a change,* I thought as I wiped the snot away from my nose.

I walked into the house and went straight to the cabinets. I needed something strong that could numb the pain that I was feeling.

Chapter Five

Akila

Three Months Later

They say time waits for no man. I had to get my shit in order fast. Losing my best friend was one of the hardest things I had to deal with. For weeks following her death, all I did was drink wine and pop hydrocodone and whatever else pills I could get my hands on. Also, dealing with the rape was a daily struggle for me. Some days were better than others. I thought about seeing a shrink, but I wasn't ready to pour my soul out to a bitch. My grades in school were dropping right before I was supposed to graduate. To be honest, my life was spiraling downhill, and I had no idea how I was going to fix this mess.

Mari's behavior had been out of control since I caught him with that bitch. At first, he kept denying that he was fucking with her until one day, he was so upset that he blurted out that he'd been fucking her. What made the situation worse for me was I inquired about that bitch and found out she was one of Richmond's biggest hoes. My homegirl knew her and how she got down. It puzzled me that my man could treat me like this over a ho that didn't really love him.

He would come and go, and I would do the same. It hurts to be around him, but until I come up with a better plan, this was how it would be for now. Even though we lived in the same house, we barely spoke. I was cool with it, though 'cause I didn't want him to ask for some pussy. I would often have flashbacks of the nigga raping me. I have no idea if I would be able to have sex with a man ever again.

I parked my car and got out. It felt weird to be back at school after taking off a few months. I was, however, excited to get back into my regular schedule because depression was slowly killing me.

"Hey, beautiful." A familiar voice startled me as I walked down the hallway to my class.

I turned around to face Tyrone. This dude was so fucking sexy. I looked at him from head to toe. I was happy to see him.

"Hey, Tyrone," I said seductively.

"Damn, shawty. I've called and texted you almost every day and got no response. How you feeling?"

"Yeah, I know. I was going through some stuff and just needed to be alone for a while. I'm sorry."

"Well, as long as you are alive and kicking, you good. Aye, yo, so you ready to let me take you out on a date?"

I let out a long sigh. I really wanted to, but Mari was in the back of my mind.

"Well, you know I'm just starting to feel better, so can I take a rain check?"

"Of course. You know I'm around, so just hit my line when you ready to take me up on that offer. You still have my number, right?"

"Of course, I do."

I smiled at him as we walked into the building and the classroom. The entire time the instructor was teaching, I kept glancing over at Tyrone. He was too busy even to notice that I was checking for him. I honestly could see us together—if only Mari wasn't in the damn picture. But wait . . . Why was I worried about a nigga who was fucking bitches and treating me like I ain't shit? Sometimes I wish I didn't love him. It would make it so much easier to fuck another nigga without feeling guilty.

I was home watching television when I heard Mari walk through the door. Normally, he would walk by and pretend like I wasn't around. But this time, he walked into the room and stood in front of me.

"We need to talk."

"Talk about what? I thought you said everything that you wanted to say." I continued watching the television, making sure I didn't make eye contact with him.

"Yo, I'm sorry for the shit I said and you finding out about ole girl, but you wrong for being gone all day."

"I told you where the fuck I was at. But don't use me disappearing as no excuse. You been running around here fucking that bitch while I sit in this house waiting on you to come home. You played me, Mari." I was getting emotional, but I was determined not to break down in front of him.

"Shawty, I'm sorry. I'm a man, and I fuck up sometimes, but that don't mean I don't love you. I love you. I do everything for you. I don't do none of that shit for no other bitch."

"You sound crazy as hell. So just because you're taking care of me, it gives you the right to cheat on me? I'm faithful. I never fucked another nigga on you. I gave you my soul, and this is how you treat me."

"Come here, baby. I'm sorry, for real. I'm sorry that I wasn't there for you when you got raped. I admit I was an asshole to you. I swear to God, my intentions were not to hurt you, bae. Just give me a chance to make it up to you. I can be a better man for you."

"I don't know, Mari. You really hurt me and carried me over that bitch. I can't do this."

"That bitch means nothing to me. I have you here with me. That should tell you I love you." He wrapped his hand around me.

I couldn't hold the tears in anymore. So I let them out on him. He wiped my tears and started kissing me all over. I tried resisting at first, but I still loved him, so my feelings were still there. This was my first time after getting raped, and I was scared.

"I'm scared, Mari. I don't think I can do this." Tears welled up in my eyes.

"Boo, there's no need to be scared. I got you, and I promise I'll take my time with you." He held me tight as he started playing with my pussy.

My mind was telling me one thing, and my body reacted another way. Before you could blink, his head was buried between my legs, and my legs were on his shoulders. I trembled as he sucked on my pussy. After I came all over his face, I got on top of him. Images of that nigga on me tried to pop in my mind, but I used everything in my power to block out those images. He was the devil, and there's no way I would let him control me like this. I started thinking of good memories of Mari and me. I smiled as I thought about some crazy but fun times. I closed my eyes and rode his dick. I don't know what I was trying to prove, but I know this bitch couldn't love him like I do. I had to remind him that I had some good pussy, and he was the only nigga that ever tasted or fucked me. Surprisingly this time, he didn't pull out.

***

It was the weekend, and I was doing laundry. Mari was out running the damn streets, and I was happy he wasn't home. Things between us had gotten a little better, but not completely good. I still didn't trust him. Each time he walked through the door, I wondered if he was leaving to go be with her. Every time we got into an argument, he would accuse me of cheating on him the day that I got raped. There were times when I wanted to break down and tell him what really happened to me, but I knew he was too arrogant to understand what I'd been through.

I heard my phone ringing. I grabbed it and saw it was my homegirl, Tesha. Even though I wasn't in the mood to talk, I knew she wouldn't stop calling until we spoke.

"Yo, bitch, I've been trying to call you. I've been worried about you. I still can't believe Ariana gone like that."

"I'm over here doing laundry. Yes, that's fucked up what happened to her. I still can't believe she's gone too." I tried fighting back the tears.

"Bitch, I ain't been myself since the funeral. I got something to talk to you about too."

"Damn, bitch. Spit it out."

"Are you at the house?"

"Yup, but you know this nigga don't want nobody over here."

"Girl, fuck him. Meet me at South Side Plaza real quick. I got to pick up some hair."

"Damn, bitch. I just told yo' ass I was washing clothes."

"Fuck them damn clothes and come meet me real quick. I need to holler at you about something."

"A'ight, man. I'll text you when I'm on the way."

After we hung up, I stood there thinking. What the fuck was so important that I had to meet her ass in person? That bitch had never held her tongue before, so why the fuck was she acting all suspicious and shit? I threw the washed clothes in the dryer and filled up the washer before leaving. I had already bathed, so I got dressed and headed out. I texted her to let her know I was on the way.

My phone started ringing, and I grabbed it.

"Hello."

"Yo, babes," Mari's voice echoed in my ear.

"Hey, you," I mustered up to say.

"What you doing?"

"On my way to South Side Plaza."

"Oh, okay. You gon' grab your nigga something?"

"Not really. Just gonna get a nail that I broke fixed."

"A'ight, yo." He hung up.

That was strange. That nigga never called just to see what I was doing. I couldn't help but wonder what the fuck was going on with that nigga for real.

I pulled into the parking lot and parked. Then I called Tesha's phone to inquire about her whereabouts.

"Where you at?"

"Girl, inside the fish market where we usually get shrimp from. You know my fat ass love food."

"Well, I'm outside. Come on out here."

"A'ight."

I spotted her as she walked outside of the fish market, holding a plate of food. The way that bitch loved food, I was surprised she wasn't as big as a cow. She spotted my car, walked over, and opened the door.

"Hey, girl." She took a seat while she sipped on her drink.

"Bitch, what the fuck was so important that you couldn't tell me over the phone?" I quizzed her while I shot her a suspicious look.

"Damn, ho, calm your nerves. You know you my bitch, and ever since our bitch . . ." She paused while she choked back her tears.

I reached over and grabbed her hand. I was pretty sure I knew what she was talking about.

"It's okay, boo. She's in a better place. I bet that fool's up there looking down on us and laughing her ass off." I felt a tear drop fall from my eye. I tried my hardest not to cry.

After a few minutes, I managed to get my feelings under control. "A'ight, bitch, so what's up with you, and what you have to tell me?" I tried to change the subject because God knows I was still hurting from losing my bitch.

She wiped her tears and took a few minutes to get herself together. "I'm good, you know, working and trying to stay out of the way. But, umm, you know you my bitch, and I fucks with you hard, right?" She looked at me.

"Yeah, and . . .?"

"Well, I don't be in nobody's business, especially no relationship shit. I got my own bullshit to worry about, but you my dawg, and I got to put you up on game—"

"Bitch, what you talkin' about?" I cut her off because I was curious to find out where the fuck she was going.

"I know Mari is your nigga, but I saw him the other day with another bitch."

"Really? Where the fuck was he at?"

"Not just any bitch, but that Spanish bitch, Dreema, and the bitch was pregnant."

I felt the world around me spinning as I tried to digest what the fuck she was saying to me. That was the same bitch that I caught him with that day.

"Are you fucking serious? That can't be his baby. That bitch is a ho anyways. Her ass be fucking e'erything 'round here." I was trying to convince myself that what she'd said was foolishness.

"I'm sorry, boo, but there's no way I could keep that from you. I asked King if Mari was fucking around with her, and he confirmed it. You know he knows e'erything that goes down in these streets."

I put my head on the steering wheel and let the tears fall from my eyes.

"Baby, I'm sorry, but I had to let you know what's going on. You know these fuck niggas ain't loyal these days. Trust me; I had my share of no-good-ass niggas." She rubbed my back.

It was like my heart was ripped out of my chest. That fuck nigga had been cheating, and not only that, but he also got a bitch pregnant? After crying my heart out and my bitch consoling me, I managed to get my emotions under control.

"Listen, boo, I'm about to bounce. I'll call you later."

"A'ight, babe. I'm here for you, and if you need somewhere to stay, you can always come stay with me."

"Thank you." I hugged her, and she got out of the car.

Then I started the car and pulled off in a hurry. I felt my chest tighten as I tried to gasp for air. The idea of another bitch being pregnant by that nigga left me nauseated. That bum acted like he wasn't ready for children. All along, he was running up in that old nasty-ass bitch raw. I felt the urge to throw up. I pulled the car over and opened my car door. Everything that I ate that morning came back up. I sat there for a few minutes. Then I closed the car door and pulled off. I wish I didn't have to go home, but I had nowhere else to go. I had a few dollars saved up, but I knew it wouldn't be enough to get my place, plus get furniture. Nobody was going to rent a place to me without a damn job.

My head started hurting as reality smacked me dead in the face. I'd relied on that nigga so much that I really didn't have shit to call my own. The tears started pouring down again as I pulled into the driveway. I sat in the car for a few minutes, trying to get my emotions under control.

That night, Mari came into the house around 11:00 p.m. and entered the room with a plate of Chinese food. "Aye, babe, I figured you were hungry, so I grabbed your favorite from Mr. Chin." He handed the food to me.

"Put it in the fridge. I'm not really hungry."

"You passing up Chinese food? That's a first. You a'ight?" he inquired.

"Yeah, I'm good," I lied as I dried my eyes.

The savage side of me wanted to confront this nigga, but all he would do is lie to my face, and it wasn't like I had proof that ho was pregnant. So I decided to stay quiet for a while until I could prove it.

He hurried to the shower as he'd been doing lately. I guess his ass was washing his ho's smell off him. I thought of getting up and checking his pants for his phone, but I quickly remembered that he had a code on his phone. So, I lay there plotting on how I would get any kind of evidence on him and that bitch.

Dreema

Present Day . . .

Mari's and my relationship was going strong. A few nights out of the week, he would disappear, claiming he was out grinding. This nigga must not know that I have three brothers out in the streets. I know damn well for a nigga on his level, he got runners, so he doesn't have to sit up in no trap house. I tried not to fuss at him because I wanted to be his peace so he could come home to me whenever that ho got rid of him. This was where he rightfully belonged.

For weeks, I wasn't feeling too well. At first, I thought it was the flu, but I didn't have a cold or fever, so I quickly dismissed that. Then Yanique and I were at the house chilling one afternoon, smoking, drinking, and eating crab legs when I began to feel nauseated. I got up quickly and ran off to the bathroom. Within seconds, my head was buried in the toilet, and all the crab legs were coming back up. I felt so weak. I rested my head on the toilet for a few moments, trying to get a little strength.

"Bitch, you straight in here?" Yanique knocked on the door.

"I'm coming," I mumbled.

I finally gathered enough strength to get up and brush my teeth. Then I washed my face and stumbled out of the bathroom. I felt dizzy as I walked back into the kitchen, where Yanique sat still ripping through the crab legs.

"Damn, bitch, what you have? The shits? Yo' ass been in the bathroom for a long-ass time," she said as she looked at me strangely.

"Girl, nah. I threw up everything that I ate." I took a seat on the stool.

"Vomit? Bitch, you got the bug, or you pregnant. Oh, hell nah, bitch."

"Girl, you trippin'. I'm on the pill, and trust me, I stay on point with that."

"Bitch, I'm not saying you don't, but if you don't have the flu bug, then the next possible answer would be you knocked up. Shit, imagine if you pregnant with Mari's baby? Bitch, you're going to be paid out the ass. You don't have to shake yo' ass for a living no more." She seemed a little too excited.

"Bitch, calm the fuck down. I'm not pregnant." I tried convincing myself that I wasn't.

"Mmmm, I hear you. You in denial. You know you look like you glowing. I was going to say something about that earlier when I came over, but it slipped my mind."

I didn't feel like going back and forth with her ass. I mean, if I were pregnant, I would know. Furthermore, my period is supposed to come Monday, so I wasn't stressing out over some shit that ain't true. I tried eating some more of the crab, but my stomach was turned, and the smell turned me off. So I decided to make myself a cup of soup instead. After eating the soup, I thought I would feel better, but it didn't help.

"Listen, I'ma go lie down. Turn the knob when you leave."

"Damn, bitch, I can tell you really not feeling good. I'ma leave now. Let me clean up real quick. I got to pick up Mama from the clinic anyways."

I sat there as she cleaned up the crabs. Finally, she put some in the fridge.

"A'ight, bitch, call me if you need me. I'll call and check up on you later."

"Okay."

After she left, I locked the door and dragged myself to the room. I cut on the air and got under the cover. I prayed when I woke up, I would feel way better than what I was feeling now.

It'd been a week since I first started feeling sick, and no matter what I tried, I still felt nauseated, and these headaches were killing me. What was most alarming is I missed my period. I kept praying that it was late, but the more days went by, the more I had to face the fact that maybe I was knocked up. I tried not to say anything to Mari before I was 100 percent sure I was pregnant.

After feeling sick all day, I pulled myself out of bed, took a quick shower, and dragged on sweatpants and a shirt. I didn't worry about my hair. I brushed it in a messy bun and grabbed my car keys. It's been days since I left my apartment, so when I stepped outside, the brightness hit me in my face. I walked to my car and got in, waiting a few minutes to warm it up before pulling off. I parked and walked into Walgreens. I looked for the aisle with feminine products. I glanced around and spotted the pregnancy tests. There were so many I was confused about which one to buy. Some of these shits were high as hell. Shit, I spotted one for under ten dollars, so I grabbed it.

I was nervous as hell as I drove back to the house. There's no way around taking this test. I needed to know what the fuck was going on with me. If I'm not pregnant, then I need to take my ass to the doctor to find out what's wrong.

I entered the bathroom, peed into the cup, then followed the steps. I put the test flat on the sink. Then I walked out of the bathroom to grab some ginger ale. I walked back into the bathroom and picked up the test. The first thing that hit my eyes was the two pink lines. I knew from reading the box that two lines mean "pregnant." I leaned against the door while I stared at the test in my hand.

My mind quickly jumped on Mari. What the fuck would he say when I tell him? I told him before I was on the pill. I didn't lie, and I've been taking my medication daily, so I was shocked at how the fuck I ended up pregnant. I walked to my room and placed the test on my nightstand. I picked up the phone to call him, then quickly decided not to. This wasn't something I needed to tell him over the phone. I would wait until he came over that night. I still couldn't believe this shit. I love

Mari and everything, so it wasn't like I was trying to get pregnant by him. Instead, I dialed Yanique's number.

"Yes, bitch? This better be important 'cause I was on the phone with my boo."

"Girl, what boo?"

"This new nigga I met the other night on Broadrock."

"Damn, bitch, you change men more than you change drawers."

"Some of us are not lucky enough to find niggas with money. So we have to keep fucking 'til we find the right one."

"Yanique, I'm pregnant."

"Bitch, I told you. I *told* youuuu," she screamed into the phone.

"Bitch, calm down. Why you all happy and shit?"

"Shit, bitch, you should be happy too. If you not, you a damn fool."

"I don't know how I'ma tell Mari."

"Bitch, call his ass over and shove the test on him. Shit, he gon' be a daddy."

My bitch was happy and everything, but she had no idea how nervous I was to tell Mari. I was scared that he wouldn't be so happy or excited. What if he accused me of trapping him?

"I don't know, Yanique. Maybe I just need to get an abortion without him knowing."

"Bitch, you a damn fool if you kill yo' baby. How many bitches you know get pregnant the first time, and it's for a money nigga? Bitch, you better wake the fuck up."

"You're right, 'Nique. I just don't want to put a rift between me and him. You know how babies change niggas."

"Trust me. He don't look like the kind that will walk away from his seed. He ain't gon' want the streets to start talking. And trust me, with my big-ass mouth, they will know if he don't take care of his seed."

"Bitch, you gon' get us killed," I chuckled.

"All right, boo, thanks for listening to me. I'ma call you tomorrow."

"Anytime, boo. You know I got your back."

After we hung up, I lay on my back, thinking of the perfect way to break the news to Mari. Then I looked at the time on the phone. It was getting late. So I decided to shoot him a text.

Are you still coming through?

Mari: Yeah, wrapping up something; then I'm on the way.

I smiled as I read his text. I love spending time with him, and each time he comes around me is like I get these fluttering feelings in my stomach. I swear I wish I didn't have to share him with another bitch. Hopefully, when he learns about our child, he'll be willing to give up that ho and let us be a family. I tried staying up so I'd be awake when Mari came by, but sleep was killing me. This was the story of my life lately: nauseated and sleepy. Finally, I couldn't take it anymore. I closed my eyes while I held the phone in my hand.

I felt the phone vibrating. When I opened my eyes and looked, I saw Mari calling.

"Hello," I said, half-woke.

"Man, I been calling you. Come open the door," he said with an attitude.

I dragged myself out of bed and walked to the door, preparing for him and his nasty attitude.

"Yo, I been calling you, B."

"I was sleeping. You *do* know I go to bed at night, right?" I shot back in an annoyed voice.

The way I was feeling, I wasn't in the mood for this nigga and his attitude. He walked off into the bedroom, and I followed him. I got back into bed while he sat there checking his phone.

"I need to talk to you," I blurted out. This might not be the best time, but fuck it. Might as well get it over with.

"Yeah? What's good?" He still didn't lift his head to acknowledge me or anything.

Okay, this is how he wants to act. So I reached over to my dresser, grabbed the pregnancy test, and placed it beside him. He looked over at it, then at me.

"What the fuck is this?"

"It's a pregnancy test. I'm pregnant."

"What the fuck you mean you pregnant, B?" he yelled.

"I don't know what you're yelling for. We fucked without condoms, the pill didn't work, and now I'm pregnant with yo' seed." I broke it down for his ass since he wanted to act like he didn't understand what was going on.

"Yo, you know I got a bitch. Why the fuck you didn't take your pill?" He stood up and looked at me.

"Nah, nigga. *You* knew you had a bitch, but you still was running up in me raw. Don't you fucking try to blame me for some shit we both responsible for."

"Yo, you right, B. So how much is the abortion?" He took a stack of cash out of his pocket.

"Abortion? Who said anything about an abortion?"

"You can't have the baby, B. I'm not ready. Plus, I'm in the streets too much."

"You're in the streets, not me, and I don't plan on killing my first child. So, you can run along to your bitch. I'm good by myself."

"Yo, you trippin', B. You really need to think about what you're going to do. Hit my line when you change your mind." He turned and walked out.

I got up off the bed and ran behind him. "*Really*, Mari? It's all good when we're fucking around, but now that I'm pregnant, you switch up?"

He stopped and turned to face me. "Listen, B. I love you and everything, but you know what it is. Part of me can't help but think you did this to trap a nigga."

"To trap you? Is *that* what you think of me? I fuckin' love you and do every fuckin' thing you asked of me. I stuff your drugs in my pussy, drive cars full of drugs from New York, and get fuckin' guns in my name for you. I do every fuckin' thing, and *this* is how you treat me? I don't see that bitch you lovin' on doing shit for you."

"Yo', you trippin', B. Miss me with all this emotional shit. You do shit for me, and I fucking take care of you. You drive the latest, wear designer clothes, and I bet that account looking lovely. I ain't gon' sit here arguing. Like I said, hit my phone."

He opened the door and walked out. I was shocked that he was behaving like this. He just fucking walked out the door like I didn't mean shit to him. I locked my door and ran back to my room. I dialed his number back to back, but he never answered. I left multiple voice messages cussing him out. I hate the way he just carried me. I know I deserve way better than this shit. I buried my head in my pillow and started crying my heart out.

It's been days since Mari and I had that altercation, and as much as I missed being around him, I decided not to hit him up any longer. I was never a weak bitch, and I don't give a fuck how good this nigga fucked me or how much money he throws my way. I ain't gon' let him carry me out in these streets. Shit, I've been making my own money since I was 16. One thing about me—I'ma get mine regardless.

Mari

Man, my life had been spiraling out of control lately. Niggas in the streets were coming at us from every angle. Akila seemed distant lately even though I told her I was sorry about the shit she went through. The worst was find-

ing out Dreema was pregnant. I was shocked as fuck when
she called me over and showed me her fucking test. I was
busting all up in her 'cause she told me she was on the pill. I
had no reason to doubt her until she screamed, she's pregnant. I told her to get an abortion, but she wasn't trying
to hear that shit. I knew then my life was about to change.
At first, I put it out of my mind, but the bigger her stomach got, the more reality hit me that I was about to have a
seed. Lately, I'd been stressed out, fearing that Akila might
find out about this baby. She was ready to get pregnant for
a while now, but I kept telling her we were not ready. So, I
could imagine how the fuck she was going to react when
she found out another bitch was having my baby.

I decided to stop by the bar and kick it with my brother
for a little while. We'd both been so busy grinding that
we rarely saw each other anymore. Tonight, we planned
on meeting up and having a few drinks, talking shit, and
shooting pool. This little spot by Shockoe Bottom was
real chill, so we decided to meet up there. As soon as I
walked in, I spotted him by the bar.

"Whaddup, bro?" I greeted him.

"I can't call it." We exchanged daps, and I ordered a
shot of Patrón with a beer.

"Nigga, you straight?" my brother asked as we shot
pool at the bar.

"Yeah, why?" I asked as I gathered the balls.

"I don't know. Your game just a little off. Normally, you
be killing it."

"Man, just a lot of shit on the brain. You remember
Dreema from the apartments?"

"Yeah, why? She used to have the strip parties all the
time, right?" He looked at me strangely.

"Yeah, well, you know she pregnant, and that's supposedly my seed."

"Ha-ha. Nigga, you trippin'. You mean to tell me you ran up in that freak raw?" He shook his head as he lined up the balls.

"Man, it was one night. We were both fucked up off the Xany, and the shit happened. Now, she 'bout six months pregnant." I took a sip of my Patrón.

"Damn, bro, I see why you stressed out. You're having yo' first seed by a certified freak. This some crazy shit. Does Akila know?" He caught me off guard.

"Nah, she don't know. That's what stressing me the fuck out. I been trying to come up with the right way to tell her, but I still can't figure it out yet."

My brother irked my soul with that statement. I mean, he wasn't lying, but shit, there was nothing I could do about it. I thought about denying that I even fucked her, but we didn't have a daddy growing up, and I wasn't going to walk away from mine.

"Shit, you only got three months, and there's no right way to tell your woman that your freak is pregnant with your baby. You know the streets talk, so you might need to handle that ASAP before one of these bitches find out and tell Akila."

"You right, bro. Shit just ain't that easy. I'll figure out something, though." I tried to convince myself.

"Yeah, well, I always tell you about fucking with these freaks. I hope you gon' take a blood test once the baby is born. Just don't take the word of a freak."

"I plan on it." I took the last sip of the Patrón and walked off to grab another one.

We played a few more games; then bro decided to call it a night. I heard his phone going off, so I knew that was wifey calling. Sometimes I wished that I could be more like my bro, faithful to one woman. But no matter how hard I tried, I could never do it. So I quickly dismissed that idea. I loved bitches, and I loved fucking different pussy.

"A'ight, bro, I'm out. Be easy." He dapped me and left.

"A'ight, bro. I'll hit you tomorrow."

I watched as my big brother disappeared out of the lounge and into the darkness. Then I pulled out my phone. I was about to call Akila, but I heard gunshots before I could hit *send.*

Pop! Pop! Pop!

I pulled out my 9 mm from my waist and dashed out the door, not knowing what was happening. All I know is my brother just went through those doors. I glimpsed a dark-colored Denali pull off in a rush. I took a quick glance around the parking lot, desperately looking to see if I could spot my brother or his ride.

"Help, over here! Oh my God, he's been shot," I heard a female voice cry out.

My heart started thumping, and I ran as fast as my feet would take me over to where the sounds were coming from. As soon as I got there, my heart stopped when I saw who was shot. "Oh God, no." I dropped to the ground as I knelt beside my brother. "What the fuck happened? Who did this?" I asked as I lifted his head from the concrete while looking around to see if I saw anything suspicious.

"Somebody call 911! They over here. Somebody got shot," I heard someone yell.

"Bro, I got you. Hang on, bro." I used all the strength that God gave me, plus more, and lifted my big brother. Then I threw him in his car. I searched his pocket and found his keys. I jumped in his car and pulled off, almost running over the nosy-ass motherfuckers who were crowded around.

When I got to the entrance, the light was red. I didn't bother to stop. Instead, I honked the horn and drove out into traffic. There was no way I would wait until the motherfucking light turned green.

"Pussy, get out of the motherfucking way," I hollered at the fuck nigga that tried to cut me off. That nigga said some shit, but I didn't have any time to waste arguing with him. If it were another place or time, I would've got out and shot that nigga between the eyes. Instead, I pressed the gas and sped down the street. I had to get my brother to the hospital. Please, God . . . My mind was racing as my hands trembled on the steering wheel. I took a quick glance over my shoulder, and I could tell it wasn't good. Blood was everywhere, and his groans were getting louder.

"Aye, bro, I need you to pull over," his faint voice said.

"Pull over? What the fuck you talking about, bro? I'm trying to get you to the hospital."

"Bro, listen to me. I ain't gon' make it, but I need you to be out here to take care of my family."

"Man, shut the fuck up talking like that. You ain't gon' no-motherfucking-where. You goin' be a'ight, you hear me?" I yelled between sobs.

"Bro, pull the fucking car over. . . ."

Man, this nigga's tripping, I thought as I pulled over. I reached over and grabbed his gun off the seat. I also took my gun. Then I popped the trunk, grabbed the duffel bag, and glanced around. I was looking to see if I saw any place where I could hide that shit, so I could come back and grab it later. I spotted an old car nearby. I ran over there and shoved everything all the way in, hoping no one would see it. I got up, looked around, and ran back to the car. Then I ran to the side where my brother was.

"Bro, hold on. I'm about to get you there."

He was choking on the blood, so I tilted his head. I quickly took off my coat and put it up under his head. He grabbed my hand. "Bro, I love you. I love you, man. Please take care of Shari and my girls . . ." his voice faded out.

"Bro, chill out. You ain't goin' no—"

Before I could finish my sentence, he grabbed my hand. His body started shaking, and he started gurgling on his blood. I held him close to me as I fought back the tears. Within seconds, he took two big gulps, and then complete silence took over. His eyes were wide open . . .

"Noooo," I screamed out with everything in my soul. Tears flooded down as I hugged my big bro, my best friend, and my protector since the day I was born.

"Bro, nah. Wake up, my nigga. Wake up." I tried shaking him, but he wouldn't move. He just lay there. I fell to my knees and just hugged his warm body. "God, please don't do this to me. Take me instead, God. Take me, nigga," I yelled out in anguish.

Chapter Six

Akila

The phone kept ringing nonstop. At first, I kept ignoring it, but it wouldn't ease up. So I finally snatched it off the nightstand.

"Hello," I answered with an attitude.

"Bae, I need you," Mari's voice said.

"What the fuck you talking about? Shouldn't you be calling your other bitches?" I didn't wait for a response. I hung up. Even though I tried not to say anything about what I heard, I wanted him to know I was up on his game.

The phone started ringing again. I knew I should've blocked that nigga from calling me. I knew I might pay for it later, but I didn't give a damn about all that. The nigga kept calling me back-to-back.

"Boy, leave me the fuck alone," I yelled into the phone.

"Kila, Rio got killed tonight. I need you to come get me, shawty. I need you, Kila."

"Boy, shut the fuck up talking stupid. It's crazy that you would come with some lie like that."

"Shawty, my brother is goooone. . . ." his voice trailed off.

Oh my God, he isn't joking. "What the fuck happened, and where are you?" I jumped off the bed while my heart started racing and quickly grabbed my Victoria's Secret Pink sweatpants hanging on the edge of the bed. Then I started putting them on while he tried his best to explain to me what was going on. I really couldn't understand some of what he was saying because he was crying, and it seemed like he was gasping for air.

"Where are you now? A'ight, I'm on the way."

I hung up, quickly washed my face, slid on my sneakers, and grabbed my purse. My adrenaline was rushing as I sped downstairs. I jumped into my car and pulled out. All my anger toward that nigga was gone right now, and all I could think about was getting to my man. I was doing 100 mph all the way, not caring if I got pulled over by the police.

I pulled up, quickly parked, then ran inside. I saw him sitting down with his head in his hand. I ran over to him. "Boo, what the fuck happened?" I sat beside him and put my arm around him.

"My brother is gone, shawty. . . . He's gone." He started bawling.

I took his head and leaned it against my chest. My heart started to hurt for him. I could feel his pain because I knew how close they were.

I finally got him to leave the hospital. The police came and questioned him, but he really didn't tell them anything that could help them find his brother's killer. I know Mari, and he wasn't the type of nigga to run his mouth to the law. I knew him well enough to know that he was already plotting how to get back at those niggas, but I was still curious to find out what really happened. That shit was crazy. First, my bitch died, and then his brother got killed. So what the fuck was going on? All these fucking killings in this city . . .

After we got home, he headed straight to the kitchen and grabbed the bottle of Grey Goose. Then he stumbled into the living room, put the bottle to his head, and started drinking it.

"Damn, they took my nigga away from me. I'm gon' kill all them motherfuckers that did this shit," he said between sobs.

My heart was hurting for him. Shit, my mind was on his brother's wife and the girls. I knew how close they were to their daddy.

"Babe, did you see who did it?" I quizzed.

He remained quiet for a few seconds. Then he spoke. "We were in the pool hall, and he said he was going home. So he left while I stayed inside. I should've walked him outside. Those niggas knew he was out there by himself. I'ma murk *all* them niggas. I put that shit on my dead momma."

"You can't blame yourself. There's no way you could've known that this would happen. Shit, if you were out there, you could've also died."

"Man, fuck that. They should've killed me instead. What the fuck I got to live for right now? Answer that. What the fuck I have to live for, shawty?" He grabbed my arm and looked me dead in my eyes.

I could tell that he was drunk, and his eyes were cold. I decided to stay quiet because I was not sure how it might turn out, especially since that nigga was drunk, hurt, and angry. So I sat there as he cried and cussed, threatening to wreak havoc on the city until he murdered everybody who had something to do with his brother's death. I knew he was serious, and shit was about to get real.

Last night was rough, and I really didn't get any sleep. After lying on the couch for a little while listening to him rant about what he was about to do, he finally fell asleep on the floor. So I got up and tiptoed upstairs. I couldn't sleep, though. I tossed and turned all night, trying to understand all this madness.

Finally, I got up, brushed my teeth, and washed my face. Then I decided to go downstairs to check on him since he never made it to bed. I was two steps down when I heard him talking on the phone. I stopped and started to listen to him, hoping that he didn't realize that I was eavesdropping. I had no idea who he was talking to at first.

"Man, shawty, I told you I fell asleep at my nigga's crib last night," he said.

"Man, go 'head on. You know my brother just got killed, and you on the phone fussing 'bout another bitch . . . I told yo' ass you ain't got shit to worry 'bout."

"Man, give me an hour. I'm coming through. Make sure you ain't got no drawers on."

I couldn't believe what the fuck I was hearing. I heard that nigga talking to some bitch and talking about fucking her. I wanted to storm down the stairs and confront that fuck nigga, but instead, I breathed and continued walking down the stairs. His eyes popped out of his head when I entered the living room.

"How long you been up?"

"I just got up. I thought you were still asleep," I lied.

"Oh, okay. Nah, I couldn't sleep. I kept seeing my brother's face and him taking his last breath."

"I'm sorry, babe. Did you contact the rest of your family?"

"Yeah, I talked to them, but you know it was me and my brother."

I looked at him, but not because of what he was saying. It was because I saw his ass for the piece of shit he really was. A few minutes ago, he was catering to some ho's feelings, and now, he was acting like everything was normal.

His phone started ringing again. He looked at it, then placed it back in his pocket.

"Who was that, and why you ain't pick it up? It might be important."

"Man, go 'head on, shawty. That ain't nobody but a fiend."

I was going to say something else, but I bit my tongue. I just looked at him and shot him a smile.

"Yo, I got to go up by this funeral home to see about my brother and then stop by his crib."

"Do you want me to go with you?"

"Nah, I'm straight. I'll be back later. I got a bunch of shit to handle out in these streets."

I looked at that lying-ass nigga like he had two heads. I was pretty sure he was going to handle business, but I knew he would see that bitch he was on the phone with. I walked off and headed upstairs. I had a plan in mind. Minutes later, he came up and got in the shower. While he was there, I quickly dressed and then got back under the covers. I waited for him to finish taking his shower.

"A'ight, shawty, I'm 'bout to bounce. Hit my line if you need me."

"Okay. Be careful out there."

I knew he had to go in the garage to get his Range Rover because he said he left his car at the bowling alley since he drove his brother's car last night. So when the garage closed, I ran down the stairs and peeped out of the window. I watched as he pulled out of the driveway and down the street. Then I grabbed my keys off the stand and ran out the door. I jumped into my car and pulled out in haste.

He was nowhere in sight, so I pressed on the gas. I know that he hadn't gone far. About two red lights down, I spotted his truck. I tried to stay several cars behind so he couldn't spot me. I maintained a steady pace behind him. I knew that he was on his way to see his bitch, and I wanted to see for myself.

I followed Mari to an apartment complex and pulled up and parked far enough away so he couldn't see me, but just enough where I could see when he banged on the door. A few minutes later, the Spanish bitch, Dreema, opened the door. That nigga was careless as hell as they stood there in the doorway, hugging each other.

My blood pressure rose as I witnessed that cheating-ass nigga hugged up on another bitch. I thought about getting out of the car and running up on them, but I remained seated. Instead, I took out my phone and snapped a few pics before they went inside and closed the door. Then I dialed his number, but he didn't answer. I kept calling his phone, but it just rang until his voicemail kept coming on. I went ahead and texted him a few times and waited, but there was still no reply.

My heart was hurting all over again. I also noticed that the bitch had a big stomach in front of her, which proved that she was pregnant. The tears started falling from my eyes as I rested my head on the steering wheel. Last night, I was there to console that nigga, but here he was, over at his whore's house the next day. I held my chest as I continued crying.

I thought about pulling off and going home, but something inside my head clicked. At first, I tried to ignore the voice, but then I started paying attention. That nigga and that bitch needed to know that I was *not* the one to play around with. For the most part, I was a calm, drama-free chick, but I learned how to bang from growing up in one of the wildest projects.

I jumped out of my car, ran to the trunk, and grabbed a bat I kept inside. Then I ran up the driveway and banged on the door. At first, no one answered, but I continued banging.

"Who is it?"

"It's Akila, bitch. I think you got my nigga up in there with you," I yelled back.

"Say what?" That bitch opened the door with nothing on but a little shirt.

"Where is Mari at?" I didn't wait for a response. Instead, I pushed past that bitch. I didn't have to go too far because that nigga was coming down the stairs wearing only his boxers and a towel over his shoulder.

"Yo, what the fuck's going on?" His face turned white when he saw me, and he looked like he just saw a ghost.

"Akila . . .Wh-what you doing he-he-re?" he stuttered.

"Yeah, that's a good question. Bitch, what the fuck you doing running up in my shit? Do you *know* who I am?"

"Bitch, who the fuck are you? A whore who done fucked and sucked all of Richmond dope boys' dick? Yes, bitch, I *know* who the fuck you are," I blasted her.

I ran up to the bitch and raised the bat using both hands. *Wham! Wham!* I lifted the bat and hit that bitch back-to-back in the kneecap.

"Shawty, what the fuck you doing?" Mari jumped forward and grabbed me.

He threw me on the floor. I couldn't breathe as I tried to get him off me.

"This bitch just fuckin' broke my leg, bae," his bitch yelled out.

"What the fuck have you done? Do you *know* she's carrying my seed?"

His words were cold as he stared into my eyes. His grip tightened around my neck. I couldn't breathe. I tried to speak, but the words couldn't come out. Instead, everything around me started spinning. *God, please don't let this nigga kill me,* I thought before I blacked out. . . .

Mari

Man, I just lost my brother, and those hoes were acting a fool. Ole selfish-ass bitches couldn't even stop for a fucking minute. All their asses are worried about is if I'm sleeping with the next bitch. Dreema's pregnant ass just been going the fuck off lately. Shit, she knew I had a bitch when we started fucking around. Now, that bitch was acting like she had amnesia and shit. She kept threatening that she would tell Akila that she was carrying my seed. I tried to warn that bitch not to do it, but every time she wanted to see me or wanted to get fucked, that was the first thing she screamed. I put that on my dead brother's life, as soon as my seed was born, I was taking him from that ho. The only reason I hadn't murked that ho was because she was carrying my seed, and I didn't want to kill my own blood. Man, fuck those bitches right about now. I had to catch myself. My fucking brother was lying on ice right now, and that was all I was worried about.

I pulled up to her crib. I knew she was only tripping because she wanted me to come over and fuck her. Shit, that pregnant pussy be hitting, though, and it got extra wet. Man, when I was up in there, I didn't ever want to come, but that pussy be gripping the dick and caused me to bust fast. I jumped out of my Range and walked up to the steps. I rang the doorbell and waited for her to open the door.

"Hey, sugar," she said as she reached over and hugged me.

Before stepping inside, I cupped her plump ass.

"Come on, daddy. You know we miss you," she said and walked away.

I walked inside and closed the door behind me. Truth was, I was only over to fuck real quick. I had so much frustration built up in me I was ready to run through that pregnant pussy real quick.

"You see how out of shape you got a bitch looking. Six months pregnant, and I'm the side chick. I swear, I should've listened to you and got an abortion, but nah, I'm the fucking fool waiting for you to leave that bitch," she spat, looking at her belly and shaking her head.

Fuck what she was talking about now. It was a little too late for this bullshit. There was no way possible she would kill my seed this far in the game. I stood next to her, admiring her sexy body. So many temptations were going on in my head. Her hot body had me wanting to fuck her ass.

"Girl, you're talking crazy with my seed in your stomach."

"Boy, bye." She tried to shove me away, but I caught her arm and wrapped it around my body.

"I'm not going nowhere," I whispered in her ear and followed with a kiss. "Bae, you know I want you in my life more than life itself." I meant every word I said just to hit the pussy, because that pregnant pussy was calling my name.

"Stop, Mari. You know I'm already knocked up, so we can't be doing it." She played like she didn't call me over there to dig deep in her guts.

"The damage is already done. What's the worst that could happen besides you knowing how much I love you?"

"But you always spitting that love mess—"

I cut her off with a kiss on her soft lips.

"But—" was all she could get out before our lips were intertwined with heavy kissing and breathing.

One hand was cuffed around her ass, and my other hand was rubbing between her wetness. Damn, her shit was warm and wetter than a motherfucker. My dick was harder than a steel pole. I freed my hand from her wetness and unbuttoned my pants, stripping down to my boxers.

Then I stepped back to admire her beautiful body and baby bump. I noticed her juices trailing down her legs. "Damn, bae," I said, ready to fuck.

She led me to the bed. Then she stood on her feet and leaned over the bed. Her chest was on top of a pillow. Her ass was spread wide, and her camel toe was purring my name. After rubbing her heart-shaped ass, I stuck two fingers inside her wet pussy.

"Damn, baby, your shit is *so* wet." I put my fingers in my mouth, tasting her goodies.

The sweet aroma had my head throbbing. I stroked myself two times before I entered her wetness. Goddammit, I wanted to shout out in tongues because, after three strokes, I was about to come. Her pussy was on fire, good as hell. I had to pull out of that good-ass pussy because I would never hear the end of the story if I busted too soon.

"What's wrong, Mari?" she asked, turning her head around and looking back at me. *This good-ass pussy,* I wanted to say.

"Nothing, babe," I replied, sticking my dick back into her wetness.

This time, I had to hold my breath and take slow strokes. I watched my dick disappear and reappear over and over. Her ass was moving like a tidal wave as she backed up that ass. I was fighting for my dear life, praying I wasn't about to come. I held on to her waist with one hand and gripped her ass with my other hand.

"Oh shit, yes, bae," she moaned. "Damn, this dick feels so good."

That was all I needed to hear to boost me up. I repositioned my hands on her shoulders to keep her from running since I had the upper hand. "Damn, yes," she moaned louder while my dick rammed into her wetness.

Each thrust I took felt like her pussy was getting tighter. She was squeezing every pussy muscle in her body to make me come. I tried to hold back, but her pussy was on fire. My head was throbbing as I exploded inside of her wetness. I wasn't finished with her ass because my dick was still hard as hell. I rolled her over on her back and scooted her to the edge of the bed. My feet were on top of my pants, which were still on the floor. I needed all the traction I could get. A nigga didn't have time to be sliding. The only sliding I wanted to do was in and out of her sloppy, wet pussy.

"You know I'm pregnant."

"Baby, like I said, the damage is already done," I replied, grabbing her by the ankles and pulling her close to me. Her legs were on my shoulders. I eased my head into her pussy and braced my hands around her knees. I penetrated in and out of her juicy pussy. Her eyes were closed, but her facial expressions indicated that it was feeling good to her.

I grinded my hips in circular motions. "Hmmmm," she moaned as I drove deeper into her. Her fingers were wrapped around the sheets. Her moans sounded like a baby kitten. Shit had me turned all the way on. My dick was so greasy from her juices that it slid in as smoothly as possible. Her round titties were bouncing, matching my thrusts. I was so deep in her stomach that it felt like my dick was hitting the baby's head, but I didn't let that stop me from driving deeper and deeper. Sweat started falling from my face.

"Shit." My body started locking down. I released my fluids inside her pussy. Her eyes rolled into the back of her head as she creamed all over my dick. Then I flopped next to her, rubbing her belly and praying that my seed was all right in there.

Some crazy shit popped off that I didn't expect to happen. I had no idea that Akila followed me to Dreema's house. We both heard the doorbell ring and looked at each other. She walked off downstairs to see who it was. After I didn't hear anything, I walked down the stairs to check on her and see what was taking her so long. I almost collapsed when I saw Akila standing in the doorway with a bat in her hand. The look in her eyes was scary. Before I could think of a way to deflate the situation, she went ham on Dreema, hitting her multiple times. I had no choice but to jump in and attack Akila. Dreema was carrying my seed, and I couldn't risk her losing the baby.

I tackled Akila to the ground, trying to calm her. I blacked out for a few seconds as I tightened my grip around her throat. It wasn't until she kept crying that I snapped out of it and let go of her. I looked at her as she scooted on the floor. Why was she here? Did she follow me to Dreema's crib?

"You're going to jail. I swear to God, I'm calling the police," she hollered.

I ran upstairs and quickly got dressed. I needed to get out of here right now.

"Baby, what you doing? You ain't got to go. We can call the police and tell them this bitch attacked me." Dreema grabbed my arm as she tried blocking my path.

"Get the fuck off me. I don't care who you call. I'm out of here." I got out of her grip and dashed down the stairs.

By the time I got to the door, Akila was gone. I ran out the door to see if I saw her, but she was gone. Next, I ran to my truck, jumped in, and pulled off. I dialed her number, but the phone just rang out. I needed to find her and get to her before she went to the police. I raced through the streets looking for her, but her car was nowhere to be found. I went to the crib, but she was not there. I grabbed a few articles of clothes and left in a hurry. Akila had threatened to call the police, and I wasn't sure she didn't follow through with her threats.

I stopped by my brother's place. He was gone, so I had to make sure niggas were not up in there doing the most. I pulled up and had some hesitation about going in, but I knew I had to get in here and handle things. My brother and I been in this business for a minute. This was the business that we used to clean all the drug money. With his death, the police would be coming around trying to see what he was into.

The building was locked up today, so I got out of the car and walked in. I locked the door behind me. Then I headed to the back office and unlocked the door. I sighed as I sat in the chair where my big brother usually sat. I logged on to his computer, deciding to look at his surveillance cameras. I went back to the last couple of weeks. I was looking to see if my brother had any kind of beef with any niggas that came up in here to get their cars done. I watched thoroughly as he conducted business with clients. I paid attention to these niggas' faces. Some were familiar, but some were complete strangers. Nothing seemed out of the ordinary, just regular business dealings.

I closed the computer and started getting angry as I saw my brother's face. This shit wasn't fair. He was always so careful. Who the fuck knows where he had been and why they killed him. Me and my brother shared everything, so if he had beef out here, he would tell me, and we would've handled this shit together.

I sat there with my hand over my face, trying to grasp this craziness and figure out an angle to take on this shit. I know somebody out there knew something, and it was only a matter of time before they started talking.

Finally, I took out some weed and rolled me a blunt. I smoked as I tried getting my emotions under control. Suddenly, my phone started ringing. I looked at it, only to see that it was Dreema, so I pressed *ignore*. After all this shit this morning, I didn't want to talk to her. These bitches were doing too much, and I needed a break from them.

When I finished smoking, I grabbed a few trash bags and threw his papers to the business in it. I then cracked the safe. He had a little over twenty grand in it. I emptied it. Then I looked around for anything that would tie him to any illegal activities. On my way out, I spotted a pic of me, him, and Mama before she died. I also grabbed that. It's fucked up how both of them were gone, and I was the only one left here now.

After taking one last glance around, I picked up the laptop and left. I set the alarm and closed the shop again. I needed to get my car from the pool hall, so I hit my nigga G up. He was the closest to a brother that I got out here and the only nigga that I feel I could trust now that Rio was gone. We all grew up together, and once Rio and I moved out here, he followed suit.

"Yo, son, where the fuck you been? I heard what happened to Rio, and I been looking for you since then," he yelled into the phone.

"Nigga, meet me on Midlothian Turnpike, right beside the BP. I'ma be there in ten."

"A'ight, bet."

I walked to the truck, threw the shit in the trunk, and got in. Before I pulled off, I looked around. Not knowing what got my brother killed, I had to be aware of my surroundings. I know I was heavy in the streets, and this

might be some shit against me. Niggas had to know that
I stayed strapped. I tried telling Rio to get a strap, even
handed one to him, but he turned it down, talking 'bout
he was a businessman and not a thug. Shit, look where
that got him. Niggas better be prepared for war 'cause
whoever killed my brother will pay—and pay dearly.

As I pulled off, I kept checking my rearview mirror.
I was making sure I wasn't being followed. Call me
paranoid, but I was checking that shit every few seconds.
Niggas gonna have to come correct to catch me slipping.

I pulled up at the BP and checked my dash to see if I
needed gas. I was almost on empty. I got out of the truck,
walked into the gas station, and paid for the gas. I saw
my boy pull up as I put the gas into the truck. He pulled
over to the side. After I finished, I drove beside him, took
a look around to make sure no police or fuck niggas were
lurking, then parked. He got out of his whip and got in
with me.

"What's good, fam? Tell me you got word on the niggas
that did this to Rio." His voice cracked as he spoke. G
was a soldier in these streets, and to see him like this was
heartbreaking.

"Yo, son, I was in the pool hall when this shit popped
off. I ran out with the gun, but all I saw was a dark-colored, maybe burgundy or dark blue, Denali pulling off. I
didn't know it was Rio until I heard a bitch screaming out.
When I ran over to her, I saw my motherfucking brother
lying there. They shot him up like he was an animal."

"Yo, fuck that, B. Whoever the fuck did this, we gon'
find them and we gon' torture them. We got to make
these country pussy-ass niggas know they just started a
war. You hear me, B? A motherfuckin' war." He pulled
his gun out of his waist.

"Nigga, put that shit away. You know the law be out this
bitch."

"Son, fuck the law. Trust and believe they can get it too.
You hear me, fam? They took my nigga away."

"I know, yo, but you actin' crazy ain't gon' do no good. I need you out here wit' me. You the only nigga I can trust, bro."

"I know it, man. Fuck, this shit is fucked up, man."

"Listen, son, I need you to throw some money out there—a hundred grand to whoever can lead me in the right direction. I need answers—and fast. I know somebody out there know something, so put the word out there."

"You want me to hit up the niggas? You know they ready to come down."

"Nah, not yet, son. Tell them to hang tight. If we need them, we'll get at them. This one is personal, so I would prefer to handle it myself. If shit get sticky, then we'll bring the squad in."

"Gotcha. I'm 'bout to be out. I know Rio just passed, but I still got some money to collect and shit. I'll hit you later."

"A'ight, son. Be easy."

"I love you, son. We gon' get these niggas," he assured me as he stepped out of my truck and walked to his car.

I watched as he pulled off. I waited a few minutes, and then I pulled off. I didn't feel like going home and definitely didn't want to deal with Dreema's shit right now. I decided to get me a room at the Holiday Inn. I needed a minute by myself to gather my thoughts. I was feeling homicidal *and* suicidal right now. Dealing with humans at this moment may not be good. But, first, I need to go get my whip out of the parking lot before they tow my shit.

Dreema

All that shit I talked about Mari and me not being no fool to him went out the window. After us not fucking with each other for a few weeks, he called me a few days ago and apologized for the way he acted. I was missing him, so I accepted his apology. He took me out for dinner and was all over me that night. He didn't come out and say he wanted the baby, but he did tell me it was my decision, and he would support my decision. That was definitely music to my ears because I was having my baby regardless of whether he supported my decision.

We ended the night fucking and professing our love to each other. I was praying he would leave that ho and let us be a family in my mind.

I didn't get any sleep last night. I was up calling Mari's phone repeatedly and texted exactly thirty times. You can say I was obsessed, but I was angry as fuck. I know he see me calling. This was a nigga that stays on his phone, so I know he was just ignoring me. I wish I knew where he stayed at with that bitch 'cause I swear on my mama I would've driven by last night. There's no way I'ma be over here pregnant and lonely while my baby daddy is laid up with the next bitch.

I know I was pregnant, and I wasn't supposed to be drinking, but I still poured myself three glasses of Pink Moscato. By the time I finished the last glass, I was drunk and more emotional. I realized he wasn't coming over tonight, and I would be alone again. I went to the cabinet to see what pills I had. I only had a few ibuprofen, so I took them, hoping that with the mixture of the alcohol, I would miscarry. Then I crawled into bed and pulled the cover over me.

I was disappointed when I woke up in the morning to find out I was still pregnant. Fuck. Why did God allow this? I snatched my phone and realized that he still hadn't called. I was carrying this nigga's baby, and he didn't call to see if we were dead or alive.

I was nauseated, so I got up out of bed and got something to eat. I had a terrible hangover, so I took a hot shower, hoping it would help. I was in the living room eating when I heard the phone ringing. I wasn't in the mood to talk to anyone right now, but the ringing continued. Finally, I got up and walked to the room, feeling irritated. It was Mari. I thought about not picking it up, but I picked up anyway.

"Hello, now you calling me? Why the fuck don't you call the bitch you spent the night with?" I asked aggressively.

"Yo, B. Shut up with all that fuckery. They killed my brother last night."

"What the fuck you talking about? Oh my God, are you serious?"

I couldn't believe what the hell he was saying to me. I know how tight he and his brother were.

"When did this happen, and where?"

"We were over at the bar at Shockoe Bottom. These niggas took my brother away, B."

I heard him saying his brother was dead, but I know his phone still worked, so that shouldn't stop him from calling me and answering *my* calls. Call me cold, but shit, that nigga was dead.

"I understand your brother dead and all, but you couldn't call me? I guess you were getting comforted by the next bitch."

"Yo, you trippin', B. I told you what happened. Man, fuck all this. I'm coming through in a few." He hung up in my face before I could respond.

About an hour later, he popped up at the house. I was still pissed off at him, but anytime I was mad with him, and he showed up, the madness went out the window for some reason. I was horny as hell. For some strange reason, since I got pregnant, I stayed wet and wanted to fuck all the time. Mari never disappoints me when it comes down to sucking this pussy, and his dick game was on point too. I done fucked plenty niggas, but he was nasty, nasty, so nothing was off-limits for him. From sucking toes and licking ass to burying his head in my pussy. He was a beast in the bed.

After he tore up my pussy, I lay on the bed trying to get up my energy again. I heard a knocking at the door. I didn't invite anyone over, so this was strange. Shit, it might be those annoying-ass church people again. I swear they might end up getting cussed the fuck out. They dead-ass wrong for interrupting me after this bomb-ass sex I just had. I only had a little shirt on, but I didn't care. Let's see the look on their faces when they see that I'm half-naked. Maybe then they'll get the picture and leave me the fuck alone.

"Who is it?" I hollered.

"Bitch, open the door and let my man out," a female's voice hollered.

Say what? Oh no, this can't be. That was the voice of the bitch that I had an altercation with a few weeks ago. Supposedly, that was Mari's bitch. Shit, how the fuck did this bitch find my house? Fuck it. Maybe this will show her ass that he doesn't want her anymore, and he was here with me. So I hurried up and opened the door with a smile plastered across my face when I came face-to-face with the other woman. *This should be interesting,* I thought.

Without me inviting that bitch in, she entered my house. I was about to give it to this bitch, but then I heard Mari's voice inquiring who was at the door. I didn't have to answer. He was almost down the stairs when their eyes locked. This was like a scene out of an epic Lifetime movie. I was so caught up in the scene between them that I was caught off guard when this psychotic bitch attacked me.

This bitch started hitting me in my knees with the bat she had in her hand. I leaped to grab the bitch, but Mari was quick to grab her ass up. He threw that bitch down on the floor and started choking her. Her ass started fighting him, but she was no match for him. After they wrestled on the ground, he got off her and ran up the stairs. That bitch got up off the ground and started cussing.

"Bitch, you better get the fuck outta my house," I yelled.

"Fuck you, ho. You can have his ass."

"Bitch, I already had him." I smiled while I rubbed my stomach.

She shot me a dirty look and ran out the door. I was pissed the fuck off as I limped to the door to lock it. Then I hopped up the stairs where Mari was getting dressed and cussing.

"You're leaving?" I questioned.

"What the fuck it look like? Yo, why the fuck you open the door and let her in?"

"Are you fucking serious right now? So, this *my* fault that yo' bitch walked up in here and attacked me? Are you fucking *serious* right now?" I looked at him disgusted.

"Yo, B, don't sit here and act like I ain't see yo' fucking face. I ain't wit' all this fucking drama shit."

"Nigga, whatever the fuck you say. You keep screaming you don't like drama, but you the one that want two bitches. I mean, how long did you think you were going to keep me and my baby a fucking secret? I know you just mad yo' ho found out you have a baby on the way."

He looked at me and walked toward the door. I jumped in front of him and grabbed his arm.

"Why you got to go? I mean, your baby is here. You don't need that bitch."

"Let go of me, B. You full of fucking drama, yo. Grow the fuck up, Dreema. You about to have a fucking baby." He pulled away from me and ran down the stairs.

I fell to the ground crying. Why the fuck was he behaving like *I* was in the wrong? I just finished fucking him, and instead of staying here with me and his seed, he ran out behind that bitch. I dragged myself off the ground and started dialing 911.

"911 operator, how may I help you?"

Right at that second, it hit me that I didn't know this bitch full name. "I was attacked. A female came to the house and attacked me," I started crying.

"Are you hurt, ma'am, and what is the person's name that attacked you?"

"Yes, I'm hurt. I'm pregnant, and she attacked me. Her name is Akila."

"What is your address, ma'am? Is the assailant still there with you?"

"No, she ran off."

After I gave her my address, I started planning on exactly what I would tell them. This bitch was going to learn that I was *not* the bitch to be played with. . . .

Chapter Seven

Akila

I lay in bed holding the pillow and crying. First, he cheated on me with this bitch, and now, the bitch is pregnant. What the fuck did I do to Mari for him to treat me like he did? I kept replaying the incident from earlier. . . . The way he jumped on me for this bitch. I rubbed my hand on my neck. It was still sore. I couldn't believe he tried to kill me over this nasty-ass ho.

My phone started ringing. I looked at the caller ID and was relieved to see it wasn't Mari. He'd been calling me since I left that ho's house. I didn't come straight home at first, though. I was so hurt and in despair, so I pulled over at Broadrock Park and sat in my car crying.

"Hello."

"What's wrong? You sound like you crying," Tesha said.

"Girl, I went to the bitch's house and found out she *is* pregnant."

"Say what? Hold on. I'm at the CVS by your house. I'll be there in five minutes."

"All right, boo."

I'm glad my girl was stopping by 'cause I needed someone to talk to. I really miss Ariana 'cause I know I wouldn't feel this alone. Five minutes later, I heard the doorbell ringing. I got up so I could let her in.

"Hey, girl." She came in and gave me a big hug.

"Hey, boo." I walked off into my bedroom.

I didn't give a damn if Mari didn't want my friends over here. Fuck him and his feelings right about now. So I got back in bed, and she sat down.

"So, what the fuck happened now?"

"I followed Mari to the bitch house, and he went in. I waited for a while; then I rang the doorbell."

"You rang the doorbell, and what happened?"

"That ho answered, and I went in. That bitch was half-naked, and to make it worse, my cheating-ass nigga walked down the stairs in his boxers."

"Bitch, tell me you beat that ass."

Before I could respond, I heard the doorbell. This was strange 'cause I didn't expect no other company.

"I wonder who the fuck that is?" I got up, walked to the front, and looked through the peephole.

Two uniformed police officers were standing outside my door. What the fuck were they doing, and what did they want? My mind started to race. Mari had all this shit up in here. Fuck.

"Who is it?"

"It's the Richmond police, ma'am."

I hesitated but decided to open it. I understood the law somewhat and knew if they had a search warrant, they would be kicking off the door and not knocking.

"Yes, may I help you?" I opened the door, trying my best not to show my nervousness.

"Akila Jones?"

"Yes, may I help you?" I looked at them.

"Please step out here. We have a warrant for your arrest."

"A warrant? What the fuck for?" I was angered and confused.

"Please step outside, ma'am."

"What's going on?" Tesha walked from the back and quizzed.

"Please step back in, ma'am," one officer ordered.

"I'm good, baby. Just stay here until I call. I need you to come get me." I shot her an assuring look.

I didn't resist because I didn't want the focus on the house. I need to get them away from here fast. So I stepped out, and they cuffed me.

"Akila Jones, you're under arrest for assault and battery on Dreema Walker."

That's when it hit me. It was about what happened at that bitch's house. Ain't this some shit. That ho popped all that shit, but her pussy ass called the police and pressed charges. I was so angry that I could hardly breathe. I couldn't think straight and just kept crying. I can't believe Mari would put me in this fucked-up situation. I swear I could never forgive him or go back to loving him after this.

I was fingerprinted and searched before being placed into a holding cell. They told me I had to wait until the following day to see the judge. That only made me angrier. They were behaving like *I* killed someone. All I did was hit the bitch a few times in her knees. If I knew that bitch would press charges, I would've given her something to call them for. Instead, I'm in this cold-ass, piss-smelling cell for tapping that bitch a few times.

I found a little space by the end of the bench and sat down. There were four other females in the same cell. Two looked like they were strung out on crack, and the other one was crying uncontrollably. I figure this was her first time locked up 'cause she looked scared. When it was time to eat, they brought in some dried-up bread with nasty-looking sandwich meat. I took one look at that shit, and my stomach started to turn. I felt like I wanted to throw up, but one glance at that nasty-ass toilet with all that toilet paper and piss on it, and I was good.

"Aye, it seems like you don't want yo' food. Can I get it?" said one of the crackhead-looking ladies as she tapped me on my shoulder.

"Yes, just take it," I said harshly. The smell coming from her body was wreaking havoc on my nose. I was happy when she snatched the sandwich and walked back to where her friends were sitting. That shit was disgusting. Why the hell would any female walk around smelling like a dump truck?

I wondered what time it was. I had asked to use the phone when I first got here, and this old bucktoothed bitch told me to wait. Well, I was tired of waiting. I needed to call my girl so that she could call a bondsman.

"Guard," I yelled.

"Cut out all that yelling," one of the crackhead bitches yelled.

"Bitch, shut your fucking face up," I yelled back.

"Or what, ho?" That bitch jumped off the bench.

I balled my fist up. I was ready to take on this bitch and her fucking crew. I had so much anger built up, I promise they were not ready for the way I was about to drag this ho. Her friends jumped up and grabbed her back.

"Come on, girl. She ain't worth it."

"You right. Fuck that bitch."

I looked at them bitches and felt pity for them. They probably were some bad bitches back in the day, but that crack had them looking tore up from the bottom up.

"Guard," I yelled again.

A few minutes later, the bucktoothed bitch appeared. She looked at me like I interrupted whatever she was doing.

"How may I help you?"

"Ain't I supposed to get a phone call? I been waiting."

"I recall telling you when you asked that you get it later," she replied in an annoyed tone.

"Well, it's now later. I need my phone call to let my people know where I am."

She shot me a dirty look but opened up the cell. I followed her out to the front, and she handed me the phone. "You have five minutes," she said before she walked away to act like she was fixing her desk.

I thought about calling Mari, but I dismissed that thought immediately. So instead, I dialed Tesha's number.

"Hello."

"It's me."

"Damn, bitch, what took you so long? I been worried about your ass."

"I know, boo. I'm down at the jail. I have to wait until tomorrow morning to go in front of the judge to get a bond."

"Damn, bitch, I'm so sorry you're going through this. I swear I'ma beat that bitch ass for doing this shit to you."

"I know, but listen, get my card out of my purse. My pin is 7879. And come to court in the morning. Look up a bondsman and call them. I need you to bond me out."

"Shit, you know I ain't got no job. So I'ma ask my mama to do it for you. You know they want the person signing the paper to have a job."

"Your time is up," the annoying-ass bitch walked up to me and said.

"Listen, boo, I got to go. Just get the purse and ask your mama. I need to get the fuck out of here before I snap."

"All right, boo. I got you."

I hung up the phone and walked back to the cell. This bitch was really enjoying the fact that she had the upper hand. I needed to get my anger under control 'cause I was trying to go home tomorrow . . . not stay in here longer than I'm supposed to.

It was hard for me to sleep sitting up. Every time I dozed off, the clicking of keys or the slamming of grills interrupted me. I was tired, cold, and hungry. I had a terrible headache that seemed to worsen by the hour. I looked over at the crackhead bitches. They were all leaning on each other, snoring their lives away. I glanced at the girl who had been crying, and she was knocked out. Shit, I know her ass was tired from all that crying. Whatever she did to be in here, I hope the judge releases her in the morning 'cause, baby, she is not about this life. I chuckled to myself. *Shit, I hope I get to go home too 'cause I for sure am not about this life.*

I wasn't sure what time it was, but I heard the CO yelling names out loud. I figured these were all the people that had court this morning. Then I heard my name and got excited. I was ready to get a bond and go home to my bed.

Mari

I got me a room at the hotel to lie low for a few days. Akila had threatened to call the police on me. I wanted to think she wasn't that stupid, but I know she was tight with a nigga. She found out I was at another bitch's house, and not just that, the bitch was pregnant.

After smoking two blunts back-to-back, I popped open the bottle of Grey Goose and put it to my head. I was drinking before my brother got killed, but now, I was drunk almost every day. I know I need to be sober to stay on top of everything. Oh my God, just thinking about my brother's death brought tears to my eyes. I got up and started pacing the room. I then opened the drawer and took out my Glock. I put it to my head and started crying harder. I needed to be with my brother.

"Oh God, I can't live life no more. Why didn't you take me and leave my brother? Huh? Why, God?" I yelled as I fell to my knees and started bawling.

I placed my hand on the trigger, but I couldn't. I just couldn't bring myself to pull the trigger. I threw the gun down and lay on the carpet, bawling and beating the floor with my fist. I just want this all to be over with, all this pain that I was feeling to go away.

I guess I fell asleep on the carpet 'cause I jumped out of my sleep from the sound of my telephone ringing. I lay there for a few more seconds before I pulled myself up. By the time I got to the phone, it had stopped ringing. I looked at the caller ID. I noticed it was my aunt calling from the Beach. They had been blowing up my phone for the last few days, wanting to know funeral plans. To be honest, I didn't know too much. My brother's wife was handling everything. I dropped her some stacks so she could get the ball rolling. This shit was too hard for me. Just the other day, we were talking about where we wanted to go for the summer. Now his funeral is being planned.

I checked my phone to see if Akila had called, but there were no missed calls from her. Dreema, on the other hand, had called me about ten times. This bitch was getting to be annoying as fuck right now. I told her ass to chill the fuck out. I was still tight as fuck with her after that shit she pulled yesterday. I was thinking getting her pregnant was a big-ass mistake 'cause this bitch was making my life hell. I called Akila's number and waited. No one picked up, so I called again.

"Hello."

"Who is this, and why are you answering Akila's phone?" I asked with an attitude.

"This Tesha. Akila is not here right now. Do you want to leave a message for her?"

"Yo, B, I don't know who you are or what kind of game you and Kila playing, but can you just put her on the phone?"

"Ain't nobody playing no game. I just told you Akila isn't here. So either you leave a message or call her back when she's available."

"Yo, B—"

Before I could finish my sentence, whoever that bitch was hung up. This was fucking strange. Why was she answering Akila's phone? See, this the shit I'm talking about with Akila. She's always screaming she's grown but insisted on playing little bitch games. I swear this bitch gon' make me hurt her. You know what? Fuck this. She wants to play games, so I'ma show her how it's done. I'ma get all my shit from her house, and we can be all the way done.

I washed my face, grabbed my keys, and headed out the door. I was still under the influence and probably shouldn't be driving, but fuck this. I needed to get to the crib. I cut the music up listening to Meek's latest album. I was all the way in my zone as I headed to the crib.

When I pulled up, I spotted her car—but wait. Another car was parked in the driveway. I parked on the street and crept up the driveway. *Hmmm, I know this bitch ain't bold enough to have another nigga in my shit.* I quietly turned the key in the door. Once it opened, I took my time stepping inside. I took out my gun and held it in my hand. I looked around the living room and kitchen, but no one was downstairs. So I tiptoed up the stairs, still holding my gun. I heard something coming from our bedroom. The door was closed. I leaned my ear on the door, listening keenly. I then busted open the door . . . but I was disappointed. Nothing was there. The bed was made up. But wait. . . . I heard the shower running. I kind of felt like a fool. I just know I was about to find a nigga up in here. I sat on the bed, shaking my head.

Then I heard the water cut off, so I sat there waiting on Akila to step out of the bathroom . . .

"Aaaawe, what are you doing here?" Akila's friend, Tesha, said as she tried to wrap the towel around her tighter. She looked frightened to see me.

"This *my* crib. What *you* doing here, and where's Akila?" By then, my mind was coming up with some crazy freaky shit. I waited to see Akila exit the bathroom, but no one came out.

"Kila, you can come out. Ain't no need to hide, B." I got up and walked to the bathroom. I just knew I was going to snatch Akila up out of there. But to my surprise, the bathroom was empty.

"Yo, B, why the fuck you in my shit, and where's Akila?" I yelled as I walked back into the room.

I stood in disbelief as I watched her bend over, lotioning her legs, revealing her pussy from the back. I stared at her with my tongue hanging out.

"Close your mouth, love. Akila is not here, and she allowed me to stay here." She walked closer to me and started kissing me passionately.

My mind was telling me to push the bitch off me. It was a setup, but my dick was moving around in my boxers, letting me know I needed to proceed. I kissed her back and started fondling her breast. I eagerly stuck one of my fingers into her pussy. Oh Gawd, that shit was tight, and she was already feeling wet. I picked her up and threw her on the bed.

She sat straight up and started unbuttoning my pants. She released my dick and started massaging my balls. She then started licking my dick. Within seconds, my dick was all the way into her mouth. I gently took her head and shoved it down a little. I closed my eyes and bit down on my bottom lip, trying not to scream out like a li'l bitch.

"Oh fuck . . . Shit. Damn." I let out small groans as I curled up my toes. The chick didn't ease up any. Instead, she continued sucking my dick like she was a pro or something.

"Aargh, fuck." I felt like my veins were about to bust out of my dick. I was trying not to come so fast with everything in me. I tried . . . But it didn't work. I held on tight to her head as my cum shot out of my dick and into her mouth. She didn't flinch. Instead, she licked and slurped every drop of my juice.

"Yo, suck it real quick," I demanded, and she did without question.

She massaged my balls and started licking all over my dick. Within minutes, I was hard again. Shit, I thought about a condom, but I didn't have one. *Fuck it. I'll just pull out. Her pussy looked clean,* I thought before I pulled her cheeks apart and slid my dick in. Her pussy was tighter than I first thought. It wasn't easy to slide all the way in, but she grinded on my dick until I got in. She wasted no time throwing the ass all the way back on me.

Not wanting her to outdo me, I grabbed her hips, pulled her back, and thrust in and out of her. I was slow fucking her. I would pull out and then slide in slowly while she jiggled her ass cheeks on my dick. I slapped her ass a few times. The sound of her ass made me hornier. Then she started throwing it back fast. This wasn't good. I grabbed her tighter and started fucking her hard and fast. I was about to bust. The veins in both heads got bigger.

"Awww, shhit . . . oweiii . . . aargh . . ." I tried pulling out, but it was too late. Some of my cum was left up in her. I pulled out my limp dick and lay back on the bed.

Shit, what the fuck am I doing? Wait, what if Akila had walked up in here just now? I sat up immediately. Tesha was sitting there smiling at me.

"Yo, B. Where the fuck is Akila?"

"Chill out, baby. Akila is down at the city jail. So you have nothing to worry about."

"City jail? Yo, B, what the fuck you talkin' 'bout?" I know this bitch was playing right now.

"Your side bitch got her locked up. Whatever happened at her house earlier, the police came here and arrested her."

"They came here? Did they come up in here?"

"No, we were in the room when they knocked. So she went to the door, and they locked her up."

I looked at her to see if she was lying, but I could tell she was dead-ass serious. "Yo, why the fuck she ain't call me?"

"That's something you'll have to ask her. She has court in the morning, so she told me to stay here and wait to come bond her out."

"This some fucking bullshit, yo."

"Calm down, baby. I mean, she's not here, and I been hearing all these good things about you. So now, it's just me and you, love." She stood up and started rubbing on my chest again. Fuck, I couldn't resist.

She ordered some Dominoes. Then we ate, drank, smoked, and fucked most of the night. With all the stress that I was dealing with, this was exactly what I needed.

Later, I stepped out of the shower thinking, *What a night I had.* As wrong as it was to be fucking my girl's homegirl, it was all good with me. I mean, we were both grown, and we wanted each other. Shit, I really hope this isn't the last time she lets me hit that 'cause that pussy was straight fire. I finished drying off, stepped out of the bathroom, and walked into the room.

"Pussy nigga, don't move," a nigga said as he pointed a gun at my face.

I couldn't see the nigga's face 'cause he had a mask covering it. Seconds later, three more niggas walked into the room.

"Yo, what the fuck y'all want?" I asked with a grit on my face.

"Nigga, you know why we here. We here for that work and that money. Now, get to it, nigga, before I bust a cap in yo' ass."

I looked at these niggas. There were four of them and just me. Shit wasn't looking good for me 'cause I didn't have my gun on me.

"Yo, nigga, ain't shit here."

The nigga raised the gun and hit me across the head. I fell back a bit, but I quickly lunged toward the nigga. I was trying to get the gun off him as he fell.

"Nigga, you better not move a muscle. I'ma splatter your brains all over this floor if you do." I felt a gun pressed up on my head.

I put my hands up as I looked down at the pussy nigga on the ground. I swear if these other niggas weren't here, I would smash his ass.

"Now, give me that work."

"I done told you niggas, ain't shit here."

"Aye, yo, I thought you said this nigga got that work and a safe up in here."

"Did y'all look? He got something up in here," this old grimy-ass bitch said.

I can't believe that I let this bitch trick me like that. This was one of the oldest tricks in the book. A bitch fuck a nigga and then set him up to get robbed.

Two of the niggas started pulling out drawers and stuff, throwing things all over the place. They even looked under the bed.

"Ain't shit here. Let's go look in the rest of the house. This nigga making major moves, so I know he got paper. The question is, where the fuck it's at?"

"Yo, hold the gun on him. He flinch, kill him," one of the little niggas said before two of them left the room.

"Trust me. I got it." He continued pressing the gun on my forehead.

Fuck what he was talking about. I waited until I could no longer hear them. I then looked at this nigga. He looked at me with a grit on his face like I'm supposed to be scared of him and that little-ass gun. It looked like a .22 that he was holding on me. I decided to take my chance. I had one shot at getting out of here alive. I lunged toward the nigga and wrapped my arm around his neck, choking him out. He tried struggling, but I squeezed tighter. He was out cold.

"Awee, awee," the bitch started screaming.

I grabbed the little gun the nigga had and pointed it at the bitch's head.

"Please don't hurt me. I didn't want to do this. They made me do this," the ho cried.

I heard steps coming up the stairs. I fired two shots in that bitch's dome before running behind the door. It was the other two, and they had bigger guns. One nigga also had my gun. One nigga entered first and spotted his nigga on the ground.

"Yo, bro, get in here," he yelled to his partner.

He came farther in, walked over, and looked at the bitch. I walked up behind him and fired a shot in the back of his head. He stumbled forward. I grabbed my gun from him and shot him twice in the chest.

Pop! Pop! Pop!

I was so caught up in killing this nigga that I didn't think of the remaining nigga. The nigga started busting at me. I tried to push the door to shut him out, and he fell backward. I ran out of the room and dashed for the door. I busted toward him, and he busted back at me, hitting me in my shoulder. I turned around and fired two shots at him, hitting him in the stomach. Then I opened the door and ran out of the house. I made it to my truck and pulled off in a rush. I saw the nigga run outside. He started firing at my vehicle, but I was gone.

I thought I got away, but I spotted the nigga's Monte Carlo coming fast behind me seconds later. I was bleeding, and that shit was hurting. I had no idea how bad it was, but I was trying to stay alive right now. His car wasn't no fast car, but traffic was out here. This nigga was coming up on me. He got to my left side and started firing at me. I pointed the gun and fired two shots into his car. His car swerved over to the side. He must've lost control 'cause his car went over. I then sped up. There were too many witnesses around. I needed to get the fuck out of here now.

"Yo, nigga, where you at?" I asked G.

"Yo, I'm at the crib. What's good?"

"Yo, I'm on my way. Make sure ain't nobody else wit' you."

"A'ight, bet."

My nigga G's crib was all the way in Midlothian. It was a good little drive, and I was in excruciating pain. I could tell I was losing a lot of blood, but I couldn't stop to check. I had to get the fuck out of Richmond fast.

After getting out of the area, I tried to maintain an average speed. I was hoping none of the drivers on the road got a look at my license plate, even though I wasn't gon' trip off that. I needed to get some medical help ASAP. I started feeling cold. Then I began to shiver. I cut the heat on, so I could warm up a little. Soon, I was beginning to feel dizzy. I was almost at my boy's crib, so I tried my best to stay focused.

I arrived at G's crib five minutes later and parked. Then I called his phone.

"Yo."

"Yo, son, open up the garage. I need to bring in the truck."

I waited a few seconds before the garage opened. He had a three-car garage, so I drove in and parked. Then I got out of the truck and walked up the stairs. He was standing at the top of the stairs looking at me.

"Yo, you good, son?"

"Nah, yo. I got shot." I stumbled to the kitchen and took a seat.

"Yo, son, you bleedin' bad. What the fuck happened, B?" He walked over to me.

"Yo, call that doctor out here."

"A'ight."

He quickly walked off, talking to the doctor. I pulled off my shirt. It was soaked with blood.

"Yo, son, rip this and tie it for me."

"Yo, this shit bad, yo. The doc says he can be here in twenty-five minutes. He had some other nigga to deal with."

"Oh shit." I was in so much pain, and it was getting unbearable.

"Yo, pour me something strong."

"I got some Jamaican white rum."

"Yeah, pour me some of that shit."

I grabbed the glass and took two big gulps. Shit, I forgot how strong that rum was. It burned my throat going down.

"Fuck, yo, this nigga needs to come on, B."

"Yo, nigga, what the fuck happened? Who we need to go kill?"

"Nigga, that bitch Tesha that you fucked before set me up. Bitch had three niggas in the crib to rob me."

"What the fuck you talkin' 'bout, nigga?" He shot me a strange look.

I went on to tell him everything that happened. Nah, let me correct that . . . *almost* everything. I left out the part where I fucked her. G had smashed her a couple of times before.

"Yo, what the fuck she doin' at yo' crib, yo? You was fuckin' her?"

"Yo, nigga, Akila locked up, and she must've left her there. I had no idea the bitch was at my crib. Yo, that bitch set me up. I had to body that bitch and two of them niggas. Me and the third nigga got into a shoot-out. I shot him a few times, and I got hit."

Before he could respond, the doorbell rang, and he hurried off. He returned a few minutes later with the doctor. I was happy to see this nigga. Hopefully, the pain will ease up after he gets this bullet out.

***

After the doctor patched me up, he gave me a shot of morphine. I was out instantly and slept for a minute. When I woke up, it was well into the night.

"Nigga, I thought yo' ass was dead on my couch," G joked as he handed me a glass of liquor.

"Yo, nigga, that was some good shit Doc gave me."

"Yeah, nigga. And he left you some Percs for the pain. He said for you to take it easy."

I looked at my arm. It was neatly bandaged up. I couldn't move it, but I was happy the pain was at a minimum right now 'cause earlier, a nigga was on the verge of bawling out for real.

"Yo, nigga, while you were asleep, I went by your crib. I ain't see no police or nothing. So, I went inside from the back. After seeing the three bodies, I got my cleanup team on it ASAP. I then torched the shit. I was parked across the street when the fire truck came, and it was almost flat by then. They couldn't save it. But the best part is nobody will ever find them niggas."

"Good looking out, bro."

"Shit, nigga, you were fucked up, so I had to get the cleanup crew out there and make sure everything was wiped clean. No trace that you were ever there. Oh, my bad, y'all's rides are burned too."

I looked at that nigga. Shit, that was a brand-new whip. Shit, Akila's car was in the garage too. Fuck. Akila . . . That bitch did say she was in jail.

"Aye, son, you still fucking that chick Mercedez?"

"Yeah, why?"

"I need her to go bond Akila out of jail for me."

"A'ight, I'ma hit her now."

I took my phone out, hit the bail bonds dude up, and let him know the situation. I told him I needed this done now. After I disconnected the phone, I finished drinking the liquor.

"Son, I need to get rid of the truck too."

"Word?"

"Yeah, too many people were around when me and that last nigga got in the shoot-out. I can't risk one of them getting that license plate and shit. Just bring that shit to the chop shop and drop it off."

"A'ight. I'ma call them, let them come tow it and take it to the shop."

We sat there kicking it and talking about how all this craziness was hitting us at once. First, my brother got murdered, and now this.

"Yo, son, I know we makin' a killing out here, but shit's getting hot. I think it's only a matter of time before the fucking Feds start looking at some shit. So I think we should get rid of all the shit we have now, close up shop, and get the fuck out of here."

"Yo, nigga, I ain't going nowhere until I find the niggas that killed Rio. Yo, if you feel it's too hot for you out here, you can bounce, but I'm out here until all them niggas dead," I yelled.

"Son, calm the fuck down. I was just looking out for you. I mean, I know them niggas need to pay for what they did to Rio, but shit *is* getting hot. We can leave for a minute, then come back to handle them niggas once shit calm down."

"Nigga, I already told you, I'm not going nowhere. So, do what you got to do." I was starting to get angry at this nigga. I wasn't feeling what he was saying at all. This shit had me side-eying his ass.

"Bro, my bad. I ain't going nowhere. You already know I'm riding all the way."

"Yo, can you check if the bitch left to go get Akila?"

He got on the phone and then hung up a few seconds later.

"They at the jail now getting her. Yo, you don't think Akila gon' trip off her house and whip being gone?"

"Yo, a house and whip ain't nothing. Tomorrow, she can go house and car shopping again."

"Just making sure. These bitches know too much. Her and that other bitch, Dreema."

"Yo, let me deal with my hoes. You need to worry about finding out who killed my motherfucking brother. With all that money, ain't nobody saying nothing yet?"

"Yo, I put it out there. I'm waiting to hear from this one CI that I be working with. He told me yesterday to give him a few days, and he'll have something for sure."

"A'ight, bet."

I was kind of tight that they burned down the crib. I had a couple of stacks in the safe. Shit, that was money that I could've used. But I quickly dismissed that feeling. I know my nigga did what he thought was best for me. I can't do nothing but appreciate him for looking out.

Chapter Eight

Akila

I couldn't help but notice that my bitch wasn't in the courtroom when I walked in. I figured she was late or something. The judge read out my charges, and I was given a bond. I looked behind me as they led me away, but I still didn't see her. I waited for hours before they transported me to the city jail. I was pissed the fuck off. I told her where my bank card was at and asked her to come bond me out. Why wasn't she here this morning? I was livid by the time I got back to jail. I was processed and given an orange jumpsuit to put on. Tears rolled down my face as I walked down the hallway with my cot.

"Here you go. M Pod," the CO said to me as she buzzed me in.

I couldn't help but notice how packed the pod was as I entered. Girls were lying around, and clothes were hanging up on the rails. The scent of burned noodles hit my nose. I walked over to where an empty bed was and put down the cot.

"Hey, you. I'm Marie, your bunkie," the white girl greeted me.

"Hello."

I didn't intend to be here for long, and I damn sure wasn't looking for no friends.

I walked over to the phone booths to wait in line for the phone. This one bitch was on the phone going off on some nigga about putting money on her books. When I tell you this bitch was laying this nigga out, she was. She hung up twice and *still* called the nigga back.

"Yo, can I get a call?" I walked up to her and tapped her on the shoulder.

"Bitch, I know you see me talking to my baby daddy," she covered the phone and yelled.

"Bitch, you done got forty-five fucking minutes on the phone. I need to use the phone." I took a step closer to her face. I had no idea who this high yellow bitch thought she was fucking with. I might not be no jailbird, but I'm from the motherfucking streets, and I wouldn't think twice about fighting this bitch.

"Baby, I'ma call you back before I have to beat this bitch face in. Love you, baby." She hung up the phone, walked by me, and gritted on me hard.

I was hoping that she would breathe hard on me so that I could whup her ass right in front of her homegirls. This bitch had no idea what the fuck I been through. I was ready to take this frustration out on somebody's child.

"You better watch your back, bitch," she said when she was by her girls.

I looked at her, shook my head, and smiled in that ho's face. I could tell she was a coward that needed an audience to be bold. I took a quick look at all three of them. Honestly, all three didn't add up to one good bitch. I walked off to get on the phone. I thought of calling Mari, but it was his fault I was here in the first place, so fuck him. I dialed Tesha's number and waited impatiently for her to pick up. She didn't answer, though. I called back three times, thinking she didn't know the number. The phone rang until the voicemail came on. I hung up the phone and walked away, feeling disappointed.

When I got back to my bunk, my Bunkie had made up my bed. "Hey, I guess you're in jail, so I fixed your bed for you." She smiled.

"Thank you." I squeezed out a smile.

I was hoping she wasn't going to keep talking 'cause I was frustrated and not in the mood for no long conversation. I climbed on the top bunk and lay my head down, facing the wall. It was hard to focus in here 'cause noise was everywhere. I felt a tear fall on my face. I quickly wiped it away and tried my best not to let any more come out. I was trying to understand why my bitch wouldn't show up and bond me out. This was so unlike her. I wondered if something bad happened to her. The fear of losing her too overtook me, giving me shivers inside.

Two days later and I was still sitting in Richmond City Jail. I didn't know anyone else's number, and I was holding out, trying not to call Mari. This was a horrible feeling, knowing I have a bond, and I have money in my account, but I'm sitting here in jail. My head was hurting, and I was hungry. The food was horrible, and I had no money on my books to buy commissary. I need to get me a lawyer to help fight these charges against me. I just need to get the fuck out of here.

It was dinnertime, and even though I didn't want to go to the chow hall, hunger was killing me. So I got up and walked with the rest of the hungry bitches. Dinner was garlic bread and soup. I drank a little of the soup just to put something in my stomach.

"Looky here, this bitch ain't eating her food. Let me guess; she thinks she too good to eat our kind of food," the bitch said while she stood over me.

I stood up and got in that bitch's face. I knew I should've stomped that bitch the first time she crossed me. Now, here she was, still talking shit.

"Bitch, you need to go find some pussy to eat on and get the fuck out of my face," I spat.

That bitch threw a punch at me, and it landed on my shoulder. I grabbed her by the neck and started throwing blows. The only thing on my mind was to rip this bitch's neck off her body. I was so pissed off I wouldn't ease up. I just kept throwing blows.

"Move out of the way," I heard someone yell. Then someone grabbed me up and held me tight.

"Let go of me," I yelled while I tried to wiggle away.

"Bitch, this ain't over yet," that ho yelled as another CO held her.

"Bitch, it better be," I shot back.

"Shut up and let's go," the CO yelled at me as she led me away.

I ran my tongue on my lips and tasted blood, so I knew I had a busted lip. That bitch lucky they broke us up 'cause I swear I wasn't done with her ass yet.

They led me off to the office, where I was given a fighting charge and put in lockdown. It didn't hit me until I was locked down, and then tears started to flow. I was mad at the bitch that I just fought. Mad at Mari for playing with my heart like he did. I was super mad at my bitch for leaving me in here. I had no idea what was going on. I've been calling her and still couldn't get no answer.

"God, please help me. You know I don't deserve none of this," I whispered as I lay on my stomach, crying. I don't know if he was listening to me, but I needed someone to listen 'cause I was feeling helpless right now. I needed to get the fuck up out of here.

I must've dozed off 'cause the jingling of keys awakened me. I sat up and saw the CO standing in the doorway.

"You need to get your things," she instructed.

"Where am I going?" I looked at her with an attitude on my face.

"You're leaving. Bond posted."

Those were the happiest words that I've heard in a week. I was so pleased that I could've grabbed this bitch and hugged her. But, of course, that wasn't a wise idea, so I jumped up off the bed and walked out the door. I followed her up to the front. My bitch finally came through for me. I knew she wouldn't let me just rot in here.

I walked up to the front, where a bondsman greeted me. I remembered him from hanging around Mari. I looked around for my bitch, but I didn't see her. A few seconds later, I saw a well-dressed bitch walk in. I guess she was for someone else.

"Akila, hey, girl," she greeted me.

"Who—"

"Mari sent me to get you. I told them you're my little sister, so just play along." She hugged me as she whispered in my ear.

I was reluctant to hug this bitch back because this was some crazy shit, and I wasn't sure she wasn't one of his bitches. Fuck it, though. I need to get out of here first, then ask questions later. The papers were signed, and the bond was paid. I thanked the bondsman, and he left. I looked at this bitch from head to toe. I could tell she wasn't no average bitch.

"Girl, why you stand there looking like that? Don't you want to get out of here?"

"Where is Mari?"

"He's at G's crib. I'm going to take you to him."

"You ain't got to do that. You can just drop me at my house."

"Mari needs to see you first."

She walked off to the parking lot, and I followed behind this bitch, not feeling her attitude. Who the fuck she think she is telling me where she's taking me? See, this bitch got me fucked up. She walked up to a Lexus truck and got in. I got in on the passenger side and sat down. She pulled off, then got on the phone.

"Hey, babes, I got her. Here you go." She handed me the phone.

I got the phone, but not before rolling my eyes at her. "Hello."

"Aye, babes, I told shawty to drop you here. I need to rap with you real quick."

"I don't have shit to say to you. I'm tired and need a shower, so you need to tell your bitch to drop me off at my gotdamn house."

"Yo, you need to chill the fuck out with that little attitude. B, some shit popped off, and you can't go the crib. So you need to come let me holla at you."

Before I could respond, he hung up. This rude-ass nigga gets on my fucking nerves. I put down her phone.

"Listen, baby, I know you getting out of jail and everything, but this disrespect ain't called for. So don't try it next time 'cause we will definitely have issues."

"Fuck all this you talkin' about. I only want to know one thing. How long you been fucking Mari?"

"Oh, I see what this is about. Honey, you got nothing to worry about. I don't swing that way. Matter of fact, if you had your hair done and you looked a little finer, I probably would be trying to get in *your* drawers."

This bitch was crazy as fuck. I don't care how the fuck I look. I don't fuck with bitches. No way my ass eating no pussy, but, hey, to each his own.

"Don't trip on how I look. You're not my type. I love dick. Yes, big, black dick."

"Ha-ha, I hear you. Don't knock it 'til you try it, but you Mari girl, so I'ma let you live."

I didn't feel the need to respond to this bitch. I didn't know her, and she must not know me either. The bitch did bond me out, so I can't be all ungrateful to her. I closed my eyes, wondering what the hell Mari was talking about. I pray this nigga didn't do no dumb shit at my damn house. Suddenly, I felt a headache coming on. I rubbed my temple, trying to ease the tension.

I felt a tap on my shoulder, so I opened my eyes. "You're here." I looked where we were. It was a huge-ass house that looked like a mini mansion with big gates behind us. She parked and got out of the car. I got out and followed behind her to the glass door. We waited a few seconds, then the door opened. G was standing in the doorway.

"Y'all come on in."

We walked inside. I spotted Mari standing in the hallway with his arm in a brace, and he didn't have a shirt on.

"What's good, babes?" He walked over to me and hugged me with his other arm.

"What is going on? Why couldn't I go to my house?" I wasted no time in asking him questions.

"Yo, come in here. We need to talk." He walked off.

I followed him to what I figured was the den. He took a seat, and I took one on the other couch. I stared at him, anxiously waiting to hear what the hell he had to say.

"Yo, what the fuck happened? Why were you in jail, and why the fuck you ain't call me?"

"Your bitch pressed charges on me, and why didn't I call you? What, you forgot the last time I saw you, you had your hands wrapped around my neck?" I lashed out.

"Yo, babes, I swear I'm so sorry. I just blacked out. For real, you know I wouldn't intentionally do anything to hurt you. I'm sorry, B."

"Yo, you sorry. You got a bitch pregnant, you beat me up in front of her, then I got thrown in jail for days, and all you can say is you sorry. You're right. You're a sorry-ass nigga."

"Yo, B, I get it. You're mad, but we've got more serious shit to focus on right now."

"What the fuck you talkin' 'bout?"

"I can't get into the specifics, but the house is burned down—"

"*What* house is burned down? What the fuck you talking about, Mari? My bitch, Tesha, was waiting there for me." I looked at him, anxious for a response.

"B, I don't know about no bitch being up in there. Some shit popped off, and we had to burn the crib down. But like I said, the less you know, the better it is for you."

I couldn't believe what the fuck I was hearing right now, and to make matters worse, this nigga wasn't answering my damn question.

"You really pissing me off. Answer my damn question, Mari. What the fuck happened at the house?" I yelled at the top of my voice.

"Lower yo' voice, B. I went to the crib, and a few niggas followed me in there, trying to rob me. I got shot, returned fire, and bodied three of them."

"You killed *three* niggas in my shit? What the fuck were you thinking?"

"Yo, B. I ain't had no other choice. The niggas were going to kill me, so it was either them or me."

"So, I was left in jail, and now I have nowhere to live? This is some bullshit." I rubbed my hand over my face, trying to calm my nerves.

"You ain't got to worry about that. I already hit the nigga up that got you the first house. He on it. He's just waiting on you to tell him what you want. And one more thing . . ."

"What is it?"

"You need to get a new car too."

"Nigga, you fuckin' trippin'. I ain't got shit to do with what you got going on. What about the fucking police?"

"Man, none of that shit can come back on you. The house can't be traced back to you or anything, and the good thing is you were locked up when all this shit popped off."

I sat there thinking of this craziness. This nigga stays in some shit, and now my shit got drawn into it. I really need to get the fuck away from this nigga fast.

He got up off the couch, walked over to me, and dropped to his knees. He took my hands in his. "Babes, listen. I know I fucked up, and I'm sorry. I swear, Akila, I will do everything in my power to make this up to you. I need you, baby."

"Need me? Where were you all the days when *I* needed you? Many nights I go to bed by myself, not knowing where the fuck you at. When I mention it to you, you say I'm bitching, and I was wrong. I wasn't wrong. While I'm at home playing the good girl, you were out fucking with that bitch. You ran up in a freak bitch raw and got her pregnant while I wanted to have a child by you. I can't ever forgive you for this."

"B, the condom broke. I didn't mean for her to get pregnant. I don't love that bitch. I love you, B. I do everything for you. I love you. I want to marry you, B, not her. That bitch don't mean a damn thing to me."

"This sounds all good and shit, but you have no idea how much you hurt me. I loved you, never cheated on you before, and this is how you do me. Now, you sittin' here telling me you're sorry. I don't give a fuck how sorry you are. I'm done. I can't be with you anymore. I deserve way better than what you dishin' out." I pulled my hands away from him. I was prepared to jump up 'cause whenever I say something Mari didn't want to hear, he would snap, and next comes the hit. Truthfully, I should've left him long ago, but I kept thinking he would change because I loved him. So now, here we are, and he got a fucking baby on the way.

"You ain't got to look scared. Trust me; I'm not putting my hands on you. The other day, I realized how much I love you and don't want to lose you. I just need one more chance to prove to you that you're the one for me."

"It took you *that* long to realize it? What the fuck you expect me to do while you playing daddy to that ape? You think I'ma lay at home wondering if you fucking your baby mama? This shit hurts my soul, and I can't live with it. We are *over*, Mari."

His phone started ringing back-to-back. He looked at it, then back at me.

"Who is that? Your bitch?"

"Come on, B, I ain't got no bitch but you."

"Yeah, right."

"I hope you change your mind 'cause I'm not giving up."

I wasn't listening to none of that shit he was spitting out. This nigga thinks he could sweet-talk me and have me falling all over him again, but this time was different. He had a baby on the way—and that was a deal breaker for me.

Dreema

I stepped out of the shower and dried between my legs when I felt something. I rubbed my hands down there again, and this time, it was sticky. I started feeling nauseated. I ran to the toilet and vomited. After washing my mouth out, I ran for my phone. I started calling Mari, but his phone just rang until the voicemail picked up. I called back three times.

Next, my water broke, and I went into labor. I quickly got dressed, got the baby bag, grabbed my keys, and headed out the door. I was having my baby at Chippenham Hospital, so I drove there. On the way, I tried calling Mari's phone a few more times but still no answer. I threw the phone into my purse and wondered where the hell he was at. The last time I checked, that ho was still locked up. Let me find out he was laid up with a new bitch . . . So soon as I dropped this baby, I was going to show my ass. It was one thing to be his side bitch, but that's about to change. I'm now his child's mother. I can't wait for my baby to get here, so his daddy can know all his little games will be over.

I made it to the hospital and parked, then walked into the emergency room and let them know I was in labor. The contractions were getting worse. Even after all the stories I heard, no one told me this shit would hurt that bad. Shit, this might be the only child that I want to have. By the time I got on the L&D floor, the pain was unbearable. Within seconds, the baby's head was popping out. This happened so fast the nurse couldn't give me the epidural. So, I was feeling every bit of the pain.

Within seconds, the nurse placed my baby on my chest. The first thing I did was look at his complexion. I let out a huge sigh of relief. Then tears started rolling down my face as I stared at the beautiful human I had created. I then remembered his daddy wasn't here to experience this feeling with me. It angered me, but I was too focused on my son right now to put my focus elsewhere.

I named him Mari Thomas Jr. We both had agreed to call him a junior. Shit, I wouldn't have it any other way. After all, this is his first child. Any bitch that came behind me will know my son is the first and only junior.

After the nurse took my baby to get weighed, another nurse cleaned me up. I was then given pain medicine. I was so exhausted and hungry. I grabbed my phone and noticed Mari called three times. I called him back.

"Yo."

"Really, your son was born, and you just now calling back? What kind of shit you on, Mari?"

"B, I was busy, and I didn't know you were going in labor. What hospital you at?"

"You know I'm at Chippenham."

"A'ight, I'll be up there in the morning."

Did I fucking hear this nigga correctly? I *know* I didn't hear him say he will be up here tomorrow.

"What you mean, you'll be up here in the morning. Your firstborn child is here."

"I heard you the first time, B, but I'm busy handling something, and I can't leave out right now. You and the baby good?"

"Fuck you, Mari. I can't fucking believe you."

"There you go with the drama. Chill out, B, and get some rest. Kiss my son for me, and I'll check on y'all later. I got to go."

I hung up, steaming hot. Here I was, in the hospital, just gave birth to our son, and he is out "handling business." I know he was lying and probably with that bitch. I called the jail.

"Richmond City Jail. How may I help you?"

"Hi, I'm calling to check if Akila Jones is there and how much is her bond?"

"Hold a sec, please." She placed the phone down to check.

"Ma'am, Miss Jones was released."

"Okay, thanks."

I fucking knew it. That bitch-ass nigga went and got that bitch out. Now, he fuckin' over there playing house and can't come see his child. I called his number again, but this nigga wasn't answering. I called about ten times, and still no response. Finally, I hit the side of the bed rail to relieve some frustration. I can't believe this nigga is doing this to me right after I gave birth to his son. Of all the shit he could've done, this really put the icing on the cake. Old stupid-ass nigga. He has no idea that I *wasn't* the one to fuck with.

My eyes were closed when I heard someone enter the room. I was getting sick and tired of these fucking doctors coming in and out at all times of the night. I wanted to yell, "*Bitch, I just had a baby. Let me fucking rest,*" but I held it in, pretending I didn't hear her enter.

I felt someone touch my arm. "Yo."

I opened my eyes and looked at this nigga. He got some nerve walking up in here like I don't know where the fuck he been and acting like shit is good.

"Really? A whole twenty-four hours later, nigga." I sat up and stared at him.

"Yo, B, I'm here now, right? Please don't bother with the fuckery." He walked over to Baby J's crib and stood there staring at him.

"You need to wash your fucking hands before you touch him."

"Yo, relax."

He walked to the bathroom, washed his hands, and then walked out. He took the baby out of the crib, then walked to the couch in the room, sat down, and looked into my baby's face. I peeped him, smiling as he did baby talk with him. I should be happy that he was here, but I wasn't. He really pissed me off when he allowed me to give birth by myself.

"What did the doctors say? Everything good?"

"If you were here, you would have known, right?" I shot him a nasty look.

"Yo, B. You seriously need to drop the attitude. I get you pissed that I wasn't here, but I'm here now. I need to know everything good with my seed."

"Yeah, everything is good. Is that all?"

"Yeah, that's all," he said and shook his head.

I don't give a fuck how he feels. Shit, that ain't even near how I was feeling yesterday. I'm done catering to his fucking feelings. He either make me and my son a priority, or I will move him the fuck up as an option. I tried ignoring him as he kissed and hugged our son. I was pissed off 'cause he behaved as if I weren't in the room. After about an hour, he got up and placed our son back in the basinet. I guess that's all the time he had to offer us. I looked at him and breathed hard.

"Yo, B. When can you leave?"

"Tomorrow, I guess."

"A'ight. Text me the time, and I'll be here." He reached over and kissed me on the forehead.

I didn't flinch. I want him to know I'm pissed the fuck off with him. It may seem like he got the upper hand right now 'cause I'm in this hospital, but he has to know I wasn't going to stay quiet for long. He will *definitely* feel my wrath soon.

It's been three days since we got out of the hospital, and I loved the bond I was forming with my newborn. I know I should put him in his crib, but I keep him on the bed with me. Sometimes, I just lie here rubbing his head and singing to him. Mari has no idea what he was missing out on. I thought he would be here with us, but he left after he dropped us off, and I haven't seen him since. He called earlier to ask if I needed anything and to tell me he'd come by later. I guess he thinks this is what being a father is all about.

I was starved. I guess all that vomiting I did when I was pregnant was finally taking a toll on me 'cause ever since I gave birth, it's like I'm always hungry. I didn't feel like waking up J and getting him dressed, so I ordered pizza and wings from Dominoes. I had been so preoccupied with being a mom that I hadn't been able to watch television. So, I grabbed the remote and started strolling through the channels. There was nothing to pique my interest. *Chicago P.D.* was the new hot show that's out. It was on On Demand, so I decided to catch up on the episodes that I missed. The pizza man came about fifteen minutes later, and I wasted no time in getting my grub on. That pepperoni pizza was good as fuck, and the hot wings were just as good. I drank a glass of cold lemonade to wash it down. I was good now. I wished I had some weed, but Mari's ass said he wasn't giving me no weed 'cause he didn't want me high when I cared for his son. This nigga just loves running his fucking mouth. I swear, if I really want some weed, I'd find a way to get it without him knowing.

I heard the doorbell ringing, so I got up and walked to the door. I looked through the peephole and saw it was Mari. I opened the door, walked back to the room, and continued watching television.

"He sleepin' again, huh?" he asked.

"Ain't that what newborn babies do?" I asked sarcastically.

"Yo, B. Is this how it's going to be? Every time I come over here, you give me an attitude?"

"I don't give you no attitude. What the fuck. You think I'm supposed to be all happy and shit? I just gave birth to our son, and you haven't been here with us. You over there with that bitch. That's *not* your family. *We* are," I yelled.

"Yo, B, I appreciate that you had my seed, but you knew I had a bitch, and you still decided to let me fuck you. I didn't mean to get you pregnant, but it happened, and I'm here."

I got up off the bed and got into his face. "Are you fucking serious right now? When I got with you, you lied, saying you were single. Then after I fucked you and caught feelings, *then* you tell me that you have a bitch. Yeah, you right. I should've stopped fucking with you then, but it was too late. I was already in love."

"B, I care about you and love that you gave me my first seed. But I can't be here every day with you like that. I got a business to run."

"Business? You *do* know I know that you got niggas that run errands for you, right? What it really is, is you have to be with that bitch. Even after that bitch attacked me—almost hurting your seed. I guess that don't matter at all."

"Yo, all you want to do is argue. I started fucking with you trying to escape drama, but shit, all you bring is drama. How the fuck you think me and you are supposed to work out when you got my girl locked up?"

"Fuck that bitch. Where the fuck was she at when I had to drive your drugs from New York when the police ran up, and I had to stuff your shit up my pussy? Yeah, that simple bitch was nowhere around. Since you throwin' her ass in my face, it's fuck you too," I spat and stared him in the face.

"You know what, B? I'm out." He started walking away.

I couldn't let him just leave like that, so I ran up behind him and started hitting him. He turned around, grabbed me by the throat, and threw me on the floor.

"Yo, you need to chill. You just had a baby." He squeezed me harder.

"Get the fuck off me. I swear to God, you will *never* see me or my fucking baby again."

"I don't give a fuck about you, B, but don't you ever try to keep my son away from me. You hear me?" he yelled in my face, spit flying everywhere.

He then let me go and walked away.

"You know, you gon' regret this. Fuck you, Mari. Go be with that bitch."

He didn't respond. He just kept walking. He opened the door and left. I dropped to my knees, crying. He was really acting this cold to me. I was in disbelief. The way he talked to me now was foreign to me. It's like he changed after his son was born. I just laid up against the wall and cried. After I finished feeling sorry for myself, I dried my tears and got up. I was done with being a weak bitch for this nigga. I dialed a number on my phone.

"Yo, shawty, what's good?"

"You know you fucked up, right?"

"What the fuck you mean? You told me to pop the nigga if he resisted, so I popped his ass."

"Yo, you a stupid motherfucker. You didn't try to rob Mari. That was his *brother,* Rio. I didn't tell you to kill the nigga. I just wanted you to get the money up off him."

"Shit, are you serious, shawty?"

"Listen, we done said too much on this phone. I'm at the house. Come see me."

"A'ight. I'll be there as soon as I finish running errands."

I disconnected the phone and sat on the bed. I had everything all planned out. Mari had just left the house, and he had over ten grand on him. I told this motherfucker what he was wearing and where he would be at. But this stupid motherfucker killed Rio instead. I know now you can't send a nigga to do a woman's job.

Chapter Nine

Akila

I forgot how hard house shopping was. Today, I looked at about ten houses and none to my liking. My last house was a three-bedroom. This time, I wanted a four-bedroom with a pool. I mean, he told me to get whatever I wanted, so that's precisely what I'm doing. And I did get me a new whip. A 2018 Dodge Durango. It was definitely an upgrade for me, and I was loving it so far. After the first night of staying at his boy's house, I decided it was best if I got a hotel room. I still wasn't talking to Mari outside of getting the house. I could tell he was aggravated with me, but I didn't give a fuck about how he was feeling. *I* was the one that was done wrong, and there's no way I'ma let him feel like I did him wrong.

Each day that went by, I prayed and prayed for strength. I was tired of crying over him and thinking about that bitch and her baby . . . a baby that should've been mine in the first place. Of all the shit he did, this hurts the most. I really didn't know how I would live with no job. I thought about getting a job, but I wasn't going to work in no fast-food place. I just need to go ahead and wait until I graduate so I can get a better job.

***

It was my first day back in class, and I wasn't enthusiastic about it. I was here 'cause I missed too many days and was too close to graduation to give up now. I was very distracted and tried my best to focus on what the instructor said. Suddenly, my phone buzzed. I picked it up and saw it was a text. I rolled my eyes before opening it. It was from Tyrone.

Hey, there, beautiful.

I smiled and looked at two seats across from me. He was sitting there looking sexy as ever. I smiled at him, trying my best not to let anyone see our interactions. A lot of these bitches were messy and loved other people's business.

"Miss Jones, is there a problem?" the instructor said, embarrassing me.

"No, sir. Everything is good." I put my head back into the textbook in front of me.

After getting called out, I was scared to look over at Tyrone. When class was over, I packed my books in my bag and grabbed my computer. I was about to walk out.

"Miss Jones, may I speak to you for a second?"

I turned around and walked to the instructor's desk. "Miss Jones, I heard what happened to you, and I sympathize. But class is coming to an end. I need you to get focused and fast. Right now, your grades are struggling, and I'm afraid if you don't bring them back up, you won't be able to graduate."

"I don't know what you heard, but I got this. I will pass this class, and I *will* graduate."

"Okay, Miss Jones. We have a test on Monday. I hope you're ready." He got up and walked toward me. He was so close that I could smell the stale coffee reeking off his breath.

"I will be. Is that all, 'cause I got to go?"

"Yes, that's all. You know, if you need any kind of help, I'll be more than happy to help you. One hand washes the other."

I looked him dead in the eyes and spoke. "No disrespect, teach, but you're an old-ass nigga with worms. There's nothing on you I would like to scratch. Now, you better get the fuck up out of my face before I walk down the hall and report you for sexual misconduct."

"Wow, wow. You're getting above yourself. Not sure what you think I was talking about, but it was nothing sexual. I'm merely a teacher trying to help his student pass her class so she can graduate."

"Yeah, right. I wonder how many of these bitches fucking you for a better grade." I shook my head in disgust. Without saying another word, I walked out. I now know that someone was telling this school my damn business. Ughh. I can't wait to finish up and get the hell away.

I was irritated that this nigga tried to make a pass at me with his old, stinking-breath ass. I don't give a fuck how desperate I was to graduate. I would never let him touch me with a sixteen-foot pole. Ughh, just thinking about it turned my stomach.

I was so into my thoughts that I didn't see Tyrone standing by the exit door.

"Hey, beautiful. I hope I didn't get you in any trouble," he smiled.

"No trouble at all," I smiled back as he held the door, and I walked out.

"We need to talk, Akila."

I stopped and looked at him. "What's going on, Tyrone?"

I couldn't deny how fine he was. I noticed he was growing his beard out, which kind of put him in a category of sexy and rugged. He also had those deep bedroom eyes that draw you in and pierce your soul.

"Akila, I know I've told you a million times how much I'm digging you. Shawty, I can't get you off my mind. All I ask is for one chance to show you that I can be the man for you."

"My life is so complicated right now that it wouldn't be fair to bring you in it."

"I'm a real nigga. I can handle whatever. All I ask you to do is give me a chance. If this is not what you want, then I'll leave you alone, shawty."

I stood there looking at him, and my heart was screaming out to him. His words sounded so genuine, and I wanted to reach out and touch his face. I searched my brain, looking for the right words to say. Before any words could get out, he took my head, and our lips locked. Our tongues danced together. We were in sync with each other as he drew me closer to him. I didn't fight it. Matter of fact, I embraced it. Chills ran through my body, and my clit started tingling.

"Ewww, y'all go get a room," one of our classmates joked as she walked by us.

I let go of his embrace and looked around, feeling slightly embarrassed.

"Wow. That was intense. You're a great kisser," he joked.

"Boy, you better stop before I get in trouble." I started to walk away.

This was crazy. I shouldn't have kissed him back. I hope no one else saw us because I would hate for Mari to hear some shit like this.

"So, you're just going to leave like this? No goodbye or nothing?"

"Tyrone, I promise this is not what you want." I continued walking away from him.

"Shawty, I promise I'ma make you mine."

"Yeah, whatever," I said before getting into my car.

I wasted no time on pulling out of the parking lot. I needed to get away from him. That kiss had me thinking all kinds of crazy ideas. This wasn't right. I shouldn't feel like this. . . .

Heard you want a nigga that's gon' please you
Suck your toes, dick you down, please you

I stood in the mirror dancing and lotioning my body as I got dressed. Kevin Gates's song was blasting through my speaker. I was feeling myself as I glanced at my body in the mirror. I was dressed in a skintight bodycon dress that I purchased from Angel Brinks. I took a glance at my ass. The way it stuck out in this dress was giving me life right now. I applied a little makeup with lip gloss and made my way out.

I was nervous but excited to see him. After he kissed me that day, I couldn't get him off my mind, so I accepted his invite to dinner. I know I shouldn't have, but I was lonely. Plus, I was feeling him and wanted to see what he was all about.

I got in my car, put his address in the GPS, and pulled off. I made sure to check my rearview mirror. Nothing looked suspicious, so I made my way to his house. He lived in Churchill by Thirty-Second Street. I wasn't too familiar with Churchill and heard a lot of messed-up stories about that section. I thought he would take me to a restaurant, but he told me he wanted to cook for me. Shit, I was sold on that 'cause I've never had a nigga tell me he wants to cook. Most niggas would prefer to take you out to eat. So, he definitely made me feel special.

The GPS let me know the house was coming up on my right. I pulled over and spotted his car, so I parked behind it. I got out of my car and walked to the house with the address he had given me. Before I could get up the stairs, I saw him standing in the doorway.

"Hey, love," he greeted me and gave me a big kiss.

This was starting to become so natural that I didn't fight it. I kissed him back. We finally let go of each other and went inside his house. I was nosy, so I glanced around to see if there was anything that screamed a female was living there. I didn't see anything visible. His place was clean and well put together.

"Come in here, shawty," he instructed, taking my hand and leading me into the dining room.

The room was filled with the sweet aroma of delicious food. I looked at the table, and there was a little of everything on it. This reminded me of my grandma's house during Thanksgiving when she was alive. I smiled as I took a seat.

"I have fried chicken, roast beef with stuffing, and red potatoes with macaroni."

"Wow, you went all out. Let me get a little of everything."

After he had dished out the dinner, we sat down and ate. I couldn't help but think about him the entire time we were eating. His conversation wasn't average. He was classy with a little bit of hood in him. That shit was sexy as fuck. The way I was feeling was like no other. I grabbed on to every word he spoke, yearning for more. This nigga was making me wet, even without touching me. *Oh God, please, take this feeling away,* I whispered inside.

"You a'ight, babes?" he asked me.

"Yeah, I'm good," I quickly lied and straightened up real fast. I was scared that he might've picked up that I was being thirsty.

"What you want to drink? I got Grey Goose, Patrón, vodka, and pineapple juice."

"Pineapple juice? What the fuck I look like? A little-ass girl? If you don't pass that Grey Goose on the rocks . . ."

"That's what the fuck I want to hear."

We started drinking and smoking. I swear the alcohol had me feeling horny as fuck. He was fine, but with the effects of the alcohol, he was nothing short of that motherfucking nigga. He reached over to pull me toward him, and we started kissing again. Before you knew it, his hand was up my dress. He pulled out one of my breasts from my bra and massaged it. I threw one of my legs up on him and started grinding on him. I purposely didn't wear no underwear, and juice was gushing out. I hoped I didn't embarrass myself if the juice ran down my legs. He pulled me over on top of him. I threw my legs over and started grinding on his dick. It was still in his pants, but I could feel it.

"Ease up real quick."

I eased my butt up as he pulled his jogging pants and boxers down to his ankles. His dick was a nice size and pretty as hell. I thought about starting to kiss it. However, I was horny as fuck, so I slowly eased down on his dick. My pussy was soaking wet, so it was easy to get his dick inside. Without mercy, I started riding him. I braced my body forward, resting my head on his shoulder while I scooted my ass in the air. I tightened my pussy muscles and rode his dick. I pretended like I was dancing in a video, moving around in circular motions. He grabbed my hips and winded up in me, hitting every inch of my pussy. I closed my eyes and just grinded on his dick. This fuck felt so good that I was hoping he didn't come yet.

"Shit, damn, boo, this pussy so good. Oh shit, I *want* this pussy." He grabbed me tighter.

I continue grinding down on his dick, flinging my ass up. While I was taking the dick, he thrust in and out of me. My body started to move in spasms. I sank my nails into his back as I tried to release everything. Then my legs started shaking as I busted all over his dick.

He picked me up and put me on the carpet. I threw my legs on his shoulders, and he entered me slowly. I grinded on his dick while he slow fucked me. Without warning, he started to fuck me harder. I wasn't going to let him outdo me, so I threw the pussy on him, matching his strokes.

"Oh man, this pussy so good, boo," he whispered in my ear.

That only boosted my ego. I totally forgot about the pain that I was feeling. I wrapped my hands around him and squeezed my pussy muscles on him. He started going faster, sweating hard and grunting out loud. Within seconds, he busted all up in me. He lay on top of me, holding me for a few seconds before getting up off me.

"Yo, shawty, you got some good pussy."

"Your dick is bomb too, boo." I had my eyes closed, trying to savor the moment. I've been with a lot of niggas before but having sex with him was so much better. It was more an emotional level—

"Don't move, pussy."

I know that voice. Wait, what the fuck was Mari doing in here? How did he get in this nigga's house? I was too scared to open my eyes. Fear filled my soul, and my body started shaking. I wished I could just disappear right now. I was naked, and this nigga was naked, and my ex-nigga was standing over us.

"Who the fuck are you, and what you want, nigga?" Tyrone said.

"Pussy, I said don't move. Try me, and I will blow yo' fucking brains out in front of this bitch." The venom in his voice was unmistakable.

"Mari, what the fuck you doing?" I finally opened my eyes and mustered up the courage to speak.

"Yo, shawty, you know this nigga?" He turned and looked at me.

"Yeah, nigga, you done fucked the wrong bitch." He hit Tyrone in the head. Blood gushed out of the side of his head, and he fell to the ground.

"Get up, bitch." He gritted hard on me while pointing the gun in my face.

"Mari, this isn't what it seems. I can explain," I started bawling.

The coldness in his eyes and how he looked at me let me know shit was about to get real up in here. I was looking for a way to get up out of here. I watched Mari. He was pacing back and forth, uttering some crazy shit under his breath while waving the gun. If I didn't know this nigga, I would assume he was on drugs by the way he was behaving.

He walked back toward me, and I used my hand to hover over my head. He grabbed me by the hair and pulled me up. "Bitch, how could you do this to me? I gave you every fucking thing that you ever wanted, and *this* is how you repay me? I fuckin' love you, Akila. How could you?" He smacked me in my face with the gun. Blood trickled down my cheek.

"Please, Mari, please, don't do this. I love you, Mari. Please, stop," I pleaded with everything in me.

"Bitch, you *love* me? How could you fuckin' love me, but you over here being a slut for this ho-ass nigga? Huh? Please fucking explain this to me. Give me a fucking reason why I shouldn't kill this fuck nigga and you."

"Mari, baby, I swear nothing happened. I was just over here because I was hurting that you got that bitch pregnant. I don't want him, boo, and he's not interested in me like that."

"I told yo' ass I was sorry. I told you that bitch don't mean shit to me. I fuckin' love you. *You* the one that I want."

I reached over and touched his face. "I know, baby. I should've listened to you. I'm sorry that I didn't listen to you, babes, but we can get out of here together. We can get us a new house and start over."

"I can't do that. This pussy nigga took what's rightfully mine. I can't let it slide, B. You know who I am out in the streets. Niggas will laugh at me if they know a bitch-ass nigga fucked my bitch."

"Baby, stop worrying about what people might say. I love you, and that's all that matters. I don't want him."

I was desperate and trying to calm him down. One second it seemed like it was working, but then he looked over at Tyrone and got upset again.

"Bitch, get off him. I know what the fuck you trying to do. You just trying to save your little boyfriend." He turned and pointed the gun at Tyrone. He was still lying on the floor, unconscious.

I jumped in front of him, putting my hand on his chest. "Stop, please. I will show you that I don't give a fuck about him. I will shoot him myself."

"You would do that for me to prove your love to me?" He looked me in the eyes.

I took a big gulp, wiped the tears away from my eyes, and looked at him. I had to make sure he believed me and had no doubts. "Baby, listen. From the first time I laid eyes on you, I loved you. I know I done said some things to you, but it was only 'cause I was scared of losing you. But I know you love me, and I love you too. I just want to show you how deep our bond is. Give me the gun, and let me show you, baby."

I watched as he lowered the gun. I reached out and slowly took it out of his hand. I was shaking, but I tried with everything in me not to drop the weapon. I carefully took hold of the gun. I gripped it tight and looked over at Tyrone. I then looked back at this nigga . . . and I turned and pointed the gun at him.

"Yo, hold up. What the fuck you doing, B?"

"What the fuck it looks like? Put your fucking hands up, Mari," I yelled, making sure he knew I wasn't playing any kind of games with him.

"Bitch, are you fucking serious? Do you *know* what the fuck you doin'?"

"Yeah, I know what I'm doing and who the fuck you are. A lying piece of shit. I should've left you alone a long time ago."

"You're a stupid bitch. You ain't got no balls to kill. Look at you. You fuckin' shakin'," he laughed.

I took a few steps toward him. "You *sure* you want to try me. I might not be a killer like you, but I damn sure ain't scared to pull this motherfuckin' trigger," I yelled.

"Stop, babe. Don't do it," Tyrone's faint voice whispered.

"Yeah, bitch, you better listen to yo' little boyfriend. He seems to have more sense than you."

"Tyrone, stay out of this. This nigga been beating my ass for years. I should've killed him a long time ago."

"I know, baby, but you're nothing like him. You're not a killer."

"Yeah, pussy, tell her."

"Baby, listen to me. We can call the police and let them lock him up."

I was torn. Here I was holding the gun on a nigga that I loved, and the nigga I'm falling for was beside me telling me to get him locked up. I really didn't want to kill Mari, but I wanted him to feel the same kind of fear that I felt every time he jumped in my face. The funny thing was, he was a hard-core killer and showed no fear.

"Yo, you better get the fuck up out of here," I yelled at him.

"Bitch, I promise you're going to regret this," he yelled as he dashed out the door.

"Babes, are you okay?" Tyrone said to me.

"Yeah. I'm so sorry about this. I'll go with you to the station to make a report, but first, I need to get you to the hospital."

"Nah, I'm straight. I'm just glad you're okay. That nigga is crazy. I can't see how you stayed with him that long."

"Yeah, I don't know either. Just know love will have you doing some crazy-ass shit."

"That's what I heard. Shit, if it's that crazy, I don't want it."

"Can you let me clean up your wound? And I still think you need to go to the hospital."

"I would go to the hospital, but a nigga ain't got no insurance. But I got some peroxide in the cabinet."

I was so angry that this had happened to him. This was all my fault. I knew how crazy Mari was. I should've never gotten involved with Tyrone. Now, his head had a big gash in it. I cleaned it up with peroxide and bandaged it up for him.

"Listen, baby, don't feel guilty about none of this shit. This is not your fault. You had no way of knowing that nigga was a lunatic. Listen, you need to stay here with me. I don't trust that he won't hurt you if you go back to the hotel."

I looked at him, and he made a valid point. I just went off on Mari, but I never thought it out thoroughly. He had a whole bunch of connects in the city, and if he wanted something done, it would be done. I took a seat on the sofa and buried my head in my hands.

Mari

How did I let that bitch play me like that? She was moving kind of funny, so I got one of my niggas to put a GPS on her car. At first, it was the regular: school, grocery store, and back to the hotel. I spotted her talking to this one nigga after school one day. Before she walked off, they started kissing. I was in rage seeing my ho kissing on a bitch-ass nigga. Now, I figured out why this bitch was so quick to walk away from me.

It was late evening, and I kept calling Akila, but she wasn't answering the phone. I decided to stop by her hotel room to see what the fuck her problem was. I was about to exit the rental I was driving when I saw her walking out of the hotel. I could tell this wasn't no grocery run 'cause of the way she was dressed like a slut. I waited until she pulled out of the parking lot, and then I followed her. The stupid bitch didn't even take time to look behind her. If she did, she would've caught me following her.

I watched with venom in my eyes as she and this fuck nigga hugged before they disappeared behind closed doors. I spotted a couple of neighbors out in their yard, so I decided to sit still until no one was around. The last thing I need is for one of these nosy motherfuckers to report some shit. I lit me a blunt while I sat waiting. Blood was boiling in my veins. The moment was now. Everyone seemed to disappear, and the darkness quickly appeared. I got out of the car and slowly crept up the stairs. I tried the door, but it was locked. I looked around, trying to figure out a way into the house. I crept back down the stairs and made my way to the back of the building. There was an old staircase that seemed like it was ready to fall apart, but that didn't sway me away. I held on and barely put my weight down. I know I would be hurt physically if this feeble structure fell apart. I got to the stairs and tried the door that was also locked. There was a window to my right. I reached over and pushed it up. Shit, this was my lucky day. I climbed over and got in. I looked around and saw the kitchen light was off. I made my way to the front. Then I grabbed my gun and held it as I crept through darkness. I was careful to keep my ears open.

I inched closer to a bedroom. Silently, I leaned my ear against the wall. My blood pressure elevated as I heard Akila's voice. They were so into each other that they didn't hear when I entered the room.

I pressed my gun against the nigga as I looked at my bitch lying there, butt-ass naked. Anger turned to jealousy, then hatred. My thoughts were filled with rage. I looked at them both with murder on my mind. How could this bitch I love and care for give away my pussy? I gave her every fucking thing. I was seconds away from committing murder, but my brother's face flashed in my head. Then a little bitch of rational popped into my mind. I need to bury him. I got to see him one last time, and if I killed them, I would probably be locked up. I can't do this.

The sweet melody of Akila's voice interrupted my wicked thoughts. She reached over and touched my face. I tried not to show it, but she did something to me. I stared deep into her eyes. Behind that pain, I knew she was a good human being. Boy, was I so fucking wrong. That bitch tricked me into giving her the gun. How could I be so fucking stupid to trust a bitch that was fucking around on me? Soon as that bitch got ahold of the weapon, she turned it on me. For a quick second, I thought she was going to kill me. But that bum said some old corny shit to her, and she lowered the gun, then ordered me to leave. I looked at that bitch and smiled. One day, we shall meet again, and trust me, it won't be pleasant.

I didn't hesitate to get out of there. I wasn't too sure that bitch or that pussy nigga wouldn't call the police on me. I jumped into my car and pulled off. I feel like a chump leaving my gun in that bitch's possession. And for that, she'll pay with her life. . . .

I was angry as fuck. I thought about going home, and that's when it hit me: I didn't have no home. I've been staying at my nigga's crib, but I didn't feel like being around no nigga right now. I thought about Dreema, but I didn't want to be around her and that baby right now. Everything was cool before the baby was born, but lately, all that bitch do is argue and fight. I decided to grab me a bottle of Patrón and some blunts. I then got me a room at the hotel. I need time to clear my mind and plan this ho's funeral.

Dreema

Mari was a straight bitch. Shit was all peachy when it was just us, but I noticed he changed ever since I had the baby. And to make matters worse, that nigga mad 'cause I got his ho locked up. Honestly, he can kiss my big, red ass for real. Me and my motherfucking baby don't fucking need him.

I bathed my baby and put him down to sleep. I was getting tired of being in this house every damn day. I swear I felt like I was about to lose it. I've been smoking weed to ease the stress, but I fucked up and fell asleep the other day. When I woke up, my son was crying, his face was red, and he had shit all over him. I knew then I couldn't be getting high like that no more. I wish I had some kind of help, but I guess that nigga was too busy chasing that old dumb-ass bitch.

I heard the phone ringing, so I got up and walked to the room to get it. "Hello."

"What's good, shawty? I been hitting you up."

"Yeah, well, you know I just had a baby, so I been busy."

"Man, yeah, whatever. I'm pulling up now."

This rude motherfucker better go on now with his nasty-ass attitude. It's bad enough he fucked up on some shit that was supposed to be simple. Now, he seems like he has an attitude. I reluctantly walked to the door and opened it. He walked in, and I locked the door behind him.

"Yo, where the fuck you been?"

"Nigga, I been here taking care of your fucking child," I responded with an attitude.

"That nigga been over here since that shit happened?"

"Yeah, he been over here. What, you think I'm going to just stop him from coming by? Boy, how the fuck you shot the wrong brother? I texted you his picture and showed you what he had on. How do you fuck up a twenty-grand lick? I helped that nigga count twenty fucking grand. All you had to was rob the nigga. But guess what?

You killed the nigga's brother, so now the nigga put a hundred grand on the head of whoever did it. Yo, I swear I should've known you wouldn't come through for me." I walked off on him.

"Yo, shawty, it was dark, and the nigga looked like the picture you texted me. How was I supposed to know they looked like twins? Shit, I can still get the nigga. It ain't too late." He followed behind me in the room.

"You know how much heat that would bring? You fucked up, and now, I ain't got shit." I sat down on the bed.

"Man, fuck that nigga. He thinks this his seed, so milk that nigga for everything he's worth. You need to do that shit fast. I'm tired of staying at my mama's house while you over here playing house with this bitch-ass nigga. You promised a big payoff, but fuck this shit. That nigga playing."

"I can't believe you right now. Are you serious? You fucked up. That was easy money, nigga. You know what I think? You couldn't stay sober enough to do what the fuck I asked you. I swear I have no idea why I keep dealing with you. You turnin' out to be a big-ass mistake."

"Yo, bitch, I ain't tryin'a hear all that shit. You don't remember who the fuck held you down before this nigga came in the picture? I'm a real motherfucking G. I bet you that nigga can't fuck you as good as I can."

"You're so sick. You worried about who fucks me the best. To be honest, none of y'all can't fuck me the way I want to be fucked. Yo, your son needs more Pampers and shit. That's what you need to be worried about for real."

"Yo, call that nigga. He big-money grip. I ain't got shit. Matter of fact, I need some gas money right now."

"Hmmm, I swear I have no idea how my pussy got wet for you."

"Yo, just give me fifty bucks so I can go, and you can go back to playing house with that old dumb-ass nigga. Wait, what would it be worth to that nigga if he finds out who got his brother killed? That's right. You *did* say a hundred grand. . . ." He smiled at me.

I was so disgusted right now. I got up and grabbed my purse. I took out two twenties and a ten and handed them to him. "Now, get out of my house and do me a fucking favor. Disappear for good."

"Damn, shawty, I was only joking around with you." He took the money and got up.

He walked over to my son's crib and kissed him. He then walked out. I followed behind him.

"I love you, shawty. Keep that pussy tight for daddy."

I didn't respond. Instead, I slammed the door as soon as he walked out, making sure it was locked. I was feeling uneasy after he walked out. See, Damion and I been fucking with each other for years. I was fucking with him when he was making money in the streets. He caught a fed case and went away for a few years. When he came home, I started fucking back with him, thinking he would get back to the money. Months turned to years, and all he seemed to get on with was that powder. He kept making promises, but nothing came through. I should've said fuck him, but I felt guilty. I loved him when he was stacking, so I wanted to stick around to see if he would get back on.

I ended up meeting Mari and had a big plan to get us back on. At first, I was just after the money, but then I started having strong feelings for Mari. With his addiction getting out of control, Damion began applying pressure on me. I needed him to stay at his mama's house, but he would come over here each time he needed money. I was scared he and Mari might meet up one day. So, I kept giving him money. It was supposed to be a big break for us the day Mari asked me to count twenty grand for him. I quizzed Mari about where he was heading. He told me he was about to meet up with his brother at the pool hall down Shockoe Bottom. I knew then it was the perfect timing.

I was so wrong. This nigga killed Rio, and we didn't get the money. I was so disgusted by him that I could barely look at him. I really wish this was Mari's son and not Damion's. I'm happy that no one outside of us knows this. I will continue letting Mari play daddy 'cause Damion's drug habit was getting in the way. He don't even look the same. His clothes look big on him, and he is just slowly withering away. The last time we fucked, I had to keep thinking why I would even allow myself to lay up with his ass. I guess it's true. You can't help who you love, 'cause as sorry as it sounds, I love that sorry motherfucker's dirty drawers.

Chapter Ten

Akila

One minute, shit was going good in my life, and then within months, my world came crumbling down. When this nigga first came into my life, I thought it was the best thing to ever happen to me. He talked a good game, his dick game was on point, and his bag was long. What else can a bitch from the projects want? Right, this nigga walked into my life . . . and brought a whole bunch of fucking mess. Now, look at me. I have nothing to show for all the shit that he put me through. I was feeling disgusted with everything right now. This was my first time out of the house since this shit popped off the other day. Tyrone was nice enough to offer me a place to stay. I thought he would be finished with me after what Mari did, but instead, he was very understanding. For the days that I've been with him, he went out of his way to make sure I was comfortable.

I put on my shades as I walked down the stairs. This was my first time coming outside since that shit happened with Mari. Tyrone was against me going out by myself, but I was not going to be no damn prisoner. If Mari wants to be stupid and do some shit to me, then let him do it. I'm not going to let him have that kind of control over me. Period.

After looking around just as a precaution, I got into the car. I was headed to the real estate office. I've been calling this bitch for days. Sometimes, she wasn't in, and other times, she was on another line. To me, it seems like bullshit 'cause before all that shit happened, the bitch was constantly calling me to let me know what houses she had available.

It took me about twenty-five minutes to get to the office on Forest Hill Avenue. I pulled up and walked in.

"Good morning. How may I help you?" the receptionist asked.

"I'm here to see Shonda Matthews."

"Is Miss Matthews expecting you?"

"No, she is not, but can you let her know Akila Jones is out here?" I looked at the bitch with an attitude.

"Sure."

She got on the phone. I couldn't hear what was said on the other end, but she quickly hung up the phone.

"I'm sorry, but Miss Matthews is on the phone handling business. Can you leave your number and a message, and she'll call you before the end of the day?"

I looked at that bitch and just started walking away. But I knew *exactly* where this bitch's office was, so I headed there.

"Ma'am, ma'am, you can't go back there," the bitch started yelling at me as I made my way to the back. I wasn't listening, and I kept walking fast. That bitch was on my heels, but I wasn't slowing down. "You can't go in there," she yelled again.

I looked at her, then pushed the door wide open. That bitch was sitting at her desk, browsing her computer.

"I'm sorry, Miss Matthews. I told her she couldn't come back here. I can call the police if you'd like me to."

"No, Alicia, it's okay. You can leave now," that bitch said without looking up from the computer.

"How may I help you, Miss Jones?" She turned her attention to me finally.

"Lady, I've been calling you for days and can't seem to reach you. The last time we spoke, you told me Mari gave you the okay, and I just needed to find the house, and everything else would be handled."

"Yes, that's correct. I was dealing with Mr. Owens, but a few days ago, he informed me that my services were no longer needed."

"He said that?" I was shocked and somewhat confused.

"Yes, Mari, excuse me. I mean, Mr. Owens told me that he no longer needed the house. So, if you're willing to provide your credit score and proof of your income, I can get you started on finding your dream home."

"How long have you been fucking him?"

"Miss Jones, excuse me, but what or who are you talking about?"

"You can cut the bullshit, bitch. How long have you been fucking Mari? I can see it written all over your face. You're another one of his side bitches."

She stood up and looked at me, then proceeded to walk around to where I was sitting.

"Your pathetic little broke ass needs to get the fuck up out of my office before I get the police to throw you out. I look at you, and I feel pity for you."

"Bitch, how about *you* put me out? Does your boss know how you're running this company?"

"Boss? Bitch, you think I really *need* to work here? I'm only here 'cause Mari needs to buy properties without going through all the paperwork bullshit. This is *my* company, bitch. To answer your question, we've been fucking around for as long as you two have been together. Now, get the fuck off my property, you silly little girl."

She walked off and opened the door, using her hand to show me the way out. I thought about punching that ho in her face but quickly remembered that assault case that I had pending.

"Count your fucking days, ho."

"By the looks of things, your lavish days are over," she smiled.

I shook my head and walked out of the office. This bitch has no idea how fucking pissed I am. I could literally beat her ass. I walked past the receptionist's desk and shot that bitch a dirty look. Both these bitches could fucking die a horrible fucking death. I was trembling all over as I sat in my car. Tears rolled down my face as the plain reality hit me. I was a fucking fool for this nigga, and I have nothing to show for all this fucking headache.

"Damn you, Mari. What did I ever do to deserve this?" I banged my head on the steering wheel.

Mari

My phone kept ringing, and I kept ignoring it. I tried opening my eyes, but it was difficult for me because of the bright light beaming through the blinds. I lay my head back down on the pillow, and that's when it hit me what day it was. It was the day to lay my brother to rest. *Shit!*

I threw off the covers and jumped out of bed. Then I rushed to the shower and took a quick wash off. In no time, I was dressed and out the door. I glanced at the time as I pulled out of the hotel. Although I wasn't ready for this, I had to be there for my man. I looked in the ashtray and spotted a little piece of a blunt. I took it and lit it. I didn't care if I walked in there smelling like weed. I had a bottle of Patrón in my glove compartment. I took it out and put it to my head, taking a couple of sips. A few seconds later, I was in a better headspace. I cut up Kevin

Gates's "Great Man." Tears rolled down my face as I reminisced on all the great memories Rio and I had. I have no idea how I will move forward without my rollie.

I put on my Cartier shades before I exited the car. Beach police were everywhere. Shit, Rio wasn't no street nigga, so I didn't understand why the fuck they were posted up. I'm glad my gun wasn't visible 'cause the last thing I'd needed was for me to get locked up right now. I spotted a few familiar faces as I made my way through the crowd. I nodded as I walked up the stairs. Neither Rio nor I were ever into church, but mom dukes used to be a member when she was alive, and my aunt still frequents here.

On my way in, a few bitches stopped me to pay their respects, and niggas saluted me also. The church was packed. I squeezed out a smile. My nigga would be proud if he saw how much of the city showed out. I walked up to the casket and stood there staring at my nigga. I felt frozen like I couldn't move. Tears started rolling down my face. I reached into the coffin and rubbed his face. "On my life, my nigga, I'm going to make sure e'ery one of these niggas pay for this shit. I got you, baby."

I felt someone walk up to me. "Come on, baby. Come sit down." It was my aunty Nene. Since our mother passed, she's been like a mother figure to us. I took one last glance at Rio, then walked off to sit by her. My chest was starting to tighten up on me. I sat and hung my head down, trying to calm myself some.

After the service, he was laid to rest in the family lot. I couldn't continue putting on a straight face, so I walked off to the car. It was then that I broke down. Every emotion that I felt came pouring down. I pulled out the bottle of Patrón and put it to my head. I didn't remove it until every drop of liquor was gone. After that, I put my head on the steering wheel. If you have never seen a grown man cry before, this was him. My heart was hurting so fucking bad. It was like someone snatched it out of my chest.

After my brother's funeral, I chilled with the family for a few, then made it back to Richmond. The Beach was where I'm from, but I had unfinished business to handle, and it couldn't wait. I thought long and hard about closing the shop, but we decided to keep it going after talking with Rio's wife. So, I called the guys to let them know they could come back to work. I stopped by earlier to let Rahu know he was now the manager and would be running the shop. I would make sure I'm there on the regular. Rio loved what he did, and letting what he loved die with him would be a shame.

My phone started ringing. I looked at the caller ID and realized it was one of the bitches I was fucking. A little bougie bitch that I had running a business so we can clean up the dope money.

"Yeah."

"Are you back in town?" she quizzed.

"Yeah, what's good?"

"Well, your little bitch stopped by earlier and wanted to know what's going on."

"Really? What you told her?"

"I ain't had to tell her shit. She accused me of fucking you. When I tell you she showed her ass off, I see why you stopped fucking with her. Bitch crazy as hell. I had to tell her that she wasn't getting no house, and that's when she snapped."

"Fuck that bitch. She lucky I don't kill her ass."

"You better chill out talking like that on my phone. I damn sure don't want to be your codefendant."

"Fuck all that. Yo, I'm horny as fuck. Let me get some pussy."

"I'm at work, sir."

"Well, I'll be through the crib later. So make sure you ready to ride this dick."

"I was born ready."

"I hear that. A'ight, I'm out."

I swear her bougie ass was as freaky as they come. I could tell she was catching feelings for a nigga. See, she was the kind of bitch to keep around. She has an MBA in business, so she knows how to work with them numbers. But to be honest, I was still in love with Akila. I can't explain why I do the shit I do to her, but I love her with everything in me. That's why it hurts so much that this bitch would fucking betray me like that. Just the thought of that bitch made my veins tighten up. I was just waiting until after my brother's funeral to set my plan into motion. That bitch will pay, for sure.

I had just pulled off from getting the rental cleaned out. I planned to find me a ride tomorrow. I saw the brand-new Range, so I think I'm going to cop that. I told my man Luther by the car lot that I was coming through tomorrow. I know he would get me right.

Dreema kept blowing up my phone ever since I got back. Damn, this bitch was becoming unbearable ever since she had my son. I swear I regret getting her ass pregnant more and more every day. I pressed *ignore* and kept driving. The ringing ceased, and then it started up again. Damn, this bitch was getting annoying as fuck. I grabbed the phone. I was ready to give her a piece of my fucking mind.

"Yo, what the fuck you want, shawty?" I yelled into the phone as I switched lanes.

"Yo, nigga, one of them done pissed you off?" G laughed in my ear.

"Man, you have no idea. I need a new set of hoes. If you know of any, send them my way."

"I got you, nigga. Where you at, though?"

"On the south; just left the shop. What's good?"

"Come by the crib real quick. I want to discuss something wit' you."

"A'ight, I'm on the way."

Something didn't seem right. The tone of G's voice let me know something was up. I immediately busted a U-turn, heading back to the highway. I racked my brain the entire ride, trying to see what was so urgent and why he couldn't say it over the phone.

I pulled up in the driveway and hopped out of the ride. His front door was open, so I jogged to the door and walked in.

"What's good, fam?"

"Whaddup?"

We exchanged daps, and I walked into the living room while he walked into the kitchen. I took a seat and started checking my phone. Dreema's ass done sent me over ten texts, cussing me out in every last one. I just cut off the phone and stuffed it back into my pocket.

G walked into the room with two glasses in his hand. He handed one of them to me, then took a seat across from me as he pulled out a blunt and lit it.

"Damn, nigga, this must be serious and shit 'cause you got the liquor and the weed on spot."

"You a funny nigga. You know, whenever we get together, we got to smoke and drink. But on the real, I need to holler at you about some shit."

"Spit it out, fam."

"I know you been fucking with the bitch Dreema for a minute, but how well do you know her?"

"What you mean? You remember the night we met her at the club. We been rocking ever since."

"Oh yeah, yeah, you right. Nigga, I got a lead on who might be involved in Rio's death." He handed me the blunt.

I took it, took a few pulls, and then looked at him. The veins in my head started to tighten up. I tried squeezing my teeth together to control my anxiety.

"Nigga, spit it out."

"Word in the street is there's a nigga going around saying Dreema set it up."

"Man, you trippin' right now. That bitch is many things, and she gets on my fucking nerves, but there's no way she had nothing to do with Rio getting killed. I don't believe that shit. You know money is involved, and they know shawty just had my seed, so they probably plotting and shit."

"Nigga, I hear you, but you know I ain't gon' come to you with no bullshit. The nigga that's running his mouth is close to that bitch. He say he got proof and shit. He said he will only talk with you, and you got to have the hundred grand in exchange for what he's going to tell you."

I sat there listening to him while trying to see if any of what he was saying made any kind of sense to me. It didn't, but he was trying his best to convince me.

"Yo, set up the meeting for tonight."

"You sure, yo? This might be a setup."

"I don't give a fuck. You can follow behind me. If it's a setup, then I guess I'm going to be ready. Do you still have those vests?"

"Yup, for sure."

"A'ight. Grab them and grab a hundred G. If it's real, then I'ma throw the money at the nigga. If he bullshittin', he gon' feel these bullets," I said as I took a few sips of the Hennessy White.

After he left the room, I leaned back on the couch. This was definitely *not* what I wanted to hear. This bitch is the mother of my son. I trusted this bitch with a lot of shit. What was puzzling is she'd only been around Rio a handful of times. Why would she want him dead? What would her motive be?

"Here you go, nigga." G walked back into the room and handed me the vest along with a duffle bag. "Yo, I just called that nigga off the burner phone. I told him to meet us by the library in the back toward the park in another hour. By then, all the parkgoers should be gone. We can't risk it by having no witnesses out there just in case some shit pop off."

"Yeah, that's cool." I was feeling all sorts of different emotions right now. I pulled a bag of weed out of my pocket and started rolling a couple of blunts. I needed to get my head in check.

I put on my gloves, made sure my gun had a full clip, and I also threw two extra clips in the glove compartment. I then put the duffle bag with the cash on the seat with me. I gave G a nod before I pulled off. I didn't know what I was going to walk into, but whatever it is, it's worth a try. I couldn't rest until I killed whoever did this to Rio . . . even if it's my baby mama . . .

I pulled into the park and drove to the back. G said the nigga would be in a blue Corolla. I spotted the car to my right as soon as I got there. I pulled in and parked. G pulled up to the left of me. He got out of the car and walked over to the nigga's car. They exchanged words, but I couldn't make out what they were saying. G walked back to his car a few seconds later, and the nigga walked to my car.

I put the window down. This nigga looked like a fiend, so I was hesitant.

"Yo, you Mari?"

"What's good?"

"I told yo' boy I got some info that might be helpful."

"Oh, word? Jump in real quick."

I grabbed the duffel bag, put it in the backseat, and then unlocked the door. He got in. I could tell this nigga was high as fuck 'cause he was twitching around.

"Yo, so what do you know about my brother getting killed?"

"Before I talk, do you have my money?"

"Yeah, if you can give me the person that killed him. Yeah, I got a hundred grand."

This snake nigga's face lit up, and he started rubbing his hands together.

"See, you don't know me, but I know you. We both been fucking the same bitch. Ain't that ironic?" he chuckled.

"Yo, nigga, speak," I demanded.

"Well, Dreema set it up. See, your brother wasn't supposed to be killed. You were supposed to get robbed, but the person mistaked your brother for you. That's how that shit went down."

"Oh, word? How you know Dreema set it up?" I looked at this nigga dead in the eyes.

"I was with the nigga that she asked to do it."

"So, you were there when my brother got killed?" I felt my blood starting to boil.

"I-I-I didn't know the nigga was gon' kill him. Dreema told us you had her count out twenty grand, and you were on your way to the pool hall. She told us exactly where and what time you'd be there. Man, I swear the nigga thought it was you when your brother stepped out. Soon as the first shot went off, I ran away. I ain't want no parts of no murder."

I heard enough. There's no way he would know about no twenty grand if that bitch didn't tell him. I had a feeling he was the shooter, though.

"Yo, why are you telling me this now? What would make me not kill you right now?"

"I mean, I'm a real street nigga, and from what I heard, you a real nigga. The only mistake we made was trusting the wrong bitch. Oh, by the way, man, you need to get a blood test. Little man is *my* son, but she gave him to you 'cause your paper longer."

"What the fuck you just say?"

"That boy ain't yours. That bitch is scamming."

"Yo, how I know you ain't just mad at the bitch right now?"

"Nigga, yeah, that bitch pissed me off something serious, but this is personal. I heard about the reward money, and I need to get back on my feet, so I hit your mans up and let him know I got what you need."

"A'ight, I believe you." I reached in the back, grabbed the duffle bag, and dropped it in his lap.

His face lit up like a Christmas tree at Macy's. "Oh shit, you really came through. I just have one request."

"What's that?"

"Can you please not let her know I told you. I want to be able to see my little man. You know, he looks so much like me when I was a baby."

"I got you. Don't you say a word either."

"You got my word, partner." He dapped me and got out of the car. I watched as he threw the bag on his shoulder and bopped to his car. Before he could open the door, though, G walked up to him and put the gun in the back of his head.

Pop! Pop!

Two shots rang out, he fell onto his car, and the bag dropped. G went to his pocket, snatched his cell phone, and then grabbed the bag. He opened my back door, threw it in my car, and I pulled off. I didn't drive fast and was careful not to bring no attention to myself. I looked in my mirror and saw my nigga behind me. I carefully drove out of the city without incident.

Dreema

It's been almost a week since this nigga Mari has answered his phone for me. I get it he had his brother's funeral and all that, but shit, his brother was dead and gone. He got a fucking son that was alive and kicking who needs him. He ain't call to see if we needed anything or nothing. I'm not going to keep playing with this nigga. If I don't hear from his ass soon, he's going to regret fucking with me.

This was strange. I called Damion's phone, and he wasn't picking up either. Let me find out this nigga was acting up too. Suddenly, my phone started ringing. I got up off the couch and ran to the bedroom.

"Bitch, what's up?" It was my rollie.

"Are you sitting down?"

"Yeah, why, bitch?"

"The police just found Damion dead. Somebody shot him up."

The phone fell out of my hand, and I fell to the ground. "Noooo! God, noooo," I screamed out.

"Dreema, get on the phone. I'm sorry, friend," I heard Yanique yelling into the receiver.

I started shaking hard. The room was spinning. *What the fuck? This can't be,* I thought.

"Why you playing with me like this? I just saw him a few days ago."

"I wish I *was* playing with you, friend. It's all over the news. I drove out there, and police all over the parking lot of the library. Girl, it's a mess out here."

"I can't believe this. How . . . Who would do him like that? He don't be fucking wit' nobody. Oh God, this can't be real," I cried harder.

"The streets already talkin', but who knows. You know he was heavy in the streets before he got locked up. You never know."

"I got to go. I can't take this."

Without waiting, I hung up. Then I just lay on the floor crying and talking to myself. This shit can't be happening right now. I felt guilty for the way I treated him the last time I saw him. Oh my God, he died before I could tell him how sorry I really was for saying all that horrible shit to him. A lump formed in my chest. I couldn't breathe, so I grabbed my chest.

"God, please, take this pain away." I felt like I was dying. *My son,* I thought.

I tried to calm myself. My son just lost his biological father, and his play daddy was MIA. There's no way I could die right now. I needed to get myself together fast. I got off the floor, stumbled to the room, and lay down. My head was pounding, and I felt nauseated.

My phone began ringing. It was Damion's mother calling me. There's no way I could talk to this lady right now. I needed to get my emotions under control before I could take on his family's stress. I threw the phone down and went back to crying. A few minutes later, the baby started crying. His cries weren't loud, but it was enough to make my head hurt more. Finally, I dragged myself out of bed and got him out of his crib.

"Hey, mama's baby." I pulled him close to me and kissed his face. I held him tightly as we walked to the kitchen. I grabbed his formula and was about to make him a bottle when I heard a knock at the door.

I took the bottle out of the microwave and rested it on the counter. Then I walked to the door. I wasn't expecting any visitors, but I got excited as I looked through the peephole. It was Mari. Why the fuck he just popping up, though? Shit, I was in the kitchen, so I might not have heard the knock.

"Guess who's here? Your pappy." I kissed my baby on the cheeks before I opened the door.

"Hey, you," I said happily.

"Whaddup?" He walked past me.

I think that was so rude, but whatever. I was still happy that he came through. I locked the door behind us as he walked off to the bedroom. I grabbed the baby's bottle and followed behind him. He was sitting on the bed smoking a Black when I walked into the room.

"You know you can't smoke up in here. The baby is too young for that."

He didn't respond. Instead, he just blew the smoke out and continued looking out into space. Something wasn't right. I guess he was still mourning the loss of his brother. Either way, he needed to get his shit together. The silence between us was killing me. He was throwing off a fucked-up vibe, and I wasn't feeling it.

"Yo, B, how long have you been dealing with me?"

"Why, you know how long. . . ." I looked at him strangely.

He stood up from the bed and pulled his gun out of his waist. "Bitch, answer my fucking question."

I tried to inch out the door, but he slammed the door shut behind us. "Mari, I don't know what the fuck you think you're doing, but you need to put this shit away," I yelled.

"Bitch, shut the fuck up. I know I done did some shit to you, but was it so deep where you took the only person that ever loved me from me? To have my brother killed?"

I almost jumped out of my skin when those words left his mouth. I tried not to show any kind of expression, but I was nervous as fuck. Wait, I need to say something to convince this nigga that he didn't know what he was talking about.

"Oh my God, Mari, you think I had something to do with your brother getting killed? That's my baby's uncle. What kind of wicked bitch do you think I am? I'm hurt that you would believe some shit like that." I started bawling hard.

"Shut the fuck up, bitch. You know, I should've seen the fucking snake you really are, but I was too blinded, and that cost my brother his life."

"Mari, I don't know where you're gettin' your information from, but that shit is a lie. I swear to you, baby, I would never do that to you. I know how much you love your brother. They're lying on me, I swear, Mari."

I know my pleas were falling on deaf ears 'cause that nigga just stood there looking at me with no kind of emotion in his eyes.

"Yo, by the way, who son is this?"

"Don't do that. I know you mad at me, but don't fucking deny my son. He looks just like you, Mari. Oh my God, this is crazy. *So now* you're questioning who my baby's father is?"

He pulled something out of his pocket and placed it on the bed in front of me. It was a recording, and I immediately recognized the voice on the other end. It was Damion's voice. Tears spilled from my eyes as I heard this nigga loud and clear telling lies on me to Mari. This was betrayal in the worst form. I couldn't believe this.

"You're going to take the word of a dope fiend over me? This nigga angry that I left him to be with you. He's a fucking liar, Mari. I hope you didn't fall for this shit. Baby, I swear he's just trying to hurt me the way I hurt him."

He raised the gun, looked in my face, and fired. . . .

I felt a sting as I fell to the ground, still clutching my son—our son—in my arms. I heard two more shots. I looked down and saw my son was hit. Blood was gushing out of my baby's chest.

"Please, my baby needs help. Please, help us," I pleaded.

"Bitch, fuck you and that baby." He stood over me and fired multiple shots.

Akila

I had to figure out something fast. Even though Tyrone offered for me to stay with him, I still needed to get my own place. Mari's bitch ass fucked me out of getting the house. I still can't believe that shit, but I was learning, with him, anything wasn't surprising anymore. The nigga was as grimy and wicked as they come.

I still was wondering what the fuck happened at my house. Shit was strange. I'd been calling Tesha's phone daily since I came home but got no response. I planned on stopping by her mother's crib to see if she knew where her daughter was. That bitch has never disappeared before, so it's strange that she did, and the timing was off. I think Mari is involved in all of this if you ask me. But fuck it, I got bigger problems to worry about now.

Tyrone was definitely spoiling a bitch. Since I've been here, he'd been cooking and catering to my every need. I swear he was trying very hard to win me over. My feelings for him were growing, but maybe not as fast as he wanted them to move. He had to understand that I was just getting out of a serious relationship, and even though we were broken up, I wasn't entirely over Mari, and it was hard to get over a man I was deeply in love with.

We were sitting at the table eating. Tonight, dinner was bacon- and cheese-stuffed potatoes. It was delicious and had me licking my fingers. This nigga can definitely throw down in the kitchen. We just finished eating, and I was drinking a glass of Pink Moscato while he was drinking a beer.

He looked at me, smiled, and then reached across the table and took my hand. "Akila, I need to talk to you about something."

"What's up, boo?" I quizzed.

"This is hard for me to say to you, but I haven't been completely honest with you."

I pulled my hand out of his grip and looked at him. *Oh shit, here this nigga go. What the fuck. Is he married?*

"What are you talking about, Tyrone?" I looked at him with a grit on my face.

"I know you think I'm just another college student like you, but I'm not . . ."

This shit was freaking me the fuck out. If he wasn't a student, why the fuck was he at my school, and why the fuck was he telling me this?

"So, who the fuck are you?"

"I'm an undercover federal agent."

"What the fuck you just say. A federal agent? What the fuck you want from me?" I jumped up from the table.

It took me a few seconds to understand what this nigga was saying to me. Here I was catching feelings for this nigga, and he fucking catfished my ass. This was some crazy shit. I looked at him and dashed out of the dining room. I needed to get the fuck up out of here. This is some shit. None of these niggas are fucking real. I felt betrayed yet again by another lying-ass nigga.

He ran up behind me and grabbed me. "Listen to me. I didn't want to do this, but I had to."

"What do you mean? Do what? So, all this is fake, how you're in love with me? Nigga, you fucked me, and now I find out this was an assignment. By the way, what would you want with me? I don't break the law." I looked at him. I was fucking disgusted.

"It's not fake. After being around you for a while, I started falling for you. This part is real. The Feds and Richmond Task Force have had your boyfriend and his crew under investigation for about a year. The case wasn't moving along fast enough 'cause he was careful, and we couldn't get anyone in his clique to talk—"

"So, y'all decide to come up with a plan. You would get close to me, and I would lead you to Mari?" The tears rolled down my face.

"Akila, he is a drug dealer and a murderer. No one is safe. You see how he came up in here the other night. He's dangerous. If you help us, we can protect you."

"Hmmm, let me get this straight. You think 'cause I let you fuck me and feed me, now I'm going to turn into a fucking rat? Lemme tell you something. He might be all that shit you just said, but he made sure I was straight all the time."

"He also beat up on you and cheated on you with multiple women. Is *that* who you want to protect?"

Slap! Slap!

"How dare you judge me? You don't know what the fuck it's like to grow up in the projects with nothing—or how many nights I went to bed without food. He saved me. Yes, we didn't work out, but I would never turn against him for you or the fucking Feds. So, you can stop pretending that you ever loved me. I was just another assignment. I'm grabbing my stuff and leaving this house."

I walked off into the bedroom, grabbed my things, and threw them in the large duffle bag. I can't believe this fuckery. How dare he do me like this? I thought he cared about me.

"Akila, we can get you into the witness protection program and give you money to start over. Then he won't be able to hurt you ever again."

"Tyrone or whatever your fucking name is, I don't give a fuck about what you're talking about. I don't know shit about Mari or what he does, and if I did know, I wouldn't tell you shit. As far as I'm concerned, you're a piece of shit yourself. I can't believe that I let you fuck me. The shit wasn't that fucking good anyways—nothing to remember. You will be nothing but a faint memory when I leave up out of here. So, Mr. FBI, unless you're going to arrest me, get the fuck out of my way." I squeezed past him and headed out the door.

"Akila, please, rethink this. Please. I can take care of you."

I didn't hear nothing he was saying. I opened the front door and pulled the hoodie over my head and the bag over my shoulder. I got to my truck and climbed in. Then I threw the bag on the backseat and pulled off.

I stopped at a gas station and filled up my tank. While waiting on the gas to finish, I checked my account.

"Your available balance is $32,000." I disconnected the phone.

After filling the tank, I got back into my truck and pulled off. *95 N isn't a bad idea,* I thought as I exited. . . .

Chapter Eleven

Akila

With my tank full, I jumped on 95 N, and it hit me that I was driving with no set place in mind. I haven't been out of Virginia except when I went to DC with my school or the few times I went with Mari to New York. I know I have a great-aunt, Eileen, that lives in Baltimore. She used to visit my grandma, but I never really cared for the bitch. She was one of those kinds that think she was better than us 'cause she's from up north, talking all proper and shit. I used to walk past that bitch like I didn't even see her. I remember her telling my grandma that she needed to watch me 'cause my ass was fast. She has a daughter named Claire. She was cool. She used to visit my grandma during the holidays.

The last time I saw that side of the family was during my grandmother's funeral. Claire's about two years older than I, and even though we didn't keep in touch much over the years, we were Facebook friends and would occasionally like each other's statuses or pictures. I hate that I need to reach out, but she was the only person I could think of off the top of my head. It wasn't like I had all this family I could call on. I didn't plan on intruding on her life. Just need a place to crash for a few days until I gather my thoughts and figure out my next move.

Suddenly, I heard the sounds of a police siren behind me. Curiously, I looked in my rearview mirror and
slowed down so they could get by since they seemed to be
in a rush. I put my eyes back on the road before me, getting ready to pull off. Then I spotted a dark-colored SUV
with tinted windows rush past me and swiftly cut me off.

"Yo, what the fuck you doing? You fucking idiot," I
yelled as I pressed down on the brake. My purse on
the front seat flew onto the floor. The SUV stopped
directly in front of me, and two dudes and a female in
suits jumped out and dashed to my truck. *What the
fuck is going on, and who are these people?* My mind
started racing hard. I hurriedly put the car in reverse and
glanced behind me, but I couldn't move. I was blocked in
from the back.

"God, please don't let me die," I started praying.

"Put the car in park and get out," the bitch ran up to my
window and yelled. She had a gun pointed at me.

"Who the fuck are you, and what do you want?" I yelled
frantically.

"U.S. Marshals! Cut the vehicle off and get out," she
yelled at the top of her lungs.

Everything around me was moving so fast. My hands
trembled as I put the car into park and then pressed the
button, cutting it off. What the fuck was really going on?
What the fuck did they want with me? I need some kind
of answers. . . .

"Get out of the vehicle slowly with your hands raised."

I unlocked my truck and slowly got out with my hands
in the air. The bitch grabbed me and threw me up on the
side of my SUV.

"U.S. Marshals. Turn around. You're under arrest for
possession of crack cocaine, possession of a firearm
during the commission of a felon, and possession with
the intent to distribute crack cocaine."

"I ain't distribute shit. Y'all really fucking tripping," I screamed.

"Don't move," one of the dudes yelled in my ear.

"We have the suspect, Akila Jones, in custody," the bitch spoke into her microphone.

I wanted to cry and fight, but I knew this would not help my situation. This was some fucked-up shit. Is this how the Feds played since I didn't help them nail Mari? Tyrone flashed in my mind. I wonder where his bitch ass was. I know he's a part of these bootleg-ass charges.

After they placed the cuffs on me, the one officer led me to the SUV that cut me off. That's when I realized people were stopping in their cars, gawking at me. They must've seen all this commotion 'cause their ass was hanging out of their windows. I saw a few pointing in my direction and whispering. I felt so violated, but I was too angry to show that I felt embarrassed.

I looked around, and that's when I spotted Tyrone's bitch ass in the far distance, looking on as the bitch led me into the police car. I shook my head in disbelief. This bitch-ass nigga done went too far now. *How could I be so naïve?* I sat there feeling like this was all a dream. Like this was happening to someone else. Tears started rolling down my face. I can't believe my ass just got arrested behind some dumb shit that I have nothing to do with. I watched as they spoke amongst themselves, even laughing at times. They were enjoying themselves while I was hurting. These bastards were as cold as they come. I see why niggas be screaming, "fuck the police." About ten minutes later, they drove off.

Instead of them taking me directly to see the magistrate where I could see the judge, their ass took me to the federal courthouse on Broad Street. I was led into a room with a massive mahogany table.

"Miss Jones, sit down. We want to speak to you," the white officer said.

I didn't say anything. I just sat there with my head resting on the table. I was trying to hold it together, but I was scared out of my fucking mind, and it was visible 'cause I couldn't control my body from shaking uncontrollably.

"Do you need a soda or anything to eat?" he asked.

"Nah, I'm good." This nigga was pissing me off. Do I look thirsty or hungry to him?

A few minutes later, the bitch-ass nigga Tyrone made his grand appearance. I looked at him as he walked in wearing street clothes with his badge hanging from his neck. I jumped up from the chair and lunged toward him, but one of the other fed niggas jumped in between us.

"So, you finally show your face, you fucking coward. *This* is what you do since I refuse to help you? Make up some bogus-ass charge against me? You know damn well I ain't had shit to do with no fucking drugs or fucking guns. You is a bitch-ass nigga, you hear me?" I screamed.

"Sit yo' ass down now. You're in a lot of trouble. However, if you cooperate with us, I can get all those charges to disappear and get you far away from here."

"Cooperate with you? What the fuck you mean, like become a rat? I told yo' ass I ain't no fucking rat, and I don't know shit," I said, pounding my fist on the table.

"From what I gathered, you've been with Mr. Owens for over two years. You haven't had a job for those years. The degree you're trying to get is funded by drug money. The house that you were living in was bought with drug money. But the most serious charge is the conspiracy to commit murder. These are some serious charges that can land you in the Feds for life. Trust me; you don't want that."

"Murder? So, you just making up shit as you go along. I ain't kill no-fucking-body or know nothing about killing nobody. I don't know shit about no drug dealing, so either fucking charge me or let me fucking go," I shouted at the top of my lungs.

"You're not thinking rationally. You're ridin' for a man that don't give a fuck about you. He made a baby on you, put his hands on you multiple times, and has something to do with the disappearance of your best friend. I'm going to take him down one way or the other. The question is, are you going to ride with him and throw your life away too?"

"You know you're sickening. How did I even allow my pussy to get wet for you? Mari might be a piece of shit, but he has more balls than you. You a fucking liar and manipulator just like him. You looked me in the eyes and pretended like you were the cure to all my fucking problems—only to turn around and betray me. Do what the fuck you please 'cause I'm done talking to your bitch ass."

He looked at me with a wicked grin plastered across his face. "Lock her ass up and charge her." He then walked out the door.

My head was pounding, and I felt nauseated. When will this end? What did I ever do to deserve this shit? God, I need you more than ever 'cause this is definitely fuckery, and I need a way out.

Mari

I took one last glance at the bitch and her son on the floor. Her eyes were wide open, like she was still looking at me. I reached on the dresser, grabbed her cell phone, cut it off, and put it in my pocket. Then I cautiously opened the door, peeped out, making sure no one was around, and calmly walked to my car. I popped the trunk, grabbed the gasoline jug, and walked back to the crib. I entered the room I had been in and started sprinkling gasoline all over. I made sure I poured most of it all over their bodies. I want them to fucking burn in hell. I stood over Dreema and finished the jug. Then I took out my lighter, lit the flame, and stood there while the fire got higher and higher. The raw smell of burning flesh hit my nose. I didn't let that bother me, though. I needed to see this through. This one was *very* personal.

Finally, I started coughing, and my eyes began burning as the room filled with smoke, but the sight of that bitch burning was far more rewarding. I stood there until the flames started traveling toward the doorway. This was my cue to get the fuck out of there. I know by the time the firefighters get here, that bitch and her bastard will be burned to ashes.

By the time I got into my car and pulled off, the building was engulfed in flames. I took one last look in my rearview mirror and drove away. That bitch got everything that she deserved. Now, my brother could finally rest in peace knowing I dealt with that ho in the cruelest manner possible. I lit me a Black & Mild as I headed down the street.

Shit was spiraling downhill. It seems like I was losing my mind ever since I lost my brother. I tried staying calm, but my mind was all over the place. The most fucked-up thing was finding out Dreema's baby wasn't mine. That bitch had the fucking nerve to have me thinking that he was mine. I know it was cold, but that bitch and the bastard had to go. She took my nigga from me, so fuck her. I wish I could've killed her a thousand times.

After everything that happened the last few days, I decided to lie low. I've done too much dirt these last few weeks, and I was praying none of this shit would come back on me. The last thing I needed was to get locked up. I just can't see myself up in no jail when I got money out here to make.

"Yo, nigga, you good?" G asked as he walked into the living room and took a seat across from me.

"Yeah, I'm straight. What's good witcha?"

"Shit, got to check on them niggas over on the East and then hit up the barbershop. A nigga been roughing it for a few days. Start looking like a homeless nigga out here."

"I hear you. I'm just gon' take it easy. Tryin'a stay low. Too much shit going on at one time."

"Yo, I can't believe you killed the baby, though, nigga. I tell you, that's some cold shit. I'll put a slug in a nigga and a bitch, but shit, I think that's where I draw the line." He puffed some of the blunt he was holding.

"Fuck that baby. That little motherfucker wasn't my blood. Shit, I did him a favor. His parent was dead, so who was gon' take care of him? Man, that bitch got everything she deserved."

"I agree. Still can't believe that bitch set up Rio to get killed. That's some grimy shit. I really thought that bitch was one hunnit. That's why you can't wife these hoes. All you can do is fuck them and leave them. Oh shit, have you heard from Akila?"

"Nah, I ain't hear from that bitch since the day I caught her at that nigga's house. I'm still shocked that bitch had the nerve to pull a motherfucking gun on me. I swear that bitch go next. She's going to pay for what the fuck she did to me. I just need to let shit die down a little before I get at her and that pussy nigga."

"Yo, you sure that's a good move? One bitch that you fucked with already got killed. If something happen to Akila, it might bring heat on you, dawg. I mean, I can't tell you what to do, and I'ma ride with you, but just think this one out."

"I hear you, but that bitch violated me, her, and that pussy nigga. I can't just let it slide."

"Yo, do you even know who the nigga is? How the fuck he just pop up out of the blue?"

"Yo, dawg, I don't give a fuck who that chump is. He fucked the wrong bitch, and that will cost him his life. So of all the pussy out there, he just happened to fall into my bitch?" I shook my head in disgust of memories of the night I caught Akila at that nigga's house.

Anger filled my lungs as I thought about Akila. How could she betray me like this? I took that bitch out of the slum, fed her, and made sure she never wanted for anything. And this bitch disrespected me by fucking a bitch-ass nigga. I'm a boss in this city. I won't become a laughingstock behind no bitch. She'll learn not to bite the hand that feeds her.

"Yo, I'm about to bounce. Hit me if you need me."

"A'ight, yo."

After G left, I got up and walked to the kitchen. I needed a drink to calm down. Knowing that bitch was with that nigga made my blood boil again. I took two gulps of the liquor, but it still couldn't calm me. Finally, I made my way to the room I was staying in at G's crib. I pulled out a bag of blow that I had in the drawer, rolled a dollar bill, and started sniffing the powder. This was a little pleasure of mine that I was careful not to let anyone know about. I sniffed a few lines and instantly started feeling better. My mood shifted from angry to happy. I was floating on cloud nine, and no one could fuck with me right now.

I was lying on my back thinking when the phone started to ring. I grabbed it and looked at the caller ID, hoping it was Akila. But instead, it was Miss Matthews, the chick I had running the real estate business. I barely called her Shonda 'cause whenever we were around people, we tried to pretend to be on a professional level.

"What's good, love?"

"You tell me? I've been calling you for days and no response."

"Last time I saw you, I told you I had a few runs to make. I don't have my phone on when I'm handling business. But whaddup, though?"

"I'm cooking tonight and wanted to see if you want to stop by for dinner and some late-night dessert," she said seductively.

"Oh, word? You know a nigga not gon' pass up no dessert," I laughed.

"Well, how about dinner at eight, sir?"

"A'ight, I'll be there, love."

"Okay, babes, see you later."

After I hung up, I tried to call Akila's phone again, but it kept going to voicemail, and I couldn't leave a message 'cause the mailbox was full. I swear she was playing with me, and I wasn't in the mood to be fucked with. Her behavior instantly blew my high. I got up and started sniffing the rest of the coke I had left on the dollar bill.

It's been days since I been out of the crib, and it felt good when the fresh air hit my face. I was slowly coming down off the coke and feeling a little paranoid. I looked around before I got into the rental. I sat in the car a few minutes before I pulled off and lit a Black & Mild to help calm my nerves. As I drove out of the neighborhood, I kept looking in my rearview mirror to see if anyone was following me. Everything seemed cool, so I made my way to shawty's house. I was looking forward to a night of fucking and taking my mind off things, even if it's just for the night.

I pulled up to her crib and walked to the door where she was waiting for me. We hugged and started kissing.

I noticed she only had a towel wrapped around her. It seemed she just got out of the shower. I walked in, and she locked the door behind us.

"I didn't expect you to be this early. I just finished taking a shower."

"Well, I guess I'm on time then."

She took my hand and led me upstairs to her bedroom. She dropped the towel, and I noticed shawty was butt-ass naked. She got on the bed with her legs spread apart while she played in her pussy.

"Man, this how you doing, huh?" I said to her while licking my lips. Her pussy was looking extra enticing. I wasted no time. I unbuttoned my pants, and within seconds, I was naked with my dick hanging. I dove onto the bed, parted her pussy lips, dug my head straight in, and started licking her sweet wall.

"Awwww, daddy. Oh yes," she moaned while I sucked on her clit. Her groans set my soul on fire. I dug my head deeper in and made sweet love to her pussy. She grabbed my hair and pushed my head deeper between her legs, almost suffocating me. But I didn't ease up none. I continued pleasing her in a very special way. Minutes later, her legs started trembling. She began to groan harder, and I sucked harder. Finally, she exploded in my mouth. I held her legs firmly as I licked up every drop of her juice.

After cleaning her off with my tongue, I placed her legs on my shoulders and inserted every inch of my manhood into her. "Aargh, damn, bae, this pussy good," I whispered to her.

"Your dick is good too, boo." She started moving her hips in circular movements. I gripped her hips tightly as she balanced her legs on my shoulders. Then I slid in and out of her slippery pussy, making sure I hit her walls the right way.

"Fuck me, Mari. Daddy, this yo' pussy. Fuck me, pleeee-ase," she screamed out while I pounded down her walls.

"You sure this my pussy, bae?" I said as I slid in and out.

"Yes, it is. I love you, Mari. I swear I'll never fuck another nigga."

I don't know what it was. Maybe it was what she just said, but I sped up my thrusts, veins in my dick got larger, and I dug deeper inside her pussy. She started screaming, but I blocked out her screaming. I was about to bust. I tried holding it in, but I couldn't hold it anymore.

"Aargh, aargh," I groaned as I exploded in her.

Shonda

I wasn't raised to be ratchet or out in the streets, acting like one of these loudmouthed bitches. My mother taught me always to remain graceful. Play my position, and the right man will come along. This wasn't no different when I met the handsome and sexy Mari.

He was a nigga with money, and I was that educated, sophisticated chick. So together, we decided to start a phony real estate business. The company was really a front to clean up his drug money and keep the Feds or whoever was sniffing around out of his business. So far, so good. He was stacking his money. I even encouraged him to open an account in the Cayman Islands. The boy was definitely paid out the ass.

See, I know he had a bitch at the house, but I wasn't worried about that ho. Didn't trip when he came to me and asked me to find her a home either. I gladly helped the bitch. What's crazy was, at first, this bitch had no idea I was fucking her man. Shit, she had bigger problems to worry about. Like Mari getting that other ho pregnant. I have to admit, this nigga was slanging dick all over

Richmond. I made sure that I got a cut out of every dollar he made and was stacking my bread right along with him. Mama didn't raise no fool. He might be slanging good dick around, but for me having to deal with his other hoes, I got to get paid out the ass.

I was in the office working today. When I wasn't doing business for Mari, I would sell houses to others. Business was definitely booming for me, and money was flowing good. I just got off the phone with a potential homebuyer when my assistant rang the phone.

"Yes, love?"

"There's a gentleman here to see you."

"What's his name, and does he have an appointment?"

"He said its official police business."

"Police?" I almost choked on my saliva.

"Yes, ma'am. Do you want me to send him back?"

"Yes, that's fine."

I was sweating bullets at the mention of police. I didn't break no law, so what the hell would the police need with me? I straightened up and prepared for whatever was about to go down. Hopefully, it was nothing major and could be quickly settled.

The door opened, and a gentleman walked in. "Miss Matthews, here he is."

I stood up and came face-to-face with a tall, dark-skinned brother. He wasn't wearing an official police uniform, so I assumed he was undercover.

"Hello, Miss Matthews. I'm Agent Jordan."

"Agent . . .?" I quizzed. I was trying not to show my uneasiness.

"Yes, ma'am, a federal agent with the FBI."

I became nervous as hell when he mentioned the FBI, but I coached myself to remain calm.

"Please, take a seat. I don't understand. Are you searching for a new home, Agent?" I asked before I sat.

"No, ma'am, but thank you. I'm here to talk to you about your business and what dealings you have with Mari Owens."

"What about my business? And that name doesn't sound familiar. Am I supposed to know him? I mean, I have thousands of clients . . . His name don't ring a bell." I pretended like I was searching my memories.

"That's strange because public records show he has bought a few properties, and you were his agent. But wait, is there another agent in this office?"

"No, it's just me, but again, I'm lost. What does my company have to do with this man you're talking about? Is he under some sort of criminal investigation?"

"No, but if you're using your company to help criminal activities in any way, I will personally come after you," he said in a threatening manner.

"Is that a threat, Agent? You know what? I think this meeting is over. Here is my lawyer's number if you have any more questions." I opened my drawer, took a card out, and put it on the table in front of him.

He got up, straightened his shirt, and looked at me. "Miss Matthews, be mindful of the company you keep. This is not going to go away, and I guarantee you, if you have dirty hands in any of this, you will also be going down. Now, have a blessed day." He got up and walked out the door.

I felt like I was about to piss on myself. I tried to calm myself. . . .

I waited a few seconds before I got up and locked the door. I was shaking out of control. I leaned on the back of the door. . . .

Knock, knock.

I almost jumped out of my skin when someone knocked on the door. "Shonda, it's me," my assistant said.

I unlocked the door and moved away from it. "Come in." I walked back to my desk, trying hard to hide my emotions. Then slowly, I took a seat at my desk.

"What's that all about? Why the Feds want to see you?"

"Your guess is just as good as mine. He was asking questions about Mari. I tried to find out what was going on, but he got disrespectful and shit, so I told him to contact my lawyer if he had any more questions."

"Shonda, I told you from the beginning that Mari was bad news. I know he put money in our pockets, but he out there doing too much dirt. Now, you got the Feds knocking on your door. Baby girl, we need to get out before shit gets bad. I watch the news. You can get charged with money laundering, racketeering, and some more shit—"

"Whose fucking side are you on anyway? Don't forget who the fuck picked you up when you were strung out on drugs when you were living in that crack house over on Fairfield. Bitch, don't think I won't get rid of yo' ass ASAP. This is *my* shit, and I decide when we quit—not you." I cut that bitch off before she could finish her sentence.

"Damn, this how you been feeling, huh? I mean, I know I used to smoke crack and was homeless as well. Yes, you picked me up, but you didn't hand me shit. I work tirelessly, sometimes twelve hours a day, helping you. I don't complain whenever you call on me, so get off your fucking high horse. I'm only looking out for you. I don't know about you, but I don't look good in no khakis. Mari don't want you. He's just using you to clean up his money."

"Get the fuck out of my office. Matter of fact, get your shit and go. Old crackhead-ass bitch," I screamed at the top of my lungs.

"I hope it's worth it. Ain't no dick that good for you to lose your freedom behind. But whatever, Miss High and Mighty. I'm gone." She walked out and slammed the door behind her.

I let out a long sigh of relief. This old, ungrateful-ass bitch pissed me off. The only reason why I dragged that bitch out of the gutta was that she used to do real estate back in the day and was good at what she does. Not only did I pick her ass up, but she's also living in a three-bedroom house that I helped buy and is driving a nice-ass car. Now, she has the nerve to speak on Mari. Fuck that bitch. She can go back to sucking on that crack pipe.

My head was pounding. I raised my hand and started massaging my temple. Oh wait, I need to call Mari. I picked up the phone and called his number. The phone rang, but he didn't answer. I called back three more times but still got no response. Finally, I hung up the phone, then turned off my computer. I grabbed my purse, cut off the light, and made my way out.

I stopped dead in my tracks when I reached my front office. Papers were all over the floor, and my brand-new desktop computer lay shattered on the ground. That bitch thrashed my shit. I took a look, shook my head, and kept walking. Today was definitely fuck with Shonda day. I wasn't going to let these motherfuckers get to me, though. I turned on the alarm, locked the office, and left. Cautiously, I looked around to make sure no one was watching me. Then I got into my Jaguar and pulled off.

Chapter Twelve

Akila

I couldn't stop the tears from falling down my face. Just weeks ago, I was sitting in a jail cell similar to this one I was now in. I was told that I was waiting to get transferred to Northern Neck Regional Jail, a holding facility for the Feds. I had no one to call or turn to. As I sat in the cold, I started thinking about my grandmother. I wish she were here because I would not be alone like this.

So much was on my mind. Like, why did that bitch-ass nigga talk about conspiracy? Truth is, I didn't know shit about what Mari did. He didn't bring me around his work, and he didn't bring it home. The most I've ever seen was when he was counting money. This is not fair. I don't deserve none of this shit. I cried as I buried my head into my lap.

"Jones, Inmate Jones," the guard yelled my name.

I felt scared. I slowly got up off the bench.

"You're free to go."

"Just like that? Do I have a bond?" I looked at him, utterly confused.

"No, you don't have a bond. You can go."

I looked at him for some kind of explanation. He was serious. He opened the double doors and let me out. I was scared to move. This seemed unreal to me. One second, I was interrogated by the Feds, and the next minute, I was walking up out of here a free woman. I was given my property. I dressed so fast 'cause I wasn't sure if this was all a mistake, and I needed to get the fuck up out of here before someone realized it was a mistake. I grabbed my phone and started walking out.

It was dark outside. Looking at my phone to see what time it was, I noticed it was 11:45 p.m. I stepped outside, trying to figure out what I would do. *Where is my damn truck?* I thought. I hope these bitches didn't put my shit in the pound.

"Akila, we need to talk." Tyrone appeared from the side of the building. I jumped at the sound of his voice.

"Get away from me. You don't think you've done enough already?" I tried to walk away.

"I'm sorry, baby. I had to bring you in. My superiors were on me. I had to bring you in for questioning. I'm so sorry. See, you're free to go now."

"Sorry? You lied. You know I ain't had shit to do with Mari and what the fuck he does. You fucking played me, Tyrone. I trusted you." My voice cracked as I fought back the tears from flowing.

"I swear to you, baby, I'm sorry. You started off as a case, but I started to get feelings for you the more I was around you. I tried to get you out of it, but they weren't tryin'a hear me—"

"So, you sacrifice me to save your fucking job? I fell hard for you 'cause you fucking came around with your sweet lies, telling me shit you knew I needed to hear. All along, you were only 'doing your job.'"

"You're wrong, Akila. I love you."

"Get the fuck away from me. I never want to fucking see you again, you hear me? Never. You just like all these other lying-ass niggas. Only difference is you hide behind that fucking badge."

"Akila, fuck this badge. I love you, shawty. I will do whatever it takes to show you. I love you. You need to let me protect you. It's not safe for you out there."

"Protect me? You've done enough. What the fuck y'all did with my truck?"

"Your keys are right here. Your vehicle is parked in the back."

"Hmm, so what was this, a ploy to scare me? To make me turn on Mari? I done told yo' ass, I ain't no rat. Ain't no bitch in my blood, and I don't know shit. Can you go get my shit so I can get the fuck out of here?"

"Where were you going when we pulled you over? You do know you can't leave the state, right?"

"What? This some fucking joke? So, I'm *not* under arrest, but I can't leave the state? I swear to God, I fucking hate your bitch ass."

"Akila, I'm not your enemy. Believe it or not, I'm in your corner."

"Boy, fuck what you talking about. Now get me my shit," I screamed, not giving a fuck if anyone heard me.

He looked at me, shook his head, and walked off. It was cold as hell outside, and I was trembling, so I stepped back into the building. When I saw my truck coming toward me, I went outside. He pulled up, got out, and handed me my keys. I snatched them and started to get in my truck. He held on to the door.

"Akila, please be careful out here. The Feds—scratch that, *I* can protect you."

"Get off my fucking door," I yelled as loud as I could, spit flying all over the place.

I yanked the door. He stepped back, and I slammed the door shut. Then I hurriedly pressed the button, put the car into drive, and pulled off. I felt a little better once I got out of the parking lot.

I was tired, cold, and hungry. I couldn't drive any-where right now, so I decided to get a room at the Holiday Inn on Broad Street. I got out of the truck and went into the hotel. I know Mari was still angry with me, and I wasn't sure he wouldn't hurt me. Also, I'm sure the Feds were still trying to bother me. I didn't trust nothing that came out of Tyrone's mouth. That nigga was a good-ass liar.

I made sure the door was locked. I even went as far as putting the chain on the door. After getting raped in a hotel before, I still get that eerie feeling. I tried to brush off that feeling. I was feeling weak and dehydrated, so I got a cup of water out of the sink. The water gave me a little bit of life but also made me aware of how hungry I was. It was definitely too late to worry about food, so I took off my clothes and flopped down on the bed.

Seconds later, I buried my head in the pillow and started crying. I was broken into a million pieces, and I have no idea how to pull myself out of this hole that I have dug myself into.

"God, please, I need you more than ever. I really need you," I cried out from the deep pit of my soul.

The ringing of my phone woke me up out of my sleep. I opened my eyes. Damn, I must've slept a long-ass time. I reached for my phone and looked at the time. It was a little after 10:00 a.m. Shit, checkout time is 11:00 a.m. I need to get my ass up to figure out what the hell I'm going to do. I looked at the phone and saw I had several missed calls. Some from Mari and the rest from Tyrone. These niggas really need to leave me the fuck alone.

I logged on to Facebook to look for my cousin so I could message her. I sent her a text that I needed her number. I then decided to shower. My clothes were still in the truck, so I ran out to grab one of the bags. This hotel was expensive as hell, so I wasn't sure if I wanted to pay for another night. The hotel I was at before was reasonable, but I couldn't risk going back there in fear that Mari might be watching it.

The feel of the hot water on my skin felt so good. As the dirt washed off my body, so did the tears falling from my face. I was so overwhelmed and lost that I let just it all out. After getting out of the shower, I dried off, stood before the mirror looking at myself, and noticed dark circles around my eyes. My face seemed like I'd added a good fifteen years on my age. This was definitely a sign of stress. I got dressed and sat on the bed, trying to figure out my next move. I cut on the TV just to see what was going on with the news.

"Twenty-six-year-old Dreema Walker and her newborn son were found burned to death at the victim's house. The police want anyone with information to contact them right away. . . ."

I didn't hear nothing else the bitch said because I was stuck looking at the face plastered across the screen. It was the same bitch that Mari was fucking with. The bitch that had his baby. *What the fuck is going on?* I thought. I kept staring at their pics on the television. I hated that bitch, but who the fuck would kill her *and* the baby? That was some wicked shit. They could've left the baby and killed that ho. Finally, I couldn't watch it anymore.

I quickly cut off the television. I couldn't help but think about Mari. First, his brother was killed. He said niggas tried to rob him at the house, and now his baby mama and his child were killed. *What if someone is after everyone in his life? Am I next?* My mind was racing at warp speed. *Oh shit, should I call him?* I was confused about what I needed to do. I didn't know how he'd act toward me if I called him, so I decided to stay out of his business. I kind of felt bad for him, though. He was losing a lot.

I decide to stay at the Holiday Inn for another night. I was kind of scared to go out just in case some serious shit was going on. I also thought about calling Tyrone, but I quickly decided against that. I didn't want to let him think I needed him in any way.

I heard a message come in on my phone, so I checked and saw it was my cousin, Claire. She sent me her number, and I quickly dialed it.

"Hey, girl, how you been?" she quizzed.

"Not good at all."

"Why? What's going on with you? Last time we spoke, everything was going good with you. You was with that dude with money and had moved into a house."

"Yes, well, a lot has happened since that time. You know I don't want to burden you down with my problems. How's your family doing?"

"Girl, nonsense. *We're* family, and if you're going through some shit, I need to know."

That was all I needed to hear 'cause the floodgates opened up as I broke down and started telling her all the terrible things that I'd been through the last couple of days. I didn't know it would feel so good to have someone listen to me without being judgmental. It got to a point where I could barely speak because I was crying so damn hard.

"Listen, baby girl, I'm sorry that you had to go through this by yourself. I wish I had known. I would've been there. So, what are you going to do?"

It took me a few minutes to get myself under control so I could speak. That was a good question. What the hell *was* I going to do? I had planned on leaving, but 'cause the fucking Feds talking about I need to stay in town, and I did have that open case against me, I couldn't leave.

"I wish I knew. I lost the house, so I'm homeless right now."

"So, cuz, you ain't got no money in the bank? I know you done stacked some coins."

"It ain't no amount to brag about. I got like thirty-two grand."

"Bitch, thirty-two grand—that's *good* money," she said gleefully.

"That ain't no money to a bitch that ain't got no job. I need to figure out something fast. I'm supposed to graduate in a few weeks, so hopefully, I'll find a job. I need a place to live 'cause this hotel shit in the way and expensive as shit."

"Boo, listen to me . . . You know I love you, and I'll do whatever it takes to be there for you. I was thinking about moving anyways, so how about I come there with you? That way, you're not by yourself, and we can figure out the madness together."

"Girl, no. I wouldn't dare ask you to do that. I just have to pull up my big-girl panties and figure this shit out."

"Nonsense. I'll be there by tomorrow evening. I stay with my mama, so it ain't like I got to give anyone no notice. And I work off my computer as a medical billing specialist, so my work comes with me. You've always been my favorite cousin, and Grandma wouldn't want it any different, so get ready to cohabitate with my crazy ass."

"I don't even know what to say. Girl, you really are a gem."

"Don't say a word. I'm going to start packing. You're only a few hours away from me, so I'll see you tomorrow evening. Text me the address of where you at."

"Okay, girl, I'll see you then."

Wow, I didn't expect to hear that from her. It ain't like we were super tight or anything like that. Nonetheless,

I was grateful that she was coming out here with me. I have no one, so knowing I have my blood coming gave me a little comfort. I felt so relieved after we got off the phone.

I didn't get a chance to put the phone down when it started to ring. I didn't recognize the number but decided to pick up anyway, hoping it wasn't Mari or Tyrone.

"Hello."

"Hello, there, Miss Jones. This is Detective McKinney. How are you doing?"

I paused. I remember her. She was the detective that came to the hospital after I was assaulted. Shit, it's been a minute since I've heard from her, and truthfully, I was trying to put that fucked-up situation behind me.

"Hello, how can I help you?" I asked with a serious attitude in my tone.

"I called to let you know we finally got Ramon Rivera." She sounded excited.

I froze up at the mention of that monster's name. I had tried so hard for months to put the rape out of my mind, and now I was pulled back into all the ugly emotions.

"Really? Where did y'all find him at?"

"He assaulted a prostitute a few days ago, and she was able to give police a description and the license plate of the vehicle he was driving. We were able to track him down at his residence."

"Okay, so what happens next?" I nervously asked.

"Well, he's charged right now for the rape of the prostitute and will be charged with your rape and the murder of Ariana Gayle. I'll keep you posted as soon as I get with the DA this week."

"Okay, thank you."

I disconnected the phone before I broke down. The mention of Ariana's name brought out raw emotions. I sat back down on the bed as I tried my hardest not to break down. Then I scrolled through my pictures until I got to my favorite pics of her and me. It was our last time partying together.

"They got him, baby. They got the bastard that took you away from me. They got him, boo." I hugged the picture close to my heart and started bawling. I missed my bitch so much. God knows I wish she were here right now. I held my chest as it started hurting, and I continued to hug the phone and just bawled uncontrollably. Life ain't fair.

It was day two of us going out apartment hunting. I went from living in the projects to living in a nice-ass house. Now, I was back to living in an apartment. It's funny how your life could change in the blink of an eye. I remember when Mari told me he got me for life. Was this what he meant 'cause this shit was for the birds?

Lately, he's been on my mind heavy. I was still in love with him, even after everything he did to me. I hate that I even got involved with Tyrone 'cause he turned out to be a piece of shit. He wasn't even worth leaving Mari for. I started to have second thoughts about fucking up with Mari, so I quickly tucked those thoughts deep down inside. There's no way I could forgive Mari for what he put me through. A baby, fucking the bitch at the real estate firm, and fucking lying about everything. It's crazy how you can be with someone and still don't know them.

"Hey, boo, you good?" my cousin said to me.

"Yes, just thinking. You know, I miss Mari sometimes."

"Cuz, fuck that nigga. I was rooting for y'all at first, but after hearing all the shit you told me, I fucking hate him, and I don't even know him. That nigga is a bitch ass, and you don't need to give him a second thought. You're too beautiful and too good of a woman to let a bum-ass nigga drag you like that. I'm here to help you with whatever. You don't need no nigga unless he's worthy of having you."

I looked at her and smiled. Even though we didn't know each other so well before, all that matters is she's here now, and I had someone that genuinely fucks with me.

"You know, I really appreciate you and everything you're doing for me. I hope this place comes through for us tomorrow. We need to get the hell out of this hotel and into our own shit."

"Girl, I'm telling you. I feel crazy living out of these bags and shit. I still don't know which bag my makeup kit is in. A bitch out here looking rough and shit."

"Shit, look at me. This weave so damn old that it's starting to knot up in the back. I need to get this shit done, plus get a pedicure. I ain't never look this rough before."

"Well, let's get this place tomorrow, and then after we get it fixed up, we can focus on having a girl's day out. Get pampered and get cute. Shit, we probably can go out to catch a drink or something."

"Sounds good to me."

I went back scrolling through Facebook. I went over to Tesha's page to see if she's been posting. It still was puzzling how she left my house, and I hadn't heard anything from her. It ain't like we had any kind of beef or anything of that sort. The first thing to catch my eye was a poster with her picture. Have you seen her? What the fuck? I continued reading a post that her mother wrote. I scrolled down to read the comments under the posts. It was people praying for her to return safely to her family. I was puzzled. Where the fuck could she be? I pulled up her number again.

"Come on, pick up, baby," I whispered, only to be disappointed when her voicemail came on immediately.

This shit was really crazy. Under the post, some people said the last day they saw her was the same day she came over to my house. What the fuck could've happened from that time to the day I went to court? I sat there thinking. I recall Mari saying some shit went down at the house. However, when I quizzed him, he was tight-lipped about what had happened. I know it was something serious for the place to be burned down.

"Oh God, no," I said out loud. I hope Mari didn't harm Tesha. She was my friend—shit, the only friend I had left. I tried not to think of anything bad. I hope she's just somewhere laid up with a nigga or something, and she'll come home soon.

Mari

I was tired of being at G's crib. Don't get me wrong; my nigga wasn't bothering me or nothing like that. I just needed to get my own. Since Shonda was into the real estate business, I decided to get me my own crib. I didn't want nothing in the city, though. I thought about something in Midlothian, or maybe going further down south. Perhaps the Chesterfield area. I decided to give her a call. I was ready to make some moves. Later today, I was about to hit Luther up to see if my new Range had come in yet.

"Hello."

"Yo, what's good? Why you sound like you asleep? You not working today?"

"Hey, Mari. Nah, I'm at the house. I was going to call you."

"What's going on? You good?" I was concerned.

"Yeah, I'm good. Can you come by the house?"

"Yeah, I'm on the way."

I hung up the phone, grabbed my towel, and jumped in the shower. I didn't like how she sounded. God, I hope this bitch wasn't about to tell me that *she* was pregnant. I just went through some crazy shit with Dreema's ass, so I definitely don't need no more drama right now.

I got dressed and headed out. G was still asleep in the crib, so I locked up before leaving. As usual, I tucked my gun in my waist and made sure no one was following. I had a little piece of a roach, so I lit it up to kind of smooth me out. Then I cut on the music, blasting Moneybagg Yo's *Reset* album. I was definitely in the zone cruising through the city. I been in the crib so long that things seemed strange out here now.

I pulled up at her crib, parked, and got out of the car. I walked up to the door and rang the doorbell. Within seconds, she opened the door.

"Hey, boo," she greeted me.

"Hey, love. What's good?"

Her behavior was kind of strange. I took a quick glance around, but everything seemed cool. I hope this bitch wasn't on no bullshit 'cause lately, bitches were the ones that I was killing. I followed her in the living room, where she took a seat. I sat across from her.

"What's good? What's bothering you?"

"Do you know if you're under any kind of investigation?"

"Nah, why you ask that?" I looked at her suspiciously.

"The Feds came to the office yesterday."

"For what? What they wanted?" I was *really* feeling uneasy now.

"Dude wanted to know what kind of business you do with me—"

"Why the fuck would he want to know what ties I have with you?"

"I don't know, Mari. I'm just as lost as you."

"What else did he say, and are you sure it was the Feds?"

"That's what he said. He basically said you're under investigation, and if I was doing business with you, I'd go down with you."

"Yo, whoever the fuck that dude is, he blowing smoke. I know how the Feds work, and if they had anything on me, they would come get me. I mean, I'm out here."

"Well, I don't know, Mari. I'm just warning you to be careful out here. If you're under federal investigation, you don't want to give them more than they already got."

"Man, I hear you, but they ain't got shit. That's why they fishing. Yo, all your paperwork and shit is in order, right? Can't nothing be traced back to me, right?"

"No, everything is done the way the lawyer told me to do it. Everything is cool on my end. But don't you think it's strange that they popped up as soon as you left that bitch Akila?" She looked at me.

"Akila? Nah, I don't think she got anything to do with this. She ain't that kind of chick."

"How you know that? I told you that bitch was only after your money. Now that the money is cut off, you have no idea what she's capable of doing. When she stopped by the office, and I told her you wasn't getting her the house, she was pissed the fucked off. You can't trust these bitches, especially no broke bitch."

"Yo, chill out with all that. I said she ain't got shit to do with anything," I said sternly.

"All right, sir. Can't say I ain't warn you."

"Yo, you need to close up whatever you got going on. We might need to chill for a while until things die down."

"I have three clients that are supposed to be closing on their houses next month. I can't do nothing before then."

"A'ight. Be careful. And if something don't seem right, make sure you don't fuck with it. Now that we got that out of the way, come give me some head," I instructed her.

She walked over to me without saying a word and dropped to her knees. I pulled my dick out of my boxers and started massaging it. She used her tiny hand and started rubbing my balls while she licked the tip of my dick. I leaned my head back on the sofa and closed my eyes as I curled my toes up in my sneakers. Shawty knew exactly how to take her time and make love to my dick. I put my hand on her head, making sure she didn't move. The tip of my dick was touching the back of that throat. I wish I could push my dick all the way down her throat.

"Shit, come here." I pulled her up. I quickly stood up, turned her to face the couch, then pulled her pajamas down, revealing her phat, round ass. I grabbed her ass cheeks and slowly slid into her. She was already wet, so it made it so much easier on me. She scooted all the way back on the dick, almost knocking me down. She was hungry for the dick, so I served her properly. I started thrusting harder and harder in and out of her. I was cutting all through her guts, but she didn't flinch. She grinded on my dick. A few times, I felt like I was about to come. I'd draw out, then slowly slide back in. That only worked for so long. After about fifteen minutes of fucking her, my dick veins enlarged. I gripped her hips tighter and pushed all the way.

"Fuck, shit, ooooh, fuck," I yelled out as I exploded inside her.

Finally, I pulled out my limp dick, stumbled to the coach, and quickly wiped the sweat dripping from my face. That was some good pussy, and a bitch that knew how to take fuck without complaint.

She walked out of the room, and I took a moment to gather my energy. Shit, I needed to smoke something, but I left the Black & Mild in the car.

"You good, boo. What was that about?" she asked when she walked back into the living room.

"What you talking about?" I stood up.

"You fucking me hard like that."

"Damn, you ain't like it?"

"I do. You just ain't never fucked me like that before."

"The dick hit a little different when the pussy wet."

"You a hot mess."

I laughed, walked out of the room, quickly cleaned off my dick, and pulled up my clothes. Then I walked into the fridge to grab something to drink. I couldn't help but notice a hat on the counter. It was a NY fitted cap. *I wonder who the hell it belong to?* I thought as I opened the fridge and poured myself something to drink.

I walked back into the living room where she was sitting, checking her phone.

"Aye, yo, who's fitted cap is on the counter?"

"Huh? What you talking about?"

"Yo, stop acting like you don't know what I'm talking about."

She looked up, then walked off to the kitchen, so I followed behind her.

"Oh, this? This my cousin's cap. He must've forgot it when he was over a few nights ago."

"Cousin, huh?"

"Mari, don't start. That's right. I said, *cousin*. What you tripping for anyways? You been having multiple bitches. You know how I feel about you, but you put me on the 'friends with benefits' category, so you can't trip if I was riding another's nigga's dick."

I leaped toward her and grabbed her by the throat. "Don't you fucking play with me. If I'm fucking you, it better not be no other nigga running up in you."

"You better get yo' fucking hands off me before you regret it," she said.

I quickly realized that I was making a big mistake. Shawty was a valuable part of my business, and I couldn't afford to fall out with her. I removed my hand off her.

"My bad, yo. You know how I feel about you, and you saying that shit just triggered something in me."

"No, nigga, fuck your apology. Listen, 'cause I'm only going to say things one time. I'm not sure what them other bitches allow you to do, but I'm not them, so don't *ever* put your motherfucking hands on me again."

"Yo, I said I'm sorry, shawty. You ain't got to do all that."

"Mari, you just need to go right now."

"Oh, it's like that? You throwing me out?" I shot her a wicked grin.

"Yes, I'm upset, and you need to go so I can calm down. I'll call you when I'm calm."

"A'ight, shawty. I'm out."

Without saying another word, I walked away, opened the door, and left. This bitch really thinks she can talk to me like she's crazy. Sooner or later, she'll learn that being educated don't mean shit to me. All my hoes got to act right or get beat the fuck up.

I got in my car and pulled off. I saw that bitch watching me through the window. Yeah, right—some fucking cousin. She ain't my bitch, but I better not catch that nigga over here. My money help pay for this crib, and the only nigga that should be up in there fucking is me.

I pulled out of the subdivision and into traffic. A few lights down, I couldn't help but notice a dark-colored SUV had been following me. It wasn't close enough for me to see who was driving, but I knew it was following me. I kept driving while keeping my eyes on the vehicle behind me. I was getting an eerie feeling. I sat at the stoplight, waiting on it to change. It was only a two-case scenario. Either it was the Feds or a pussy nigga following me. My bet, it wasn't no Feds. I made a quick turn as soon as the light changed. Then I pulled my gun out of my waist and put it in my lap. I looked behind me but didn't see the truck, so I figured I was wrong. I chuckled to myself. I had myself riled up for nothing at all. Suddenly, I realized I was at a dead end, so I put the car into reverse to turn around.

Pop! Pop! Pop!

I grabbed my gun and started busting back while reversing in speed. The same truck that I spotted earlier was coming at me and still busting. A nigga on the passenger side of the vehicle was aiming a machine gun at me. Instantly, I saw death knocking on my door. Survival skills kicked in, and I started emptying the clip. I couldn't see behind me, so I crashed into a parked car. I didn't have no choice but to crawl over the backseat and jump out of the vehicle. I bent down and ran alongside the cars parked on the sidewalk. I still had my gun in my hand as I dashed down the street.

I saw the SUV speed down the road. I ducked down low until it passed me. Then I pulled out my phone and dialed G's number. I was preoccupied on the phone . . . until I felt something hit me. I looked up, and it was the nigga with the gun shooting at me. I raised my gun to bust back but quickly realized that I was out of bullets and the other clip was in the car. I tried to run, but my leg was hurting. I knew I was about to die, so I started praying silently. Then I heard police sirens in the background. I would be worried any other time, but I knew I was hit pretty bad, and if I wanted to live, I needed to get to the hospital soon.

I looked around and spotted a trash can in front of someone's house. I used all my strength to walk to it. I dug under the trash and put the gun in it. Then I jogged away so the police wouldn't be suspicious. My phone started ringing.

"Hello," I faintly said. "Yo, I got shot—" was all I managed to say before I collapsed to the ground.

Chapter Thirteen

Akila

I finally got the phone call I was waiting on to hear about the house I wanted to rent. We were so happy. We rushed over there to meet the landlady. It was on Warwick Road. It was a three-bedroom house with a nice big backyard. It wasn't like the place I lost, but it was not that bad. It would have to work for now. We signed the lease and did the walk-through. Everything was straight. It even had a fireplace, which was cool 'cause I love to sit by the fireplace in the winter. We decided to move in right away. We didn't have any furniture, but tomorrow, we planned on going furniture shopping.

"Let's go to Walmart real quick and grab two blow-up beds until tomorrow," I said to my cousin.

"OK, cool. Let me use the bathroom first." She walked off to the bathroom.

My phone started ringing. I dug into my bag and pulled it out. *What the fuck he want?* I rolled my eyes as I noticed it was G, Mari's homeboy. I hate that I gave him my number. I pressed *ignore* and was about to put the phone back into my bag, but it rang again.

"Listen, G, you ain't got no business calling me. I ain't got shit to say to your boy," I blurted out into the phone.

"Yo, shawty, Mari got shot. I'm on the way to the hospital. I don't know if he's going to make it."

"What? You serious?"

My heart stopped for a quick second. Don't ask me why I care, but I can't help how the heart reacts. I started feeling sick.

"What hospital he-he-at?" I stuttered.

"MCV. I know y'all beefing, shawty, but I thought you would want to know. I know y'all still love each other."

I hung up the phone as I leaned against the wall for support, feeling nauseated. Oh God, this can't be happening. I know we're not together, but I still love him. I don't want him to die.

"Cuz, you all right. Why you look so pale?"

"Mari got shot and might not make it," I squeezed out as I rushed to the bathroom.

I made it just in time to put my head in the toilet. The number one I had at Chick-fil-A came back up. I didn't feel too good. After emptying my stomach, I sat on the floor for a few minutes. I felt like the wind was knocked out of me. Finally, I held on to the wall and stood up. I realized that I didn't set up the bathroom yet, so I didn't have my toothbrush. Instead, I used some water and rinsed out my mouth. This news really fucked me up like this. I walked out of the bathroom and found my cousin was standing in the hallway.

"I was just coming to check on you. You good?"

"Yeah, I think I got sick after hearing about Mari."

"Why? It ain't like y'all together or nothing. Shit, he might be better off dead. That way, you ain't got to worry 'bout shit."

I turned around and looked at her. That was some cold, trifling shit to say. "Why would you say that? Regardless of what we went through, he's still the man I fell in love with. That's cold as hell." I shook my head in disgust.

"Girl, I ain't mean it like that. But after how you tell me he treated you, please don't expect me to feel any kind of pity for him. Karma is a bitch, and sometimes when you do people wrong, it comes right back at you."

"Listen, I got to go. You can put the nearest Walmart in the GPS and go get some stuff if you need to. I'm going to the hospital."

I didn't wait for a response. I walked out the back door and to my SUV. I put the car into drive and pulled off. I was still troubled by Claire's statement, but I shifted my focus to Mari.

"God, I know I don't always come to you, but please, I'm coming to you as humble as I know how. Please, let my baby pull through. Please, God, I will forever be good to you," I prayed aloud.

My grandma was a praying woman and had always told me that you need to drop to your knees when things get rough and give it to God. I couldn't drop to my knees right now, but I hoped he heard my cries. I sped down the streets, running a few stop signs. At one time, I almost hit a car. I honked the horn like the bitch was wrong. I didn't care about anything but to get to the hospital to see Mari.

I pulled into the parking garage and frantically searched for a space. This shit was packed to the max. I went around and around. I thought about just parking the car behind another car and running out. I knew I'd probably get towed, but that was the last thing on my mind. Before I could take that action, I spotted a little old lady walking to her car. I wished the bitch would hurry up instead of taking baby steps. I was an emotional wreck and wasn't thinking rationally.

"It took yo' ass long enough," I said as she backed out her car. I wasted no time as I pulled into the parking spot. I turned off the engine, grabbed my purse, and got out of the truck. Once I spotted the elevator, I ran over to it. Quickly, I pressed the button and waited as I pulled out my phone and called G's number.

"Yo."

"I'm here. Where are you?"

"I'm in the emergency room, shawty."

"Okay." I hung up the phone and got on the elevator. I stood by the door, waiting for it to reach the first floor. As soon as it stopped and the door opened, I ran out, spotted G pacing back and forth, and ran into his arms.

"I'm sorry, shawty."

I let go of him and looked at him. "Is he going to be all right? Who the fuck did this to him? Where were you at?" I bombarded him with a bunch of questions while I started hitting him in the chest.

"Shawty, he in surgery right now. I was at the crib. I don't know who the fuck did this to him." He grabbed me and wrapped his arms around me.

"I can't lose him. I know we beefing, but I love him," I admitted.

"We ain't gon' lose him. Yo' boy is a fighter. Trust me. He back there fighting. We just need to be strong for him," his voice cracked.

We stood there hugging and crying for a few minutes until we let loose. Finally, I walked over to some chairs to sit down. My stomach was still queasy, and my head was pounding like I took a savage beating.

"Yo, shawty. I promise, soon as my boy make it out, he gon' tell me who the fuck did this to him. I swear I'ma deal with that shit. I already lost Rio. I can't lose my dawg too." He wiped tears from his eyes.

I reached over, grabbed his hand, and squeezed it. "Do you think the same niggas that killed Rio are responsible for shooting Mari?"

"Nah, I doubt it. But you never know."

"Well, I hope whoever it is, you find them and let them pay."

I ain't never want nobody to get killed, but it's different when it's the man you love that's fighting for his life.

"Kila, I want you to know that no matter what you and Mari went through, he loves you, shawty. You the only woman that he brags about on the regular."

"No disrespect, G, I know that's your boy, and you will lie for him. Mari couldn't love me and carry me the way he did. I mean, this nigga had a baby on—"

Before I could finish that sentence, I remembered that Dreema and the baby were killed a few days ago.

"Wait. Did Mari know the bitch Dreema and his son were killed?" I looked at him.

"Yeah, we heard about it. But you know he had stopped fucking around with shawty after she got you locked up. Then a few days later, she told him that wasn't his seed."

"What? That wasn't his baby? Oh my God, so this nigga was claiming a fucking baby that wasn't his?" I shook my head in disbelief. This was some crazy shit.

"Well, when Mari gets better, he can tell you exactly what happened. I don't know the full details and shit, but I know the nigga love you. Sometimes, niggas just be fucking up and shit."

"I hear you, but I done forgave him too many times, and all he do is continue making a fool out of me. I really don't know why I'm even here." I started thinking.

"Shawty, you're here 'cause you love the nigga. Trust me; once he pulls through, he's going to make things straight between y'all. Right now, we just need to hold on to hope and send some positive vibes his way. Homie ain't got no real family but us."

"Yeah," I whispered under my breath.

After the rush and I had time to think, I had mixed feelings. I had completely walked away from him and his foolishness. But as soon as I heard some shit, here I was crying over him. I tried to push the negative thoughts out of my mind for now. I really need him to pull through.

It was hours later, and we were still sitting there waiting. I was feeling weak, and my stomach was touching my back, but I wouldn't dare leave to get anything to eat. I got up and walked up to the receptionist.

"Hello, is there any update on Mari Owens?"

"Are you family?"

"I'm his fiancée," I lied.

"Hold on a second."

She got on the phone and spoke to someone. "Ma'am, he's still in surgery. The doctor will be out to speak with you soon."

"All right, thanks."

I walked back to where G was and took a seat.

"What they say?"

"She talking 'bout he's still in surgery. I swear I'm having a bad feeling about this. It's been hours since he's been on the operating table."

He didn't respond. He just sat there with his head buried in his hands. I could tell he was feeling hurt. Mari was lucky to have a nigga that cared about him like this.

I saw a Filipino doctor walk through the double doors into the emergency room. He walked to the receptionist and said something. Then she pointed to where G and I were sitting.

We stood up right away and walked toward him. "Are you the doctor for Mari Owens?" I asked.

"Are you immediate family?"

"I'm his fiancée, and this his brother," I blurted out.

"Well, Mr. Owns was hit pretty badly. He just got out of surgery, and he's stabilized now. He's in the ICU. He's not out of the woods yet. He was lucky to get here when he did. The next twenty-four hours are very critical in his recovery. We just have to hope and pray. The doctors here at MCV are some of the best in the country, so I'm confident he is in good hands."

"Can we go back to see him right now?"

"Yes, follow me, but he's heavily sedated, so you only can have a few minutes with him. After that, he needs rest to build up his strength again."

He led the way, and we followed him upstairs. I was thrown off when I saw police officers at the door. I could tell G was feeling uneasy, so I grabbed his hand as we walked into the room. Mari was hooked up with tubes all over him. He was swollen and dark purple compared to his normal complexion. Tears dropped out of my eyes as I stood over him. He reminded me of when my grandma was in the casket. My heart was hurting seeing him like this.

"Homie, I need you to pull through. We got shit to do, my dawg. You can't leave me like this," G said in between sobs.

I couldn't get no words out. I reached over and touched his hand. I was hoping he would know this was me. However, he didn't move none. He was lying up there like a statue.

"OK, guys, let him rest. You can check with the desk to see when you can visit tomorrow. Like I said, we're monitoring him closely and will contact you all if there are any major changes."

Part of me didn't want to go. I wanted to stay with him, so he could know I was right here with him.

"Come on, shawty. The dawg is a fighter. He ain't going anywhere."

We were on the way out the door when the officer stopped us.

"I have a few questions to ask you guys."

"About what?" I quizzed.

"Do you all have any idea of what happened to Mr. Owens?"

"No, I don't. I only got a call that he got shot."

"What about you, sir?" He turned to G.

"I don't know nothing. I just heard he got shot, and I came here to see him."

"Well, Mr. Owens's brother, Rio Owens, was killed over a month ago. Do you think the shootings are related?"

"Like I said, Officers, I don't know 'bout no shooting."

"Here's my card. If you hear anything or think of anything, please give me a call." He handed me the card.

I took the card, and we walked off. I was as curious as the officer if Rio's death was related to Mari getting shot. But Mari was not awake, and he was the only one to answer this question. I couldn't help but wonder why the officer was posted up. I know Mari's name was ringing bells in Richmond, so I'm pretty sure they were aware of who he was. This was strange that Mari got shot and didn't bust back. And if he did, where was his gun? So many questions were flooding my mind, but again, only Mari knew the answers. If G knew anything, he was tight-lipped about everything. I didn't expect anything different. They were as close as niggas could get.

"Aye, I'm going to go home for a little while. I have my cousin down here with me, and I need to go check on her. Please call me if anything changes."

He wrapped his arms around me. "Shawty, he's going to be straight. Get some rest, and I'll hit you up later. I'ma be up here just in case. I hit up the rest of his fam in the Beach. They should be here soon."

"OK, boo."

As I walked off, I couldn't help but think. For all the years that I've known G, I've never seen him this emotional. As far as I've heard, he was a stone-cold killer, so to see him this emotional was really crazy.

I dried my eyes as I made my way to my car. I was an emotional wreck. Mari didn't even look like himself. Whoever did this was trying to kill him. I remember all those days I begged him to leave the streets alone. He kept saying the streets were his life. I wondered what it would take 'cause he done lost his brother. Will it take him losing his life? Sad, but he won't be here to tell it if he doesn't pull through this. The thought of him dying made my soul hurt. I pulled my key to open my door when I saw a shadow approach me.

This was the last fucking person I wanted to see, especially at a time like this.

"What are you doing? Are you following me?" I quizzed.

"Akila, we heard what happened to Mr. Owens."

"Okay, and what? You're here to check if he dead or not?" I opened my truck.

"I told you he's under investigation, so we came down to see if we could gather anything."

"Tyrone, you don't have no fucking heart. That boy in there fighting for his life, and all you can think about is your fucking investigation. I swear I'm so happy that I don't fuck with you anymore 'cause you colder than ice."

"I'm sorry you feel like that, but you know for yourself Mr. Owens is a stone-cold killer. What about the people that *he* killed? What about your friend that went missing? What about the families of these victims? By the way, did you know Dreema Walker and her newborn son were killed? You think all this is a coincidence? Come on, Akila. You're not so naïve."

"Tyrone, I don't care about none of this shit you saying. If you have all this proof that Mari killed all these people, why are you here bothering me? Why haven't y'all locked him up? You know what? I'm getting tired of this harassment. I'm going to find me a lawyer first thing in the morning."

"I warned you, Akila, stop being around this criminal. I'm going to take him down, and if you're anywhere around, this time, I'm going to charge you."

"You know, Tyrone, this sounds personal to me. I think you're mad 'cause Mari fuck me better than you did."

I slammed my door, and before he could respond, I started the car and pulled off. His ass was becoming a nuisance to me. I still can't believe that I fell for him and actually thought of being with him. I hurried up and pulled out of the parking lot after paying the ticket. I hate the fact that the Feds might be following me around without me knowing.

It was around 4:00 a.m. when I got home. I totally forgot that I didn't eat all day, but once I went in, there was no way I was going out again. I tiptoed past Claire, who was sleeping on a blow-up bed on the living room floor. I saw there was another pumped-up bed, but I didn't have the energy to move that shit right now. I walked into my room, took off my jacket, threw it on the carpet, and lay down. I was mentally drained and needed sleep right away.

Hours later, I heard a knock on the door. I lifted my head, then flopped it back down. My head was still pounding, and I was still nauseated.

"Yeah?" I yelled out.

Claire pushed the door and peeked her head in. "What's up?"

She walked in and sat down beside me on the carpet. "Cuz, I just want to apologize about yesterday. I know I came off a little harsh. Is he going to be all right?"

"Well, he had surgery, and he's still in the ICU. What time is it? I need to go back to the hospital." I sat up and grabbed my phone.

"I'm sorry, boo. I hope he's okay. I don't want nothing to come between our relationship. I know I might come off judgmental sometimes, but it's out of love. After all that you've been through, I just don't want you falling back into the same situation."

"I know you mean well, cuz, but you have to understand that I'm grown and capable of making decisions. I admit that I might make some fucked-up ones sometimes, but I can accept that and learn from them."

"I understand, boo. Like I said, I apologize."

I jumped up and ran to the bathroom. I started vomiting, but nothing was coming up but a bitter liquid. *What the fuck is going on?* I thought as I washed my mouth out. After I was finished, I walked back into the room. She was still sitting down.

"You all right, cuz? You don't look too good."

"I don't know what the fuck is going on. I been feeling ill since yesterday."

"What kind of sick?"

"Yesterday, I was vomiting, and just now, I keep trying to vomit, but I don't have anything on my stomach, so I kept bringing up some bitter, green shit. That shit is nasty as hell."

"Hmmm . . . Wait, cuz. When was the last time you seen your period?"

"I'm about to see in a few days. Why?" I shot her a strange look.

"Girl, it sounds like you're pregnant. That bitter shit is what comes up in the mornings when there's no food on your stomach."

"Girl, bye. I ain't pregnant. It's probably that food that I got from Chick-fil-A."

"Hmm, I hear you. Well, you need to get something hot on your stomach, but I suggest you buy one of those pregnancy tests from Family Dollar."

"Girl, I would know if I was pregnant, and I'm not. Anyway, we need to get some furniture up in here, plus some pots and pans. What did you get from Walmart besides the beds?"

"Girl, that's all I could get. A bitch is broke. I'm waiting to get this check from my job. I barely got gas in my car."

I was shocked when she mentioned she was broke. If I'm not mistaken, she often bragged about how she was making lots of money numerous times when we talked. This shit didn't make sense. What was the point of her moving all the way down here if she knew she was broke? I was starting to feel irritated as fuck, but I tried to conceal it so she wouldn't see it. I only have a few dollars, and I can't take care of another grown woman.

"Girl, I'm going to take a shower and see if I could shake this feeling."

I got up and walked over to where I had my clothes in a few big black garbage bags. I stood there and shook my head in dismay. A few months ago, I had a closet, drawers full of clothes, and over thirty pairs of shoes. Just like that, I lost everything. I felt sad, so I tried to brush it off. I began digging in the bags. I needed something to put on.

"Girl, let me go find me something to put on too." She got up and walked out of the room.

I was happy she had left. I could finally breathe without her being all up in my space. I love having her here with me, but her statement about being broke rubbed me the wrong way.

After picking out what I was wearing, I decided to give G a call. I cut the shower on as I waited for him to pick up the phone.

"Yo."

"Hey, G, it's Akila. Are there any changes with Mari?"

"What's good, Kila? I just left from up there. Yeah, he woke up, but he's still in critical condition. This morning we had a scare. He flatlined twice and shit, but the doctors were able to bring him back—"

"Oh my God, are you fucking serious? Why you ain't call me and let me know this?" I cut him off. I started to shake. This wasn't the news that I was trying to hear this morning.

"I know you was tired, shawty, so I figured you was getting you some rest. The family up here too."

"I'ma run some errands and shit, and then I'ma be up there. Please call me if anything else happens. You know I'll be there ASAP."

"A'ight; got you."

After he hung up the phone, I placed it on the sink and got into the tub. *Oh God, Mari, you have to pull through.* I swear my heart can't take this right now. I started bawling so damn hard that I was shaking uncontrollably.

I decided to go to Value City Furniture down on Broad Street. By the time the cashier rang up the bill, it was almost four grand. Yes, you heard me. Four grand 'cause Claire wasn't lying. She didn't have a dollar to put toward getting furniture for the house. The furniture would be delivered in three days. The next stop was Walmart. I ended up spending another grand on bathroom and kitchen stuff. I was tired of spending already. When I was with Mari, I didn't have to spend shit. I recall when I was shopping for the house, he dropped over ten grand and pretended like that wasn't shit. I didn't have it like that and wouldn't pretend like I did.

"Hey, boo, what you trying to eat?" Claire asked as we left the Walmart parking lot.

"We can stop at South Side Plaza and grab some fish and shrimp from the fish market."

"Is their fish good? I don't like eating from strange places."

"Well, that's what I want. Ain't nobody said you have to eat that." I came off a little stronger than I meant to.

"Girl, you sure you good? You snapping and shit. I ain't mean to offend you."

I tried to calm my nerves. I didn't know what was going on with me, but I felt on edge.

"Cuz, sorry. I just don't feel too good, and I got some more fucked-up news about Mari."

"He's going to be all right, right?" She looked at me.

"I don't know, cuz. His boy said he flatlined twice this morning. I know I said all that shit about him, but I still love him. I swear I don't want to lose him," I confessed as tears fell onto my arm.

"Oh no. Well, I know God can work miracles. Cuz, I'm here to support you no matter what you're going through. Let's pray, girl . . . He's going to pull through."

"I just can't lose him. I swear I feel like we have so much more to talk about. I want one more chance to sit and talk with him," I cried.

By the time we got to the fish market, I had managed to get my crying under control. I grabbed me a three-piece lake trout with French fries and some steamed fish. All that shit she was talking about earlier, and she copped her a two-piece croaker. We then decided to go back to the crib.

After I ate, I decided to head to the hospital. On my way out the door, my cousin stopped me.

"Hey, boo, do you want me to come with you?"

"You ain't got to, but I appreciate it, boo."

"Cuz, I want to come to support you. Let me be there for you."

"A'ight, come on. I know you don't like him, so don't come up there with nothing negative."

"Cuz, oh my God, give me some credit, boo boo. I know I'm ratchet, but not *that* ratchet," she busted out laughing.

"Uh-huh. I'm not fooling with you today." We walked out of the house together, and I locked the door.

On the way to the hospital, I tried to prepare myself mentally. It was heartbreaking when I saw him yesterday, and I wasn't sure what to expect today. I really hope my cousin stayed in her place 'cause I would hate to check her over Mari.

After giving our names to the front desk, the nurse made sure we had permission. That was strange to me, but she explained that the police had to approve who could come and go to his room because he was a shooting victim. We made our way to the elevator. After we stepped out of the elevator, I walked to his room. Shit, I forgot to call G to let him know I was on the way. I've only seen some of Mari's family once when we went to Virginia Beach.

His door was closed, so I knocked, then entered the room. I spotted G sitting down when I first walked in, but suddenly, I heard a female's voice. I walked farther in and stopped.

"What the fuck your ass doing up in here?" the bitch realtor said. She was sitting on the bed beside Mari.

"Bitch, you better get the fuck on. Mari is sick up in here, and I hate to take it there with you. G, you better get this ho." I turned my attention to him.

"Yo, Shonda, you need to chill out, shawty. My nigga right here fighting for his life. He don't need no beef around him."

"I understand that, G, but *why* is she here? The last time I saw Mari, he told me he was done with her. Trust me. He would not want her here."

"Bitch, you don't get to decide who visits him or nah. Excuse me, are you his wife or something?" my cousin chimed in.

I see where things were getting out of hand. "I can't believe Mari would fuck around with you. You ghetto as fuck hiding under that fake shit. I love Mari and respect him to not beat your ass up in here, so I'ma leave. G, please call me when this ho leaves. Come on, Claire." That bitch was yapping off at the gums, but honestly, I wasn't listening to none of that shit.

I walked out, pissed the fuck off that bitch was there and had the nerve even to address me. *Mari really knows how to choose them,* I thought as we stepped on the elevator.

"Cuz, I swear I want to beat that bitch ass. Who the fuck is she?"

"One of Mari's hoes," I said as we walked to the parking lot.

My day just got fucking worse. I have no idea why I don't just say fuck him and stop dealing with this bullshit. All this fucking headache ain't worth it.

Shonda

I sat on the bed, looking at Mari. Part of me felt sad that he was fighting for his life, but the other side of me was pissed off. This nigga was a liar. He just told me he didn't fuck with the bitch no more, so you should've seen my face when that bitch walked in.

Yes, I get it that we ain't no couple yet, but shit, we fuck without condoms, and we do everything couples do. I sat in the shadows long enough watching bitch after bitch come in and out of his life. Fuck that. Now was *my* time to get my shine with him, and there's no way I'm going to let this old slimy, snake-ass bitch weasel her way back into his life.

I know we had an argument when he left the house, so it wasn't strange when he didn't pick up when I called. I waited for a few hours, then I called again. There was still no answer. Something didn't seem right to me, so I called his boy G's phone, and that's when he informed me that Mari got shot down the street from my house. I almost fainted. Even though G was still on the phone, I had to put it down while I got my crying under control.

He told me he was in surgery, and it didn't make sense for me to come up there. That was kind of weird. Now I'm thinking, he didn't want me up there 'cause this ho was up there. These niggas are full of shit. I looked over at G sitting on the chair, browsing his phone.

I got up off the bed and walked over to where he was sitting.

"G, let me ask you a question. If Mari is done with that bitch Akila, why the hell she came up here?"

"Yo, shawty, I don't know that man's business. As far as I know, he ain't with either one of you, so what's the problem?"

"The problem is I do everything for y'all. Shit, did he tell you the Feds came to see me? I ain't gon' risk my freedom behind a nigga that's still entertaining his old ho."

"The Feds? What the fuck you talking 'bout, shawty?" He put down the phone and looked at me with his face made up.

"Yeah. A day earlier, some agent came to the office wanting to know what dealings my company had with Mari. Yesterday, Mari stopped by the house, and I told him about it."

"Oh, word? Damn, they didn't tell you anything else?"

"Nah, I asked Mari if he knew he was under investigation, and he said no."

He stood up and rubbed his hand over his head. "Yo, this some bullshit. I told Mari that we need to lie low for a few, but that nigga hardheaded, yo."

"Yeah, I told him the same thing. I think I'm going to contact a lawyer 'cause I need to know why the company is associated with him. I make sure all my paperwork is right. Nothing should connect me to you guys."

"Yo, it's just stress after stress. We need to get the fuck out of this town. Go back home or bounce up north. This shit is hot out here."

The nurse walked in, so the conversation was over. She went over to Mari and took his vitals.

"Nurse, is everything looking good?" I asked.

"Yes, well, everything is looking good so far. He's still not out of the woods yet, but he's receptive to the treatment. Mr. Owens is fighting hard to stay with us. Before long, he will be able to walk up out of here, I'm sure."

"Thank you, hon. I hope so. I can't wait to take him home." I rubbed Mari's hand.

After the nurse left, I took a seat beside Mari again. "Hey, you, how you feeling?" I asked when I saw him awake.

"Thirsty."

I reached over and grabbed a cup. I filled it with water, put the straw in it, and put it to his mouth. Damn, he was right. He was thirsty 'cause I had to pour him another cup of water.

"I'm so happy you're feeling a little better. Soon, you'll feel much better, boo."

G stood up and walked over to the bed. "Good to see you awake, homie. It was getting kind of boring sitting in here with no one to talk to."

"Dawg, you know they got me on that good shit. I can barely stay awake. That shit be having me floating and shit." Mari squeezed out a smile.

"Okay, y'all. I got some errands to run. I'll be back in the morning. G, call me if anything happens."

I leaned over and planted a kiss on his lips. They felt like cardboard from the way they were dry. I didn't care, though.

"I love you, Mari."

"A'ight, shawty."

"G, call me."

"A'ight, shawty."

I was tired as hell. Ever since I found out he was shot, I haven't been able to get any sleep. I was physically and mentally exhausted. I needed something strong to drink and a relaxing bath.

Mari

This was the second time in a month niggas tried to take me out. I know my mama was up there guarding her baby boy 'cause this time, I knew for sure I wasn't going to make it. I was shocked when I opened my eyes and realized I was in the hospital. I guess mom dukes and Rio were protecting me.

"Yo, dawg, I know you tired, and I don't want you to stress, but can you tell me anything? Did you see the niggas?"

"Nah, dawg, I was coming from Shonda's crib. A couple of lights down, I spotted a SUV following me. I thought I was tripping, but I made a right turn to make sure. I figured I was in the clear when I didn't see the vehicle behind me. But I was wrong. They came down the street busting at me when I looked to the right. I started busting back, but the nigga had a shotgun. I couldn't go forward, so I tried reversing. That didn't go well 'cause I was shooting, trying not to get shot. I ended up crashing. I jumped out of the car and ran down the street. That's when the nigga saw me and started shooting again. I ran out of bullets, and I wasn't left with no choice. Them niggas hit me up, yo."

"Yo, dawg, somehow, I feel like them niggas was watching you. You didn't get a glimpse of them niggas' face?"

"Nah, 'cause the nigga that shooting was wearing a ski mask. The truck was tinted, so I couldn't see shit. Yo, I swear I just want to wreak havoc on this entire city so these coward-ass niggas can show their fucking hands."

"Yo, dawg, I been up here with you making sure shit straight, but best believe, soon as I touch the streets, shit gon' get real. Niggas done violated enough. It's time to fucking let loose on these Richmond niggas. It don't even matter who behind the shit. I'ma snap on e'erybody. I'm done playing around," he yelled.

"Yo, chill, dawg. You know where we at, and we'ont need no witnesses and shit." I tried to calm him down a little.

"Yo, dawg, I love you more than life itself, and when niggas fuck with you, they fuck with me. They done took Rio from us. I ain't gon' sit around and let them take you too. Yo, we need to send a strong message to these bitch-ass Richmond niggas." He paced back and forth.

"I feel you, dawg, but right now, I need to feel better so that I can get the fuck up outta here. I can't do shit. I can barely move. Yo, how is e'erything going in the streets?"

"E'erything good. I brought up my brother, Marvin, here to help me run shit until you back on yo' feet. He's just waiting to get word on who did this shit. We gon' let them know Beach niggas out here."

"OK, bet. Aye, Shonda told me some shit about the Feds came to see her and shit. I didn't get a chance to holla at you. It was right after leaving her house that I got hit."

"Yeah, she told me about it. Shit seems bogus, though. Like, why the fuck would the Feds go to her? She runs a legit business. I don't know, bro. Maybe someone just trying to spook shawty into not fucking with you. You think Akila could be behind that?"

"Nah, I mean, I know they had words the other day, but I doubt Kila would play them kind of games."

"Nigga, I'ma need for you to stop having so much faith in these hoes. The last couple of bitches turned out to be fucking snakes. You got to start treating these bitches just like you treat these niggas. The first time they move funny, get rid of that ho. Why you think I don't try to wife none of these hoes? I can't trust them. I barely go to sleep around a bitch. And if I do, I hug that bitch so tight, it's impossible for her even to breathe, much less move. I ain't playing them games with these old trifling-ass hoes."

"Well, I'm done with bitches for now anyway. I need to focus on getting my strength back. I'ma go extra hard for 'bout six months, put some of this money into a couple of more businesses, and let that bubble. I swear, ever since I got shot, I been thinking hard on my next move."

"I feel you on that. Sometimes, I feel like my days are numbered. Like, I feel I won't be around to have no seed or live past 35. But I guess that's just how it's set up when you living the life of a thug. That's why I live carefree now. I buy what the fuck I want, fuck when I want to, and just live to the fullest 'cause after losing Rio, I know anything is possible. Rio was a cool-ass dude that was all about his family. He wasn't into the streets like us, and look what happened. This shit ain't fair, bro."

I just lay back thinking. G was a hothead who drinks and smokes all day, but he was spitting some real shit right now. I was trying my best to stay awake, but this morphine had me feeling tired as hell.

"Yo, bro, did you talk to Akila?"

"Yeah, I hit her up to let her know what happened to you."

"Oh, okay. So she ain't come see me?"

"She did. She was in the emergency room with me the first day. Earlier, while you were sleeping, she stopped by, but she and Shonda got into a heated argument. So she ended up leaving."

"What the fuck. To be honest, bro, I don't know why Shonda bring her ass up here. It ain't like we a couple or anything. We just fucking."

"I hear you, but you treat these bitches so good, they be thinking y'all are together. I think you messed up any chance that you might have with Akila. She left here pissed off. Even threatened to beat up Shonda."

I just shook my head in disbelief. Here I was fighting for my life, and instead of these hoes acting right, I'm learning they were up in here cutting up. I ain't going to lie. I was hoping to have Akila by my side. She's probably still angry with me, but after me almost losing my life, this might be my chance to get her back finally. Shit, even if it means me pretending like the helpless victim. I want to get her back one way or another.

After G left and the nurses were out of the room, I decided to give Akila a call. She might not take my call, but I was willing to take the chance. She was here earlier, so I had hope.

"Hello."

My heart jumped a few beats, and I felt like dancing around when I heard her sweet, luscious voice.

"Hey, you," I mustered up all my strength to say.

"How are you feeling?"

"In a lot of pain. Doctor said I was lucky. I could've died."

"Boy, you had me scared. When G called me, I must've done 100 mph to the hospital. I swear I didn't give a fuck if I got pulled over. I swear you don't know what you did to me."

"I'm sorry, love. It ain't like I planned to get shot or nothing like that. The niggas ambushed me, but the good news is doctors said I'm going to be all right. I guess I had some angels watching over me."

"Yeah, I guess so. Well, now that you're feeling better, I can breathe."

"Akila, I want to see you. I thought when I woke up I would see you right by my side." I cut to the chase.

"Mari, I know you're not well, and I'm not trying to be mean or anything like that, but we're not together. Plus, earlier, when I stopped by, your bitch was there. Matter of fact, she told me I didn't have no right to be there."

"Akila, I don't care what that bitch said. She is *not* my bitch, and you had every right to be here. Shawty, I swear, I told God that if he let me get out of this, I'm going to be the b—"

"Listen, Mari, I'm happy that you didn't die, but all that other shit is irrelevant. Matter of fact, I got to go. I'll text you later to see how you doing." She cut me off before I could finish the sentence.

All I heard was the dial tone in my ear. I laughed to myself. Shawty really was carrying it like this while I'm at my lowest? I would've never done her like this. I wanted to feel angry, but that wouldn't make sense. I know if I want to get her back, I need to play it cool even when I want to snap and go off on her.

Chapter Fourteen

Akila

Talking to Mari brought up so many different emotions in me. I wanted to be upset with him, but since he almost died a few days ago, I wanted to hold him, let him know I forgive him, and we're going to be good. I don't know about all that, though. We were not good. Now that everything was out in the open, I realized that he was never faithful to me. As much as I want to be there for him, that shit hurts like hell.

I couldn't sleep. I twisted and turned all night. Mari was on my mind. A few times, I got up and thought about going back up to the hospital with him, but each time that crazy thought ran across my mind, I quickly talked myself out of it. My mind was strong, but my heart was weak for Mari. I was really scared that I might do something stupid, like running back to him.

"God, help me, please. I don't need to go back there," I silently prayed.

After days of vomiting and barely being able to get out of bed, I decided to run to Family Dollar and grabbed one of those cheap pregnant tests that they had up front over the counter. Sitting on the toilet, I kept staring at the two pink lines that ran parallel. I rested my head on the edge of the face basin, trying to make some sense of what was happening. My period didn't come, and this was a first for me. For as long as I can remember, I've never been late. I could feel a tension headache coming on as I took one last look at the pink stick.

I pulled off some toilet paper and wrapped the stick in it before disposing of it in the trash can. Then I finished using the bathroom, washed my hands, walked out, went into my room, and got back into bed.

This can't be. I slept with Mari, and then I slept with Tyrone. Oh God! I rubbed my hand across my face as the dark truth hit me. I wasn't sure. I couldn't be sure who I was pregnant by. I recalled the first time Mari busted in me, and then when I slept with Tyrone, we didn't use no condom. I grabbed my phone and pulled up my calendar. I was trying to remember the dates that I slept with both men.

What have I gotten myself into? I've always been careful, but here I was in a fucked-up situation. For years, I wanted a baby real bad. Never had I thought that when I finally got pregnant, I wouldn't be sure who the daddy was. I was already feeling sick physically, but I was also feeling mentally drained. Finally, I couldn't take it any longer. I threw the phone down and pulled the cover over my head.

"Cuz," I heard Claire yell my name as she knocked on the door.

"Come in." Sometimes I forget that we're living together.

"Cuz, when was you gon' tell me you knocked up?"

"What you talking 'bout now?" I said in an annoyed tone.

"Girl, I found this in the trash." She showed me the pregnancy test that I threw away yesterday.

"What the fuck, girl? Are you going behind me and digging in trash and shit?" I glared at her with a disgusted look on my face.

"You ain't been cleaning, so I'm the one that's doing it. I was emptying the trash in the bathroom, and this fell out. Girl, I told you, you was knocked up, but you act like I don't know what I was talking about."

"I just found out, and I didn't think I needed to report to you. Girl, you're my cousin, not my damn mama."

"I'm your *older* cousin, so I have to watch over you. Congrats on the baby, by the way. I'm about to be a god mama. I'm too excited for you. Ummm . . . Whose baby is it?"

"What you mean?" This bitch was going a little too far with this shit now.

"I don't know. Remember you told me you was with Mari, then you started fucking with the Fed dude. Shit, unless you used condoms with one and let the other come in you—"

"Girl, bye. What are you, a damn PI? I know who I'm pregnant by."

"Oh, OK. Well, you need to get to the doctor soon. They need to give you something for that vomiting."

"OK." I kept it short and sweet.

She must've gotten the drift 'cause she silently walked out of the room with no other words. I pulled the cover over my head. This headache and nausea were wreaking havoc on me. I just needed it all to stop right now.

It's been weeks since I last seen Mari, but a day has not gone by that I haven't thought about him. I did call G almost daily, trying to check on his recovery. He told me that Mari was moved out of ICU and into a regular room. G also relayed his recovery was coming on well, and he

might be coming out this week. I was genuinely happy
for him and happy he would be able to make a speedy
recovery.

Being pregnant had me scared as hell. I made a doctor's
appointment and learned I was eight weeks pregnant. I
thought by getting my expected due date, I would be able
to pinpoint which one of these niggas got me pregnant,
but I can't figure this out for the life of me. I was caught
up in some ratchet shit and couldn't figure my way out.
I also thought about having an abortion, but that was
out of the picture. For years, all I wanted was to have a
baby, and there's no way I was going to kill my first child.
I couldn't stop the tears from falling. I rubbed my hand
across my stomach. I need to get it together, if not for me,
for the life that's growing inside of me.

This was my first day back in school since all that shit
went down with Tyrone and me. As I walked into the
classroom, I was kind of nervous. I held my head down
as I made my way to my seat. I glanced over to where
he would normally sit and then quickly looked away. I
wonder if the school knew he was working undercover.
There's no way they didn't know.

The instructor walked into the room, and I tried my
best not to make eye contact with him either. The last
time I was here, we had that little altercation. I hope he
learned his lesson and stayed in his fucking place. I only
had a few weeks before graduation, and even though my
grades were not the best, I think I had enough to pull
through. I was banking on bettering my future with this
degree.

Suddenly, I felt drowsy, and my head fell a few times.
This wasn't good because I needed to catch up on the
lessons that I'd missed.

"Miss Jones, are you sleeping in my classroom?" I heard that bastard yell.

I quickly opened my eyes, feeling embarrassed. "No, I'm not sleeping. I was not feeling well, so I hung my head down a little. I'm still paying attention to what you're saying."

"I'm sorry to hear that you're not feeling well, but maybe you should excuse yourself and go to the nurse's office."

"I don't need to go to the nurse's office. I can manage," I said in a high-pitched, disrespectful tone.

"We'll talk after class, Miss Jones."

I wanted to yell "fuck you" to his bitch ass, but I calmed myself down. I realized that he was provoking me to act out. There's no way I would give him the satisfaction his old wrinkled ass was seeking.

While his back was turned, I quickly glanced at the time. Only fifteen minutes were left in this class. I was hungry, nauseated, and tired as hell. I hurried and did the assignment.

"Well, this is it, guys. We have a test coming up Friday. Please come prepared, as this will determine if you graduate. Miss Jones, we need to talk."

Here this fuck nigga goes again with this talking shit. I swear, yo, I need to report his ass for harassment and get it over with. I watched as everyone left one by one.

I walked up to his desk and stood there with an attitude. Finally, he walked over to me.

"Miss Jones, I don't know what has gotten into you lately, but your behavior in my classroom is very unprofessional and disrespectful."

"What . . . What are you talking about? Ever since I turned down your little advance, you've been coming at me. *You're* the professional. How about you keep it like that? Like I told you, I don't know how many of these bitches you done fucked to up their grades, but I'm not them. I have brains and don't need to fuck my way to the top."

"I've been teaching for over twenty years, and I've come across your kind more than a few times. You turn up your nose at an older man like me and cling to the young thugs that ain't got nothing but a hard dick and a bunch of little bastards running around. Don't you act like that pussy is gold."

He took a few steps toward me. Then without warning, he grabbed my neck and tried kissing me. I instantly started to flash back to when I was in the hotel. I reached for his balls and latched on to them, squeezing them with all my might.

"You bitch! You're going to pay for this."

"Not before you do."

I let go, then used my Chromebook to hit him upside the head twice. He stumbled back while he held on to his crotch. I dashed out of the room and ran straight out of the building. I knew I was safe once I got outside. Finally, I stopped to catch my breath and to get myself together.

"You a'ight, girl? You look like you just saw a ghost," Shayla, one of the few chicks I deal with, asked me as she walked up to me.

"No, I'm not. That bitch-ass nigga just tried to rape me!" I yelled while fighting back the tears.

"Who?" She looked around.

"The damn instructor Greene."

She wrapped her arms around me. "Come on. Let's sit on the bench for a second. You're still shaking, girl. What happened?" she quizzed.

"He told me he needed to talk to me, so I stayed behind. Then this nigga tried to kiss me."

"Baby, you need to go to the counselor and report his ass. You can't let him get away with it."

"I don't have no proof. I'm just a student, and he brags that he's been teaching for years. They're not going to take my word for it. He'll just accuse me of coming on to him."

"I'll go in there with you. But, wait, I ain't seen Tyrone in his class today. Is he sick 'cause he's always here?"

"Girl, that's another topic."

"Oh wait . . . Did y'all break up? I didn't mean to intrude."

"Long story, just know you won't be seeing him in class anymore."

"Wow . . . Okay. Promise me you'll think about reporting Greene. But, listen, I got to run. You sure you're going to be okay?"

"Yeah, I'm sure. My truck is right over there."

"A'ight, chica. Here, take my number. Call me if you ever need to talk or grab a bite."

"Thanks, girlie."

We exchanged numbers and parted ways. I made my way to my truck, still trying to calm myself. I thought about what she said about reporting Greene, but honestly, I just need to get home and get in my bed.

The next day, I was moved to another class. I didn't even bother to find out why. I was happy that I wouldn't be dealing with Greene anymore. This was a female teacher, and she was pretty cool. I wasn't going to be here for much longer, so I decided to focus on graduating.

Claire

It's funny when bitches were making lots of money and living the high life, you couldn't hear a word from them. Not even a conversation on social media. But as soon as they fall, they all in the inbox asking for the number. My ass sat there for a good ten minutes, debating if I would call this bitch or not. My ass knew there had to be a reason for her to reach out to me. So being the nosy bitch I was, I called her ass, and, boy, was I right. The bitch was down and out and needed someone to talk to. And guess who that was? The same old cousin that she never paid any attention to.

I would see the pictures of her living the high and mighty life, shopping sprees, the latest designer clothes, and showing off the new nigga. I used to look at that nigga and wish I had one like him. But I guess bitches only post the good shit on social media 'cause, boy, was I shocked to find out the nigga was cheating on her, even beat on her a few times. I guess him spending money on her was enough for her to put up with his fuckery.

I fought so hard not to show the smile on my face when she was telling me how much shit she's been through. The craziest shit I heard, though, was when the bitch told me the Feds were involved. So, this bitch was scared. Shit, ain't no need to be scared now when you were spending all that money and living the good life. I'm pretty sure they had a cot for her in one of those prisons.

I might be coming off as a hating-ass bitch, but I'm not. I hated bitches that feel like their shit could make patties. I really didn't know the bitch that good. True, we were cousins, but the few times we spent around each other, she's always made me feel like I was beneath her. I really don't know why 'cause the bitch wasn't prettier than me. I damn sure was a bad bitch while her ass was just regular.

After talking to the bitch, I learned she had some money in the bank. I was kind of broke, and the nigga Jaquan that I was fucking just broke it off with me. I was devastated when he came home and told me it was over. Five fucking years I rode with this nigga through his prison stint, putting money on his books, and visiting him every weekend. I could barely get out of bed to shower or eat for weeks. Depression was hitting me hard. This was the change that I needed to start over and probably see what's up with one of these Richmond niggas. I heard these niggas' money out here was long, and they had no problem spending on bitches. Shit, I was here for it all. After messing with Jaquan's broke ass for so long, it's only fair that I snatch up one of these money niggas. The thought of that made me smile.

The ringing of my phone dragged me out of my thoughts. I looked at the caller ID, and it was my bestie, Maria. I sure missed her crazy ass. Soon, I'll let her come down to visit. Then maybe she can move down here too.

"Whassup, bitch?"

"Hey, boo boo, how is it going in the Rich City?"

"Bitch, I ain't get a chance to explore the city yet, but soon, though. I plan on getting pampered this weekend and hit the scene."

"Uh-huh. So, where is your cousin? How y'all getting along?"

"Girl, that bitch at school. I forgot to tell you that stupid bitch is pregnant."

"Pregnant? For who, the money nigga?"

"Bitch, you're not going to believe this. She don't know if it's for him or the Fed nigga that she was fucking."

"Bitch, close the front door. You're lying," she yelled in excitement.

"Best friend, you know I don't tell no lies. Bitch, I just sit back, waiting for this disaster to happen. So much shit going on, but wait until that baby is born. That's when the *real* drama will start. I'm here for it all, biiiitch."

"Girl, I don't blame you. If she treats you the way you say she does, then that bitch deserves everything she got coming to her. Shit, you didn't have to move out there to help her. I told you, I would say fuck that ungrateful-ass bitch and move back home."

"Girl, nah, 'cause I'm trying to get over Jaquan and find me one of these niggas with money. If her ass was lucky enough to find Mari, I know I can find me one. I just need to get out there. Anyway, I hear that bitch car pulling up. I'ma call you later, bitch."

"A'ight."

I hung up the phone and made my way to the living room. I quickly cut on the television, propped my legs up, and waited.

"Hey, you. What's going on?"

"Hey, cuz. How was school, girl?" I inquired.

She walked in, flopped down on the couch, and started to take off her shoes.

"Girl, let's just say I'm ready for this class to be over already."

"It's that bad? If you want, I can help you with your homework and stuff. I ain't the brightest, but I know a little sump'n sump'n."

"Thanks, girl. I got it. I'm just happy school will be over before I have this baby."

"I know you are. Have you spoken to Mari?"

"Nah, about what?"

"I just thought you would tell him about the baby."

"Nah, I love him and everything, but telling him about this baby would only be an invitation for him to come back into my life. I've been trying to get over him. It's not easy, but I'm trying. Sometimes, I want to run to him, but each time, I'm reminded of the bitch he got pregnant and all the other shit he did to me. I'm living in a fucking three-bedroom house because of him. That nigga really fucked up with me."

"I hear you, cuz, and I support you one hundred percent in whatever you do. I admire your strength to walk away from him for good. Trust, you and the baby gon' be good."

"Aye, cuz. How come I haven't seen you working since you got here?"

"Work? Oh yeah, girl. I be working at night when it's quiet. I got to keep the money flowing."

"Oh, OK, 'cause the rent is due in a day or two, and I need your half."

"Girl, don't worry. I got you."

"A'ight, boo. I'm about to lie down."

"Okay, cuz. Get you some rest."

I rolled my eyes so damn hard. I'm surprised they didn't get stuck in the back of my head. Whew, that bitch almost caught me in a lie. I was a pro at this 'cause my mind was too fast for her slow country ass.

I heard her close her door. Then I got up and walked into my room. I had a plan. I wasn't sure how I would execute it, but I was determined to see it through. My darling cousin will learn sooner or later that I wasn't the one to be fucked with.

Mari

Three Weeks Later

I was released from the hospital an hour ago. I decided to stay at Shonda's crib so she could help me while I recovered. I was doing way better than before, but I was still in pain. The doctor gave me some Percocet, so I should be good.

"Well, babe, it ain't much, but make yourself at home. What the Mexicans say, '*mi casa, su casa,*'" she said as she helped me up the stairs.

"Appreciate it."

This pain kicked my ass. I sat down on the bed, trying to catch my breath. Those stairs knocked the wind out of me. I was eager to get my strength back. Shit, I missed being out in the streets handling business. Me not able to move around like I want to was in the motherfucking way.

My phone started to ring. I grabbed my jacket and took the phone out. It was G calling.

"Yo."

"Aye, bro. I'm at the door."

"A'ight."

"Yo, shawty, go let G in for me."

She shot me a strange look before she walked off. I don't know what that was about, but I'm sure I'll find out later.

A minute later, G walked into the room. "Welcome home, bro."

"Thanks, yo. I'm happy to be up out of that hospital. I mean, the nurses were nice to a nigga, but the food was horrible. Plus, I need to get back into the swing of things."

"Yeah, for sure. I still think you shoulda came to the crib."

"Bro, I know I could've, but shawty said I could come here, and she'll cater to a nigga. You know I couldn't pass up that offer."

"Nigga, you can barely walk, and here you go thinking about some pussy. Yo' ass ain't learn yet." He busted out laughing.

"Nigga, my dick ain't hurt." I laughed out.

"You a fool, yo, but I'm happy you feeling a lot better. I feel kind of lonely out here without you. My brother out here with me, but it's not the same, fam."

"Bro, the doctor say a few weeks of physical therapy, and I'll be brand new. I'm ready, homie. So enough about me. Any word in the streets 'bout them niggas?"

"This what I heard. The nigga Damion that we popped, he wasn't at the park by himself. His brother was parked in the cut. Supposedly, he saw e'erything that went down."

"So, you telling me this pussy nigga's brother shot me? Yo, where that pussy nigga stay at? He want smoke? I got all the motherfucking smoke for that nigga. Fuck that. Where his mama stay at?" I yelled.

"Calm down, bro. I'ma handle the shit. I was waiting to run it by you."

"Bro, I know you want to handle it for me, but this is personal. This nigga violated me, and I want my face to be the last one he see before he join his bitch-ass brother. I'm done playing wit' these clown-ass niggas."

"A'ight, bro. Well, you know I'm ready to go whenever."

"Already, bro."

"Aye, bro. You ain't hear from Akila? I been callin' her, but it seems like she blocked me or something."

"Yeah, she hit me up a few times asking about how you doing. I doubt she would block you. She seems really worried about you."

"Hmmm, yeah. The last time we talked, she seemed irritated. Then she quickly hung up. When I called the next day, the phone kept going to voicemail."

"Well, my nigga, you might've fucked up with a real bitch this time."

"Yeah, I know she still love me. Shit, I'm that nigga that fucked her and let her squirt all over the place. I spent tons of money on her. Trust me; she out there without anything. Sooner or later, that bitch will come crawling back to daddy. Trust me. That bitch-ass nigga she fucking with can't fuck her like I do. I see that weakness in that nigga's eyes."

"Yo, I still can't believe you went up in that nigga's shit. Yo, what if that nigga had a gun and started blasting at yo' ass?"

"Fuck that nigga. He's a bitch."

"Yeah, me and you know that scared niggas are dangerous as fuck. But you're right. Fuck that nigga. His bitch ass can get it, for sho'."

We sat there talking about the business and what's been going on in the streets. I was eager to get back out there. I know G got it, but I was the face of my business, and I know niggas rock with me hard as hell.

"Yes, daddy, fuck meeeee," Shonda screamed as she held on to the headboard and squeezed her pussy muscles down on my dick while riding me.

I cuffed her ass and pulled her down on the dick. It's been over a month since I fucked, and it showed. It was barely a good ten minutes, and I was ready to bust. I tried to hold it in, but shawty was being greedy with the dick. Fuck it. I decided to let it out.

"Fuck, I'm coming, babes," I whispered.

"Let it all out, boo. Come all up in this wet pussy. Yes, daddy, let it out," she said seductively.

I gripped onto her hips and exploded all up in her. Maybe I should've waited until I got my strength back to fuck 'cause I was in pain, twisting and turning. I done popped about five pills, but the pain didn't even budge. Times like this, I wish I could drive so that I could get my hand on some blow. I know this would help the pain. But instead, I lay on my back, thinking I really need to get better.

This was my first day with the physical therapist, and I was looking forward to it. Shonda pulled up to the facility and helped me out. I was walking way better than before. Soon, I won't be needing anyone's help.

"Hello, we are here to see Tamryn."

"Good morning. You must be Mari Owens. Come with me. Tamryn is expecting you guys. I must tell y'all, she is very good at what she does. Trust her methods, and she'll have you in superb shape in no time."

I smiled as we followed her a few offices down. She knocked on the door before we entered.

"Tamryn, this is Mr. Owens, the patient you were waiting on." She then walked out.

"Mr. Owens and Miss Shonda. Welcome to the South Side Rehabilitation Center. Please have a seat so we can get started. Mr. Owens, I've read your files that were submitted, and I have to say, you're a fighter. I'm going to tell you a little of what we do here at SRC, but first, I need your insurance card so I can bill the insurance company for services."

"I don't have no insurance."

"You don't—"

Before she could say another word, I cut her off. "Listen, Tamryn, just let me know how much it is, and Shonda will cut you a check."

"Mr. Owens, from what I'm reading, you'll need about six weeks of intensive care. These treatments are not cheap. I can try to find a facility—"

"Again, Tamyra, no disrespect, but what is the total cost?"

"Okay, let me put your care plan together, and then I'll let you know."

"A'ight, cool."

We talked for about twenty minutes. I was examined by the doctor and then given a step-by-step treatment plan. Tamryn walked back into the room with a folder in her hand.

"So, the doctor spoke with you, and he also gave me a copy of treatments you will need to get up and run again. Each session will cost $504, and you would need around ten sessions minimum."

"Shonda, make sure the lady gets paid."

Tamryn looked at me, shocked. I smiled to myself. This bitch thought she was dealing with a regular-ass nigga. I wonder how she feels when she sees that I was a nigga with some money.

"Babes, I got to meet up with a client. You'll be here for about an hour, so I'll be back to get you."

"A'ight, yo."

"OK. Mr. Owens, are you ready to put in some work?"

"I was born ready."

That statement was very premature 'cause pain was busting my ass each exercise that she required of me. I wanted to quit, but I wasn't no bitch, and I sure wasn't going to fold in front of no bitch.

"You're doing great, Mr. Owens."

I love the way my name rolls off her tongue. I thought I would get an old, white-headed lady when the doctor suggested physical therapy. Instead, I was shocked when I laid eyes on Tamryn. She was slender, but I soon noticed she had a phat ass when she bent over.

I felt an erection when she stood close to me, showing me a technique. Shit, I tried to take my mind off her phat ass, hoping my dick would go down. I hurriedly used my hand to adjust myself when she turned to get her clipboard.

"Are you okay?" she asked me with a smile.

"Yeah, I'm straight, love. Aye, I was wondering if I could take you out sometime, though?"

"Huh? You talking to me?" she asked while pointing to herself.

"We're the only ones in the room, love, so, yeah, I'm talking to you."

"Isn't that your woman that left earlier?" She gave me a shocked look.

"Nah, me and shawty cool, that's all. But don't worry 'bout all that. I'm tryin'a take *you* out."

"I don't know about all that. I think it's against company policy to go on dates with patients. So, no, I can't risk my job."

I looked at her and smiled. I could tell she's playing hard to get. From the look she was giving me, I knew she wanted to give me the pussy. I inched closer to her to the point where I could smell the mint candy on her breath. I could feel her breathing faster. I took her chin into my hand.

"What the fuck is going on?" Shonda's voice startled me.

"Yo, chill and lower your voice," I demanded. I was hoping she wouldn't create a scene.

"Chill out? What the fuck was you doing, kissing this bitch? I leave you to run errands, and this what y'all doing? Where's this bitch boss at?" She started to walk off. I grabbed her arm with a tight grip.

"Yo, chill the fuck out. Ain't nobody was kissing. Shawty was only trying to help me."

"Help you? Let me the fuck go. Dr. Rowe needs to know this bitch crossed the line. What kind of facility are they running? A whorehouse?" she said at the top of her lungs.

I wasn't trying to hear that shit. I hung on to her and pulled her until we were out of the building.

"Let go of me."

"Bitch, quit acting stupid," I yelled in a serious tone.

"*Bitch?* So you calling me out my name for this bitch you just met?" she quizzed while pulling away from me.

"You know what? You want to be out here acting like one of these stupid-ass girls, so go ahead. I'ma get my shit out of yo' crib. I'm done dealing with this old weak-ass shit you doing." I started walking away.

"Are you serious right now? I caught you in a bitch face, and you want to act like *I* done you wrong? You know what, nigga? Do what the fuck you please." She followed closely behind me.

I waited for her to unlock the ride. Then I got in. I was pissed off that this bitch came back when she did. I was this close to getting this bitch's number. Now, I doubt I'll ever be able to get it. This bitch in the motherfucking way for real. I shook my head in disgust as I stared out the window, picturing me banging the nurse from the back. Shit, my dick started to get hard again.

Chapter Fifteen

Akila

My grandmother used to warn me about growing up too fast, and back then, I thought she was speaking a bunch of gibberish. Now, I can look back and say Grandma was on to something. This pregnancy was kicking my ass. The vomiting was the worst. There are days when I can barely get out of bed. I wish that I wasn't doing this alone, but it is what it is. I know I need to pull up my big-girl panties and do what I need to do for me and my child.

I'm kind of excited that I get to know the sex of my baby next week. I can start shopping for him or her. In my heart, I'm hoping it's a girl, but if it's a boy, that's also cool. As long as my baby is healthy, then I'm good with it.

Ring, ring.

As soon as I stepped out of the shower, the ringing of my phone startled me. I walked over to the dresser and looked at the caller ID. Unknown. Who the fuck is calling me from an unknown number? Fuck that. I'm not answering. Shit, I'm behind on a few bills, so it might be the bill collector. I done heard stories about them harassing folks. Oh well, they would have to wait until I figured out what the fuck I was going to do.

I dropped the towel and started lotioning my body, making sure I massaged my stomach. Then I felt a kick. I placed my hand on the spot, hoping to feel another one. Then the damn phone started ringing again. I looked over at the phone and stomped over to grab it.

"Hello," I yelled in an annoyed tone.

"Akila, it's me, Tyrone. Before you hang up, I just want to talk to you."

"What the fuck do you want? I thought I made myself clear that we have nothing to talk about. I was hoping that you would get the hint and leave me the fuck alone. Don't you have some crime out there that needs your attention?" I was ready to hang up in this nigga's face.

"Akila, I know you're pregnant. I just want to know if it's my baby. I want to be there if it is."

"Me being pregnant is none of your fucking business, and no, it's not your fucking child. I'm warning you, stay the fuck away from me before I hop my black ass down to the fed building and make a complaint against you."

I didn't wait for a response. I hung up. Then I took a seat on the bed, trying to get my breathing under control. How the fuck did this nigga know I was pregnant? I haven't seen him since the day at the station. Was he stalking me? This shit was starting to become creepy as hell.

I got dressed and decided to head out. It's been days since I've been out of the house. My fridge was looking empty, and I needed food. I grabbed my phone and purse, then walked out of my room.

"Hey, girl," I greeted my cousin, who was laid in her favorite spot watching television. This seems to be all she did all day, every day.

"Hey, cuz. Where you off to, girl? You need some company?"

"Nah, I'm straight. About to go by Walmart to pick up a few things for the house."

"Oh, okay, girl. Call me if you need me."

I didn't respond. I just kept walking. I love my cousin, and I was happy she's here with me, especially now that I'm pregnant, but she has started to become a burden. Before coming down here, she said she was making money. Now she's here, and she doesn't contribute to anything. So, I have to keep using up my little savings to pay these bills. I ain't going to lie. I'm sick of this shit. I'd rather struggle by myself than have a grown-ass woman living off me. I be trying to give her a break, but I don't know how much longer this will last.

I pulled out of the driveway while checking out my surroundings. After what Tyrone said, I wasn't sure this nigga wasn't following me around. I rolled the window down, letting some cool breeze in. Then I cut the music on and just let my mind wander freely.

Doing grocery shopping wasn't one of my good qualities, but a bitch was hungry, and I needed to feed my baby. So I grabbed a few packs of chicken wings. It's been a minute since I had baked chicken. That used to be one of my favorites that my grandma made when she was alive. I had my headphones on listening to Moneybagg's latest album, *Reset*. I swear this nigga was gangsta, and his voice be making wet.

Suddenly, I felt a tap on my shoulder. I dropped the can of corn in the cart and turned around. It was this nigga G. Wait, what the fuck he was doing here? I started feeling nervous. Was Mari also here too? I scanned the area around me.

"Yo, Kila, what's up? I thought that was you."

"Hey, G. How you doing?" I spoke softly.

"Yo, what the fuck? You pregnant? Do my boy know you pregnant?"

"No, your boy don't know I'm pregnant, and I don't think it's his business," I politely responded.

"Akila, look, shawty, I know my nigga hurt you, but you can't say he don't love you. If this his seed, he needs to know about it."

"Look, G, no disrespect, but it's *not* his fucking business. Now, I got to go."

I hurried off without hearing what else he was saying. I pushed the cart quickly, going to the register that was open and wasted no time putting the groceries on the belt. Within minutes, I was up out of there. I practically ran with the cart to my truck. I threw the groceries in the back, pushed the cart to the side, and climbed into my car. Then I pulled out of the parking lot, hoping he wasn't following me.

This was straight bullshit. Of all the people I could've run into, I had to run into him. I knew he was going to tell Mari that I was pregnant. This was another stress that I didn't need right now. I slammed my hand down on the steering wheel. This day can't get any worse. First Tyrone, now this nigga.

Before I pulled into my driveway, I checked my rear-view mirror to make sure no one followed me home. Everything was clear, and I hurriedly pulled into the driveway. I let out a sigh of relief when I got inside the house.

"Cuz, you good? You look like you seen a ghost."

"Girl, I just ran into Mari's boy at the grocery store. He saw I was pregnant."

"Are you fucking serious? You *know* he's going to tell."

"I know. I don't need Mari thinking this his baby. I swear I just want to be left alone. Let me have my baby in peace."

"Girl, this some messy shit. Let me go get the groceries."

"Yeah."

I walked off into my room. I really didn't want to hear what my cousin had to say right now. It's my life and my decision.

Mari

It's been months since I got shot, and even though I was up and about, some days, the pain was kicking my ass. I tried to hide it 'cause I didn't want to come off as no weak nigga. I started popping the Percocet and even started fucking with the blow. See, I ain't no junkie, and soon as this pain goes away, I'll stop fucking with that shit. I took a few more drags, then folded the dollar bill back up. I was careful not to let Shonda know what I was doing 'cause I didn't want motherfuckers in my business.

My phone started vibrating in my sweatpants. I pulled it out while trying to stay calm.

"Yo," I said to my boy.

"Whaddup, yo? I thought we was going to handle some business today?"

"I was just going to call you, my nigga," I lied while I bounced all around the room.

"Yo, bro, guess who I just seen?"

"Who, nigga? You know I'm not good at no guessing game." I was getting irritated. This nigga was messing up my high.

"Akila, nigga. And guess what else . . . She pregnant."

"She wha-what?" I stuttered.

"You heard me, nigga. She got a big-ass stomach in front of her."

"You sure that's who you seen?" I asked.

"I was in Walmart, and I saw her shopping. We talked for a minute."

"Did she ask about me? Did she tell you who she pregnant by?"

"Nah, but she seemed nervous when she saw me. I figure she didn't want me to tell you I seen her."

"Yo, bro, that might be my seed. If it is, why the fuck she ain't call me and tell me?"

"Maybe it ain't your seed. Remember, she was fucking that other nigga."

"Yeah, but shit, I want to know for sure."

"I don't know all you did to shawty, but it's like she don't fuck with you. I still tell you, she was the best bitch you had. No disrespect to Shonda, but Akila was genuine."

"Yeah, I hear you. Listen, I'ma come see you in a few. Where you at?"

"I'm by South Side Plaza now, but I'ma be at the spot in an hour."

"A'ight."

I took a seat on the edge of the bed. Yo, this shit just brought out a lot of raw emotions. Who the fuck is Kila pregnant by? Is it me, or did she make that square-ass nigga run up in her raw? I pulled out the dollar bill and sniffed a few more lines. This shit can't be happening. That's *my* bitch. We were supposed to be together forever.

"Hey, babe." Shonda walked into the room.

"What's good?"

Damn, that was close. I didn't hear the garage door go up. I folded the dollar bill behind my back and stuffed it into my pocket.

"Are you okay?" she said as she walked over to me.

"Yeah, I'm good. You know how them Percocet be having me."

"Babe, I think it's time you stop taking those. You don't want to get addicted to them. I have an uncle who was

in a bad accident, and he started off with Percocet, then
gradually started sniffing powder."

"I'm *not* your fucking uncle. I sell blow—I don't sniff
that shit. Doing drugs is for weak-ass niggas, and I damn
sure ain't one."

"I'm sorry, babe. I wasn't saying you one. I was only
telling you about my uncle."

This bitch just added to my aggravation. I went to
the closet, grabbed an outfit, and then jumped into the
shower. I couldn't seem to get Akila out of my head. I
need to find out where she's staying at. I need answers.
After I got dressed, I grabbed my keys and my phone and
started walking out of the room.

"Where you going? Damn, nigga, I just got here," she
said.

"I got to meet up with G. We got some business to
handle."

"You always got business to handle. Ever since you
been feeling better, you don't be home anymore. How
you think we're supposed to work out if you're never
here?"

"Yo, don't you have a company to run? How the fuck
you think the bills get paid if you want a nigga up under you twenty-four seven? Listen, I'm not no nigga
that's going to lay up under no female. If that's what
you're looking for, you got the wrong nigga."

"Hmmm . . . I'm starting to think *you* the wrong nigga.
Period."

I took a few steps back toward her. "What's that supposed to mean?"

"I mean, we don't do shit no more. Not even fuck. Lately,
when I try to have sex with you, you draw away or make
up some dumb-ass excuse about why you can't. I ain't no
fool. I notice everything, even when I don't say shit."

"Shawty, I done told you, I have a lot of shit on my mind. I can't focus on no pussy when I got street shit to handle. If you can't understand that, then, oh well."

"Yeah, that ho must be making you feel special. But don't worry. You'll get tired of her ass soon, and you'll be crawling back to me in no time."

"Ha-ha, you know you crazy. You actually believe this shit you saying. Listen, I got to go."

As I walked down the stairs, I could hear her cussing, but I didn't stop. This bitch was starting to get on my fucking nerves. It's time to get my own crib ASAP. There's no way I'm going to let no bitch dictate my moves. That pussy ain't that damn good. I plan on checking on the crib when I get back. I think that bitch was dragging her feet 'cause she wants a nigga up under her. It's time to get the fuck on.

I pulled up on my boy at the new detailing shop we opened. At first, I kept my brother's place running, but going there was getting to be too much for me. Even to this day, I can't believe he's not here no more. I decided to open up a new shop, bringing his workers over here. I then rented out the other shop.

I got out of the truck and walked into the shop. I greeted the fellas working and then made my way to the back. I walked into the back office, and G was sitting there smoking a blunt.

"Whaddup, bro?" I greeted him, and we exchanged daps.

"Coolin', fam. You want to hit this?" He passed the blunt to me. I took the blunt, then sat on the couch.

"Yo, I got the money from the weekend. I figure we can count it together and go through the numbers."

"All that shit gone?"

"Hell yeah, the workers ran through that shit. The workers saying that was straight raw."

"Yeah, my boi told me it was good shit straight from Colombia. Shit, the way it's going, we gon' need to double up on the next order."

"Yeah, the only thing with that is traveling from Texas with that shit. My boi brought the first order but told me in the future we got to go get that shit."

"Oh, word? We just gon' have to figure that shit out. Remember, there's not too many niggas we can trust out here. I rather keep this on the low. Don't want to fuck up the cash flow."

"I hear you, bro."

We counted the money to make sure everything was straight. Then we rapped about how we would continue taking over the city.

"Aye, bro, I need someone to find out where Akila staying now. I know she ain't really got no family, so I know she still in the city. I need to find out where ASAP."

"Nigga, I thought you was tight with ole girl, and y'all was taking y'all relationship to the next level."

"Yo, I'm tired of that bitch. Lately, I don't even want the pussy. It's like my dick won't even get hard."

"Nigga, you a fucking fool. I know this nigga. He a PI. He probably can find out where she at. I'ma need basic info to give to him. Nigga, don't say I ain't warn you. If you find her and find out that ain't yo' seed, you gon' be hurt, nigga."

"Man, fuck all that. I ain't worrying 'bout no feelings. I just want my bitch back, and if it means using the baby as a way to get her back, then, oh fucking well."

"Yo, nigga, you a dangerous dude. I ain't never under-stand how a foul nigga like you can get all the bad bitches, but a good nigga like myself always getting the ugly bitches." He shook his head and started laughing.

"That's 'cause you ain't sucking that pussy good. Nigga, I eat pussy, ass. I even let a bitch piss in my mouth," I busted out laughing.

"Nigga, you fucking sick. And to think we just shared blunts." We both busted out laughing now.

His phone started ringing so he answered it. I grabbed the duffel bag with the cash and threw up the peace sign before I walked out of the office. Before leaving, I stopped in the front to check on the workers. After that, I left, threw the bag on the seat, and pulled off.

I was on the way to the crib, but once I got on the Powhite Parkway, I noticed a black SUV, probably a Denali or a Suburban, behind me. After getting shot, I was more on point of my surroundings. I kept my eyes on it as I continued blasting Kevin Gates, "Luv Bug," thinking of all the shit I want to do to Akila. Shit, the old people say pregnant pussy is the best pussy.

I was about to turn into the subdivision when I noticed the truck was still behind me. I made a sharp turn, but the truck continued down the street instead of turning. I guess I was wrong. I wasn't being followed. After getting shot, my ass be on edge.

It's been over a week, and I still didn't get any news about Akila's whereabouts. I tried not to show it, but I was anxious and irritable at times. All this fucking money and connects I have, and I can't find the bitch I want. I grabbed my phone. It's been months since I logged on to Facebook. I ain't no social media kind of nigga, but I still had my account. I clicked on Akila's name. "Add Friend." *She unfriended me. Damn,* I thought. That shit kind of fucked me up a little. I threw the phone down and went to the kitchen to grab a drink. I took two big gulps of the Patrón. The liquor burned my throat going down, but I welcomed it.

"We need to talk," Shonda walked in and said.

Damn, this bitch just won't stop, I thought. I took another sip before turning around to face her.

"What's good?" I quizzed in a nonchalant tone.

"I'm tired of this, Mari."

"What you talkin' 'bout?"

"This, old stupid-ass relationship. You treat me like shit. You come and go whenever you feel like. This ain't how it supposed to be, so if this ain't what you want, you just need to say that so I can get the fuck on. I'm too good of a woman to get treated like this."

"Okay." I walked out of the kitchen.

"Okay? After all the shit that I've done for you, *this* is how you act? You know what? I should've left you with that other bitch. Y'all deserve each other."

I stopped and turned around, facing her. "Listen, don't call her no bitch no more. Oh, and I'll be gone before the weekend."

"Ha-ha, you checking me about that ho. I see why you acting all funny lately. Nigga, if you wanted that bitch, you should've said that. I ain't hard up for no nigga."

"Well, get the fuck out of my face then, bitch. Matter of fact, I'ma 'bout to get the fuck out now. I'll come get the rest of my shit tomorrow. Oh, and that company . . . Make sure you got money. I'm done dealing with yo' crazy ass, old dramatic-ass bitch."

I walked back down the stairs and pushed past that bitch. She grabbed my shirt and started crying.

"Is *this* how you gon' do me? I love you, Mari. We're good together. We make moves together."

"Shawty, I'm sorry, but I can't do this shit no more. You deserve a good nigga, and obviously, I'm *not* that nigga. Listen, I'ma leave you some money. You gon' be straight."

"You think I want money? I *had* money way before I started fucking with you. You think I did all this for money? I risked everything—even my fucking freedom—to be with you," she bawled.

"Shawty, trust me, I get that, and I'm sorry, but this ain't gon' work. I'm not focused on no relationship right now. I'm in these streets too much."

"I'm pregnant. I'm pregnant," she cried out.

"You *what?*" I looked at her suspiciously.

"That's right, Mari, I'm pregnant with *your* child. I just found out two days ago, but we been fighting so much, I was waiting on the right time to tell you."

"How far along are you?" I looked at her flat stomach.

"I took the home pregnancy test. I need to make a doctor's appointment."

"A'ight, I got to go. Let me know when it is so that I can go."

"You can't go, Mari. Me and my baby need you," she yelled out.

"Yo, shawty, you need to kill it."

"Kill it? You talking like it's an ant or some shit. It's our baby that was made out of love," she cried.

"Shawty, I got to fucking go."

I shoved her off me and opened the door. Then I practically jogged to my car. I jumped in and reversed out of the driveway. I saw her standing in the doorway, but I just turned my head to the street and sped off.

I couldn't wrap my head around what the fuck she was saying. Is this a lie, so I'll stay with her? Either way, I don't want no fucking baby with her. She needs to get a fucking abortion ASAP. I want Akila back, and I can't allow anything to get in the way this time.

Shonda

Tears rolled down my face as I crumbled to the floor. I just told this nigga I was pregnant, and his response was "kill it." I never thought he would be that cold toward me after all we been through.

There was no way I would just sit back and watch him run back to that bitch. That bitch could never love him the way I do. I love him and have shown him repeatedly, but I guess that wasn't enough. How the fuck he's going to tell me he's moving out? I can't believe what I heard. I had to share him once, but I'll be damned if I'm going to share him with another ho again.

I finally stopped crying and pulled myself onto the couch. I needed a drink and not just any drink. I needed a strong one. I walked upstairs into my bedroom and grabbed my laptop. If Mari wants to play, well, let the games begin. I pulled up his offshore bank accounts. Time to move some money around. This street nigga will soon find out I'm not the dumb, naïve college girl that he thinks I am. I'm not here to play with this nigga.

It's been days since I heard from Mari. I held the phone to my ear as I listened to his voicemail come on. I've left him over twenty messages, and he still has not called me back. Where the fuck was he at? I need to find him, I thought as I threw the phone down, grabbed the pillow, and buried my head in it. The tears flowed freely as my chest tightened. I can't believe Mari was treating me like this after everything I gave up for him. I helped him when no one else was there for him, and *this* is what I get? The tears wouldn't stop flowing, and my cries got louder.

"Fuck you, Mari. You will see—you'll see that I'm *not* one of these stupid bitches," I cried out. "You-you'll see," I yelled out.

I couldn't sleep last night. I just kept pacing back and forth. There were times when I stood by the window with my head against the windowpane, hoping he would pull into the driveway. But nothing happened. My feet got tired, so I stumbled to the bed. It was about 4:00 a.m. when I finally lay down and dozed off.

My head was pounding hard. I walked over to the cabinet and grabbed me the pill bottle. I took out two of the Aleve, took them, and walked back to my bed. Then I heard my phone ringing and wasted no time grabbing it up. But I was disappointed. It was one of my clients. I really wasn't in shape to handle business. I'll call her back tomorrow or something. I threw the phone back on the bed and sat there thinking. That's when something hit me. I pulled out my drawer, looking for a card I put in there a few months ago.

"Ha-ha . . ." I laughed.

When I was given this card, I thought about throwing it in the trash. At the time, I knew there was no way I would use it, but look at God. I might just need to reach out. After all, we might have a common enemy. I found the card and looked at it. . . . Desperate times call for desperate measures, and I was *very* desperate. I grabbed my phone and dialed the number on the card.

"Hello," a male voice answered.

"Hey, I don't know if you remember me, but you gave me your card awhile back."

"Yes, sure. What can I do for you?"

I started feeling nervous and thought about hanging up.

"Hello, are you there?" he asked.

Claire

"I'm hittin' that ass from the back, lovebug; Say this
dick just turned her out, and it's a love drug . . ."

I grinded my hips side to side in a circular motion
while listening to Kevin Gates's latest song, "Luv Bug."
It's been over four months since I got dick or even got
my pussy sucked. Who knows what tonight might bring.
Just in case a bitch got lucky, I made sure I shaved and
washed my pussy extra good. The thought of getting
fucked sent shock waves through my body. I was tired of
using my bullet. It was time for me to feel a man's touch.

I finished getting dressed and applied a little makeup. I
was looking sexy as fuck. I turned my ass around to look
in the mirror, grabbed my purse, cut off my room light,
and closed my door. Then I knocked on Akila's door.

"Come in," she yelled.

Sure, I thought, and I rolled my eyes. I opened the
door with a huge smile plastered across my face.

"Hey, cuz, I'm going to step out for a minute."

"Really, all dressed up? Let me find out you have a
date." She shot me a strange look.

"Well, I met a friend, and we're going for drinks." I
smiled from ear to ear.

"OK. Where y'all going?"

"I think he said some lounge down by Shockoe Bottom."

"Well, cuz, please be careful. You know these Richmond
niggas are crazy, and if anything feels funny, call me. I
might be pregnant, but I'll still come up with something."

"Girl, I'ma be good. I have a feeling we're going to hit
it off well. Who knows, I might not come home tonight."

"Go on with yo' bad self. Let him use a condom. You
don't want to end up like me, knocked up."

"Byeee, I'm gone. Love you. I'll call you if I'm staying
out."

"A'ight, girl. Lock the door behind you."

"Okeydokey."

I closed the door, then sashayed out of the house after locking it behind me. I was looking forward to my date tonight. It's been over a week since we started talking on social media. I plan on putting this tight, wet pussy on him tonight. He ain't going to have no choice but to wife me. I smiled at the thought of that. Life would definitely change drastically for me.

The GPS let me know I had reached my destination. I found a parking space and parked, then took a few seconds to check my hair and makeup. I made sure my lipstick was popping, making my lips more attractive to kiss. After that, I got out of my car and straightened my clothes before putting on my sexiest walk and entering the building. I took a quick glance around and saw my date sitting by the bar. He wasn't hard to recognize 'cause, baby, that man was fiiiiine. He saw me and stood up. I walked over to him, and we hugged. I held on a little longer than I anticipated.

"What's going on, beautiful?" he asked while pulling out my chair.

"You're what's up, handsome," I replied in a sexy, seductive voice. I took a seat beside him and couldn't stop staring at him. He was a fine species of a man with a bit of roughness around the edge.

"What you drinking, love?"

"Hmmm . . . Let me see . . ." I glanced around the bar and waved for the bartender.

"Yes, how may I help you?"

"Can you make me a fruity drink? Nothing too strong."

"Sure. Do you like rum? I can make you a Jamaican Rum Punch."

"Yeah, that will work."

I noticed my date got him a shot of Patrón along with a beer. We started talking. This was strange since I'm normally shy when I first meet a man, but here I was, sitting up here, vibing with this nigga like we've known each other for a lifetime. I couldn't stop staring. I had to admit, he was much finer in person than the pics that he posted on Facebook.

Lord, his voice was giving me the chills. I had to cross my legs because my pussy was throbbing through my thong. Lord, I hope pussy juice doesn't spill out on this dress that I'm wearing. I would hate for the embarrassment. How would I explain that it wasn't piss, but instead, pussy juice? We continued talking about our lives and how we were interested in getting to know each other.

"So, I know you said you're not in no relationship, but do you have any kids?" I asked him, then took a sip of my drink.

"Kids? Nah, I ain't been that lucky. What about you? Do you have any crazy baby daddies that I need to know about?"

"No, sir. I don't have any of those. I guess you can say I need a husband first. But I won't be anyone's baby mama. I ain't tryin'a be like these other chicks out here. I need to know we're going to be a family."

"I hear that. I can respect it. You're a woman that knows what she wants. Ain't nothing wrong with that."

"It's getting late. What do you plan on doing for the rest of the night?" I probably was coming off strong, but I believed we wasted too much time talking about irrelevant bullshit. Truth is, I didn't give a fuck if he had a baby mother or not. I'm not worried about no bitch. I'm just trying to get in where I fit in.

"I mean, I was trying to see what's up with you and shit. We can get out of here and go somewhere more private if you like." He waved for the bartender. "Let me get the tab, please."

"That sounds like a plan." I smiled.

He paid the tab, and I watched as he walked over to a few niggas. I checked my phone to see if I had any missed calls. There was none, which was great. I didn't want to talk to anyone while I was on this date and definitely not my annoying-ass cousin.

"You ready, shawty?" he said as he walked over to me.

"Yup, let's go."

We walked out of the lounge and into the parking lot. He stopped and turned to face me. He was so close to me I could feel his breath all over my face. I wanted to grab and kiss him, but my inner self was trying hard to control my ho tendencies.

"I was thinking about getting a room. We can drink, smoke, and chill."

I shot him a sneaky look . . . "Sounds good," I chuckled.

"Follow me then."

"Alrighty."

I got in my car and followed him. He got on Broad Street. I was hoping he wasn't taking me to no bull-shit-ass motel. My worries were put to rest when I saw him pull into the Hilton on Broad Street. I pulled into the parking space beside him and parked. I sat in the car and waited to see what he was doing. He got out of the car and walked over to me.

"Yo, here's some money. Go get the room. I'm waiting on my boy to pull up real quick so I can handle something." He handed me two crisp one-hundred-dollar bills.

Then he walked off to his car, and I grabbed my stuff and got out of the car. I twisted my hips from side to side as I walked into the hotel entrance. I was 100 percent sure he was paying attention to how phat my ass was. Shit, that was my best asset—Phat ass with a tiny waist and DD breasts.

After paying for the room, I made my way to the elevator. I texted him the room number. *This is nice,* I thought as I flopped down on the bed. I rubbed my hand over the sheets, thinking all sorts of dirty things. The magic I want to happen tonight will be going down on this bed. I decided to freshen up in the bathroom before he came up. The first thing I did was stick my two fingers in my pussy and then to my nose. I know it's probably gross, but shit, I had to make sure my shit was still fresh for when I sit on his face. I can't afford no nigga to clown me because of no musty pussy.

Thirty minutes passed, and this nigga still didn't show up. I started to feel slightly upset. This was our date night, so I don't understand why the fuck he was handling business. That shit can wait. I'm trying to get fucked and sucked on.

I must've dozed off. When I heard the door open, I jumped up and straightened my hair. He walked into the room and threw his keys on the table.

"My bad, yo. I had to handle something right quick."

"That's fine," I lied.

I was no longer upset now that I saw his ass. He took off his shirt, revealing his toned, tattooed-up body. Then he took a seat on the bed and started rolling a blunt. After that, he took a liquor bottle out of the bag he carried in the room.

"My boy just gave me this. I know you probably don't fuck wit' no hard liquor."

"Shit, I need something to drink, so I guess I'll be drinking that."

We sat drinking and smoking. I started to cough uncontrollably. I'm not going to front. I'm not no smoker, but I was trying to hang.

"You straight?" he quizzed.

"Yeah, yeah," I managed to say in between coughs.

"This that loud, shawty. You got to take your time."

I had no idea what a damn loud is, so I assumed it was his way of saying it's some good weed. I passed the blunt back to him. That was it for me. Now, I took a sip of the drink.

"Damn, shawty, you ain't no smoker, I see," he chuckled.

"You're so right. I thought I was dying," I laughed.

He took a few more pulls before he put down the blunt. Then he started looking at me in a very seductive manner while he began rubbing on my thighs. Before I could react, his hand was all the way up my skirt. This was feeling so good. I wasted no time. I leaned in toward him and started kissing him. My body tingled all over as he leaned me down on the bed and inserted his fingers into my wet pussy. I started grinding on his fingers as we kissed passionately.

Within minutes, we were butt-ass naked. I thought he was about to eat my pussy when he grabbed my legs. Instead, he threw them on his shoulders and inserted his dick slowly into me. My body shook as I slid down on the dick. He slowly slid in and out, each time causing me to gasp. My pussy was hungry for the dick. I was loving the way he was taking his time with me. I prayed this feeling would last forever. My muscles got tighter as I grabbed him closely. My legs started shaking as I exploded on his dick. He held me close and started fucking me faster. It was then I felt the full effect of his dick. It was huge and thick. I cringed each time that he sank deeper and deeper into my guts.

"Yes, fuck this pussy, baby," I screamed. I was trying to get him excited so that he would come. I loved the dick, but my pussy was under intense pressure. I needed a break.

"Fuck, I'm about to bust," he yelled out as he fucked me harder.

"Come on, baby. Bust all up in this pussy," I yelled back.

I was sure he was about to come all up in me, but he pulled out and busted all over my stomach. *What the fuck is that for?* I thought. We lay there for a few minutes before we got up and showered together. We were both beat, so we got into bed. No words were spoken. I think we were both lost in our thoughts of each other. *I could really get used to this life,* I thought before dozing off.

I opened my eyes and looked around. Shit, daylight was peeping through the curtains. I looked over to the side of the bed. He was still asleep. I got off the bed and tiptoed to the bathroom. I forgot how hard he fucked me until I started peeing, and my pussy started burning like hot pepper. I hurried and got up, grabbed a washcloth, then wet it with cold water. I placed it between my legs. I needed to cool down this burning.

I checked my phone to see the time. It was after 10:00 a.m. Shit. I saw about five missed calls from my cousin. I thought about calling her back, but fuck it. I was a grown-ass woman. I don't need nobody checking up on me. She'll see me when I get in the house. Hopefully, it won't be today.

About an hour later, he woke up and sat up in bed, checking his phone.

"Hey, sleepyhead," I teased.

"What's good, shawty?" He got up and walked to the bathroom.

I lay in bed, thinking I was starved. I remember I didn't have any dinner the night before. I hoped he was planning on taking me to breakfast.

"Yo, I got to go," he said when he walked back into the room. He then grabbed his clothes and started to dress.

"Really? I thought we would go to breakfast. I'm starved."

"My bad, shawty. I need to be somewhere in another twenty minutes. I tell you what, though. I'll buy you breakfast, and next time, I'll make it up to you."

"All right then. I guess I'll get dressed."

I tried not to show it, but I was disappointed. After the night we had, I hoped he would want to spend the day with me.

"Here you go, shawty. I'll hit you up later." He handed me $300, kissed me on the lips, and walked out of the room.

Shit, I was happy for the money 'cause a bitch was broke, but I would rather spend time with him. I guess I need to get my ass up and get dressed. It was almost checkout time. I got dressed and made sure I had my phone and charger.

My pussy was still hurting when I walked, but it was so worth it. Being in his presence really showed me a different side of fucking with a street nigga. I realized then I'd been fucking with the wrong kind of street nigga. This was the life I wanted, and I plan on doing whatever it takes to get it.

Chapter Sixteen

Akila

I was tired of paying these damn bills by my damn self when I had another grown-ass bitch living under the same roof. I was starting to think this was a bad idea to ask her to come live with me. Since she's been here, I haven't seen her work, and when I ask, she lies to my face. The food we eat, I buy it. The toilet paper and soap to wash her ass, I bought it. I was at my breaking point. I got up out of bed. We needed to talk. She either needed to start contributing, or she could move back to Maryland and let me continue struggling by myself.

I got up, grabbed my robe, and walked out of the room. I knocked on her bedroom door. I waited but got no response. I continued knocking, but still nothing. I then tried the door. It was locked. I shook my head and walked out to the living room. She wasn't there either. I walked to the kitchen and opened the back door. Her car was gone. I locked the door, got me some milk, and warmed it up. This heartburn was killing me. Old people say your baby's head will be full of hair when you have bad heartburn like that. I really hope so 'cause I don't want no dry-headed, monkey-looking baby. I had to rub my stomach. I hate to think like this, but it's the truth. I grabbed the cup of milk and made my way back to my room. Then I picked up my phone and called her, but it went straight to voicemail. I left a message.

Just checking on you. Let me know if you good.

I hope she was all right. I tried to warn her about these Richmond niggas and how treacherous they were. Some of these niggas will fuck you, then turn around and kill you. Oh well, her ass grown, so she should know what she's doing.

I decide to do some online shopping. I told my doctor I wasn't interested in knowing the sex of my baby, so I started buying unisex clothing, so whatever sex pops out, I will be good on the clothing. By the time I was finished shopping, I'd gotten the crib, car seat, and a swing. This was good that I got the big things out of the way. I only have two months left, and I want to make sure I have everything before going into labor.

As I lay there thinking about labor, my mind wandered to Mari. I feel in my heart it was his baby, but how can I be sure when I let Tyrone fuck me around the same time? I still can't believe that I was so gullible and let him fool me like that. The fucking Feds. I hate that I'm not sure who my baby daddy is, but what can I do? I don't plan on involving either one in my child's life. But I'm not going to lie. I do miss all the things Mari used to buy me, and I miss the bond we once shared. I felt tears well up in my eyes, so I quickly pushed that shit back. There's no need to cry over him. We are over, and that's it.

Suddenly, I heard the door open, so I jumped up off the bed and walked out. I saw my cousin come in, heading to her room. I stood in my doorway with my hands crossed.

"Hey, girl."

She looked startled.

"Hey, I called you."

"Yeah, I was with ole boy. Girl, he is so fine, and he is paiiiid out the ass," she screamed.

"That's good. I was a little worried about you. You got to be careful out here."

"I hear you, girl, but he's a sweetheart, and he got a big dick. Bitch, my insides still hurting from last night."

"Hmmm, you so crazy. Listen, cuz, we need to talk."

She opened her door and walked in. "Yeah, what's up, boo?"

"You know I been holding these bills down by myself. I thought you were going to help me, but you have not. I've been going through my little savings. I don't know long it's going to last."

"Girl, you can always hit Mari up. There's no way you should sit up struggling when you carrying his baby. Shit, you should hit up both them niggas. Let both of them give you money. It ain't like they gon' to find out that the other one is paying you."

"Girl, I ain't trying to do all that. I just want to know when you're going to start paying your half of the rent and help buy some groceries around here."

"Damn, cuz, you really putting pressure on a bitch. Look, here go $200. I'll give you some more by the weekend." She went into her purse, took out some money, and handed it to me.

I looked at what she was handing me. "Cuz, come on now. You been here for over six months, and I've been carrying all the weight by myself. What am supposed to do with $200?"

"If I had more, I would give it to you. Trust me; I've been working. These people just playing around with my check. But now that I'm dating, I should get some money. Don't worry, cuz. We about to be straight."

I was getting upset, and I didn't want to come off disrespectful, so I walked away and into my room. I closed the door behind me and threw the two bills on the dresser. This bitch was turning out to be a fucking burden, and I needed to figure out something fast. I didn't get a chance to sit down when my phone rang. I was still feeling angry, so I answered it without looking at the caller ID.

"Hello," I said, then let out a long breath.

"Hey, girly," Shayla said.

Damn, it's been a minute since we've spoken. She ran on my mind many times, but I've been dealing with this pregnancy so much that I just cut off everyone.

"Hey, chick. How you been?"

"I'm doing good. I was thinking about you earlier and said to myself, we haven't spoken in a while. How are *you* doing?"

"Girl, where do I start. . . . I'm knocked up."

"Hold up. Wait . . . You pregnant?" she said excitedly.

"Girl, yes. I found out a few weeks after I left school."

"Oh man, well, congrats, girl. Is it a boy or girl?"

"I'm not sure. I wanted it to be a surprise."

"I know I'm asking a lot of questions, but how far along are you, and did you have your baby shower already?"

"Girl, I'm almost seven months, and you know I don't have no family or friends out here."

"True, but fuck that. I'm your family now. I got to run to the gym, but I'ma call you when I leave. I'm going to get some stuff for the baby. You don't have to go through this alone."

"All right, girl, thank you."

That conversation really touched my soul. Lately, I've been feeling down a lot. I wish my grandma were here. I can't lie. I often wondered where in the world is the bitch that gave me life. How did she get up and just walk away from me? I pray to God I'll be nothing like her ass and never leave my child out here like this.

Enough thinking about that sorry bitch. It was crunch time. I need to get all my baby stuff together before I fuck around and go into labor early.

Mari

"Yo, dawg, you ready?" I turned and asked G.

"Let's get it, fam."

I pulled off in the old, beat-up car that I bought from a junky a few days ago. After putting that money out there, we finally got word on where the niggas stayed that shot me. We knew that the main nigga owns an old bingo spot on Hull Street, so we decided not to waste any time and get these niggas handled.

"Yo, let me see the pic of that nigga again."

He pulled out his phone and showed me the nigga's picture. I looked at the picture and made a mental note in my head. I saw the resemblance to the fuck nigga we killed. I made my way down the highway and was definitely in a zone. The only thing on my mind was murder.

I pulled into the parking lot and saw a few cars parked. I immediately spotted the dark-colored SUV that followed me that day. The same one the niggas that shot me were driving. I didn't have any doubts that the informant was correct with the info he gave us.

I didn't cut off the engine. We sat in the car for a few minutes, scoping out the scene. It was dark outside. No one was walking around. I looked around to make sure no camera was visible. Then I pulled the mask over my face, and G did the same. I checked my gun and made sure it was loaded and ready to shoot.

"Let's get it, bro."

I exited the vehicle and took the lead. I held my gun at my side as I ran to the side of the building, quickly opened the door, and dashed inside.

"Yo, who's Buck?" I yelled out while I pointed the gun at the group of men sitting at the table playing dominoes.

"You heard the man. Where the fuck is Buck?" G yelled out in an aggressive tone.

You could tell by the look on their faces that they were terrified. Then I saw a shadow walk from a curtain, and without blinking, I knew it was the nigga I was looking for.

"What the fuck going on out here? What is this, a robbery? Y'all got to be bold coming up in here like that. Y'all must not know about Buck from South Side."

I looked that nigga in the eyes and aimed my Glock. *Pop! Pop! Pop!*

"I guess you ain't heard about *me,* pussy." I walked up on his bullet-riddled body and pressed the gun on his temple.

Pop!

By then, the rest of niggas started making a bunch of noise. G began firing at them. Within seconds, they were all dead. I peeped out the window to see if there was any action outside.

"Let's go."

We walked out of the building, trying not to arouse suspicion that a bloodbath had taken place inside. We got into the car, and I slowly crept out into traffic, disappearing in the dark.

"Yo, hit that nigga up that gave us the info. Let him know I got the other half of the money for him."

"Where you want to meet at?"

"Tell him to meet us on Walmsley Boulevard behind the BP gas station."

I listened as he told the nigga where to meet up. One thing I learned being in this business . . . You can't trust no nigga and definitely can't trust no nigga that will sell another nigga out for no money. *All* loose ends need to be tied up.

"Yo, dawg, that pussy nigga didn't see that one coming, huh?"

"The fuck he thought? They was gon' touch me, and there's no repercussion to it? I might not be from here, but this *my* motherfucking city now."

I pulled up at the BP and made sure I went in the back way. I pulled over and lit a Black while we waited. About three minutes later, a car pulled up and parked beside us. I saw a crackhead-looking nigga get out.

"Yo, over here. Get in," G yelled and waved to the nigga.

The nigga got in the backseat and started running his mouth right away.

"Yo, we got to get the money from the safe house. We didn't want to drive around with that much money. Take a ride with us real quick, and we'll drop you back off at your car."

"Okay, that's fine. So, did you all take care of business?" he quizzed.

"Yeah, good looking out, fam. Aye, you ain't mention it to nobody, right?"

"Nah, hell no. These niggas can't be trusted. Plus, I didn't want nobody to know I got this little change. I'm about to take this and get the hell out of town."

"Oh yeah? Where you heading to?"

"I got a sister down in Alabama. She been asking me to come out there, but the timing wasn't right. I think I'ma go on down there now. Richmond is getting hot with all these killings. Ain't nothing out here for me."

I pulled over to the side of the street that was pitch black.

"What's going on, fam?"

"I think we got a flat. I'ma check it out."

"Shit, let's check it. Come on, homie. We gon' need your help."

I got out and bent down to see what was going on with the tire.

"Pop the trunk. See if there's a tire in there," I yelled.

Old dude walked over to where I was standing and bent down to check the tire. I pulled the gun up and fired one shot in the back of his head. He fell over, and I fired two more shots. Then we jumped back into the car and sped off.

We went back to G's house, and I got into my truck and drove behind him. We had to get rid of this old hoopty ASAP. We found a spot behind an old warehouse. I made sure the inside was wiped down properly, then doused the vehicle with gasoline. We watched as the fire consumed it. After that, we jumped into the truck and drove off. We had to get away fast before someone called the police.

We finally got out of harm's way. Then I turned the music up all the way. I was listening to Yo Gotti. I was feeling relieved. The niggas that shot me finally met their maker. Maybe now I can sleep better at night 'cause I haven't been able to sleep lately.

"Now, we can focus on getting this money, fam."

"You already know. It's a new day tomorrow."

My phone started ringing, so I pulled it out of my pocket. It was Claire, the new chick that I was fucking.

"Hey there, beautiful."

"Hey, boo, what's up?"

"Nothing new. Just out handling some business. What about you?"

"Just lying here thinking about you and that bomb-ass dick."

"Yo, chillll. You know I'm around niggas. I can't be getting no hard-on."

"I'm sorry, baby. I just really miss you, and my pussy is throbbing for your dick. Can I see you tonight?"

"I'm out right now, but I tell you what. I'll hit you in an hour. Can I come to your crib?"

"I told you I stay with my old grandmother, and she's not having that. We can just meet at the room if you don't mind."

"All right, that'll work. I'll hit you back."

"Okay, boo. I can't wait."

I disconnected the phone. Shawty was definitely growing on me. At first, I was just trying to fuck, but the more time I spent around her, the more I started liking her. It was like she was a whole different vibe. She always positive and don't stress me out like other bitches.

"Yo, nigga, who the fuck is that? It sounds like a nigga in love and shit."

"Stop playing, dawg. Me, in love? That's some funny shit. The last bitch I loved is Kila."

"Yeah, I hear you, dawg, but I see how you smiling e'erytime your phone rings. Who is this new bitch?"

"I met her on Facebook. We had drinks, and let's just say, I been tapping that ass ever since."

"So, you telling me you met a random bitch on Facebook? Dawg, be careful. Bitch might be the police. You can't put nothing past them motherfuckers."

"I get you, but shawty ain't 12, plus I don't discuss no business with that bitch. I'm just there to fuck her and make her feel good."

"A'ight, fam, as long as you straight."

"We good, trust me. She wants to meet up tonight. I'm beat right now, so I'ma chill for a few, then meet up with her."

"A'ight, nigga. Can't say I ain't warn yo' ass. Shit, you might be the next victim on *48 Hours*," he chuckled.

"You see this, nigga. Don't think I won't blow a bitch brains out if she even seems like she on some foul shit."

"Uh-huh. Aye, we been caught up with all this other shit that I forgot to tell you. The PI nigga said he found out some info on Akila."

"Oh, word? Did he get the address?"

"I didn't even have time to ask him that. He called when we were in the middle of something the other day."

"Oh, OK. Well, get back at the nigga and see what he got. I need to find shawty ASAP."

"So lemme get this right. You with this bitch, but you still want Akila? Nigga, that's why yo' crazy ass stay in some shit. And let's not forget that crazy bitch, Shonda. She been quiet, but I know she over there cooking up some shit."

"Nigga, just get me the info. Let me worry about these hoes."

I got up and walked off. I needed to take a quick shower and put on fresh clothes. After the day that I had, I need to get out of the house and celebrate some . . . and get some fire head in the process . . .

Shonda

I've been on pins and needles lately. I know it was only a matter of time before Mari finds out that some money was moved out of his account. I know I was playing a dangerous game, but to be honest, it was a risk that I was willing to take.

I slid into my pencil skirt, put on the skintight shirt, then slipped into my Gucci pumps. From the looks of it, you would think I was heading to the office, but wrong. I have an important meeting today with a federal agent. I got some things to share that might pique his interest.

I sprayed on some perfume and took one last glance in the mirror. I was pleased by my appearance. I'm not sure why I was so adamant about looking good as hell today, but I was. I want to walk into this meeting looking and feeling like a million bucks.

I locked up the house, got into my car, and pulled out of the garage. Then I pulled up the address that he sent me. I put it in the GPS and pulled off. I pulled into the Marriott on Broad Street, gave my keys to the valet, and sashayed inside. I pulled out my phone to call him, but I quickly saw him walking toward me. He didn't look like no Fed. Instead, he looked like a regular nigga out in the streets.

"Good morning, Miss Matthews. I'm glad you could meet me."

"Good morning. It's definitely my pleasure."

"Come this way. I got us some privacy in the conference room."

He led the way, and I followed closely behind. Then he closed the door behind us, and we took a seat across from each other.

"So, you said you believe we can help each other. I'm curious to know what you're talking about." He gazed into my eyes.

"Well, when you came to my office awhile back, you told me you were investigating Mari."

"Oh yes. And if my memory serves me right, you told me you were not aware of what I was talking about. So, did you have a change of mind?"

"Well, back then, I was in love with him. I didn't know he was using me. Come to find out, he has a girlfriend, and I was only doing his dirty work." I kind of choked up while I spoke.

"Oh, I see. I'm very familiar with Mr. Owens, and you're correct. He is very popular with the ladies."

"Well, I know a lot, and I'm ready to help you. The only request I have is to keep my name out of it. I'm sure you are aware he's a dangerous man, and anyone who is against him always ends up dead."

"Well, Miss Matthews, if you decide to help bring him and his crew down, the Bureau and I will guarantee your safety. If you feel better, we can provide you with the witness protection program."

"Oh, hell nah. I see those on television all the time. I'm not walking away from my life. I just need to know he'll never find out I'm helping you."

"I promise he will never know you're helping me."

"Oh, another thing. Is there some type of cash incentive for helping y'all? I read somewhere that you can get paid for helping the Feds."

"Yes, you're correct. As far as how much it is, I'm not sure. I would have to talk to my superiors, and they will make the final call. Now, tell me what you know and what evidence you have."

He took a recorder and placed it on the table.

"Wait, hold up. No one else is going to hear that, right?" I looked at him. I was starting to feel unsure about this.

"No, this is just for me and my superior. I can't just go to them and say a person told me so-and-so and don't have any proof. I tell you, you're doing the right thing. We are investigating Mr. Owens in a string of murders, and you may be next. From my studying his profile, this man is dangerous, and he uses females. When you are no longer beneficial to him, trust he won't think twice about getting rid of you," he warned.

His face was somber when he spoke. I could tell he was a low-life nigga who probably thought he was using me. But I was on to game and looking at the bigger picture. I didn't waste no time, so I started singing like a hummingbird. I even added some shit that I didn't have proof about. I know I had to make sure Mari will be buried deep down under the jail. If not, my life could be in danger.

"I fully understand. I just have to make sure my family and I are good. He knows where my mama and daddy stay. I wouldn't be able to live with myself if anything bad happened to them."

"I can assure you nothing will happen to them or you."

Now, I was ready to lay it all out on the table. I had a lot of info about Mari and his boys. I was the one that was driving out of town with him when he would go meet with his connects. I was also the one that laundered his money through my business. See, niggas be thinking they fucking over a bitch when, in reality, he just fucked himself.

I spent the next couple of days cooped up in the house. I was scared to go outside, not that there was any kind of danger. I was feeling paranoid. It's been awhile since I moved money out of Mari's account into mine, and I still haven't heard from him. I knew the Feds would be all over him and his business, so I deleted everything that linked me to him. I also contacted the clients that I had to let them know I was taking an indefinite leave of absence.

I grabbed the phone and called my cousin. I wasn't sure how she would react because we hadn't spoken since the day we got into that heated argument. I waited for her to answer the phone.

"What the hell you calling my phone for, Miss High and Mighty? What, the nigga finally left you?" she spat.

"Girl, whatever. You know me better than that. Anyway, lower your voice. I ain't calling you for none of that. The Feds want to talk to you."

"Feds . . . talk to me? What the fuck for? I ain't did shit, and I damn sure don't know nada. Girl, don't call my phone 'bout none of that."

"Wait, the Feds know we were cleaning the money for Mari, and they just want to talk to us. You don't want to get charged with money laundering, right?"

"I ain't launder shit. I worked for you. Whatever you and him got going on is y'all's business. Like I said, I'ont know nothing else."

This crackhead bitch was pissing me off. She knows why the fuck I hired her and what was going on. Matter of fact, she rode with me a few times to NY to pick up some work.

"All right, keep on playing crazy. Doing fed time ain't no joke. I'ma cover my ass. It's up to you what you want to do."

"No, bitch, it's up to *you* to keep my name out of your shit. If you don't, Mari ain't the only one going down 'cause you just as dirty as his ass."

Before I could respond, this old filthy-ass bitch hung up the phone in my face. I should get dressed, head over to my auntie's house, and drag out this bitch. I had to smile, though, 'cause this what my ass gets for looking out for family. I threw the phone on the bed and started massaging my aching temples.

Chapter Seventeen

Akila

"Girl, I'm so happy you could meet for dinner. How are you feeling?" Shayla asked as I took a seat at the table.

"I'm good, girl. Just this baby killing me and shit. I'll be happy when it's over."

"I ain't never been pregnant before, but I heard from my sisters that it can be horrible on the body. Well, look at like this, it will be well worth it when you see that beautiful face."

"You know what? You're right. That's the only thing that keeps me going. I don't know how some bitches be having a bunch of kids. I think this might be it for me. I can't go through this again."

The waitress approached the table. "Hello, ladies, can I get y'all two something to drink?"

"Well, I'll get a Bahama Mama."

"I'll get a glass of water please."

This heartburn be killing me, so it's best I stay away from the juice or sodas. I did take my nausea medicine, hoping this will help while I'm out.

"So, have you heard from Mari?"

"Girl, no. After I found out he wasn't who I thought he was, we went our separate ways."

"So, he don't know about the baby?"

"Huh?"

"I'm sorry. I assumed he's the baby father since you two were together."

"He is not . . . Just say I'm the Virgin Mary." I busted out laughing.

"Girl, you are too funny, but that will work. I know you say you were not doing no shower, so I went ahead and bought you some stuff for the baby. There's no need for you to go through this by yourself. Also, here is a gift card to Target. You can get whatever you want." She reached in her purse and handed me a gift card.

After the waitress brought back her drink and my water, we ordered our food. I stuck with baked chicken and mashed potatoes. I hoped I would hold it down, at least until I leave. We continued talking in between eating.

I saw a shadow approach our table. I looked up and realized it was Tesha's mother. I haven't seen her in a while. I was a lousy friend 'cause I promised I would keep in touch, but I haven't. My life's just been so hectic I can't really keep up with what was going on.

"Akila, I thought that was you," she said with a devilish grin.

I stood up to hug her. "Hey, Miss Bell, how you doing?"

"Don't you dare touch me. I'm still looking for my daughter. Y'all were like sisters, and I ain't seen yo' face not one damn time. All the searches we done did, and you nowhere to be found. My mind tells me you have something to do with her disappearance. My daughter told someone she was going to stop by your house, and next thing, your house is burned down, and my daughter just disappeared off the face of the earth."

I took a step back. I know she was upset. Shit, what mother wouldn't be, but I had nothing to do with Tesha's disappearance.

"Miss Bell, I know you are hurting, but it's unfair to blame me. I was locked up when Tesha disappeared. I spoke to the police and was cleared."

"Bitch, fuck you. You and that drug-dealing boyfriend of yours are responsible for my daughter's disappearance. Watch your back, bitch, 'cause as long as I'm living, you're going to pay. You *will* pay, you *hear* me—you fucking murderer? You *killed* my daughter," she yelled before storming off.

I turned around and noticed the other patrons were looking attentively and whispering to one another. I looked at Shayla before I sat down again.

"I'm sorry about that. We can leave if you want to."

"Girl, you straight. I thought I would have to get up and beat on this old bitch. She has no right to accuse you of some shit that she has no proof about. She was *way* out of line for that."

"You know, I fully understand her frustration, but I was locked up, and I did talk to Tesha on the phone. She was supposed to come bond me out but never showed up. I tried calling her and got no response. I was in the jail for days before Mari bonded me out." I started shaking while tears rolled down my face.

"You getting upset like this can't be good for the baby. You know you ain't got nothing to do with this, so fuck her. She could've talked to you like a civilized person. Instead, she had to act all ratchet and shit."

The waitress arrived with our food, and we started eating. I was still visibly hurt and had lost my appetite. I tried not to break down at the table.

"You need to put something on your stomach. Feed the baby."

"I know, right?"

While we ate, my mind was all over the place with crazy thoughts. I knew something happened at my house because Mari burned it down, but what exactly happened? I had tried inquiring about it a few times, but he brushed me off or was evasive with his response.

Could Tesha have walked in on something Mari was doing? Could he have killed her? My head started hurting from all these thoughts. I took a sip of the water and tried to calm myself.

After we finished eating, the waitress brought the tab. I started going in my purse, but Shayla grabbed my hand.

"Girl, I invited you to dinner, so I got it."

"You sure?" I quizzed.

"Yes, I'm sure. You already have had a rough night. You need to relax."

"Thank you, girl. I really appreciate you."

She paid the bill, and we walked out of the restaurant. Then she went into the trunk of her car, grabbed three big bags, and handed them to me.

"Here are the things. If you need anything else, please don't hesitate to call me. Plus, I'll be checking on you daily. Consider me your new best friend."

"You make me want to cry. This pregnancy been so rough, and I have no one. I love you, girl."

"Well, that's what friends are for. Plus, I work and ain't doing too much with my money. Go on home and get some rest."

We hugged, then got into our separate vehicles. Tears welled up in my eyes. This was the first person outside of my grandma who made me feel special without wanting anything in return. I tried not to get close to females since I lost Ariana, but I see Shayla's heart was good, and I needed her in my life. I dried my eyes before I pulled off. Whew, what an eventful night it was.

I was happy to see my cousin wasn't home. I was tired and in my feelings. I didn't feel like dealing with her. Lately, all she kept talking about was her new mystery man, and I'm not jealous, but I got too much shit going on in my life and wasn't in a happy place.

I got into the house, used the bathroom, and climbed into bed. I was tired, exhausted, and needed to rest. I placed my hand on my stomach, trying to refocus my thoughts on my baby. When everything around me fails, I know I got to be strong for my baby.

It was early in the morning, so I got up and tiptoed to the kitchen. The plan was to make me some scrambled eggs and a toasted bagel. This baby be having me craving shit that I don't eat on the regular, like eggs. I hated them growing up. I remember my grandmother used to scold me 'cause every time she made eggs for me, I would wait until she left the kitchen, then I would throw them in the trash. Finally, she stopped making me breakfast, and I didn't have to waste her food.

I was happy that I made it back to my room without waking up my cousin. While I ate, I jumped on the internet and started looking for any article related to Tesha's disappearance. She's been heavy on my mind since the altercation with her mother. I know I didn't have anything to do with her disappearance, and Mari is not saying anything. Let's see if I can find anything that can put my mind to rest.

Mari

The streets were in turmoil after what went down with the nigga Buck. I mean, what the fuck did they expect? They shot me and left me for dead, but I guess God wasn't ready for a real nigga. As I drove down the road, I couldn't help but think about my brother. A day hasn't gone by where I haven't thought about him or missed him. A tear fell down my face as I thought about my right hand. I wish I could keep killing that bitch over and over. Rio was my brother or more like a father figure, and the day I lost him, I lost a piece of my soul.

I pulled up at the new trap we have on Porter Street. I know the niggas were already inside by the number of cars parked outside. I looked around cautiously before I jumped out of my truck and made my way in. I was getting tired of changing traps, but I know it's important to stay off these pigs' radar.

I walked into the front room, where niggas were sitting, smoking, and chatting. "The bossman is here," G said loudly.

I moved around the room, greeting everyone and exchanging daps. I don't trust a lot of people, but these five niggas in the room were definitely family. We been rocking together for a minute, and they have proven their loyalty to me time after time.

"All right, fellas, I called this meeting 'cause shit is getting hot in these streets. When I got shot, I got back at the niggas that touched me. Now, that seems to have a lot of these South Side niggas in their feelings. I'm saying this to say, be prepared for war. Y'all know how grimy and sneaky these Richmond niggas can be. Don't let them catch y'all slipping. For the time being, I don't want y'all going to handle any kind of business alone. Always bring someone with you. When coming to the trap, circle around at least twice before you pull in."

"Boss, no disrespect, but you talking like we scared of these pussy niggas. We straight killers out here."

"Jah, that's that attitude that will get you killed. Brave niggas don't fire guns. It be the scared, pussy niggas that will kill you. You can't be too cocky. That will blind your judgment, young nigga."

"I ain't tryin'a hear that shit. These niggas pussy. They don't want to see me."

I looked at him. I saw myself in him ten years ago. This was dangerous and risky, so I pulled my Glock out.

Pop! Pop!

I fired two shots into his body and heard motherfuckers gasping.

"Yo, what the fuck . . . He was a youngin'," Dre yelled out.

"He was a fool. You need to follow directions in order to lead. Now, y'all clean this shit up and get rid of the body."

I looked at them with a grit on my face, and as I walked out of the room, I looked down on the fresh white tee I was wearing to make sure there was no blood splattered on it. Then I put the gun back into my waist before I got into my truck.

I hate that I had to end that little nigga's life. I really liked his drive and tenacity, but he showed weakness in following orders. That was something I couldn't allow on my team.

My phone started ringing. I looked at the caller ID. It was G. I know he probably was calling about what just happened. To be honest, he was my nigga, but I didn't feel like explaining shit to no one right now, not even him.

After a long-ass day of handling business, I decided to meet up with shawty for drinks at the bar. I took a seat and glanced around.

"Hey, handsome, can I join you?"

The voice sounded familiar. I looked up. Oh shit . . . It was the therapist from the rehabilitation center. The same one that Shonda got into it with.

"Hey, there, beautiful. How you doing?"

"I'm good. After what happened with your girlfriend that day, I never thought I'd run into you again."

"Nah, that's history. That chick is no longer in my life."

"Hmm . . . Really?"

Now, Claire walked up in the middle of our conversation. "Hey, baby." She smiled, leaned over, and kissed me. "Oh, excuse me. You are . . .?" She turned to Miss Tamryn.

"Hello, I'm Tamryn. I was just leaving."

"Oh, so soon? Why don't you join us for drinks?"

I looked at Claire and then back at Tamryn. I wasn't sure what was going on, but shit, let's see how it plays out.

"Are you sure? I mean, I don't want to intrude on y'all's privacy."

"That's bullshit. I don't mind, and I know Mari wouldn't mind either. Right, baby?"

"Huh?" I pretended like I wasn't paying attention.

"I was telling her that you wouldn't mind if she joined us for drinks."

"Sure, she good."

I took a few gulps of my Patrón. I wasn't sure what Claire had up her sleeve, but I planned on staying out of it.

All three of us started drinking and talking. I could tell the therapist was getting tipsy 'cause she started talking more loosely.

"So, Mari, is this your new girlfriend? I have to tell you, I like her better than the other one."

I almost choked on the liquor 'cause I was caught off guard with her question.

"Yes, love, I'm the new girlfriend, but I can tell you have a crush on him too," Claire giggled.

"Who me? Nah. We're just old friends," Tamryn said nervously, and then she took a sip of her drink.

"Girl, relax. It's OK. I tell you, he do have some good diiiiick. I mean, you know the kind that will have you *screaming*." This chick was insane. She was talking about my dick like I wasn't sitting here.

"Is that soooo?" the therapist said.

"I tell you what. How about we get out of here? And if you let me taste between your legs, I'll let you ride his big black dick. I promise you will *love* it."

"I don't know. I ain't never got my pussy licked before."

"There's a first for everything, and I can assure you, once you feel this tongue on that clit, you won't have *any* regrets." Claire grabbed Tamryn's head and started kissing her.

I saw the waitress shoot a look over where we were seated. Shit, I was enjoying the show. My dick started standing up in my jeans. I used my hand to adjust myself. They finally let loose.

"Let's get out of here, babe," Claire whispered in my ear.

I pulled out a wad of cash and put it on the counter. The waitress looked at me and smiled, giving me the thumbs-up. All three of us walked outside and then split up. We decided to go to the Marriott on Broad Street. I kept thinking about fucking these two bitches on the way over here. Shawty did surprise me 'cause I wasn't aware that she loved bitches. Shit, this was the kind of bitch I love. We can be on those levels, fucking bitches together.

After we got into the room, we smoked and drank. I sat on the bed, taking in the beautiful sight in front of me. Two bitches going at it. At first, Tamryn was acting shy, but being the teacher Claire was, she caressed her. And before you know it, her legs were wrapped around Claire's neck, and she lay there screaming out.

My dick was hard, so I started massaging it down. It was my way of telling him to chill out. His time was coming. Boy, was I correct. Both bitches took turns sucking my dick, and I took turns eating their pussy. We went on for about two hours. If I die right now, I would be the happiest nigga. After busting the third time, my body gave out. I excused myself to the bathroom. I took out the dollar bill in my pocket and started sniffing some blow. I waited a few seconds for it to take effect, then put the bill back into my pants. I looked in the mirror and checked if my nose was clean. After that, I exited the bathroom. Both of them were sprawled out on the bed. By now, my energy level was elevated, and I couldn't stay still. I took a swig of the liquor and a few pulls out of the weed. I was trying to bring my high down some. I couldn't risk these bitches noticing my sudden change of behavior.

I was asleep, but I could hear my phone buzzing. I reached over and pressed the *ignore* button without fully opening my eyes. I was tired, and my head was pounding. I closed my eyes again. The plan was to catch a little more sleep, but the phone started going off again a few seconds later. I ignored it until it was impossible to ignore it any longer.

"Yoooo," I said without looking at the caller ID.

"Yo, nigga, I been calling you and shit. I thought something was wrong. I ain't hear from you since yesterday."

"My bad, yo, but I been busy."

"Busy or not, bro, you know we stay in touch. That's the rule."

"You right, fam. I'm about to get up now. So, what's up, though?"

"I got an address for Akila. I don't know if it's right, but he said it is."

"Oh, word?" I jumped up and walked over to the bathroom. This was definitely the news I was waiting to hear for over a week.

"Yeah, bro. I'ma text it to you when I get to the crib."

"A'ight, fam. I'ma take a quick shower and hit you back."

I used the bathroom, then walked back into the room.

"Hey, you, we need to talk," Claire said as soon as I walked in. She startled me 'cause a few seconds ago, she was asleep. *Not all shut eyes are sleeping.* My mama's voice echoed in my head.

"Yo, what's good, shawty?" I put my phone down and looked at her.

"We've been fucking around with each other for a minute now, and we be together whenever you're not working. I think what I'm trying to say is, don't you think it's time to make it official?"

"Official?" I looked at her for some kind of understanding.

"Yeah, like you keep telling me you like me and shit, and we fuck all the time. Don't you think it's time you make me your only girl and probably let us get our own place together? I mean, you can't come to my place 'cause I don't live alone, and I'm tired of these hotels. I mean, it'd be cheaper, and we can be together more."

"Yo, shawty, you cool, and I'm definitely digging you, but I don't want to move too fast. Our relationship is fine the way it is right now. Why change it?"

"Why change it? Do you have another bitch that you fucking or something?" she stood up and yelled out.

"Yo, chill out with all of that. Ain't no other bitch. I'm feeling you, and I'm with you. I'm just not ready to be living with no female right now."

"You know what, Mari? It's all good. Niggas like you rather chase these no-good-ass bitches out here than cuff a real woman like me. What else could you be looking for? I got a tight, wet pussy. I suck yo' dick good, and I ride that dick good."

"Yo, chill out with all that. I ain't chasing nothing. I mean, we good just the way it is. I don't want to change anything."

My phone started buzzing. I looked down and saw it was a text from G.

"Yo, let's talk about this later or something. I got to run."

"Are you serious? You leaving in the middle of a conversation? You acting like what I have to say isn't important? Y'all niggas kill me with this bullshit."

"Yo, shawty, I said I got to go. If you can't understand that, then maybe you need to lose my fucking number," I yelled before taking a few steps in her face.

I grabbed my phone and gun, then started walking out. I have no idea why bitches be starting off sweet at first, but the minute they get the dick, they turn into deranged, crazy bitches. I was *not* the nigga for this bitch to play with.

I got into my truck and opened the text that G sent me. So Akila's ass was on the South Side. Shit, how was she able to stay out of my path this entire time? Oh well, I got an address now, so she can't hide anymore.

Claire

I sat on the bed of the hotel room, trembling as he walked out the door and slammed it behind him. Tears rolled down my face as I tried my best not to let them out. I can't believe that Mari handled me like he just did. It's been weeks since we been fucking with each other, and I never saw this coming. I really thought I had him locked in. I mean, we been chilling, he ate my pussy and licked my ass, so I assumed I was his girl, and he was ready to make it official. I fucked him good, sucked his dick, and often licked *his* ass. I was hoping that he would see how much I cared for him and would forget about all them other bitches. I see I was wrong 'cause the minute I mentioned "let's make it official," his entire mood changed.

He didn't even care to finish the conversation. He just up and left without giving a fuck about my feelings.

Suddenly, I heard a knock at the door. I got up, hoping he had changed his mind and returned to apologize. I opened the door and was disappointed. It was the cleaning lady.

"Sorry to bother you, ma'am, but it's checkout time," she said in her best English accent.

"Bitch, I know what time it is," I yelled, then slammed the fucking door in her gotdamn face.

I wiped the tears away from my eyes and grabbed my stuff. The bitch was still standing by the door as I shoved past her. "Stupid-ass bitch," I mumbled under my breath as I waited for the elevator to come to the fifth floor.

By the time I pulled up to the house, I was beyond exhausted. All that fucking and sucking last night had me drained. On top of that, I was feeling angry that I did all that for that nigga, and he didn't appreciate it. I mean, I don't mind eating pussy. I've been eating pussy since I was 14 when I first ate my best friend, but what I did last night was all for him. I know my bougie-ass cousin would have never done no shit like this for him. Yet, he spent lots of money on *her* ass.

I quietly opened the door and walked in. I was almost in my room before I heard her voice.

"Damn, bitch, you're never around anymore, huh? It seems like that nigga got you on lock."

"Girl, you ain't the only one that can snatch up a dope boy," I replied sarcastically.

"Hmm, I hear you. I hope you plan on snatching some more money from him. If you out with him all night and fucking him, he need to be throwing some paper your way. Pussy ain't free, and you damn sure got some bills piling up."

"Listen, cuz, I hear you, but I'm beat. Can we finish this conversation later? I'm too tired right now." I leaned on the door to emphasize how exhausted I was.

"Oh, a'ight."

I was happy when she walked back into her room. Then I opened my door and fell in. Within seconds, I took my clothes off and got into bed. I was still furious at how Mari treated me earlier. I checked my phone to see if he called or texted, but he didn't. I was disappointed all over again. Tears welled up in my eyes, so I allowed them to flow freely now.

I was awakened out of my sleep by the ringing of my telephone. I looked at the caller ID, and it was my bitch. I was happy to talk to her. Maybe she can help lift my spirits a little.

"Yes, bitch?"

"Damn, yo' ass sound tired as hell. Don't tell me you was up all night."

"Girl, yes, I was up fucking and sucking on that nigga, and we had a bitch in the room with us."

"Ho, you lying. You telling me you and that nigga had a threesome?"

"Yes, bitch, that's *exactly* what I'm telling you. That shit was lit too. That bitch had a phat, juicy pussy."

"I can imagine that nigga ain't gon' let your ass go now. He done lucked up and found him a freak."

"Bestie, I don't know 'cause his ass was acting all funny this morning. I think it's time that we made our relationship official, but he was not feeling that shit."

"Bitch, I thought you were going to take it slow and try to get as much money out of him as you can."

"I was trying that, but I can't help that I fell hard for the nigga. That dick is so fucking good that it had me gone."

"Bitch, I love you to death, but that's the problem. You fall in love too damn easy. Don't forget what happened with your ex. You got to know how to chill and play your cards right. You can't expect shit to happen overnight. Bitch, he sounds like a good catch. Don't fuck around and run him off before you get some shit up off of him. Fuck them feelings you got. That shit only gon' get you hurt and broke. You need to think big and see the whole picture, not just a tiny portion. Bitch, this opportunity only comes once in a while, so you better get your head all the way together and get out of your feelings. All them feelings going to get you is a wet ass and a beat-up pussy."

I sat there with my head bowed and my tongue hanging out of my mouth. I know she was always the friend that would let me know when I was wrong. This, however, was going over the extreme. She was handing me my ass.

"Damn, bitch, you didn't have to go that hard. I mean, shit, if you wasn't my bitch, I would think you trying to carry me."

"Calm your nerves, bitch. I love you, and you're my ace, but if you don't get it together, you gon' run that nigga off to the next bitch—or better yet, into your cousin's arms. You know you don't want that."

"Hell nah, I don't want that nigga to go back to that bitch. She don't know how to treat him like me. I need to come up with a plan."

"A plan? Oh no, bitch, what's spinning around in that big-ass head?"'

"Bitch, I got a plan, but I got to think some about it. I got to go now. I'll call you later."

"Claire—"

I hung up without answering her. My eyes lit up as this crazy-ass idea popped up in my head.

Shonda

I had to pee, so I got up, grabbed my robe, and wrapped it around me before I tiptoed to the bathroom. I was careful to be quiet, so I didn't wake up my new love interest. As I sat on the toilet peeing, I smiled to myself. I still had it in me to fuck a nigga to sleep. Last night, after fucking for hours, he lay down and started snoring within minutes. Here it was morning, and this nigga was *still* asleep.

At first, I was hesitant to fuck him 'cause all we had was a business arrangement. But after our first meeting, I could tell he was attracted to me. I admit he was cute but more like a clean-cut nigga. Much different from the thugs that I'm used to fucking with. Being with him was also personal. He was the same nigga that Mari caught his bitch with, and, boy, he hated him. While I was fucking him, I smiled 'cause I can imagine how hot Mari would be if he found out I was also fucking him.

I washed my hands and walked out of the bathroom. He was wide awake now. I smiled at him as I leaned over and kissed him on the cheek.

"Good morning, beautiful. I had a great night last night."

"I'm glad you did. There's plenty more where that came from." I winked at him.

"Woman, you're one of a kind. Where you been all my life?"

"Wasting my time with all them all no-good niggas, but here I am now, baby."

"I love that, but you know we got work to do. And when we're around my people and shit, we have to be careful, so no one catches on that we have something going on."

"So, what, I should be your little secret?"

"Babes, you showed me a great night, but we can't let a fuck jeopardize a case that we been building for years. This is the furthest we have come to nabbing this evil and his crew. I just can't be the one that fucks it up. I hope you understand what I'm saying to you."

"Okay, I understand what you're saying. I'm cool as long as you get me out of here before Mari finds out that I'm working with y'all. That nigga don't care who he kill, whether it's kids or women. He's dangerous. . . ." My words trailed off.

It gives me chills thinking about how dangerous Mari was. Yes, when I was with him, it didn't matter what he was doing. But I know if he ever finds out about me betraying him, I will end up the next dead bitch.

"Listen, don't you worry. We have you going in front of the grand jury in the next week or so. And you must be prepared to leave immediately after the indictments come down. I don't know how much you know about the witness protection program, but it's a whole new identity. Everyone and everything you know will have to be a thing of the past. You will assume a new identity, and your life will begin all over. That means no one—even your closest family—will be able to contact you."

As I heard him talk about the witness protection program, I thought about getting up and getting the fuck out of here. Lawd, my mama and my daddy . . . How will I explain to them that I won't see them again? That will break my mama's heart.

"I know it will be hard, but you can do it."

"Is it too late to change my mind? I mean, it ain't like I went in front of the grand jury or anything like that."

"Babes, I already told you that they were willing to indict you on multiple federal charges. The truth is, Mr. Owens wouldn't be able to run his business and clean up the money without you and your company's help. It's good you're cooperating with us. If you could only get your cousin on board as well. . . ."

"This is so fucked up. I see how y'all work. Pressure the little people to get to the head niggas. It's like jumping out of hot water into the fire. Either way you take it, I'm fucked."

"Don't look at like that, baby. At least with you, you know you can live a comfortable, long life. With Mr. Owens, your mother will be planning your funeral. You don't want to put your family through that."

"Well, I got to go. I got some things to get together."

"Baby, listen, I know you scared, but I'm just a phone call away. If you feel any kind of way or feel threatened, don't hesitate to call me. I'm out in the field this week, but you can reach me."

He got up off the bed and walked into the bathroom. I was feeling so conflicted. I wanted to get up and run, but run where? The truth is, it's too late to back out, and I didn't want to die.

I decided I needed to change my locks. I had taken my keys from Mari, but I wasn't too sure that he didn't make any copies. I know he had eyes and ears in this town, so I wasn't sure anyone saw me when I went into the fed building. Mari used to joke that he has Richmond PD on his payroll, and I thought he was just flexing, but I still was worried that it might be true.

I pulled into my gate, then into the garage. I looked around nervously to make sure no one was inside. Quickly, I locked the door behind me and breathed out loud. *Fuck.* I headed straight to the kitchen, grabbed a gin bottle, turned the bottle to my head, and took two gulps. I needed this to calm my nerves. My hands were shaking uncontrollably. I took another swig before closing the bottle.

Finally, I walked into the living room and kicked off my heels. This had been a rather eventful day. I went for a meeting with the Feds and somehow ended up in bed with one of them. The crazy thing is, I've never fucked an officer before, much less the Feds. But I have to admit, that was some good sex.

My phone started buzzing, instantly taking me out of my thoughts. My eyes popped open when I realized who it was. Wait—we haven't spoken in days, almost a week, so why was he calling me?

"Hello," I answered weakly, pretending like I was asleep.

"Yo, what's good? I thought you was gon' get back to me about the baby situation."

"Huh, what baby situation?"

"You said you pregnant, right?"

"Oh yes, yes. I'm sorry I was in a deep sleep. I tried to get a doctor's appointment, but I couldn't with my doctor. I'ma try a few other doctors later."

"Yo, we need to talk. How about I come through in a while?"

"I don't know if that's a good idea, Mari. I mean, after what happened last time."

"Listen, B, I'm sorry for the way I acted. I was under a lot of stress. I just want us to talk."

"Okay, if it's just talking, then that's cool. I'm here. Let me know when you on the way."

After I hung up the phone, my mind started thinking all kinds of crazy shit. Mari ain't been calling me, so why he called me out of the blue acting all nice and shit? This didn't sit right. I grabbed the phone and dialed Tyrone's number.

"Hey, dear."

"Listen, I think Mari knows," I said frantically.

"Hold on. Calm down. Knows what?"

"That I'm working with y'all."

"That's impossible. The only ones who know anything are me and the three people that were in the room with us. They been in the bureau longer than I have and are very trustworthy. Unless that guy is Miss Cleo, he doesn't know shit. Did he contact you?"

"Yes, he just called talking 'bout he wants to see me later on."

"What did you say?"

"I said no at first, but he insisted."

"That's good. You need to be cordial with him. You don't want him to become suspicious. You know how these thugs are."

"Yeah, you right. I guess I have to appear normal around him."

"Listen, can I come by and put a bug in your house and a minicamera?"

"A camera . . . What the hell?"

"I mean, you can drill him and get him to talk to you. Reveal some things that can help us."

I got really quiet on the phone. This nigga got some fucking nerve. He don't really care about me. All he cares about is making a fucking case. *What the fuck did I get myself into?* I thought.

"Listen, babe, I got to run. I'll be over there in a few."

Before I could respond, he hung up. I put my hand over my face. This is *not* good. I thought about calling Mari and telling him not to come, but I knew that would only raise suspicion. This is not turning out the way I envisioned. Me trying to pay back Mari might do more harm than good to me.

So, I waited and waited, but Mari never showed up. This made me even more suspicious. He called me out of the blue to come see me and then was a no-show. I tried calling him numerous times and got no answer. Something wasn't sitting right with me.

I thought about gathering my things and leaving the state, maybe the country. I had enough money to live comfortably on an exotic island. The grand jury was tomorrow, and even though Tyrone kept trying to convince me that everything was okay, I had my doubts. I've learned everyone could be bought if the price was right.

I dressed in a black Armani pants suit with a black pair of Gucci heels. I felt like I was going to someone's funeral dressed in all this black. Truth is, after getting a good night's sleep, I was ready to bury Mari. I did too much to help him for him to just throw me away like garbage.

Tyrone was parked outside, waiting for me. I think they knew how much danger I might be in, so he decided to escort me. I locked the door and walked out of the house. I made my way down the driveway, careful not to slip. I was so caught in my thoughts that I didn't see the shadow that emerged from the left side of my garage.

Pop! Pop! Pop!

Chapter Eighteen

Akila

I glanced around my room. There were baby things everywhere in boxes and bags. The crib took up most of the room, leaving little space for everything else. This was bullshit. Here I was struggling in this small-ass room while Mari was running around with money. It really angered me that he didn't keep his word and let me get the house he promised after burning down my shit.

I had no idea how I would manage *after* I had the baby. The bills were piling up, and after buying all this baby stuff, my account was dwindling down fast. I was sick and tired of talking to my cousin. Her ass was pissing me off 'cause I shouldn't have to keep asking her for money. Shit, she keep on bragging about this dope boy she's fucking, so why ain't this nigga helping her? I'm kind of curious about why she ain't bring him around. Sometimes, I think her ass lying.

My stomach was touching my back, so I got up and decided to get something to eat. Before I could walk out of the room, I heard my phone ringing. I picked it up and looked at the caller ID. I shook my head before I answered.

"Hello."

"Kila, what's good with you?"

"Mari, what do you want?" I asked, making sure he knew I wasn't pleased he called me.

"Listen, shawty, I know I'm the last nigga that you want to hear from, but can you just hear me out? I promise I won't call you back after this if you don't want me to."

I took a seat on the bed, rolling my eyes so hard it hurt. I was shocked that they didn't get stuck in my head.

"What do you want, Mari?"

I could feel my baby kicking. I guess whenever I get upset, my baby could feel it too. I rubbed my stomach to calm my baby.

"Akila, since you left me, I haven't been the same. I can't do nothing without thinking about you. I didn't know then, but I know now you're the love of my life. Shawty, I need you in my life. We were so good together, and even though you ain't saying it, I know that's my baby you carrying."

"Hold the fuck up. I never told you I'm pregnant by you. And as far as all the other shit, don't you think it's a little late for you to be sorry. Where are all the bitches that you carried me for?"

"Baby, listen, I mean, Kila. I was fucking them bitches, but they don't mean nothing to me. I love *you*, shawty. I want my family back. I mean, you can't tell me that you don't think about me. Like, shawty, we were a team."

I was sitting there trying my best not to let this nigga get into my mental, but it was hard. I hate to admit it, but I never stopped loving him. I just tried my best to suppress my feelings for him. So, him trying to bring them back up was painful.

"Listen, Mari. I would be lying if I say I don't love you. I mean, you were the only nigga that I've known. You knew that, and you used it to your advantage. While I was being good to you, you were out there fucking and disrespecting me. You know how stupid you made me look out here among these Richmond bitches? You violated me in *every* way possible, so, no, I don't give a fuck about none of those old fucked-up-ass memories."

"Akila, listen, I get what you saying, and as long as I'm breathing, I'll try to make it up to you. Shawty, I just need one last chance. I swear you leaving me made me realize what I lost. Fuck all this money and clout. I miss my queen. I won't be complete until you come back to me."

"Boy, I swear you should be a pastor 'cause of all this preaching. But don't forget, I know the *real* you, and all this fuckery is only another one of your cons. Listen, I'm hungry, and I need to feed my baby."

"A'ight, listen. Meet me on Midlothian. Let me take to you to lunch. If you don't want to see me again after lunch, I promise I'll walk the fuck away."

I sat there, and it's crazy that I was even entertaining what he was saying. But I missed this man. I missed the way he used to spoil me. Shit, even more, I missed his money. I missed the shopping sprees and spending what I wanted when I wanted to. Here I was struggling, barely making it. Shit, call it greed, but something clicked in my head.

"Yes, I'll have lunch with you. What restaurant?"

"We can go to Red Lobster. I hope that's still your favorite restaurant."

"A'ight. I'ma get dressed. I'll text you when I'm on the way."

"Shawty, thanks for this. I love you, girl."

I didn't respond. Yes, I agreed to have lunch, but professing my love to this nigga was taking it a little too far. There was no way I was letting him back in my life as my man. Right now, I'm just thinking of a way to survive.

I hung up the phone and dashed to my closet. That's when reality hit me that I can't fit in none of my cute-ass clothes, not with this big old stomach.

"Hmmm." I needed to find something, so I went through my closet to see what I could get into. Finally, I found a pair of slacks and a sweater. I hope it don't hug my stomach too much. Truth is, I needed a new wardrobe, but I couldn't really afford it. Buying clothes for my baby was way more important. I looked in the mirror. This head needs to be done too.

It's kind of sad how lately I just been letting myself go. I used to be the bitch that lived at the hair salon and nail shop every weekend. Ever since I got pregnant, I only been twice. I swear some shit needs to change 'cause a bitch like me used to be on top of her game. Well, this ponytail will have to do. It ain't like I'm trying to impress him.

I took one last look in the mirror. I looked halfway decent. I grabbed my keys and phone, locked my door, and walked out into the living room. My cousin was lying on the couch watching television.

"Hey, you."

"Hey, cousin. Girl, where you going?"

I walked around to the couch and took a seat by her. "Girl, you ain't goin' to believe who called me."

"Bitch, who, the Fed nigga?"

"Nah, hell no, not him. Mari."

"Mari? What the fuck that nigga wanted?" She sat up and gave me a shocked look.

"Girl, chill. He called me talking 'bout how he miss me and ain't been able to focus since I been gone."

"And don't tell me you falling for those lies. Why you ain't hang up the phone on him? Girl, that nigga is a

fucking user, and you shouldn't believe nothing he said."
She seemed visibly upset.

"Girl, calm down. I didn't say I believed him. I just told
you what he was saying. You know, I think every time I
talk to you about him, you get upset."

"Girl, every time you mention him, my blood boils
'cause you told me how he carried you. That nigga don't
deserve you."

"I get that, boo. All I'm doing is meeting the nigga for
lunch. It's not like we're going to be fucking or nothing
like that. Plus, a bitch is getting broke, so he might throw
a few dollars my way. I ain't never turn down no money."

She shook her head and looked at me in a disgusting
way. "Bitch, you tripping. I wouldn't take a dollar from
him. All money isn't good money, and his money damn
sure ain't good. You taking his money only gives him the
impression that you want him back. But, hey, you grown.
I can't tell you what to do. Just be careful. You know how
dangerous that nigga and his crew is. Not only that, but
also remember the Feds trying to pull you into his dirt.
Cousin, I love you and the baby and just want y'all safe."
She reached over and rubbed my shoulder.

My phone started ringing. I checked and saw it was
Mari.

"I'll be back," I whispered before getting up.

"Hello."

"Letting you know I'm on the way."

"A'ight, I'm leaving now."

Damn, this nigga was pressed. I walked out of the
house and got into my SUV. As I pulled out of the yard, I
couldn't shake the crazy thoughts I had. I think somehow
my cousin is jealous of me and Mari. Every time I mention his name, she gets kind of angry. I mean, I know she
loves me, but she got to calm down.

As I got closer to the restaurant, I started getting bubbles in my stomach. I haven't seen him since that shit happened between him and Tyrone. I remember that night he was spitting fire and threatened my life. Could this be a way to get his revenge on my life? I'm glad I decided to meet him in public. I mean, he would have to be out of his mind to try some shit in broad daylight.

I pulled up and parked. I wasn't sure what he was driving, so I dialed his number.

"Yo."

"I'm here. Where are you?"

"I'm pulling in now."

That was so much like him. Whenever he would meet someone, he would park somewhere and wait on them to pull up first. That way, he would know who was in the vehicle and if they're on some fucked-up shit. I checked my face in the mirror. My lip gloss was still popping. I was so preoccupied I didn't see him walking up.

Knock, knock.

I looked, and it was him knocking on the glass. I opened the door and got out.

"Hey, beautiful. Looking good as usual." He leaned in and hugged me. My body tensed up because I didn't know if he would kill me right here. I didn't trust him, and this was starting to feel like a big mistake.

I released myself out of his grip, and we walked into the restaurant. It felt so awkward sitting across from the man who I gave my heart to, and then he ripped it out of my body.

"You look great. How you been doing?"

"Thanks, and I've been doing good. What about you?"

"I'm good. Out here, still trying to make it. You know it's rough with my brother gone and all, but I still got to maintain."

"Yeah, I know how close y'all were. I can't say time will heal your pain, but it will get better."

Before he could respond, the waitress walked up, ready to take our orders. I was starving, so I wasted no time ordering my food. I know I probably appeared like I was famished, but I didn't care. I ordered a steak meal and shrimp. He ordered lobster.

"Babes, I'm glad you decided to meet with me. I miss you, Akila."

"I hear you, Mari, but it's too late for that. I'm pregnant, and I need to focus on my baby."

"Do you know what you're having?"

"No, I didn't want to know. I kind of want to be surprised."

"Be honest. Is that my baby?"

I wasn't expecting that question, so it caught me off guard. I looked at him. His face was dead-ass serious.

"I don't know."

"You don't know? How many niggas did you have running up in you raw?"

"*Excuse me?* How *dare* you talk to me like this. You know, this was a big fucking mistake coming here." I got up and dashed outside.

"Hold up, Akila. Hold up. I'm sorry, babes. I didn't mean to."

He grabbed me from behind and pulled me toward him. Then he wrapped his arms around me. I didn't know how to react. I wanted to fight, I wanted to run away, but his strong arms held me. Instead, I collapsed in his arms. Tears spilled out as I leaned on his shoulder.

"I'm sorry, babes. I love you, and I want you and the baby. I want both of you," he whispered in my ear.

Those were the sweetest words I have heard in a minute. It didn't matter they were coming from him. I just needed to hear someone got me.

After a few minutes of us embracing, I pulled myself away from him. Mari had just hurt my feelings . . . again. This showed me he was still a disrespectful-ass nigga.

"I need to go. This was a bad idea. I'm sorry."

"Akila, please, baby, don't do this. I love you, and I'm a better man now, shawty."

"It's too late for us, Mari. I can't allow myself to fall you for again." The tears rolled down my face as I spoke.

I didn't waste no time. I walked to my ride and jumped in. I shouldn't have come here. I thought I had all my feelings under control, but I see everything was still raw. It's like a wound that never heals. I pulled off, and I was careful not to look back. Since I was starved, I decided to hit up the fish market at South Side Plaza. I was ready to eat now. Then I heard the phone ringing. I took it out and saw it was Mari.

"Hello."

"Yo, you good? My bad. I didn't mean to upset you. Akila, if you don't want me as your man, let me be your friend. Shawty, I could tell you could use a shoulder to lean on. Let me be there," he pleaded.

"Hmmmm, I hear you. Well, I'm going home now. I had enough drama for one day."

"Yo, so can a nigga get an invitation? I mean, I ain't gon' do nothing to you."

"I don't live by myself. I live with my cousin, and I don't think she would be okay with a man coming over."

"Cousin . . . I ain't never heard about no cousin. A dude or a chick?" he quizzed.

"I said a girl." I shook my head.

"Oh, okay. I don't want no other nigga poking my baby head."

"*Your* baby? I told you, I'm not sure."

"Yo, I don't give a fuck. That's *my* seed, and you gon' be my girl again one day. I know I got a lot to prove, so I'm okay to be in the friend zone until then."

"Boy, I ain't trying to hear all that shit you saying. I got to go."

"Wait, you ain't going to invite me over?"

"I'll think about it and call you."

"A'ight, babes. I love you."

I hurried and hung up the phone. My emotions were all over the place. Mari had a way with words and always managed to pull me into his web of deceit. I'm trying hard not to fall for it this time, but on God, it was hard as hell.

I walked into the house, hoping my cousin was in her room. Wrong. Her ass was popped up in her favorite spot.

"How was lunch?"

"It was okay."

"Just okay? You fucked him, didn't you?"

"No, I didn't. Girl, you tripping. I'm tired."

I kept on walking. I really was in a good mood and didn't want her negative vibes. I walked into my room and locked the door behind me. Then I hurried and took off my clothes and got under my covers. I was smiling from ear to ear. This was indeed a very adventurous day.

Claire

Niggas love playing with fucking fire. Only thing is, Mari is playing with the wrong fucking bitch. I've been calling this nigga and texting him for days, and all I get is a few words. Most of the time, his ass telling me he working. I texted the nigga at 10:00 a.m., and he texted back that he was in NY. So, you should've seen my fucking face when my cousin walked in the living room telling me she's going to lunch with Mari. So, either this nigga lying that he's in NY or they done created some kind of spaceship that could get this nigga to VA in twenty minutes. Old lying-ass nigga has no idea he just got busted.

I tried to talk this old dumb-ass bitch out of going to see him. Her ass wasn't tryin'a hear what I was saying. I was getting angry, but I was careful not to show it. I have a plan, and for it to work, I couldn't show my hand just yet. Dear old cousin is in for the shock of her life.

There's no way they were going to enjoy no lunch. So I kept texting him, and when that didn't work, I started calling him. If I knew Akila, I figured she was getting sick of his phone going off like that. An hour passed before I heard her coming in. I knew then I would get the full hundred on what was going on, but this bitch acted like she had an attitude. Her ass was holding out on me, but not for long.

I heard my phone ringing. I snatched it up and looked at the caller ID. It was Mari.

"Hello." I pretended like I was sleeping.

"Yo, shawty, what the fuck, yo? I got over twenty-five missed calls from you, followed up by texts. Man, I told yo' ass I was up top handling some business."

I was sitting there listening to this old lying-ass nigga spit game to me. I wanted to scream "stop lying" at the top of my lungs, but I held in my anger and continued listening to him.

"Well, it would be nice if you call me back at least once. I mean, just the other day, we were inseparable, and now, suddenly, I can barely get a hold of you. If you fucking some other bitch and don't want to be bothered, please let me know so I can get the fuck on."

"Shawty, I swear your motherfucking attitude in the way. You need to get that shit in check for real."

"Boy, whatever. I ain't trying to hear all that damn lies you spitting out. The next bitch might believe you, but not me. You act like you a real nigga, but you keep doing sideways shit."

"Man, I'm trying not to disrespect you, but you keep coming out of yo' mouth foul, so I ain't got no choice but to carry yo' ass. Matter of fact, this conversation over. I got to meet up with the niggas at the bar."

I sat there with the phone at my ear. I couldn't believe this old disrespectful-ass nigga hung up the phone on me. I started breathing heavily. I was pissed the fuck off. The last nigga that tried to carry me had to learn the hard way. I was trying not to take it there with this nigga. Truth is, though, he didn't leave me no choice, but I'll show him that I'm the wrong bitch.

I got up and started pacing the floor. I walked over to the window and just stood there staring. Tears rolled down my face. I done did everything in my power to get this nigga to love me, and this is how he carried it.

I rushed to my closet, pulled out a sexy dress that barely covered my ass, and a pair of Kenneth Cole knee-high boots. I then went to the shower. I'm glad my cousin was still in her room 'cause I had no words for this bitch after how she behaved earlier.

As I washed between my legs, I couldn't help myself. I stuck my fingers in deep. I know this nigga was missing this sweet pussy. It's been a week since we fucked, so I know he was missing it. I just need to remind him. I slowly lotioned my body, then slid into my dress. I turned around and took a long look at my ass. It was round and filled out the dress, just the way I love it. I grabbed my purse and keys before I headed out the door.

My mind was racing. This nigga said he was going to play pool, and I know exactly what spot him and his niggas be frequenting. I cut the music up. Megan Thee Stallion's "Hot Girl Summer" was playing. Bitches be hating on her, but shawty was securing the bag, plus she bagged Moneybagg's ass. So, she was definitely doing the damn thing.

I pulled into the parking lot. As usual, it was packed, so I circled around until I found an empty space. This was one of the spots Richmond niggas be cooling at. If the police want to grab a bunch of niggas, this was definitely the place to come.

I did a once-over in the mirror. Everything was still in place. I got out of the car. I know Mari gonna be shocked to see me, but, oh well, he'll be a'ight. I looked around to see if I spotted his truck. I didn't see it, but I walked in anyway. I glanced around the room. It didn't take me long to spot him. He was sitting down at the bar, him and some other niggas. I didn't let that deter me. As I got closer, though, I noticed a bitch was standing in the midst. I walked a little faster, almost like I ran over there.

"Excuse me." I tapped the female on the shoulder.

"Who the hell are you?" the light-skinned bitch said as she turned around to look at me.

"I'm Claire. This my nigga you all up on."

"This yo' girl?"

"Man, what you doing here, shawty?"

"The question is, who is this bitch all up on you?"

"Shawty, chill with all that. We were just having a little talk."

"Really? I see you got drama going on. I'll catch you another time, papi," she said before shooting me a dirty look.

I guess the niggas sensed some kind of beef 'cause the boys walked off, laughing and talking.

"Yo, what the fuck you doing? Why you here?"

"I'm here to see you, nigga. We need to talk."

"Man, if I wanted to talk, I would've stayed on the phone with you. I'm here to chill wit' the niggas."

"Chill with the niggas, huh? I'm pretty sure you was just all up in that ho's face. If I didn't show up, you probably was going to fuck her."

"Man, you trippin', shawty. I ain't worried about no pussy. You see how you acting? I ain't got time for no shit like this."

"I'm pregnant!"

"You what?" He picked up the glass and took a sip of his liquor.

"You heard me. I missed my period, and I took the test. Yup, I'm pregnant," I lied.

"Man, this some crazy shit."

"Yeah, it might be, but since you the only nigga I'm fucking, *you* the daddy."

"So, you plan on having it?"

"Yeah, I plan on having my baby. I don't believe in no abortion."

He just sat there. It was cool in the bar, but I could see sweat beads on his forehead. I watched as he rubbed his hands over his face. I took the seat across from him and just stared at him. I was thinking of what else to say, just in case he hit me with a barrage of questions.

"Yo, I'ma go holla at my niggas, and then we can leave."

He got up and walked off. I watched as he stood with them talking. I also saw the stanking-ass bitch walk over to him and whisper in his ear. I thought about rushing over there. I done warned the ho, so she's just being disrespectful at this point. Before I could react, though, he walked over to me.

"Let's go." He grabbed my arm.

"I'm coming." I snatched my arm away from him.

I could tell by his demeanor he was pissed off. I didn't give a fuck, though. What he thought was going to happen when he blew me off like that? Sorry, Mari, *no one* treats me like this.

Mari

When I hit Akila up, I didn't think she would agree to meet up with me. I was happy as fuck when she agreed to meet me for lunch. Seeing her brought up all kinds of unsettled feelings. I remember the night when I caught her with that nigga. I had to bite down on my bottom lip so hard that I could taste blood. I tried to keep my emotions under control 'cause I didn't want to scare her off. As strange as it sounds, I still love her in a crazy way. I know if I want her back, I had to humble myself and pretend like I was cool with the shit she was saying. When I asked her whose baby it was and she told me she didn't know, that shit set fire to my soul. The craziness inside of me was telling me to get my gun and kill that bitch. I mean, I done took care of this bitch, sent her back to school and e'erything, and this bitch had the nerve to give the pussy away to that lame nigga. I know I shouldn't have said that dumb shit to her, but I plan on working hard to get Akila to trust me again. Work that I'm willing to put in.

After a stressful week, police running up in one of the traps and us losing some work, the fellas and I decided to hit up the pool hall. It was time to play some pool and strategize. With so much happening around me lately, I've been thinking hard about leaving this area

and taking things back down to the Beach. Things ain't
the same since my brother left. Even though the people
responsible for his death are gone, I still feel angry. Some
days, I can't function 'cause of the hurt I feel.

We sat at the bar, drinking and chopping it up. I
spotted a cute Spanish chick with a phat ass on her, so
I waved for her to come chill with us. After all the shit I
was going through with bitches lately, I should be staying
clear of anything with a pussy, but I can't help it. Plus, I
was smoking and drinking. I ain't gon' lie; I was ready to
smash her ass.

I must've been there for about an hour chilling, enjoying the music and vibing, when I spotted a familiar face.
This wasn't the person I was trying to see 'cause I know
she was coming with drama. This bitch was definitely out
of line when she tapped shawty on her shoulder. I just
wanted to yank her ass up and throw her against the wall.
But I held it 'cause a nigga wasn't trying to go to jail, not
tonight anyway.

I was ready to flip on this bitch until she said the
fucking words that I'm tired of hearing. The bitch told
me she was pregnant. My head instantly started to hurt.
This the second bitch in a few weeks that was telling me
they pregnant. This shit can't be real. I took a sip of Grey
Goose, trying to calm myself. I watched as she sat across
from me, staring me down. I knew that shit could get
crazy in here, so I decided to leave. I need to get this bitch
out of here, probably talk some sense into her.

I walked over to where my niggas were playing pool.
"Yo, I'm about to bounce."

"What the fuck, dawg? I thought we were going to chill?"

"My bad, yo. This bitch trippin', and I don't want to
beat her ass up in here. I'ma catch up wit' y'all in the a.m."

"Hey, cutie, hit me up when you want a *real* woman,"
the Spanish chick whispered in my ear.

I smiled at her and winked. "I got you, mami."

"A'ight, nigga. Be safe."

We exchanged daps, and I walked back to where Claire was sitting.

"Let's go." I grabbed her arm.

She snatched her arm away from me and started to talk shit. This bitch was really trying me. I walked off before I ended up dragging her up out of here. When we got outside, I grabbed her.

"Yo, what the fuck you acting like this for?"

"Let me go, boy. You think you was just going to knock me up, then say fuck me?"

"Man, ain't nobody doing that. You got mad 'cause I told you I like how our relationship is right now. I didn't see anything wrong with it, but you ain't want to hear that shit. So, you start trippin'."

"Boy, let me go. I ain't no fucking fool." She tried to get out of my grip.

I saw a few people walking in, and they were staring hard, so I let her out of my grip.

"Man, let's go," I said before walking off.

"Where we going?" She stood there pouting.

"Man, I'm going to the crib. Follow me."

I jumped in my car and pulled off. I was beyond pissed that this bitch brought her ass up here with this foolishness. I didn't even want to be with the bitch anymore, so to hear her say she's pregnant was fucked up.

I pulled into the gate and waited for her to pull in. Then I locked the gate behind her. I got out and opened the door. She followed me inside. I headed straight for the kitchen. Even though I was tipsy, I needed more drinks in my body. I took a pack out of my pocket, opened it, took a little on my picky finger, and sniffed it up. I did it two more times before tying up the bag and putting it back into my pocket. Then I stood at the counter, letting the drug marinate in my brain. The blow hit my brain and instantly put me in a happy mood, a mood that I was hoping this bitch didn't try to fuck up. Then I picked up the bottle of Grey Goose I had on the counter and put it to my head.

"What are you doing?" She walked up on me, startling me.

"Man, I ain't doing shit," I replied with an attitude. I put the bottle back on the counter and walked out of the kitchen.

The blow had me geeking, so I really couldn't stay still. I was hoping the alcohol would bring me down some. I walked into the living room and turned on the television. I forgot football was on tonight, and my favorite team was playing.

"Why you invite me over here if this is how you gon' act?" She confronted me in an aggressive manner.

"Yo, bitch, why the fuck you keep coming at me like this?"

"Bitch? What the fuck? How dare you call me out of my name like that."

"Yo, shawty, I'm sorry, but all you want to do is argue. I'm sick of this shit. To be honest, if you pregnant with my seed, you need to kill it 'cause I don't want no kids. Plus, looking how you acting all ratchet and shit, I can't fuck with you like that."

"Wow, I can't believe what you're saying to me. So, I was just a fuck?"

"I ain't saying you was just a fuck, but you been acting crazy and shit. On some real shit, I'm tryin'a see what's up with my ex-bitch, and I can't have no drama around me."

"Yo' ex-bitch . . . You talking 'bout Akila? The bitch that's pregnant with another nigga's baby?"

"Hold up. How the fuck you know about her? I never told you about her." I looked at this bitch in a deranged manner.

"Yeah, nigga, I know all about you, her, and how she left you for the Fed nigga. So, it's funny how you in my face claiming her fucking baby like it's yours. It seems like you a bigger clown than I thought."

"Bitch, what the fuck you talking about?" I was trying not to jump on this ho.

"Nigga, your precious Akila is my cousin. We live together, nigga. How the fuck you think I know about you and her?"

"You grimy bitch! Wait, Akila set this up?" I jumped up and grabbed this bitch by the throat.

I started squeezing her. "Get the fuck off me. Everybody saw when I left with you."

"Bitch, I'll kill you and wouldn't give a fuck who seen what. Now, get your dirty, stinking pussy ass up out of my shit." I let go of her.

She wasted no time. That bitch bolted out of the crib. I opened the gate as I saw her backing out. Then I locked my door and took the bag out of my pocket. I wasted no time doing lines of coke. I was high out of my mind. I felt like I should've killed that bitch, but I know it wasn't a good move. I need to be more careful. The last two bitches that I killed, I didn't think it out. I just acted out of rage.

I remember Akila telling me she lived with her cousin. I grabbed my phone and pulled up Akila's number. She didn't pick up, so I called right back. I need to talk to her ass. These bitches think they gon' play me. The phone kept ringing, but she didn't pick up. Fuck that. I still had the address that G had given me. I scrolled in my messages and found it. Then I grabbed my keys and headed out the door. My blood was boiling. Just when I thought that Akila and I were on the way to being good, she and this bitch was on some bullshit.

On the way to her crib, I tried to figure out what the point was of letting her so-called cousin fuck with me. Yeah, I threw a few dollars the bitch's way, but it wasn't no major paper. Nothing for these two bitches to floss with. The fucked-up part is all Akila had to do was fuck back with a nigga, and she would've got anything she wanted. See, now, these bitches done fucked up.

I pulled up at the address on the phone. Shit is crazy that I've driven past the crib numerous times and had no idea this was where Akila was hiding out. I cut off my lights and slowly pulled into the yard. I peeped two vehicles. I know one belongs to Akila and the other car belongs to the bitch Claire. So, the bitch wasn't lying when she said she was Akila's cousin.

I walked to the back door and knocked hard. I had my gun in my hand, hidden behind my back. No one answered, so I banged harder.

"Who is it?" I heard Claire ask.

"Yo, it's Mari. Open the fucking door," I yelled back.

"Boy, why you come here? You need to go."

"Yo, open the door before I kick it off."

"What's going on? Who's at the door?" I heard Akila ask.

"Girl, we need to call the police. I think it's your ex."

"My ex? Who, Mari?"

I then heard the locks clicking, and the door flew open. Akila was standing there with her big stomach hanging out. Her stupid-ass cousin stood beside her with her mouth wide open. I stepped inside with my gun still behind my back. I locked the door behind me, then looked at both the bitches while taking a quick glance around the room.

"Mari, what the fuck are you doing here? How did you know where I live?" Akila asked with a strange look on her face.

"Why the fuck don't you tell me? You and this bitch tried to play me." I took a step toward her.

"Boy, what the fuck you talking about? This my cousin from Baltimore. Y'all never even met." She looked at her cousin, then looked back at me.

"Bitch, you can cut the act. She your cousin, and you and me used to be together. Then this bitch popped up out of nowhere, and we started fucking."

"Wait, hold the fuck up. What the fuck you talking about? Y'all was fucking? Is *this* the nigga you been fucking?" she turned to Claire and asked.

"Cousin, I can explain. I didn't know this was the Mari you was talking about. I can explain."

"Oh my God! Bitch, how could you do this to me? Mari, did you *know* this was my cousin?" she looked at me and yelled.

"Nah, I ain't know this was your fucking cousin. But it's hard for me to believe that you didn't know either. This bitch hit me up on social media and just started flirting with me."

"You grimy bitch. I sit here and tell you everything about me and him. I ask you to come down here 'cause of what I was going through, and you go and *fuck* with him?" Akila started tearing up.

"Bitch, chill with those fake-ass tears. You know damn well you didn't fuck with me when you was living your high and mighty life, but soon as you got played, you find me. Bitch, I never liked your ass since we were young. But who had to come save yo' old dumb ass? Yeah, I listened to yo' little pitiful stories, and then it hit me. I deserve some of the money you keep bragging about that he used to spend on you. Yeah, his ass fell for me. Yeah, we been fucking ever since. And yes, bitch, this the dope boy I was bragging about. He ate my pussy, licked my ass, and fucked me good. How the fuck you feel about your baby daddy fucking me while you lay your dumb ass in your room?"

Before she could finish talking, Akila jumped on her and started pounding that bitch's head on the table in the kitchen. I put the gun in my waist and tried to grab Akila, but her grip on that bitch was strong.

"You bitch. You done tried the wrong one," Akila screamed while she repeatedly banged the bitch's head on the glass table. I saw blood spilling out, and I knew then it was getting serious.

"Yo, get the fuck off her, Akila," I yelled at the top of my lungs. I grabbed up Akila and snatched her away from that bitch.

"Get off me, nigga. This *your* fucking fault. You fucked this bitch—my fucking cousin." She fought out of my grip. I wanted to throw her against the wall, but I knew she was pregnant, so I tried my best not to hurt her.

I let go, but it turned out to be a big fucking mistake. Claire ran up on her and started throwing blows to Akila's stomach in a split second. Akila grabbed a big knife lying on the counter and started stabbing her cousin in her chest. I grabbed her and squeezed her hand until she let go of the knife as I watched Claire fall to the ground. Even then, Akila was like a possessed demon. She was still cussing and raging with anger, trying her best to get out of the tight grip I had her in.

"Help me, help me," her cousin said between soft sobs. She lay on the floor, holding her chest.

"Bitch, fuck you. I hope you die, ho," Akila yelled.

"Yo, shawty, chill." I couldn't let her go 'cause I didn't trust that she wouldn't jump on her cousin again.

"Nigga, let me the fuck go. I can't believe you and this bitch played me like this. I fucking hate you, Mari," she yelled before she started bawling. I carried her to the living room and sat her on the couch, still holding on to her.

"I need you to listen to me. You stabbed your cousin pretty bad, and we need to figure out what to do. If she dies, you're going to jail. Do you understand what I'm saying?"

She sat there looking at me, but it seemed like she was far away. I've never seen her like that before, and this was scary.

"Listen, stay here. I need to go check on her. Don't move, Akila."

She still didn't respond, so I slowly let her go and got up. I dashed into the kitchen, where Claire was struggling to breathe. Her breaths were getting further in between. I knew she was on her way out. She just lay there grunting and staring at me. I pulled out my gun and fired two shots in her chest. It was best to put her out of misery.

"Yo, fuck. This is fucking crazy," I mumbled before I walked back into the living room. Akila was sitting there sobbing loudly and shaking.

"Yo, shawty, I need you to quit all that fucking crying and get back to earth. Your cousin is lying dead on your kitchen floor, and we need to figure this shit out."

The word "dead" must've gotten to her 'cause she looked at me. "She dead?"

"Yeah, you stabbed her multiple times. She dead, shawty."

"I ain't no killer." She started sobbing again.

I grabbed my phone and called G.

"Yo, nigga, what's good?"

"I need you to come through. Got some garbage that needs to go out. Remember the address you gave me for ole girl?"

"Yeah. A'ight. Cool. Say no more."

I hung up the phone and lit a cigarette. I ain't got no problem killing the bitch, but the fact that she's Akila's people and Akila's involved makes the situation sticky. I looked over at her, and she had stopped crying. She got up and walked to the kitchen.

"Oh my God!" She started crying, and seconds later, she began throwing up.

"You good? You shouldn't be in here."

"I don't feel too good. I need to go to the bathroom."

I followed her to the bathroom, where she buried her head in the toilet, letting everything out of her stomach. I wasn't sure if she was throwing up from the pregnancy or because she saw her dead cousin lying on her kitchen floor.

Chapter Nineteen

Akila

This was the reason why I didn't trust no bitch . . . but my cousin, though. I poured my soul out to this bitch, and she turned around and sought out Mari. I felt so fucking stupid. I remember sitting there telling this bitch my business and how she pretended like she hated Mari. Tears welled up in my eyes. To be honest, at first, I was sad that she was dead. But the more I think about how the bitch betrayed me, that ho deserved everything that she got coming to her. Old grimy-ass ho really tried me.

It's been three days since the incident happened, and here I was at Mari's house. There's no way I could've stayed in that other house, plus Mari and G had to clean up. I tried to ask him questions, but he told me I didn't need to know anything but just to know I'm good. I know Mari and his niggas been killers, so I'm sure they got rid of all evidence, including the bitch.

My phone started to ring. I didn't recognize the number, so I didn't answer it. The phone rang again. *Who the fuck is this?* I thought.

"Hello," I answered, hoping it wasn't no debt collector 'cause my ass was behind on a bill or two.

"Akila, how you doing?" a female voice asked.

"Who is this?"

"This Eileen, Claire's mother. Have you seen my daughter? I've been trying to reach her since Thursday, and her phone just keeps going to voicemail."

I felt an instant headache. Sweat started forming on my forehead even though the place was chilly. I quickly gathered my thoughts. I needed to think straight. I've thought of the police questioning me, but I didn't plan on hearing from her mother, who was also my cousin.

"No, she left the house, told me she had a date, but she never returned. I just assumed she and her dude were spending time together. Plus, I been over my baby daddy house and haven't heard from her."

"Hmmm, that's strange. She did tell her friend she was going to meet that guy she's dealing with, but we haven't heard from her since. That is so not like her. I don't have a good feeling about this. I just hope she's OK."

"I'm pretty sure she's good. From what I can tell, she's really into that dude. So they probably just spending some time together."

"All right, you probably right. By the way, how you doing? It's almost that time for the baby to come, huh?"

"Yes. I can't wait."

"Well, that's good you have your cousin there with you. I got to run, but if she contacts you, please let her know her mother is worried, and she should call me immediately."

"OK, I sure will."

I hung up the phone. I felt suffocated, like I couldn't breathe. I know I could be a liar, but this was hard for me, talking to this lady, knowing full well her daughter was dead and in some manhole or probably worse.

I heard the door open, and Mari walked in. We haven't really been talking a lot since I came to his house. I think it was the shock of what happened. Plus, it wasn't like him and I were together. He told me that I could stay in his bedroom or one of the guestrooms, so I chose the guestroom. I didn't feel comfortable sleeping in his bed. Didn't want him to think we were anything other than homies.

He walked into the living room where I was sitting down. I was scrolling on Facebook, trying to see if anyone posted on Claire's page. The last post on her page was the one she posted talking 'bout "He gives me butterflies in my stomach." I quickly got off her page 'cause my blood started boiling again. That bitch was a straight snake.

"What's good, shawty? How you feeling?"

"I have a slight headache. Claire's mother called me, asking if I'd see her daughter."

"Really? What you say?" He walked over and took a seat beside me.

"I told her I hadn't, plus I wasn't home."

"Yeah, that's good. Aye, you gon' need to move your stuff. You are welcome to stay here, or you can get your own crib. I'll pay for it, of course."

"Hmmm, you acting all extra nice and shit. How come when we were together, you didn't act this nice?"

"Shawty, you trippin'. No matter what you think about me, I've always held it down for you. You can't even lie about that."

"I have a question. How do you go around killing people and still walk around like nothing happened? I mean, since this shit happened, I ain't been able to sleep. I keep seeing Claire's face when I close my eyes."

"That's 'cause you ain't a killer. Anyone can become a killer if they're pushed. You need to push that shit out of your mind and don't even think about it no more. If anything was to come up, I want you to put e'erything on me. I did it. You don't know anything about that shit. I doubt it will ever come to that 'cause first, they would have to find a body and prove that bitch ain't just run away. At the end of the day, that bitch went out and never came back. You don't know. I don't care how they force you to say anything. You don't know nothing."

"What about her car?"

"Don't worry 'bout none of that. All you need to worry about is delivering a healthy baby boy."

"Boy, whatever the fuck you say. I feel in my soul it's a girl."

"A'ight, I put a couple of bonds on it. It's a little dude. Don't be shocked when that ding-a-ling come popping out," he laughed.

I couldn't help but smile at him. I sure missed him and the good times we used to share.

"Shawty, I miss you. I miss us. I sure hope you give me another chance. I'm getting ready to give up these streets and move back to the Beach. I hope you'll join me. We can take all this money I made and start a couple of businesses."

Shit sounded good, but I know I couldn't fall for the fuckery. Mari can't be trusted, and I didn't want to allow myself to fall into his web of deceit again. That's what my head was telling me, but my heart was screaming for him. My pussy was squinting around in my underwear. It's been months since I fucked. But hearing his voice and listening to him speak that good shit, I wanted to fuck.

I guess we're on the same page. Don't ask me how it happened, but our lips were locked within seconds, and our tongues stuck into each other's mouths. I missed this, so instead of fighting it, I held on to his shoulder and allowed him to have his way. My clothes were off in no time, and he knelt in front of me with his head buried in my pregnant pussy. My legs shivered as he sucked on my clit. That nigga sucked my pussy like he was starving for a five-course meal.

"Awwww, owwwww," I cooed in his ear.

He didn't ease up none. He took that as a cue to bury his head deeper inside my wet pussy. I bit down on my bottom lip as I tried not to come, but he made it hard for me. I grabbed his head and pulled him in closer to me. I wrapped my legs around his neck as my body started shaking. The veins in my forehead bulged, and I tried to control my scream. I couldn't hold it any longer. Finally, I exploded in his mouth. That didn't deter him. He locked on to my clit and licked up each drop of my cum. My pussy was as shiny as a newborn baby's ass when he finished.

Even though I just busted a nut, I was still horny. I needed to feel his long hammer up inside of me. But instead of doing that, he got up and walked out of the room. I was left confused. What the fuck was this nigga thinking? How dare he get up and leave me hanging like that? Talking about salty, a bitch was salty that I didn't get the dick. I got up, put on my underwear, and walked out.

I heard him in the kitchen, so I walked in there to confront him. He was standing there on his phone.

"What the fuck was that all about?" I asked with an attitude and my hand akimbo.

"What you talkin' 'bout, shawty?" He shifted his attention away from the phone.

"Boy, you know damn well what I'm talkin' about. You just gon' suck my pussy and then leave me hanging? I mean, your phone call was more important?"

He didn't respond. Instead, he placed the phone on the counter, walked over to me, and pulled my underwear down. He then shoved me to the counter, bent me over, and got behind me, sliding up in me with force. I squirmed as the dick hit my stomach. Being pregnant and not getting fucked on the regular damn sure made my pussy much tighter. A few strokes later, it was wet enough, and the dick could move around more freely. He grabbed my hips as he thrust in and out of me. I braced myself and poked my butt out.

Oh, I miss this dick so much. This nigga knows *exactly* how to please this pussy. My pussy was responding to his dick like it was moving on the same beat. My soul loved this man right now, and my body surrendered to his every command. I felt his veins enlarge, his strokes got fiercer, and he grabbed my hips tighter.

"Aarrghh," he groaned before he exploded inside of me.

Boom! Boom! Boom! Three noisy sounds echoed loudly. It was like fire or an explosion. Mari pulled out of me and ran in the direction the sound was coming from.

I ran behind him to see what the fuck was going on. That's when I stopped dead in my tracks. The front door was off the hinges, and people in FBI uniforms were standing there with guns pointed at Mari lying on the floor. I used my hands to cover my breasts and put my legs together. Here I was, naked as the day I was born, and all eyes were on me.

"Don't move," a female FBI agent yelled.

As if I had anywhere to move to. All kinds of crazy ideas ran through my head. Were they here for me 'cause I killed Claire? *Oh God, my baby,* I thought.

"I need to get my clothes." I looked at the bitch with an attitude.

"I said don't fucking move."

"House clear," I heard a familiar voice yell.

The footsteps got closer, and soon, I was standing face-to-face with the nigga I used to fuck. The nigga that's possibly my baby daddy.

"Miss Jones, I see you didn't take heed. We gave you a chance, and you ran straight back into the arms of this killer and drug dealer." He shook his head in disgust.

"Boy, fuck you. Can I get my fucking clothes?" I spat at him.

"Gonzalez, take Miss Jones so she can get dressed. I don't think this is any way for a young lady to be in front of the fellas."

The female bitch came over and snatched my arm. "Where're your clothes?"

"In the living room," I replied with an attitude.

I quickly got dressed under the watchful eyes of the bitch. I know this wasn't good, and to be honest, I was scared as fuck.

She led me back out to the hallway, where everyone stood. By now, they had Mari up, and handcuffed.

"Mr. Owens, you're under arrest for gun possession, murder, racketeering, drug trafficking, and money laundering."

"Well, well, Mr. Owens. I told you I was coming for you. Looks like we finally got you," Tyrone said while smiling in Mari's face.

"Bitch nigga, fuck you. You still mad that I took my bitch back from you."

"Mr. Owens, where you're going, you'll never see the streets anymore, so pussy should be the last thing on your mind. I think someone else will soon be banging your bitch. Now, take this scumbag out of here and read him his rights."

"What you want me to do with her?"

"Take her down to the jail to see what she knows. And if she gives you a hard time, arrest her ass too."

I couldn't believe what I was hearing. This nigga was still in his feelings and would use his power to intimidate me.

When we stepped outside, lights were everywhere. It seemed like the whole police force was present, along with the FBI, ATF, and helicopters flying overhead. This was a scene fit for the movies. They were behaving like Mari was the mob or something. I looked around to see if I could get a glimpse of Mari, but I couldn't find him. I'm not going to lie. I was scared and trembling inside. I tried my best not to show it, but a bitch was terrified 'cause I wasn't sure what would happen this time around.

I sat restlessly in the interview room at the federal building. This room was similar to the one I was in before. I was cold, hungry, and my stomach was hurting so bad. I rubbed my hand across it, silently praying that everything was okay with my baby.

I lay my head on the table as the tears flowed down my face. I wasn't hurting physically, but I was hurting mentally. These last few days have been nothing short of hell on earth. I didn't deserve none of this shit. I had left Mari the fuck alone, and here I am, right back into some bullshit that I have nothing to do with. Life just ain't fucking fair. The tears started flowing harder.

I heard the door open, but I pretended not to hear it. Someone walked in, but I didn't care to know who it was. These bitch-ass niggas know damn well I wasn't doing shit, so they were only being nasty. I ain't never sell no fucking drugs or kill—

My thoughts were interrupted when I heard a chair pulled out. I lifted my head. My nose was runny, and I can only assume I looked a hot fucking mess. But as soon as I realized it was this nigga, I wished I had kept my head down.

"Hello, Akila," he said with a slight grin plastered on his face.

"What the fuck do you want? I see this is all a fucking game to you. Damn, was the pussy that great that you have to go through all this shit?" I gritted on him.

"Don't flatter yourself, sweetheart. You're just as guilty as that slimeball boyfriend of yours. The only reason why yo' ass ain't slapped with all these charges is because of me. I'm saving you 'cause that could be my baby in your stomach. By the way, once you have the child, I will be getting a court-ordered paternity test, and I will be going for full custody if it's mine. I can't trust you not to bring my child around these lowlifes you be hanging with."

"Yeah, right. Do your superiors know that you were fucking me? Do they know you jeopardized their entire case behind pussy? You can fuck with me if you want, but I promise you, you won't ever get my child."

"Do you really think I give a fuck about this job? I've been undercover for years. I will sling this dick to any bitch like yourself to squeeze whatever information I need. Your little naïve ass was too quick to slide in the sheets with me, and I admit it. I fell for you. I mean, you suck dick good, and that pussy . . . Oh boy, that pussy is *oh* so good," he bragged while licking his lips.

"Nigga, fuck you. Do what the fuck you want to do. I'm sick of yo' ass," I yelled at the top of my voice. Not sure where I got the strength from, but I've had it with this bitch-ass nigga. I got up and flipped the fucking table on him. "Fuck you. I fucking hate you. Charge me or let me fucking go. Matter of fact, get me a fucking lawyer. Y'all don't have shit on me," I yelled.

I was scared of being charged. These were the fucking Feds we're talking about, but I was tired, mentally and physically. That nigga stood there looking at me like he was shocked. Suddenly, I got dizzy and felt a sharp pain. Something was running down my legs. I reached down the leg of my tights. It was soaked with a sticky substance.

"I need an ambulance, nigga," I yelled.

"You're not going anywhere until I'm satisfied that you're not holding back anything."

"I'm going into labor. Get me a fucking ambulance," I yelled as I collapsed to the ground.

"Oh shit." He dashed out the door.

"God, please protect my baby." I was weak, and my feet buckled under me. I was having contractions, and they were hurting as bad as hell.

"I'm here, Akila, baby. I don't know much about this baby thing, but the ambulance is coming, babes."

His voice made me sick, but I was in too much pain to cuss him out. I just need to get to the hospital to deliver my child.

I gave birth to a beautiful baby girl I named Malikah Akayla Jones. She weighed seven pounds, five ounces. After I thanked God for a safe delivery, I waited for everyone to exit the room, then I sat there quietly. She was beautiful. Her skin was caramel and smooth. She had little chinky eyes with fat cheeks. I was trying my hardest to figure out who she favored. I looked closely at her, and I could see Mari. Or was it that I wanted to see Mari's features in her? I really couldn't tell whose child it was. I used to talk shit about bitches that were in the same situation. Never did I imagine that this would be me.

After the nurses took Malikah to the nursery, I decided to take a nap. I felt so alone. I really never imagined that I would be alone when I gave birth, but what's a bitch supposed to do? I had to pull up my big-girl panties and be the best mother possible.

Epilogue

Akila

Two Days Later

"Girl, she's beautiful. Oowee, you giving me baby fever," Shayla said as I got into her car. I didn't know who else to call; plus, she has really been there for me lately.

"Girl, it's your god-baby, so you're welcome to come get her whenever you feel like it."

"Yes, you know I work a lot, but I'll be there to get her as soon as I get a day off. That's crazy what you were telling me about Mari. Did he call you?"

"No, not yet. To be honest, I'm not sure if I want to hear from him. So much shit surrounds this nigga. I can't go through this again. I'm a mother now, and I need to be here for my child. You know?"

I was saying all this good shit, but to be honest, I felt terrible, guilty, that I was not there for him. I used to spend his money, and he just covered for me on some shit . . . Shit that could land me in jail.

"Listen, baby, I know your heart's hurting, but you loved him at one point. I ain't never been locked up, but I have a brother who was in these streets. He told us all the time it's a lonely place, especially when you have no one there. I'm not saying do it now, but one day, drop him a line or two. Plus, he might be your baby daddy. Baby girl will appreciate it one day."

"I hear you, girl. I'm just so tired right now. I just want to rest and lie up with my baby."

"I hear that. Well, if you need me, just call me, and I'll come."

She pulled into the yard, and I got out. I took out the car seat and brought my stuff inside. Shayla honked the horn before driving off. I opened the door and walked in. My nose picked up an unfamiliar smell right away. I panicked. I thought about running, but before I could reach the front door, I saw a shadow step from behind the hallway door.

"Hey, girl, I've been waiting for you."

"What the fuck are you doing in my house? How you got in here?" I asked while I hung on tight to the car seat.

The last time I saw this bitch was when she bonded me out of jail, and that encounter wasn't too pleasant. Now, she was standing in my living room acting like we old buddies and shit. This shit didn't sit right with me. Was she here by herself? I took a quick glance around, being careful not to take my eyes off her for too long.

"Relax, sweetheart. By the way, cute baby." She walked over to me and looked in the car seat.

"You didn't give me an answer. So what are you doing in my house?"

"Mari asked me to stop by."

"Why would he do that?" I looked at her suspiciously.

"Well, you know they got him, and he might never see these streets again. They got the clique, and I'm on my way out of town. He asked me to drop this off to you and wanted me to tell you he loves you."

She lifted a duffle bag and shoved it to me. The bag was heavy, so I quickly put it down. I had no idea what was going on.

"Why would he do that?"

"Listen, I don't know what the nigga see in you 'cause he could have done way better. But truth is, this nigga has always loved you. So take that shit and get the fuck out of here. Word is some bitch is snitching, and they have inside information on a lot of shit. I'm out of here 'cause a bitch like me is too good to be going to anybody jail. I don't care how much pussy in there to eat."

She shot me a dirty look, put her shades on, and sashayed out the door. I looked down at the bag, opened it, and froze. Stacks of cash were there. Not no little bit of money, but a duffle bag full of hundreds. A note was on top. I opened it up.

"I hope this gets to you. Shawty, take this and get the fuck out of here. Take care of my baby and know daddy will forever love y'all."

Tears dropped out of my eyes as if I could hear the words coming out of his mouth. Emotions filled my heart. I love him and hate him at the same gotdamn time. I quickly wiped the tears. I needed to get the fuck out of here.

I ran to my room and grabbed two boxes of Pampers and some clothes out of the baby's closet. Then I grabbed two of my outfits, took the stuff to my truck, and put my baby in. I then grabbed the duffle bag and dragged it to the car. After that, I pulled off on the road.

"God, please direct my path," I whispered before I started driving. I kept looking in my rearview mirror. Maybe I was paranoid 'cause the last time I tried to leave, the Feds got me.

I felt relieved when I made it downtown and saw the sign, 95-South. I jumped on it. I heard great things about Atlanta. I didn't have no family or anyone, but I had my daughter and a duffle bag full of cash. It was all I needed to start my life over. I took one last look in my rearview mirror. People say home is where the heart is, and this was no longer my home.

I cut on the radio. I didn't want to hear no noise in my head right now. Baby girl was still asleep, and I needed to take this moment to figure things out.

"Breaking news . . . Police have confirmed that drug kingpin, Mari Owens, was stabbed to death in the shower at the Richmond City Jail. Details surrounding his death are sketchy, but we will bring them to our listeners as soon as we get more information. The jail is on lockdown, and authorities are asking everyone to stay away from it."

I pulled over and held my chest. This can't be true. I opened my car door and started throwing up. My body felt weak, and my head throbbed.

"Mari . . . Mari . . . how . . . why . . ." were all I could mutter out.

God, this is too much to bear. I could hear his words clearly in my head. *"Kila, get out of here."* I wiped my mouth, started the truck, and pulled off. I'm not sure how I would make it to Atlanta, but I had to get the fuck out of *here.*